What Lurks Below

Bruce E. Norris

Published by Hemingway Publishers

Cover design by Hemingway Publishers

ISBN: Printed in the United States

Nature said it couldn't be done.

Man made it happen.

A new terror lurks below the surface…

What Lurks

Below

By

Bruce E. Norris

Table of Contents

About The Author

Bruce E Norris is the author of Escape Socotra Island...dead men still tell no tales and The Springs. He lives in South Florida with his wife and family.

Contact: <u>brucenorrisbooks@aol.com</u>

1

It was a quiet evening on the calm waters of the Port Everglades Harbor. The hot sun had slowly gone down with its beautiful display of red, yellow, and orange colors. A light breeze kicked up, cooling the air from another hot summer's day in South Florida.

A beautiful full moon was leisurely rising from the east as Captain Virgil Goodman smoothly ran one of two tugboats through the basin and out through the jetties to the open sea. The two tugboats slowed and turned around no more than a quarter mile out and sat idling, waiting to meet the large Panamax-size container ship approaching from the East.

Captain Virgil was a handsome, rugged man with a five-foot-ten-inch frame, piercing green eyes, and an athletic build. He had a dark, leathery tan from years spent on the water.

Born in Wichita, Kansas, the son of a loving mom and dad, Virgil and his younger sister Donna had a happy childhood. This would soon change as Virgil's father was the proud owner of a full-service automobile station. Being one of the most reputable mechanics in town, the elder Mr. Goodman tried to groom young Virgil to follow in his footsteps.

Virgil wanted no part of the auto business and made it

known, much to the chagrin of his father. Working on car engines in the freezing cold winters, always scraping a knuckle or two on some stubborn bolts and a constant sore back, was not one of the top ten choices he wanted to do with his life. In fact, he couldn't wait to finish school and get out of Kansas altogether.

Finally, at the age of eighteen, Virgil and his buddy Don Henderson had saved enough money to buy a shrimp boat down in Louisiana. The two of them scraped a respectable living for a couple of years, shrimping off the Gulf Coast until they began to get on each other's nerves, which is always the case when working and living in tight quarters with the same person day in and day out.

Finally, after too many nights on Bourbon Street, they sold the boat and went their separate ways. Virgil wouldn't give a second thought of working on dry land and wound up in Florida, landing a job as a deckhand on a tug-boat in the Port of Miami. After studying hard and demonstrating his skills on the water, it wasn't long before he acquired his Captain's license and became Captain of a tugboat at Port Everglades in Fort Lauderdale. Within two years, he found the lady of his dreams and married her. They quickly started a family and became proud parents of a daughter and two sons.

Don Henderson, on the other hand, was less enthused about

working on a boat ever again. He was more of a get-rich-quick kind of person who was always looking for the next big thing to show the world. Virgil was always quick to chide him about wanting to be the next P.T. Barnum. The last he heard from Don was when he telephoned from the Philippines and said he was researching large crocodiles.

As the nine-hundred and sixty-five-foot container ship slowed its approach a mile outside the port, the port's pilot boat met it, and a ladder was dropped down the side. The pilot quickly scuttled up the stairs and made his way to the bridge, relinquishing the captain the duty of piloting the ship into the port.

The two tugboats waited on either side of the inlet, preparing to throttle up and meet the ship as it cruised through the jetties. Virgil watched the pilot take control of the ship and slow down to meet the tugs. He returned the binoculars to the table just ahead of the steering wheel and scanned the water in the inlet to make sure all pleasure boats were out of the way of the incoming ship.

The container ship cruised between the tugboats and continued toward the inlet as the tugboats throttled up to catch it and secure the lines.

Suddenly, Captain Virgil spotted what looked like a large log drifting toward the port side of the tugboat.

"Hey, Skip! Keep an eye on that log," he shouted out the window to his deckhand, pointing at the object. "I don't want that thing in the propeller when we pass by."

"Okay Cap!" replied Skip, sitting on the gunwale, closing his latest issue of Playboy, and standing up to see where the log was.

The tugboat matched the speed of the ship, following alongside as the other deckhand, Bill Brighton, prepared to throw up the hawser line. Skip relaxed on the port side of the tug and watched the log. The more he watched it, the more he began to realize it wasn't a log. In fact, it looked like it could have been the top section of Captain Nemo's submarine. When the object looked like it was on a collision course with the tugboat, Skip was ready to shout up to Virgil. Before he could utter a single word, he was startled to see that the log changed course and swiftly moved in the opposite direction and vanished under water completely.

"What the hell was that?! Hey Cap, the log was on a collision course with us until it turned and hauled ass toward the jetty on the Sandy Beach Parkside."

Virgil ignored him as he was focused on working the massive ship. Forty-five minutes later, the ship was docked at its berth, and the lines secured. When the tugboats backed away and headed back toward their dock, Captain Virgil called Skip up to the bridge. Skip promptly dropped the hawser line that he was carefully stowing and made his way up the ladder.

"Cap, did you see that floating thing?"

"No Skip!" he spat out. "I wasn't watching that damn log, and I want you to stop drinking on the goddamn job!"

"Easy Cap, I wasn't dri…"

"I simply ask you to watch a log, and I see you running around and shouting like a banshee," he paused to let it sink in before continuing the scolding. "Somebody's going to see you doing this and report that there's alunatic working on my tug."

Before Captain Virgil could say another word, Bill stepped into the wheelhouse.

"Hey Captain, it looks like there's one hell of an incoming tide this evening. Either that, or I'm so tired. I'm starting to see things," he said, rubbing his eyes and yawning.

Virgil rolled his eyes off Skip and gave Bill a condescending look. "What?"

"After we backed away from the ship and started heading back, I was looking out through the jetties and saw that big log coming straight through the inlet like a torpedo. When I wiped my eyes to make sure I wasn't seeing things, the damn thing disappeared," he explained, reaching for a towel and drying the ocean spray from his big, burly arms.

The Captain crossed his arms and glared at them for a moment, wondering if they thought he was gullible enough to fall for some prank.

"Okay…What the hell are you two talking about?"

"Look Cap, I know it sounds silly, but I saw it with my own eyes. I kid you not, that freakin' log was more than twenty-foot long and cruisin' straight into the harbor," Bill replied, holding his hands out and dropping the towel.

Skip and Bill were one of a kind. Never one's to pass up an opportunity to pull a prank or tell tall tales. If they knew the listener was hooked on their stories, they'd go on for hours.

Skip Long was a young-looking, blonde-haired twenty-eight-year-old from Alabama. His slender build and charming good looks covered his school of hard knocks background underneath. He divorced his wife of four years after he caught her having an affair with his best friend.

In and out of jail for petty misdemeanors since high school, his father accused him of being a good-for-nothing, pot-smoking bum who would never amount to anything.

Finally, after being fired from his latest job as a restaurant dishwasher, he decided to cut the family ties and run down to Florida. He survived for a while playing acoustic guitar in small bars in Key West until he had a run-in with a bar owner who refused to pay him one night. When told that he drank more than he earned, Skip smashed the guitar on the man's head and nearly beat him to death. The next morning, he escaped with his hangover to Fort Lauderdale, where he learned there was a warrant out for his arrest.

After bumming around for a few days, he jumped at the offer to work as a deckhand on the tugs.

Bill Brighton, on the other hand, was a tough, hardworking ex-bricklayer from Pennsylvania. With arms the size of a regular man's legs attached to a five-foot-seven-inch frame and a bald head, one look gave the impression you were looking at Mr. Clean from the commercial ads.

Married to a slim, petite wife for ten years, Vicki gave birth to a petite, healthy daughter named Lisa, and it wasn't long for the head of the family to decide to pick up and leave his construction job of fifteen years and move to greener pasture. Always quick with a joke and a smile, the thirty-five-year-old father was more like a gentle giant than the intimidating hulk people portrayed him to be, and he easily filled the open position offered as a tugboat deckhand when he moved to

What Lurks Below

South Florida.

"Okay," said Virgil, "Let me get this straight. Skip, you saw the log move out of our path...against the current? Do you really expect me to believe that?"

"Sounds crazy Cap, but that's exactly what I saw."

"Right," Virgil replied skeptically. "And Bill, you saw it cruise through the inlet like a torpedo...not more than five minutes ago?"

"Sure did," he replied, dead serious.

"Uh-huh, I'm sure you did," Virgil replied, picking up a pair of binoculars and scanning the harbor. After a moment, satisfied there was no mysterious log floating in the basin waiting to sink a boat, he replaced the binoculars and turned to face the two jokers.

"Bullshit," he concluded. "We don't have another job until eight-thirty tomorrow morning. I suggest you two get some sleep," he said in a firm tone while Skip anxiously searched for his magazine.

It was useless to argue with the captain. Virgil was the best tugboat captain in the company. Unlike the other captains, he was considered one of the boys and became good friends with the crew. When one of the crew would mess up on occasion,

Virgil would back them up one hundred percent instead of writing a report on them. The crew well respected him and when things were slow, he'd even drink with them. He made one thing clear, though: they would do as they were told and stay in line while working.

"Sure Cap, whatever you say," Bill answered, looking over at Skip and shrugging his shoulders.

The two men walked off the bridge and leaned on the railing, waiting for the captain to dock the tug. Virgil stood at the wheel, guiding the tug between two other tugs at the dock, and watched the deckhands as they stood talking. Deep down, he knew they must have seen something out there, but it just didn't add up.

An hour later, Virgil was in the galley sipping a hot cup of coffee and thinking about the slow evening ahead. It was the first evening in two days the crew was actually going to get some rest. The work schedule and the pay were good, but sometimes working one week on and one week off left them feeling tired and haggard, especially the last couple of nights when they worked one ship after another.

"Hey Virge, what's doin'?" asked Chuck, the engineer, as he stepped into the galley after a refreshing shower. Dressed in a dark green polo shirt, a tan pair of casual shorts, and a well-worn pair of boat shoes, he looked more like a fishing guide than a tugboat engineer. His job required that he stay down in the engine room during the boat's operation, making sure the three-hundred-horse-powered diesel engine kept running smoothly.

Chuck McClowski was by far the friendliest man on the crew, never thinking twice to help a crew member in need. The forty-two-year-old stood five-foot-ten with a medium build and a dark, tanned, leathery face, which made him look like he had spent all his life on the water. He was born and raised in South Florida, marrying his high-school sweetheart at the young age of twenty-one. He and his wife Terry had thought about but never had kids and for some reason, never wanted to talk about it when the conversation came up. Chuck walked through the galley, poured himself a cup of coffee, and refilled the Captain's mug.

"Thanks Chuck. Looks like we finally have a slow night," Virgil said, closing his log book and taking a sip from the hot mug.

"Good, I think I'll turn in early," Chuck replied with a yawn. "I'm going to get up early and take a dive under the tug. I want to check the tail shaft and kort nozzle."

"What's the problem?"

"No problem, just maintenance. It's been a while since I checked for Barnacles and whatnot."

Chuck was known to be overly anal about the upkeep of the aging tug-boat. He kept the engine room squeaky clean and all moving parts well-greased.

"Sounds good. I think I might go down there with you and try out my new regulator."

They sat in the galley for an hour, talking and drinking coffee with shots of apricot brandy before calling it a night. Virgil climbed the stairs up to the wheelhouse and turned the VHF radio down a notch. Standing by the windows, he finished his last shot of brandy and looked out across the basin. The water was smooth as glass, and it looked like every star in the sky was lit.

Turning off the overhead light, he turned and made his way to his room just behind the bridge. As tugboat captain, he had to sleep with one ear tuned to the radio so that he could hear what was going on in the port at all times.

At two o'clock in the morning, the harbor was quiet. A light breeze kept the mosquitoes away as the Captain slept with the windows fully open.

Suddenly, the radio woke Virgil from a light slumber like a firecracker in a museum. The call came from a small sailboat returning from the Bahamas.

The sailboat captain was calling the Harbormaster to report that he nearly hit what looked like a large tree branch barely poking out of the water as he entered the jetties.

Virgil sat up in his bed and cursed his bad luck. Listening half asleep, he heard the Harbormaster respond, saying he will notify the Jackson Towboat Company and have it removed before it became a danger to other boats.

Fair enough, Virgil thought, and slid back between the sheets and fell asleep.

Rick Manditto was not in a good mood. His boss called his cell phone just as the party was picking up. He had second thoughts about answering the call, but after bragging to his friends about his new job, he felt inclined to answer.

And now, there he was, cruising through the port at three o'clock in the morning, half drunk and looking for a floating palm tree. What a bunch of crap, he thought.

He slowed the boat and scanned the area where the sailboat reported the floating debris but couldn't find any sign of a tree or log anywhere in the vicinity. Feeling groggy from the beer and shots he drank, he figured he'd take a quick dip to invigorate himself. The ebb tide barely stirred as Rick put the boat in neutral and turned off the motor. He removed his shirt and jumped over the side, the salt water refreshing and warm. Floating on the side of the boat, he thought to himself that if he hadn't been drinking, he'd probably never jump in the water in the middle of the night.

While holding on to the ladder attached to the stern, he leisurely relieved himself before climbing aboard.

With a sudden feeling of sheer terror, he was dealt a heavy blow that knocked the breath out of him. As he put one foot on the bottom rung of the ladder, something snatched him and carried him away from the boat in giant vise-like jaws. Rick's mind was racing as he couldn't believe this was happening to him. He felt a sharp pain running through his entire torso when he realized he was in the jaws of some kind of predator.

Fighting to get free, he let out a guttural scream as the giant reptile lifted its massive head out of the water, chomping down and swallowing Rick whole. The entire attack lasted fifteen seconds. The reptile descended below the surface, and the agitated water returned to calm.

Less than two-hundred yards away, Captain Virgil was awakened by the loud, blood-curdling scream. He quickly jumped out of his bunk and stubbed his toe on the doorjamb leading into the wheelhouse.

"Ouch! Goddamnit!" he shouted as he crashed through the bridge door and reached for the floodlight. He cursed out loud as he scanned the harbor, looking for any signs of trouble.

"What the hell was that?" Chuck asked, rushing out to the bow with a flashlight.

"Good, you also heard it. I thought I was dreaming," Virgil answered, massaging his toe which was quickly turning black and blue.

"I don't see anything but that towboat out there waiting for a customer," Virgil said, focusing the high-beam light on the towboat drifting in the middle of the channel.

"There's the culprit," Chuck smirked. "I bet it's that crazy Manditto kid."

"He's not at the wheel," replied Virgil, squinting through binoculars. "The lucky dog must be lying on deck with his latest score," Chuck smiled, shaking his head and remembering what it was like to be young.

"I think you hit the nail on the head Chuck," Virgil said, shutting off the spotlight. "Next time I see that son of a bitch, I'm going to scream in his ear, see how he likes it." he continued, limping back to his bunk.

Chuck stayed out on deck for another minute, trying to scan the tow boat with his tiny flashlight.

2

Susan Thomas was last year's prom queen. She had an athletic build on her five-foot-nine frame with curves in all the right places. She had long, straight blonde hair framing beautiful blue eyes and a nose that looked like a model's dream. Her voluptuous lips seemed to curve slightly upward at the ends, making her look like she was always up to something. A deep, dark tan complemented the look of an all-American cover girl for Surfer magazine.

She made it clear to her friends and classmates that she would never tolerate being stood up on a date, no matter who it was. If it ever happened, she made it known to him and his friends that, as far as she was concerned, he would be treated like he never existed.

She sat quietly at her kitchen table, staring at the phone. *"If Rick thinks he can make a date with me and not show up, he's got another thing coming,"* she said to herself, trying not to choke up and become teary-eyed. She jumped from the table, stormed over to the phone, and began dialing.

"Hello...Mrs. Manditto? Umm...My name is Susan. Is Rick there?" she asked, not doing a good job holding back the tears.

Mary Manditto knew all about Susan Thomas from the

stories other moms told at the bingo hall. From all the gossip, she pictured Susan as way too licentious for her good son. The last thing she wanted was Ricky to entertain people like her. After all, Ricky was a good boy.

"Well, look, honey," replied Mary. "Rick is a very busy young man. He told me he was going to a party last night and wouldn't be home 'til late. He's still sleeping, and I don't want to wake him up."

"Yes, but..."

"If it's important, I'll go wake him up," Mary cut in, detecting the girl's voice starting to quiver.

"No, no," she sobbed. "No thanks. He was supposed to meet me last night, but I showed up late, and he was gone... I guess he forgot about me."

"Okay honey, I'll tell him you called," replied Mary, happy her son dumped her but wondered where he went when he left the party.

"Oh...Wait a minute," she sniffled. "Please don't tell him I called... Bye."

Susan hung up the phone and slowly walked to her bedroom. Standing in front of the mirror, she disrobed and looked at herself with satisfaction, *"Well Ricky... You lost your chance,"* she murmured to herself.

Rick Manditto thought he was God's gift to the female race. He was the all-star high school quarterback on the school's champion football team who went out with every pretty girl on the cheerleading squad at one time or another.

With jet-black hair, dark brown eyes, and a chiseled jaw, he looked like a young Burt Reynolds, only taller. At six-foot-five, he could never walk inconspicuously into a room.

During the summer vacation, Rick was able to land a job at Jackson Towboat Company. His father, Ben, was a good friend of Bob Jackson, the owner.

Ben and Bob had been friends for more than twenty years. They met while working as lifeguards on the Fort Lauderdale beach. When Mary became pregnant with Rick, Ben decided to become a paramedic where he could earn more money.

Bob remained a lifeguard until he unwittingly stumbled on the towboat operation. One day on the beach, he ran into a guy who told him he was selling his towboat operation in South Carolina to settle down in South Florida. When the U.S. Coastguard ceased to respond to non-life-threatening calls, a light bulb went off in Bob's head, and he ended up buying the company cheap and moved it to Port Everglades, where he would give the two towboat companies already in business a run for their money.

Five years later, Bob Jackson Towboat Company was one of the most trustworthy marine assistance providers in South Florida. Consisting of five thirty-foot boats rigged for towing and stationed at a dock within five minutes from the mouth of the harbor, his business boomed.

As a favor to his friend, Bob hired Rick to work as a towboat operator throughout the summer.

Rick thought it was an easy enough job. A small boat breaks down, and he zooms over to the rescue. And with a little luck, he helps a damsel in distress and becomes her knight in shining armor. Yes, what a great summer job.

Mary Manditto hung up the phone and walked down the hall to Rick's bedroom. With Susan still on her mind, she still couldn't think of any reason why her wonderful son would associate with her kind.

The door was closed, so instead of risking the chance of disturbing her tired son, she returned to the kitchen and started making pancakes. After all, it was Rick's favorite breakfast, especially after those late-night get-togethers with his friends.

At eight-thirty, the phone rang again. Mary rushed over to pick it up before it could wake Rick.

"Hello?" she answered.

"Good morning, Mary, this is Bob," he replied, sounding all business-like. "Is Rick around? I need to talk to him."

"Well... he's still sleeping. Can I have him call you when he gets up?"

"It's almost nine o'clock, Mary. I've got to ask him something important about work last night," he replied, his patience wearing thin.

"Okay, hang on a minute, I'll wake him," she replied in an equally testy tone as she put down the receiver and walked to Rick's bedroom. With one hand on the doorknob, she gently knocked on the door.

"Rick dear, wake up. Your boss is on the phone and wants to talk to you... he says it's important."

She knocked again when there was no reply and slowly opened the door. "Ricky honey, it's time to..." she froze in her tracks. Rick was not sleeping in his bed; he was gone. In fact, he's been gone all night. His bed was still neatly made by his mom like he hadn't slept in it at all.

She had a gut feeling that something was terribly wrong. Rick was a good boy and never stayed out all night. He had too much respect for his parents to not at least call if he was staying at a friend's house. No, something was terribly wrong.

Mary frantically ran back to the phone.

"Bob! Rick didn't come home last night! I have a feeling something bad has happened!" she cried out.

"Okay, okay," Bob intervened. "Don't worry, Mary; you know how kids are these days."

"Not my son. He would never do something like this. Something's wrong," she replied, sounding like she was having a panic attack.

"Wait a second, Mary; I called Rick early this morning. It sounded like he was at a party. I told him to report to work and move a tree or something floating near the harbor entrance," he said, trying to calm her.

"It was his night off," she stated in a perplexed tone.

"Yes, I know. I thought he could use the extra cash. I'm going to call around. I'll give you a call when I find him, okay? Oh, by the way, is Ben there?"

"Ben's at work. And please, give me a call when you find Ricky," she replied sorely.

"I will, Mary, and don't worry, he's a big boy," replied Bob.

Mary hung up the phone and slowly walked over to the front window, peering out towards the driveway in hopes of seeing Rick's car pull in.

3

Captain Virgil was sitting in the wheelhouse, preparing to work his first ship of the day. Sipping a cup of coffee, he looked down at his throbbing, black and blue toe, now swollen like a balloon.

Bill walked out of the galley and started up the stairs leading to the wheelhouse. He stopped and leaned on the railing, "How's the toe, Captain? Chuck told me you smashed it pretty good last night."

"I'll live," Virgil replied in an irritated tone.

"Chuck said you guys heard a scream? I think I heard it too," he continued, leaning forward to get a glimpse of the toe.

Virgil stopped drinking his coffee and leaned outside the window, "I'd be surprised if you didn't. It sounded like somebody was getting pulverized. I looked around and figured it came from a Jackson Towboat sitting in the channel," replied Virgil, reaching in his shirt pocket and taking out a pack of Camel cigarettes.

"Yeah, I figured it was nothing," replied Bill, scratching his bald head and heading back down to the galley.

When Bill walked away, Virgil carefully slipped a sock on his throbbing toe and painfully slipped into a pair of leather clogs. He was about to grab the binoculars and scan the port when Skip came walking through the door, "G'morning Cap, Have you by any chance seen my magazine?"

"No, no, I haven't, Skip," he replied in a painful tone. "I've been up here nursing my bruised toe."

"Oh yeah? What happened?" Skip pretended to care. "You look like you're in a lot of pain."

"I banged my toe last night when I heard a loud scream. I think it was that dumb-ass Rick kid on the towboat. He must have gotten too carried away with his girlfriend," Virgil replied, tired of talking about his toe and walking away from the window.

"Damn, I'm sorry to hear that, I slept like a baby," Skip grinned. Virgil was glad he walked away. If he was still hanging out the window, there was no doubt he would have reached over and knocked him out.

"This is Harbor Patrol to Jackson Towboats. Come back," a voice sounded on the VHF radio.

"This is Jackson Towboat Company. Come back," said Margaret Jenkins, the dispatcher.

"This is Officer Randy Taylor. It seems that one of your

towboats is drifting a half-mile out off Hammerhead Reef. Over."

"Are you sure it's one of ours?" Margaret inquired as she leaned over the desk and peered out the window, noticing a boat was missing.

"Affirmative," the officer replied with a stern tone. "Not only that, but it seems your vessel had drifted over some divers. They were pretty upset when they called to report it, to say the least. They boarded the boat after screaming for the captain. After they boarded, they looked around and the boat was empty."

"Okay, I'm sorry. The logbook shows nobody has gone out today yet, but one boat is missing at the dock," she replied suspiciously. "I'll get somebody out there right away, over."

"Ten-four, I will remain at the scene, over and out."

Margaret Jenkins was an attractive lady in her mid-forties. Although she had a steady boyfriend, she realized nothing more would come of it, and her search for the right man would continue.

Originally a legal secretary, she met Bob one afternoon when he came into the office to discuss legal business with his new towboat company. A few minutes into the meeting, Bob realized the lawyer was a pompous, supercilious jack-ass and walked out. He struck up a conversation with Margaret, and the two hit it off immediately. Impressed with her friendly smile but straightforward demeanor, he invited her out for coffee after work.

After a couple of hours of conversation, Bob realized how unhappy she was working for the lawyer and asked her to work for him. With her knowledge and know-how, she could practically run the business while Bob focused on running his boats. She accepted the offer and has been in the business ever since.

Within five minutes, Bob parked his big four-wheel drive Ford pickup in the gravel parking lot and jumped out. Sprinting through the office door he nearly knocked Margaret to the floor when he bolted down the hall and into his office. She regained her balance and followed.

"Bob! Are you alright?"

"Yeah, I heard the radio call. One of my boats drifting aimlessly outside with nobody in it," he replied, out of breath, grabbing a pair of boat keys and storming back out toward the boat dock.

"The log book shows that Rick didn't return this morning."

"I know. It doesn't sound good. I just talked to his mom and she's all upset."

"Oh my God, I hope he's alright," she stated solemnly.

"I'm sure he is. I'm going out to Hammerhead Reef and meet the officer. I'll radio when I find out what's going on," he shouted as he jumped into a boat and cranked up the twin motors.

Bob untied the lines and steered the boat through the port. It was the beginning of another beautiful day, and he had to weave around all the boat traffic. The sky was clear, and the water was smooth as glass. It seemed that every recreational boater in town was cruising around aimlessly with a drink in their hand. Fifteen minutes later, he cleared the jetties and gunned the engines. He looked in the direction of Hammerhead Reef and quickly spotted the patrol boat.

Officer Randy Taylor had tied his patrol boat to the unoccupied towboat and was writing his report when he looked up and saw Bob slowing down to meet him.

Randy had been a Police Officer for sixteen of his thirty-eight years. Ten of those years had been spent in and around the port. Standing six-foot tall and weighing one-hundred and ninety-six pounds, he rarely had trouble with unruly characters trying to overpower him during his numerous drug bust operations. His wavy blonde hair and tanned, weathered skin gave him the appearance of a man who spent all of his waking hours outdoors.

Known for the no-nonsense way he carried himself, he treated everybody, including criminals, fairly and with due respect. Since switching from a patrol car to a boat, he's been involved with everything from shootouts with high-speed boats on the high seas to picking dead bodies out of the water that had been floating for days. A confirmed bachelor, his family and friends had noticed how he had become a bit callused.

Bob slowed the towboat and, idled alongside the empty vessel and tied a line to the cleat. He shut off the motors and leaped to the deck of the unoccupied towboat, "Good morning, Officer," he said, shaking Randy's hand.

The Officer clicked his pen closed and put it in his shirt pocket. "Good morning, any word on the where abouts of your worker?"

"No, I just got off the phone with his mother; she said he didn't come home last night. I stopped at my warehouse and the office before I heard your call," replied Bob, looking around the empty boat.

"How reliable is your man? Was he ever mixed up in drugs or anything?"

"No, no, he's a good kid; I have no idea why he'd do

something like this."

"I've got a bird in the air scanning the area," said Randy, referring to a helicopter. "I'm hoping it doesn't spot something. If you know what I mean."

"Yeah, I hope he doesn't find anything either," Bob murmured.

The two men looked around the boat, trying to find a clue as to what happened to Rick. The officer noticed the ladder was extended in the water and wondered if Rick might have gone in. "Maybe the line got tangled in the prop," he said, pointing to the ladder.

"I doubt it. Rick is pretty good. I don't think he would have tangled the line, but who knows? I can't imagine why he'd put the ladder down."

Bob followed Randy back to the patrol boat and filled him in on the job Rick was called to do.

"Maybe this kid was drunk and went back to the party. Maybe he thought the towboat was docked when he left it," Randy threw in for good measure. "No, he's a pretty trust worthy kid. I've known the kid for years; his father's a good friend of mine."

"You said you called his house, and his mother is upset about him not returning home," Randy confirmed, taking his pen out again and writing.

"Correct, she's in hysterics right now."

"I wonder if he's done something like this before."

"According to his mom, he's never done anything like this before. She insisted that her son's a good boy, never stayed out all night unless he called."

"Of course not. All moms think their kids are saints," Randy answered. Bob opened a storage box, pulled out Rick's duffel bag, and looked inside, "This isn't good," he said to himself as he retrieved a set of keys. "These belong to Rick," he grudgingly continued, showing them to the officer.

"No, it doesn't look good at all," replied Randy, reaching for his radio. He grabbed the mic and wasted no time calling the Coast Guard, requesting another helicopter to help in the search. He then reported to his headquarters and relayed the information, requesting more patrol boats to keep a lookout.

"Okay, Bob, I've got the Coast Guard and patrol boats searching for Rick. In the meantime, I want you to tow this vessel back to your dock. I've got CSI waiting there to try and help figure this thing out."

Bob held his head low and tried to take in the whole scenario,

"Okay, Officer, thanks for calling a search."

Captain Virgil Goodman and his crew were heading out past the sea buoys to bring in another ship. A half-mile out, he slowed the tugboat, turned toward shore, and put the tug in neutral.

The ship was still about three miles out, so Virgil picked up a pair of binoculars and focused the lens toward Hammerhead Reef. He found it odd to see the three boats tied together, especially one of them being a patrol boat.

Virgil met Officer Taylor a few years back, and they talked on occasion, usually about things pertaining to their jobs. He had a few minutes to burn and decided to give the officer a call.

"Harbor Patrol, this is Captain Virgil Goodman of the tugboat *Horizon*. Come back."

Randy looked over Bob's shoulder and saw the tugboat drifting outside the inlet and grabbed the radio.

"This is Harbor Patrol. Come back, Captain," he replied in an official tone.

"Am I speaking to Officer Randy Taylor? Over."

"Affirmative Virgil, working another ship, I see. What can I do for you? I see you're tied to the towboats out there. If it's got anything to do with last night, I may have some information for you."

Randy and Bob looked at each other with a puzzled look. "When are you free to talk?" replied the officer.

"In about an hour, after this ship. I'll be free until three-thirty this afternoon."

"Thanks, Captain. I'll stop by after you're finished working that ship I see coming in."

"Ten-four, over. *Horizon* standing by on sixteen, over and out."

Forty-five minutes later, Captain Virgil gently docked the tugboat at its usual spot, where it shared the dock with two other tugboats from the same company. Chuck shut the engine down as Bill and Skip tied off the lines.

Virgil filled out the log book, then stepped out of the wheelhouse and made his way down to the galley. Skip was busy making bacon and eggs and was elated to see that he found his Playboy magazine hidden under the bacon in the refrigerator.

A few minutes later, Bill walked in, shaking his head with a grin on his face, "Oh, you found your magazine?"

"Yeah, thanks, pal," replied Skip, glaring at Bill as he learned he had hidden it.

They had just finished their breakfast when Officer Randy Taylor pulled the patrol boat alongside the tug. Bill walked out of the galley and grabbed the line. Virgil followed and welcomed the officer aboard. Shaking hands and talking casually, he led the officer up to the wheelhouse. Chuck looked out of a porthole from the engine room and saw the patrol boat. He cleaned the grease from his hands and made his way up to the wheelhouse to see what was happening. He knocked at the door and heard Virgil tell him to enter.

"Thanks for stopping by, Randy," Virgil said. "No problem, Virgil. What's on your mind?"

"I saw you tied to the towboat and I noticed helicopters flying overhead like they're searching for something."

"Yes, there seems to have been an accident, and a captain of one of the towboats is missing," Randy replied, looking out of the big windows.

"Thought so," Virgil guessed, looking over to Chuck. "Did you two see something last night that might help?"

"No, we heard something, though," answered Chuck.

"We heard a horrendous scream around three ten this morning. Chuck and I dashed out and scanned the area with the floodlight. The only thing around was a Jackson towboat drifting in the middle of the cut," Virgil explained.

"Three ten?" replied Randy, retrieving a small notepad from his breast pocket.

"That's right."

"And there were no other vessels out there? Nothing looked suspicious?" the officer continued the investigation, scribbling down the information.

"No, just the towboat. We kept the beam on it for about ten seconds and didn't see anybody. We figured it was that young kid fooling around with one of his girlfriends," Chuck replied.

"Okay, thanks for the information. I'm on my way to check the surveillance tape. You've saved me valuable time sifting through the tape. I'll cue it up to three o'clock and see what happens," Randy said, heading for the door.

"You've got cameras in the port?" Virgil asked in surprise.

"Sure do," Randy answered with a cocky smile. "Ever since the nine-eleven attacks. Port security wants to make sure nobody tries to turn one of these crude tankers into a bomb."

"Let me know if something shows up," Virgil said with a concerned look. Randy didn't have a clue what he meant, but Chuck looked over and knew exactly what he was talking about. He was referring to the occasional slow nights when the crew would sit out and have a few beers on the dock.

"Okay, Virgil, I'll let you know what I find," replied Randy. He walked with a purpose to the side of the tugboat and jumped back to the patrol boat.

He cranked the motors as a forty-five-foot speedboat sped past and left a wake that nearly slammed his boat into the tug.

"Damnit! Look at that SOB!" shouted the officer as he turned on his blue lights and sped off in pursuit.

"Sure hope he doesn't catch us drinking on those tapes," said Chuck with a dour expression.

"Nah, Randy's a good man. He'd have warned us if those cameras were aimed at us," Virgil replied with confidence.

4

Officer Randy Taylor retrieved the tape from the main building overlooking Port Everglades and went directly to the station. He walked briskly through the hallway leading to his office and shut the door. Not wasting any time, he quickly put the tape in the machine, cued the tape to three a.m., and pushed play. After a minute, he pushed the fast-forward button until he saw the towboat come into the picture.

He zoomed in on the boat and noticed Rick Manditto was by himself, ruling out the possibility of a party getting out of hand.

He watched as the boat slowed when it neared the entrance to the port and scanned the water with a search light. The vessel idled slowly out of the jetties as it continued searching the water.

He paused the tape when he saw Rick turn off the motor and extend the dive ladder before jumping into the water. "What the hell is he going in the water for?" he murmured. He watched as Rick swam around the boat and began to climb up the ladder.

He wasn't prepared to see what happened next and fell out of his chair as his mind couldn't comprehend what his eyes were seeing.

****

Virgil and Chuck checked each other's dive gear before falling backward into the water. Chuck dove straight down to the stern of the tugboat while Virgil continued to the bottom.

Sixty feet below the surface, Virgil spotted the grey sandy bottom littered with beer and brandy bottles. He made a mental note that he would send Skip down to clean it up at a later time. He continued along the bottom, testing out his new regulator and watching a school of large barracuda patrolling the area.

Chuck checked the propeller, rudder blade, kort nozzle, and tail shaft. Satisfied that everything was in good working order, he looked around for the captain. Visibility was only about thirty feet, and Virgil was nowhere to be found. Chuck searched for his bubbles with no luck and decided to head for the bottom.

Virgil spotted Chuck and thought he'd have a little fun. Holding his breath so his engineer couldn't find his bubbles, he leisurely snuck up behind him. Staying just beyond the grey wall of sight, he was getting ready to pull on Chuck's fin and give him a jolt.

Suddenly and without warning, something plowed into his

weight belt and knocked the wind out of him. Virgil doubled over in pain and tried to catch his breath. Chuck turned around when he heard bubbles escaping and hastily swam over. He made eye contact with Virgil and saw that he was hurting. Taking a quick scan around the area, he didn't see any predators or anything out of the ordinary and wondered if the good 'ol Captain was pulling a prank. To be on the safe side, he held Virgil's arm as they ascended to the surface.

"What the hell happened down there, Virge?"

"Something hit me," replied Virgil, gasping for air.

They swam on their backs to the dock, where they climbed up a fixed ladder. Standing on the dock with his air tank still on his back, Virgil wasted no time taking off his weight belt and examining it.

"Missing any body parts?" Chuck asked as he followed behind and took off his air tank.

"Wow! Check this out," Virgil replied, holding the weight belt out and pointing to a chunk taken out of a weight. "I think I just got slammed by a barracuda."

"Jeez! That would have left a nasty wound," Chuck said in amazement, rubbing his thump where lead used to be.

Chuck and Virgil contemplated on how lucky he was to

escape the razor-sharp teeth of a barracuda when Bill stuck his head out of the galley and yelled over to the dock, "Hey Captain, Officer Taylor called and wants you to stop by his office and check out the video he's got!"

"Did he forget I'm on duty!" he replied rancorously, annoyed that the officer thought he could summon him whenever he wanted. "The good officer must have seen something of interest," he continued, looking over to Chuck with a slight frown.

"Right, I'll tell him to blow it out his..."

"Sorry, Bill, I'm still reeling from this torpedo blow to the hip," Virgil cut in, rubbing his side. "Tell him I'll be over in about an hour."

Bill didn't know what the hell the Captain meant but waved him off and awkwardly returned to the phone while Virgil and Chuck gathered their gear and leaped back onto the tugboat.

Virgil rechecked the work schedule, and nothing had changed. They were free of ships until early evening.

Virgil asked Chuck if he wanted to join him and watch the tape at the patrol office. Chuck couldn't care less about the video because he was sure it would turn up nothing but he decided to go along just to get off the tugboat for a while.

The two pulled into the patrol office parking lot and were surprised to be greeted by Officer Taylor and Bob, owner of the towboat company. Randy's face was ghostly pale and Virgil quickly surmised that whatever he saw on the video was not good. Chuck thought they were caught on camera drinking on the dock.

They were quickly ushered to the office, and Randy shut the door behind them.

"Okay, guys, prepare yourselves for this," Randy muttered as he anxiously put the video on and closed the window blinds.

"Did you see the tape, Bob?" Chuck inquired, speaking to him for the first time in the five years that he knew of him.

"Not yet," he replied, making no attempt to introduce himself, as he took a seat and made himself comfortable.

He was expecting to see Rick Manditto doing something foul on the video and thinking how he was going to explain to his father why he got himself fired.

Officer Taylor sped the tape forward to the scene where the towboat entered the picture. Bob saw Rick drinking a beer and swore to himself, thinking the officer was making a big deal out of nothing.

They continued watching without saying a word; Virgil had

an impatient look on his face and looked like he was ready to leave. He wondered to himself why he was suddenly involved with police work.

They watched as the towboat stopped in the middle of the inlet, and Rick dived into the water. What they saw after that paralyzed the senses like never before.

They watched as Rick swam over to the ladder and started to get out of the water. Suddenly, something enormous violently snatched him from the ladder and carried him away from the boat. It lifted its gargantuan head out of the water with Rick in its massive jaws and chomped down on its prey as Rick let out a horrific scream. Blood gushed out everywhere in a torrent before the predator retreated under the surface, and the ocean returned to calm.

Astounded from viewing the tape several times earlier, Randy stood up and walked over to the VCR, turning it off. The other three men sat speechless; you could hear a pin drop as they sat in disbelief.

Chuck tried to get up from his chair, but his legs wouldn't move as tears welt up in Bob's eyes, "What the hell is that?" he murmured.

Nobody answered as Virgil somberly stood up and walked over to the window with his hands in his pockets, too numb to reply.

"What the hell are we going to do about that thing?" Chuck blurted out. Randy stood and composed himself, gathering his thoughts, and replied, "First, I've got to close the Port to all small vessels and notify the mayor. Then I've got to hire somebody to catch that damn thing."

"You might want to close the beaches and notify the dive boats as well," Virgil found his voice. "We think we saw that thing outside the jetties in open water yesterday. Skip, Bill, and I. We thought it was some kind of log." Randy replayed the video and freeze-framed the scene where the predator had its head out of the water.

"Take a good look and tell me what you think it is," Randy instructed. "It looks like a very large alligator," Virgil hastily replied.

"That's what I thought," replied Randy, "But I've never seen an alligator with a head like that. I mean...Look at those teeth; I've never seen so many... Look at the size of the damn thing! Its head looks about six feet wide!"

"I can only imagine how big the damn thing is," Bob contributed.

"I used to hunt gators," Randy said gravely, "That monster's got to be at least twenty-five feet."

Nobody replied. They just looked at the officer as if he was making a bad judgment call or maybe had no clue as to what he'd just implied.

"A twenty-five-foot alligator in the Port?" Bob questioned.

"Sounds impossible, but we've just seen something on that tape, and it sure as hell isn't small," Chuck replied, dumbfounded.

"As Randy said, it doesn't look like an ordinary alligator. Notice the snout extends a bit longer than a gator; the head is exceptionally wide, but beyond the eyes, it tapers out," Virgil added.

"Yes, the son of a bitch looks like a prehistoric monster," Chuck muttered. "Okay, I've got my work cut out," Randy Taylor said, opening the blinds and escorting the men out of the office in a hurry. "I've got to close the beaches and the Port to small vessels, visit the Mandittos with the bad news, and hire a hunter to kill that beast."

"Good luck, Randy, we'll keep our eyes open," Virgil replied solemnly. "I'm going to need it."

It was now early afternoon, and Mary Manditto was keeping busy preparing dinner. Frustrated that nobody would believe that Rick wouldn't stay out all night without phoning her, she felt pain in the pit of her stomach. Something was wrong, and nobody could change her mind.

Her husband Ben was home now and tried to calm her nerves, explaining that Rick was at that age now where kids are so caught up in things that they sometimes don't make it home on time, especially when they're with friends and girlfriends. He assured her that he'd be stomping through the front door any time now, apologizing that his cell phone didn't work. He tried to hide the fact that he was worried sick.

He poured Mary a glass of wine and a scotch on ice for him and sat on the couch, surfing the television channels for a baseball game.

He stopped flipping channels on a cooking show and took a sip of his drink when the doorbell rang. Mary bolted for the door, hoping it was Rick with a story of how he lost his keys and cell phone.

Composing herself first, she opened the door as Ben walked up behind her. Her heart skipped a beat when Officer Randy Taylor and Bob Jackson gave a half-hearted smile and asked to come in.

"Hello Bob, come on in," said Ben, motioning with his hand to enter, swallowing hard as Randy walked past. "Is there some kind of trouble, Officer?"

Mary felt a lump in her throat and a sinking feeling in her

stomach when she noticed the morose faces of their guests.

"I'm afraid we'd better have a seat," Bob cut in and followed his friends to the couch. "I asked the Officer if I could come along and tell you personally."

Officer Taylor remained standing with arms crossed, his head lowered and a hand on his chin.

"What is it, Bob? Tell me," Mary demanded with a quivering tone.

Bob could feel tears well up in his eyes and put his arm around Mary, and he took a deep breath before answering, "Ricky had an accident," he said flatly. "He was attacked early this morning by a large alligator."

"Is he going to be alright?" Mary cried out with alarm.

Randy walked over and put a hand on Ben's shoulder, "I'm sorry...he didn't make it."

"My son is dead?" Ben questioned, tears flowing.

"I'm sorry...I'm so sorry," Bob said despondently. "Ricky was attacked by a large reptile over by the jetties."

"A large reptile? An alligator at the jetties?" Ben's voice trembled.

Mary tried to stand up. The look on her face was something the men would never forget for the rest of their lives. Her mouth was gaped wide open, but nothing came out. The look of horror on her face was wraith-like. Her eyes were the size of golf balls as she looked over to Ben and fainted.

Randy rushed over to her and felt for a pulse. Satisfied she didn't have a heart attack, he spoke in his walkie-talkie and called for an ambulance.

"Was it quick?" Ben cried out in despair, kneeling by his wife and stroking her head.

Randy looked over to Bob, and their eyes met, "It was quick," replied Randy.

"Was my son in any pain?" Ben continued, his voice getting angry.

Once again, Randy and Bob's eyes met, "I'd like you to come down to the station tomorrow and take a look at the tape," replied Randy, skirting the question.

"I'll bring him over tomorrow, Randy," Bob replied, trying his best to comfort his heart-broken friends.

Within minutes, an ambulance arrived and the paramedics were in the house attending to Mary. Randy gave them a brief explanation of the situation, offered his apologies, and quietly walked out the door. No matter how many times he had to go through things like this, and there were many, he considered it the worst part of the job.

5

"C'mon ya, little freak," Jimmy said to his little brother Steve.

"I'm coming, I'm coming. Why do you always have to call me names… jerk," replied Steve, walking hastily behind his older brother, trying to keep up.

"Because you always have to tag along with me…freak boy."

It's been three years since their father suffered a fatal heart attack. Their mother, who hadn't worked a job since she'd been married, found herself working two jobs around the clock in order to keep a roof over their heads. As it turned out, Jimmy Butler wound up becoming a full-time babysitter for his little brother. Before their father passed away, the two boys were inseparable and always played together, but Jimmy was now seventeen years old and getting into girls. He loathed the idea of looking after his little brother, especially when he tagged along everywhere he went.

It was seven o'clock on a sunny Saturday morning. Jimmy set his alarm clock and gingerly tried to sneak out of the house without Steve and meet a girl from his class. He was nearly out the front door when Steve poked his head out of his bedroom door and asked where they were going today.

Jimmy stood at the front door with his shoes in his hand and realized he couldn't win, "Beach...We're going to the beach," he said, rolling his eyes.

Steve's face lit up with a smile as he ran from his bedroom wearing his brand new orange and yellow flowered bathing suit.

"You knew we were going?" Jimmy marveled.

"Yup, I heard you on the phone last night talking to some girl," he replied, slipping into his flip-flops.

"C'mon, dork," said Jimmy, shrugging his shoulders.

The two brothers hopped on their bikes and headed to Sandy Beach Park. The sun was already heating things up and it looked like it was going to be another scorcher.

"So...Who is she?"

"Nunyer," replied Jimmy, picking up the pace while Steve struggled to keep up.

"Nunyer? What kind of name is that"?

"Nunyer business, that's what," Jimmy laughed and peddled faster.

"Funny... None of your business..." Steve sighed, embarrassed he fell for the joke.

They raced their bikes across town, jumping sidewalk curbs and speeding through stop signs until they finally made it to the beach. Jimmy was already locking his bike to a tree when his little brother arrived and crash-landed into a garbage can.

"Smooth move goofball!" Jimmy laughed.

"It's not funny...I scraped my elbow," Steve whimpered. "You'll live, ya little baby."

A couple of tourists watched the two brothers carrying on. One, a middle-aged lady, offered Steve a band-aid as she gave the evil eye to the older brother. Steve put the band-aid on his elbow and thanked her before rushing off to catch up to his brother, who was walking down the beach.

"Where is she, Jimmy?"

"Shut up, jerk, she's not here yet."

"Why don't you look over by the Indian head statue? Isn't that where you guys said you'd meet?"

"Jeez! Were you listening to the entire conversation on the phone?" replied Jimmy, acting like he didn't forget the meeting spot.

"Most of it, until I heard all that kissy kissy stuff and got sick."

"Shaddap!... Yer such a dork," replied Jimmy, shoving his

hand on Steve's forehead until he fell back.

"Hey, Jimmy! Over here!" Jenny Jennings shouted, waving her arms excitedly.

Jimmy looked over and waved back. He ran over to meet her with his little brother trailing behind.

"Wow! She's pretty," Steve blurted, causing Jimmy to blush.

Jenny was wearing a bright yellow bikini and had her long black hair tied back in a ponytail. Originally from New York, she moved to Florida with her family during the mid-school year. She was featured in a few clothing catalogs and became the envy of the girls in her class. Quick with a smile and eager to make people laugh, she made friends easily.

"Hi Jimmy, who's your friend?" she smiled, knowing it was his little brother.

"Nobody, just my little dork-faced brother," he replied, grabbing Steve in a headlock.

"Don't hurt him, Jimmy. He's a cutie," she said tersely, sticking up for the little man.

Jimmy let go of his brother and gave Jenny a big hug and kiss for what seemed to Steve to last forever.

"Jeez, that's gross. I thought you two were going to suck each other's face off...Ugh!" Steve said as he pretended to vomit.

What Lurks Below

"Shut up, squid!" replied Jimmy, smacking him on the head.

Jenny let go of Jimmy and gave him a dirty look as she put an arm around Steve, "Ahh, leave him alone you big bully," as Steve rubbed his head and tried not to cry.

"I hope you're not planning on picking on my new friend all day," Jenny said in a nice way but meant every word.

Jimmy got the hint and felt a little stupid for acting like that to his little brother. Most girls wouldn't want their boyfriends to run around babysitting, but Jenny was different.

The three of them walked down to the shore and dropped a blanket close to the water. Jenny liked Jimmy but couldn't tolerate him acting like a bully to impress her. She hoped she got through to him and made it clear that she didn't want to see him picking on his little brother.

*****

By nine a.m., Captain Virgil and his crew had already worked four jobs. While Bill and Skip were doing some on-deck maintenance, Chuck was busy in the engine room, greasing and cleaning parts. The Captain was in the wheelhouse when he got a call from Officer Taylor, requesting that he and Chuck meet him at the mayor's office around noon if the work schedule permitted.

Virgil was becoming irritated with the fact that the officer was involving him with the towboat fatality, but once again checked the updated schedule to see if it was clear to meet.

Chuck walked into the wheelhouse and saw the captain reviewing the schedule, "How's the day looking, Virge?"

"Looks like we're clear until five-thirty."

"Good, gives me time to clean the engine room."

"Officer Taylor asked us to meet him at the mayor's office at noon."

"Swell, if this keeps up, I wonder if he'll put us on the payroll."

"Don't hold your breath," replied Virgil wryly.

At a quarter to twelve, Virgil and Chuck were on their way to meet up with the officer at the mayor's office. Skip conned Bill into sneaking off the tug for a couple of hours and having a few drinks at the Anchor Bar.

The Anchor Bar was located a block away from the Port entrance. It was a seedy local bar whose patrons included the usual locals mixed with visiting sailors, bikers, hookers, and a variety of others that worked in and around the area. When Skip wasn't working, he could usually be found sitting on a stool at the end of the bar.

Bill and Skip walked in, and the bartender shook his head disapprovingly, knowing the men were supposed to be working.

"Skip! Bill! How you two crazies doin'?" the bartender asked.

"Good Carlos, all is good," replied Skip, parking himself in his usual spot, "What's the latest round here."

"Same ol' crap. Oh, by the way, Officer Tammy stopped in here about an hour ago and told me she viewed a videotape at the station. She was vague, but she said something about a sea monster attacking somebody in the inlet."

Bill and Skip looked at each other and shook their heads. They were told not to say a word about the tragedy. Carlos concluded that he wasn't going to get any information from them and excused himself, walking to the other end of the bar to serve a pair of hookers that looked like they had a rough night.

An hour passed, and the two men were getting inebriated. "I sure hope they catch the damn thing," Bill slurred.

"They will. They've got no place else to go," replied Skip with a smile, craning his neck to get a look at the hookers.

"What do you mean? It can be allusive," replied Bill with a puzzled look. "Nah, I've seen their kind before," replied Skip, still eyeing the ladies. "You what?"

"Yes, sir. Just 'cause they got a pretty face, they think they can go anywhere, anytime," said Skip, his elbow slipping off the bar.

"Are we talking about the same thing, you drunk bastard?" Bill questioned. "I'm talking about the sea monster," he continued, trying to fix his blood-shot eyes on Skip.

"Wha?... Oh, that thing," cracked Skip. "I thought you were talking about those ladies."

Carlos saw what was going on and walked back over before things got out of hand, "Okay, you scalawags, I think you guys should get back to work," he said implausibly, removing the empty shot glasses of bourbon.

"Sure thing, Carly, whatever you say. Just keep 'em drinks comin'," Skip garbled. "This is our lunching hour."

"You two have had enough. When Captain Virgil finds out you're drunk, he's gonna come in here and kick my ass!" Carlos complained.

"If you don't give us another drink, I'm gonna kick your ass," Skip replied in his best John Wayne imitation, causing Bill to laugh so hard he fell off the bar stool.

"Jees Billy, you're drunk," Skip said, looking down and

seeing Bill sprawled out on the floor.

"Just help me up, Skippy."

Carlos and the hookers broke out in laughter as he gave in and refilled their glasses. Bill slid back on the bar stool, and they toasted another drink.

"Ah, much better," Bill said blissfully as they downed another shot. "Now, what were we talking about?"

"Chicks," replied Skip, winking at the ladies of the night. "You sure?"

"Yup, just 'cause they got a pretty face, they think they can get free drinks."

"What? That's rid...ridicu...ridilicious!"

Bill stopped talking when he realized what he had said. Skip looked at him with a staggered look, "Hey, did you make that word up?"

"Sure did. They're not just delicious...they're redilicious!" Bill laughed and looked over at the two ladies, who were starting to feel uncomfortable.

At that point, the entire bar broke out laughing. The two hookers were so embarrassed; they got up and stormed out without leaving a tip.

"Alright, guys, that's enough," said Carlos. "You can't chase away the patrons."

Carlos took the shot glasses away quickly and replaced them with hot coffee.

"Wow, thanks, boss," Skip said.

"Carlos is doing the right thing, Skip. Sober up, and let's get back to the tug," Bill replied, drawing a surprised look from the bartender.

"Cheers."

*****

The ocean was calm, and the pelicans were flying in combat formation, cruising the beach and occasionally bombing unlucky beachgoers. As they flew down the beach, they appeared to zero in on three kids lying on a spread-out beach blanket.

Steve saw them coming and slowly got up from the blanket. He told Jimmy and Jenny he was going to cool off in the water.

"Be careful," Jenny said with a loving smile. "Get lost," Jimmy snarled.

Steve couldn't hide his wicked grin as he jumped into the water and turned to watch the pelicans. He watched as Jimmy and Jenny were so busy kissing and whispering sweet nothings to each other that they didn't notice the pelicans until it was too late.

Splat...Splat...Splat...The birds successfully hit their target. "Ah, shit!" Jimmy yelled, jumping up.

"Aaauugghh!" Jenny cried at the same time.

Jimmy was standing in water up to his shoulders, laughing his heart out until he accidentally gulped down a quart of saltwater.

"Oops! Sorry guys," he shouted as he spat out the water. "I should have warned you when I saw them coming!"

"You idiot!" Jimmy shouted, white and green slime oozing down his back. "I'm gonna drown your sorry butt!"

He stopped yelling for a second as he noticed the water swirl close by his brother, followed by a wake headed toward the jetties. For a brief moment, goosebumps ran up the back of his neck until he reasoned that it was probably a school of fish. A few other people on the beach also saw it and stood up, pointing at the water. When the ripples diminished, they sat back in their easy chairs and went about their business.

Jimmy raced down to the water and jumped in, followed by Jenny. He swam underwater until he reached Steve, grabbing his head and dunking him underwater. Steve got away and broke the surface, but before he could take a breath, Jimmy jumped up, grabbed him in a headlock, and pulled him under again.

"Laugh at me, will ya! Ya, little freak!"

"Aaagh! Stop it, Jimmy! I can't breathe!" Steve howled.

"Ha ha, jerk! It's time to pay," Jimmy laughed as he dunked his brother again.

"Stop it, Jimmy, or I'm going home!" Jenny yelled, grabbing his arm. Jimmy was showing off again at his little brothers' expense. But when Jenny threatened to leave, he let go of Steve and gave him a kick, causing him to cry out in pain. "Okay cry baby, you get to live another day."

Steve cleared the water from his eyes and swam over to Jenny. She could see that by the look on his face, the little guy was having a rough day. "Don't worry, Stevie, I'll protect you," she smiled, patting him on the head.

Jimmy was rinsing the pelican droppings off his shoulders while Steve splashed the muddle off Jenny's back. Jimmy gave a sullied look, catching Jenny's eyes as she smiled and winked at him, as if to say it was alright, the little guy's just trying to help.

6

Officer Randy Taylor was waiting for Captain Virgil and Chuck outside the mayor's office. At five 'til twelve, Virgil's van pulled into the overcrowded parking lot and drove right past the parking attendant without stopping for a ticket. Virgil spotted Randy leaning on his car, shaking his head.

"What are you doing, Captain? You've got to stop and get a ticket before parking in here," the officer bleated.

"Put it on the mayor's tab," Virgil shouted with a cocky attitude as he parked the van next to the officers' car.

Virgil and Chuck got out of the van and met with Randy. "You've got a bad attitude, Captain Goodman," said Randy.

"It could be worse," Chuck replied, keeping pace with the captain as heblazed toward the office.

"Let's make this quick. Taylor, Chuck, and I are on the clock," Virgil stipulated, taking no notice of the officers' ranting.

The mayor's office was busy with the everyday dealings that kept the town on track. It seemed everybody was in the building but the mayor.

"Take a seat, fellas. I'll call you when he's ready," the secretary said non-chalantly.

"I bet Myers isn't even here," Virgil growled at her, leaning over her desk.

"He'll be in shortly," she replied, a little put off by the comment. "Tell him he knows where to find me...on my time," Virgil snarled. "Give him a few minutes, Captain," Randy retorted.

Virgil gave him an imposing look and replied, "We'll be at the tug," and walked out.

"Whew, what's eatin' him?" he asked Chuck.

"He doesn't think much of the mayor," he replied, following Virgil out the door.

Officer Taylor took a seat and impatiently waited for his appointment. Fidgeting in his chair, he was also ready to walk out. He had a busy day ahead of him, but he couldn't get anything started until he first talked to the mayor.

"Excuse me," he said to the secretary, "Are you sure Mr. Myers knows I'm waiting to see him?"

"I spoke to him last night, sir," she replied irritably. "It's Saturday morning, he said he'd be here."

Nearly an hour and a half later, Mayor Nick Myers waltzed through the front door.

"Hello, Molly," he cheerfully said to his secretary as he

walked past Randy like he wasn't there.

"Good day, Mr. Myers. You sure seem to be in good spirits today," she replied with a gratifying smile.

"Well, my dear," he stopped short and turned to face her, "That's because I had just finished my best game of golf ever. I scored a ninety."

Randy couldn't believe his ears. He made it clear that he had to talk to the mayor and that it was extremely important. He jumped out of his chair and stormed down the hall, where he caught the mayor by surprise.

"Excuse me, officer..." said the secretary. Too late, he grabbed him by the arm, forced him into the office, and slammed the door shut.

"Just what the hell do you think you're doing, Taylor!" the Mayor demanded.

Officer Randy Taylor tried to be a patient man, but after waiting for nearly two hours to discuss a life-threatening matter, he blew his top.

"Listen up, Nick," he replied, jabbing him in the chest with his pointing finger, "What I'm about to say is very important."

"You've always been a bully, Taylor; I should have fired you long ago," he replied, rubbing his flabby chest.

"There is some kind of monster swimming around out there that attacked and killed a towboat operator inside the jetties. I'm closing the Port and surrounding beach areas to small boaters."

"The hell you say! I'm not closing..."

"Just sit down and watch this tape," Randy interrupted as he rolled a cart with a television and video tape player closer to the desk and inserted a videotape inside.

The mayor sat in silence as the officer fast-forwarded the tape until the towboat came into view.

"That's Bob Jackson's towboat," Randy pointed eagerly. "I'm aware of it," Myers hissed.

The mayor sat motionless until he saw the part where the reptile attacked, "Damn it! Damn it all to hell," he shouted, more pissed off than shocked, which seemed a little peculiar to Randy.

Randy fell back in his chair, still unable to grasp what he saw. Oddly, he noticed the mayor jump up and start pacing by the window, deep in thought.

"Well damn it, Taylor, that looked like a scene from Jaws. We'll hire a couple of hunters and catch that damn thing," he said without a hint of remorse.

"It's not a shark, Nick. It's some kind of prehistoric alligator or something," the agitated officer retorted.

"Whatever it is, I want it caught as quickly and quietly as possible. I don't want to scare the tourists away."

"You don't think they'll notice when the Port and beaches are closed?"

"Close a section of beach near the jetties. The Port stays open," he ordered.

"What!"

"Make up some bullshit story about toxicology tests being the reason for closing the beach for a couple of days. Tell them the seagulls crapped in the water too much."

"I don't think you understand exactly what's going on here, Nick!"

"I know exactly what's going on!" the mayor roared back. "Now get the hell out of my office before I fire your ass!"

"You're making a big mistake!" Randy snapped, flinging the door open and storming out.

"Close the damn door!" he screamed to no one, as Randy was already gone.

******

After a lunch break at the Sandy Beach Burger Shack, Jenny suggested they take a walk on the jetties. Her favorite thing to do at Sandy Beach Park was to walk to the very end of the jetties, which extended out nearly one hundred yards and wave at the boats cruising in and out of the inlet.

The park was located on a small barrier island between the Intracoastal and the ocean. It had one of the most beautiful beaches in South Florida. It included trails along a creek that ran the length of the island called Rumrunners' Creek. The ocean side had one of the most clandestine beaches in the area. The parking lot was hidden by large Australian pine trees and sand dunes, where a boardwalk led to the uncongested beach.

Jenny took Jimmy by the hand and started walking along the beach toward the jetties.

"Maybe Steve can wait for us on the beach," she whispered in his ear, trying to get cozy.

It was against Jimmy's better judgment to stay away from home all day without calling or checking in with his mother, which she drilled into his head. At the risk of looking like a little kid who had to be home, he had to think of something quick.

"Nah, we'll have to walk out there some other time. Me and

the little dork have to get home. I've got baseball practice in an hour," he lied.

Steve looked up and gave his brother a weird face, "No, you don't; you don't have practice until next Tuesday."

"Shut up, numb nuts! You don't know nothing," Jimmy snarled.

"See? You don't have practice 'til Tuesday," Jenny purred, smiling at Steve, and continued on to the jetties.

Jimmy looked torn between admitting that he had to go home and check in with his mom or keep up with his racing hormones and follow Jenny.

"Okay, let's go," the hormones won as he raced Jenny to the large boulders extending from the beach.

When they made it to the rocks, they stopped running and carefully walked out to the end with Steve following close behind. Jenny reached into her handbag and retrieved the remains of her hamburger.

"Here you go Steve, feed this to the seagulls," she instructed, hoping it would keep him busy enough so she could steal a kiss from his brother.

Eighteen feet below the surface, on the inlet side of the rocks, the vast predator rested on a rocky shelf, awaiting prey. The colossal reptile measured a startling thirty-five feet long. It was a wonder how nobody had spotted it thus far, as it had been lurking in the area now for over a week. A ferocious predator, it had no enemies. It was at the top of the food chain. Its eight-inch conical teeth protruded from its jaws like a grotesque bear trap. Its blackish-brown hide was extremely thick and was protected with what looked like armored plates called Scutes.

Since its arrival to the area, the monstrous reptile seemed to like this spot best for hunting. Within the past week, it had been feasting on large snook, unsuspecting pelicans, curious porpoises, sharks, hapless manatees, and most recently...a human, which it recognized as the slowest and easiest prey. The mutant creature had a never-ending appetite.

"C'mon, Jimmy, I'll race you back to the beach!" Steve said playfully. "No way, goofball, if you slip on these rocks, you'll kill yourself."

Steve shrugged and gave up trying to get him to play. Any other time, they would have raced back, but now that he was with his girlfriend, he was no fun at all.

"Ooh yuck!" Steve screamed as he stood up and felt his backside. He was so busy watching his brother and Jenny fooling around that he hadn't noticed that he sat on the bloody remains of what once was a pelican.

"Ooh, what is that!" Jenny screamed in revulsion.

"Looks like it used to be a pelican," Jimmy muttered, getting a closer look at the blood, guts, and sinew hanging off the bone.

"Gross, I got blood all over my butt!" Steve cried out.

"Serves you, right twerp. You should watch where you sit," Jimmy snickered.

Steve carefully crawled down the rocks so that he could splash water on himself and clean the mess off of him. He slipped on the slimy rocks and fell into the water. Jimmy saw it happen and rushed over to make sure he didn't hit his head on a rock.

Climbing down as low as he could go without falling in, Jimmy reached out and shouted, "Grab my hand, butt-head."

The rocks were slippery with algae, and Steve quickly found out that the only way out of the water was to grab his brother's hand.

"Hurry up, turkey, before you get slammed on the rocks by waves," Jimmy said as he looked out and saw a set of swells coming in.

The gargantuan reptile's eyes sprang open when the boy fell

into the water. Little stubbles on its body called Integumentary Sense organs detected the pressure change in the water. It slowly moved to where it was directly under its prey and waited, preparing to shoot straight up and catch its prey off guard.

Possessing extremely good vision, the revolting creature became agitated when it saw two more objects of prey on the rocks, possibly trying to steal its food. It had to act swiftly as it targeted the thing splashing in the water and primed to spring into action.

"C'mon, dumb ass, hurry up!"

"I am. Just wait a minute," Steve replied as he finished cleaning himself. "Listen, snapper head, big waves are coming! Grab my hand!" Jimmy shouted with apprehension, eyeing the set of incoming swells.

Jimmy reached down and grabbed his brother by the wrist. As he pulled him up the rocks, he caught a glimpse of the reptile shooting up from the depths with its mouth wide open.

"Steve!" he screamed, yanking his little brother out of the water with all his strength.

Both brothers fell back on the rocks as the monster soared out of the water like a missile, its enormous jaws snapping shut and missing its prey by inches, or so Jimmy thought.

"Whoa! It missed us; let's get outta here!" Jimmy frantically screamed as the hideous reptile gripped onto the jetties.

But all was not well. One of the big eight-inch teeth protruding from the massive jaws caught Steve and sliced him from his right thigh to the top of his head.

"C'mon Stevie, run!"

When his brother didn't respond, Jimmy looked down and was horrified to see Steve's entire right side covered in blood. It's okay, little brother, you just cut yourself on the rocks, he thought.

With a rush of adrenalin, he scooped Steve up in his arms and ran toward the beach, leaving a stunned Jenny standing like a statue. He stopped when he heard his brother try to scream, but all that came out was a sick, gurgling sound.

Jimmy thought he had pulled his brother out of danger in the nick of time but failed to see that one of the reptile's teeth sliced through Steve like a scalpel, severing his jugular vein. He watched in horror as his little brother tried to scream, staring at him with wide, unbelieving eyes.

"Oh no, no, no...Stevie!" he screamed out, laying him on the rocks as he began shaking repulsively with convulsions.

Jenny screamed out for help. Her knees were shaking so

badly that she couldn't run.

Jimmy picked his brother up in his arms again and started running for the beach, crying hysterically, as the enormous reptile scuttled to the top of the rocks and gave chase.

For a brief moment, it looked like the reptile was going to run past Jenny, but it stopped abruptly and turned on the girl. The people on the beach jumped up in awe when they heard the blood-curdling scream. People shrieked and cried as they witnessed the horrendous reptile maul Jenny. They could do nothing but watch as the reptile's jaws clamped down on her torso and shook its head violently until she was torn in half. Some of the men acted like they were going to run to her rescue as the reptile continued to devour the poor girl, only to fall to their knees and vomit.

Jimmy finally made it to the beach and set his brother in the sand. Quick-thinking beachgoers ran over and wrapped towels around Steve. Exhausted and bleeding from falling all over the rocks, Jimmy collapsed and started to go into shock.

Steve's pale, lifeless body had bled out. His blank eyes stared up at the people gathering with a look of dismay.

Boats that were coming and going through the inlet had stopped and couldn't believe what they were seeing. The hideous monster was standing on the rocks, chomping the bloody flesh that used to be Jenny. Some boaters tried to get the monster's attention by blowing horns until the beast turned to face them, and they quickly sped out of the way.

Twenty minutes later, paramedics arrived and attended to Jimmy when, all of a sudden, he sprang up and crawled over to a blanket that was now covering his little brother. The pain and guilt set in on him as Jimmy realized little Stevie wasn't coming home. All of the petty name-calling was not for real. He loved his little brother and wished he could tell him now.

Police arrived with boats and a helicopter, firing shots at the grotesque reptile to no avail, as the bullets appeared to bounce off the thick hide. After a few shotgun blasts, which did little more than irritate the creature, it crawled back into the water, swam under the startled boaters, and vanished in the depths.

Officer Randy Taylor was still seething about the run-in with the mayor when the call came through the radio. He quickly made a U-turn and headed back to the mayor's office.

"Dispatch, this is Officer Taylor," he vexed sternly. "I'm on my way back to see the mayor. I want full details of the attack when I return."

"10-4, we'll have the report within the hour."

Randy was raving mad when he stormed through the mayor's office and demanded to see him.

"One moment please, Mr. Myers is on the phone," the secretary implored.

The officer walked past her, ignoring her plead, and stormed through his office as he hung up the phone.

"Taylor, I see you left your manners behind and figured you could just walk right in here," the mayor said derisively.

"Stuff it, Nick, there's been another attack."

"Yes, I know. I just heard about it."

"And what are you going to do about it?"

The Mayor nervously sat back in his chair and folded his hands in front of him. Finally, he stood up, walked over, and closed the office door.

"Okay, Randy, close the beaches, but only for twenty-four hours."

Randy gave him a nasty look before replying, "Twenty-four hours, maybe more."

"Twenty-four hours is a lifetime in this tourist town. If the tourists can't swim and go boating, they'll go elsewhere," Myers retorted.

"Have you got some trappers in mind?" asked Randy, ignoring the mayor's idiocy.

"I just got off the phone with Chief Bhim, the trapper who owns the Wildlife Sanctuary in the Everglades."

"You've got to be kidding!" Randy hissed. His resentment toward the Indian trackers was well known.

"I've used them before," Myers replied smugly. "They'll capture their reptile in no time."

"You've got to be joking, Nick! Those damn Indians are a bunch of drunks! Last time they came around, I nearly arrested the whole lot of them!"

"Is that so? I do recall that they captured that alligator out of a residential swimming pool in less than two hours!"

"I don't know what was worse, the alligator in the pool or the drunkin' Indians causing the riot at the Anchor Bar!" Randy shouted, feeling more and more uneasy about the whole situation.

"Bhim and his crew are doing the job," the mayor said flatly.

"I hope you know what the hell you're doing Nick," Randy replied, opening up the door and walking out.

He walked to his car with a thought weighing on his mind. *What did Nick mean when he said, "They'll capture their reptile?"*

7

Chief Bhim was the leader of a small tribe of Seminole Indians living at a tourist attraction called the Everglades Sanctuary. He was sixty-two years old with a husky build that showed no signs of aging on a six-foot frame. His complexion was like worn leather from years in the sun. He claimed to be a descendant of the first Seminole tribe on record.

The tribe lived in small houses built out of wood on the outskirts of the Sanctuary. It was located in the heart of the Everglades, where the tribe rescued animals and caged them in a zoo environment where tourists could take an airboat ride out and visit.

The Chief and ten of his best hunters were now headed for town to hunt for the elusive reptile. They arrived late in the afternoon and met with Officer Randy Taylor at the patrol station located inside Port Everglades.

"Chief Bhim, glad you and your men are here," Taylor lied, shaking the Chief's hand as they sat down.

Bhim barely grunted in return, as he loathed the officer as much as the officer detested the Indians.

"Before we get started, I want you to take a look at this

video," Randy continued in a cordial manner. He closed the window blinds and played the video.

As the monstrous reptile came into view, the officer watched their faces and observed how they weren't alarmed, confirming to himself that maybe they knew more about this beast than they were willing to discuss.

When Randy turned off the video and opened the window blinds, he turned to Chief Bhim and waited for a reaction.

Bhim sat staring at the blank screen for a few moments before saying, "What I've just seen is no ordinary alligator. I will capture that creature... but I want more money," he said flatly.

"Take it up with the mayor," retorted Randy.

"I also want no obstruction from the law. My people will not be arrested or abused in any way while we're here."

Randy couldn't control his anger and went off in a rage, "I will arrest any one of you who do not follow the law. What happened last time you were here was a complete fiasco, and I will not tolerate it. You and your boys here will capture that damn beast as quickly as possible and get the hell out of town! Understood?"

"I'm sure Nick won't see it that way," Bhim replied bitterly, referring to the mayor as if they were buddies.

Randy calmed down and spoke in a low tone, "Kill the reptile, I'll double the money," he promised, opening the door and indicating that the meeting was over.

The officer's hands were tied. He needed the creature captured quickly and was not about to squabble over money. He knew the chief would get his way no matter what. He detested the thought of the Indians living in the Everglades free of charge without even paying taxes and now coming to his town demanding more money.

He sat brooding in his office, thinking about the meeting that just took place, how the hunters watching the video weren't surprised like others who saw it. It was almost like they'd seen it before; he could have sworn he overheard one of them whisper a name for it.

Not even twenty minutes passed when the phone rang. Randy broke his train of thought and answered, "Officer Randy Taylor, how can I help you?"

"The Indians get free rein of the town while they're here," ordered the Mayor.

Nick Myers, ignoring any hint of niceties.

"As you wish," replied Randy, submitting to a winless battle.

What Lurks Below

He slammed the phone down and began to wonder if maybe the mayor was somehow involved with the reptile, the way he was trying to keep it a secret and hiring Bhim so fast. Maybe he's in cahoots with Bhim and the Sanctuary. Maybe that damn thing came from the Sanctuary?

His thoughts were broken when his secretary knocked on the door to report a topless lady jogging down the beach.

****

It's been years since Ben Manditto had been seen drinking at the Anchor Bar. Now, after the untimely death of his only son, he left his grieving wife at home and entered the bar.

The usual lunchtime crowd was there, and the food and drinks were flowing. Ben walked into the dark room and adjusted his eyes, spotting an empty bar stool in the corner, and headed for it.

"Benjamin Manditto? It's been a long time. What brings you here?" asked Carlos, the bartender, smiling and extending his hand to shake with the elder man.

Ben ignored the hospitality and hung his head low. Carlos withdrew his hand and grabbed a bottle of Makers Mark, remembering Ben's favorite whiskey.

Ben looked up with a pale, gaunt face and drank the shot

before answering, "I'm here because Rick's dead."

Carlos' heart sank when he realized Rick was the victim of the reptile attack and was stricken with grief.

"Ah, Ben, I'm so sorry," he replied remorsefully, pouring another shot.

Ben ignored him and downed the shot. Carlos left the bottle with Ben and walked away to attend to the other patrons.

As Ben sat there draining the bottle, he reflected on earlier times with his son, remembering how proud he and his wife were. They wanted nothing but the best for him, scraping and saving for his college education since the day he was born. He wanted to give his son the things in life that he never had, and now it was gone... all gone.

Polishing off the bottle and feeling the effect, Ben wondered what it was all about. Why did this happen to such a wonderful son? Why was he sitting in this dingy bar and his son dead? Why can't they find his body for a proper burial? It just didn't seem fair.

"I'll have another," he slurred, raising his empty glass as he stood up to go to the restroom. He wobbled over to the restroom door and tried to push it open. It wouldn't budge. He thought about it for a minute and finally realized he had to pull it open.

"Open up, you goddamn door," he mumbled to himself as he entered.

"Easy Pops," came the voice of a stranger standing at the urinal.

"Who the hell you callin' Pops!" Ben roared, noticing a skinny little man about half his age.

There was no reply. Frank Scully had seen his type before. Frank was a regular at the bar and was feeling a bit drunk himself. He perceived in the stranger's tone that the man was looking for trouble. He decided to shut up, finish his business, and walk out in one piece.

Ben staggered up to the urinal next to the man, "I said, who the hell are you calling pops, you skinny faggot?"

"Easy, old man, I didn't mean to get you hot," scoffed Frank.

Ben unzipped his fly and began to urinate. He turned to the man next to him and started to say something but forgot what he was thinking.

Suddenly, Frank screamed out in horror, "Hey! What the...?"

Ben was facing the man and peeing on his pant leg, "Oops, sorry, partner," he chuckled. "See what happens? You talk crap, and people mistake you for a toilet."

Ben broke out in uncontrollable laughter and urinated all

over the floor. Frank quickly zipped up and tried to kick Ben in the groin but slipped on the wet floor and fell flat on his back. Ben jumped back and wanted to kill the little man but was so drunk he fell down and rammed his knee into the man's chest.

"Uughh! Get the hell off me!" he screamed in pain, pushing Ben against the urinal.

The two drunks began rolling around on the pee-covered floor, trying to kick each other to death, when Carlos burst through the door and broke up the fight.

"Stop it, Ben!" he shouted, grabbing him by the arm, "You're only making matters worse!"

Ben pulled his arm back and was ready to hit the bartender. Carlos saw it coming and gave him a right hook to the stomach, ending Ben's tirade immediately. Doubled over and trying to catch his breath, he felt embarrassed. He slowly stood up and walked to the sink and washed his hands. Carlos helped Frank up and walked over to the door.

"You two fight again and I'll kick both your asses, got it!" he turned and pointed a finger, then walked out as if nothing happened.

Ben tried to apologize, but Frank wouldn't hear it. Still feeling embarrassed, Ben staggered back to his bar stool and ordered another drink. Five minutes later, Frank came out of the restroom and walked past Ben without saying a word. He smelt like a urinal.

After a few more drinks, Ben was deep in thought again. In such a short time, he'd gone from being the proudest man in the world who seemed to have it all: a great job, a great family, and a son with a bright future to a broken man who lost everything.

He started to blame himself for his son's untimely death. When offered the towboat job, Ricky shrugged it off at first until dear 'ol dad told him it would be a good experience. Always trying to please his father, he changed his mind and took the job.

"Last one, Ben," Carlos said, breaking Ben's thoughts, "Last one... Go home and be with your wife."

"I'll go home when I'm good and ready!" Ben retorted, gulping down another shot.

Carlos shook his head disapprovingly and walked to the other side of the bar. He felt bad for the man and decided to leave him alone and let him drink where at least he could keep an eye on him. After he's had his fill, he figured he would call him a cab and pay the fare.

Unexpectedly, Ben stood up and gazed at his drunken

reflection in the huge mirror behind the bar and shouted, "You dumb sonofabitch! You killed Ricky!" and proceeded to throw his empty shot glass through the mirror, shattering it to smithereens.

The smashed mirror made a mess behind the bar as it collapsed through a glass shelf holding a stock full of liquor bottles. The entire bar went quiet as the startled patrons looked on in dismay. Carlos ran from behind the bar and grabbed Ben by the arm, forcefully removing him from the bar stool. Before Ben could protest, Carlos had thrown him out the front door and onto the sidewalk.

"Go home and sober up, you drunken sod! You come back in here and I'll have you arrested!" he shouted, losing what little patience he had.

Ben picked himself off the sidewalk and straightened his clothes. Pointing a finger at Carlos, he retorted, "I should feed you to the reptile that killed my son! You'd be like poison and kill that thing for sure!"

"Get outta here, ya drunk bastard!" Carlos shouted. "Go home to your poor wife!" he continued as he slammed the door shut.

Ben staggered down the sidewalk towards home. He didn't really want to face his heartbroken wife in his condition but couldn't prolong it any further.

Fifteen minutes later, he stumbled to his front porch and fumbled through his pockets for the keys. He became irritated when he looked through the window and saw the house was dark. Mary always had the lights on at dusk. He finally opened the door and turned on a living room light.

"I'm home, Mary," he mumbled, tossing the keys on the coffee table.

No answer. He wondered where his wife had gone. Staggering to the kitchen, he opened the refrigerator and found that his dinner was also missing. He sat at the kitchen table and pondered the day's events. Before he left, the house was full of family and neighbors offering their condolences and grieving for Ricky. It was too much for him to handle and he just got up and left. Now feeling a bit remorseful, he wished he'd stayed home to comfort his wife.

Now, the house was empty – completely empty. He walked outside and stood on the sidewalk, searching up and down the street to see if Mary was talking to neighbors. Seeing no sign of her, he returned to the house and grabbed a beer. Brooding at the kitchen table, he figured that she must have gone to her sister's house.

He stood up and stumbled to the telephone, trying to figure

out what he was going to say to Mary or if she would even talk to him. Dialing the number, the bathroom light down the hall caught his eye from underneath the closed door.

"Mary?" he called out. "Mary honey, are you in there?" he asked again as he hung up the phone. He straightened up and ran his fingers through his hair, trying to put himself together.

He walked down the hall like a man on a mission, carefully bumping into the walls and repeating the word 'damn.' Leaning on the bathroom door, he quietly turned the handle and peeked inside to see Mary in the tub and the room glowing with lit candles.

"Mary... I'm sorry I walked out," he said as he walked over and knelt down beside her. "We'll get through this together, honey. I promise. I was an idiot for going to the bar," he confessed, running his hands on her shoulders.

She didn't make a sound; Ben figured his poor wife was so exhausted that she probably cried herself to sleep. He gently tried to wake her, but she was literally dead to the world.

"Come on honey, let's get you to bed," he tried to say with compassion but slurred every word.

He leaned over and kissed her on the cheek, noticing for the first time that she was ice-cold. Startled, his heart skipped a beat at the same moment that he noticed an empty bottle of sleeping pills on the floor.

"Oh no!" he gasped, his mind unable to comprehend the tragedy. "Wake up, Mary! Wake up!" He promptly leaned over to pick her up, but she felt like a two-ton anchor. He lost his grip on her and fell backward, hitting his head on the toilet.

Dazed, confused, and way too drunk, he tried to stand up but stumbled head-on into the shelf containing five large candles. His long-sleeved shirt ignited in flames before he knew what happened. Screaming out in pain, he tried in vain to rip his shirt off. By now, the shower curtain was also on fire. He looked back at his wife, who seemed to be eerily at peace, and made a dash for the door. Once again, he slipped and smashed his face on the sink, knocking him unconscious.

Glenn Tibbits, a neighbor who lived down the street was walking his dog past the house and saw the smoke billowing out the windows. He rushed next door and banged on the door. A lady in a night gown opened the door as far as the chain lock would allow.

"Call nine-one-one! The house next door's on fire!"

At that instant, the door opened wide, and a large man in a bathrobe peered down at the intruder, "If you're lying, I will shoot you," he calmly said, waving a three-fifty-seven magnum like Dirty Harry.

"Lying?! Take a look for yourself!" the man with the dog said, losing control and pointing at the burning house.

The lady smelt smoke and dashed outside to take a look, "My God! The Mandittos' house is burning!" she screamed as she ran with the stranger to the house while her husband called the emergency number.

They kicked through the living room window and climbed inside, shouting for the occupants. The smoke-filled house made it almost impossible to breathe as they rushed to the bathroom and saw Ben on the floor. They quickly picked him up, carried him outside, and lay him on the swale next to the road.

"He's not breathing!" the neighbor cried out.

"Here comes the paramedics," Glenn pointed out as three paramedic trucks and a fire engine came rushing down the street.

Within minutes, the entire neighborhood was outside, watching the commotion. Glenn and the next-door neighbors were giving statements to the police as they saw the paramedics cover Ben with a blanket.

"Poor Ben," the lady sobbed in her husband's arms. "I wonder where Mary is."

Glenn felt the lump in his throat as he pointed to the firefighters coming out of the house with Mary's body. Most of the neighbors ruefully turned and walked back to their homes, deeply saddened and unable to understand how the Manditto family could come to such a tragic end.

8

The sun was up for nearly an hour, and Captain Virgil Goodman was already up reading the paper. Even though he was trying to enjoy his week off, he rarely slept past eight.

Suddenly, there was a loud knock at the door. Now what? Who the hell can that be at this hour, Virgil thought. He quickly and quietly jumped up to answer the door before another knock came. To his surprise, he was standing face to face with his old buddy, Don Henderson. The same person he hadn't seen or heard from since they split Louisiana quite a few years back.

"Donald! What a surprise," he whispered. "Come on in." "It's good to see you, Virge. Why the whisper?"

"Family Don. I've got a wife and kids sound asleep upstairs," Virgil replied, leading Don into the kitchen, where they sat down at the table.

"Wow, you've got family," Don said, acting surprised. "You're the lucky one."

"Yeah, I'm the lucky one. We all have to grow up sooner or later," he said, looking at Don with a sinister grin. "So, what brings you here at this ungodly hour 'ol buddy?"

"Well, Virgil, it's a long story, a long, unbelievable story."

"Okay, that explains why you're here so early in the morning, so let's hear it," Virgil replied cordially, pouring more coffee and wondering what kind of scam his old pal was up to now.

"Oh, congratulations, by the way," Don said, quickly changing the subject. "I heard you are a tugboat captain."

Virgil set his coffee cup down on the table and looked Don in the eye, trying to figure out what he was up to before replying, "Thanks. What do you mean you heard I was a tugboat captain? Who were you talking to?"

"Nobody in particular, Virge; I just got in town last night and went to a place called the Anchor Bar. I asked the bartender if he knew you, and he sent me here," Don answered, noticing the quizzical look on Virgil's face.

Virgil's mind was hard at work. What was Don Henderson, a man he hadn't seen in years, doing at his house at this hour? After all these years, why would he just happen to drop by?

"Okay, Don, let's have it," he cut to the chase. "Why, after all this time, are you making a social visit at seven-thirty in the morning?"

Don looked up in surprise, "Hell Virge, I see you still have that skeptical mind working twenty-four hours a day. After all this time, I come to visit my buddy, and you want me to cut to the chase?" he questioned, shrugging his shoulders and holding his hands up.

"Because I know you didn't just stop by to say hello. Remember? I'm quite aware of your strange fascination with alligators in Louisiana, and I hope, for your sake, that you have nothing to do with a large mutant-looking reptile that's eating people around the jetties," he replied with a glare.

Don was defeated. Virgil was always quick, adding two and two together, and this time, it was no different. His former buddy saw right through him. His first thought was to throw his hands up in the air and walk out the door. He sat for a moment, staring across the table before getting up and leaning on the counter with his back toward Virgil.

"Okay, Virge... you win. What I'm about to say can't leave this room, understood"?

Virgil didn't answer. He leaned back in his chair, crossed his arms, and waited for Don to continue.

Don waited for a reply but continued when he was sure he wouldn't get one. "It started when we left the shrimp boat. You took off like a bat out of hell, but I stayed behind and did a little research on alligators and crocodiles. I thought it would be fascinating if the two mated."

"You've lost your mind," Virgil cut in. "Why would you think of such a thing?"

"Because it's never been done," Don answered flatly. "When I found out it could not be done naturally, I became determined more than ever to make it happen."

"What would you gain?" Virgil glared.

"What would I gain? Can you imagine the people that would flock to see a large, monstrous reptile, a freak of nature? I'd make millions! Headlines reading, *Nature said it couldn't be done, but man made it happen.* I'd be famous!" he ranted.

"Another P.T. Barnum," Virgil said sarcastically, "How the hell did you do it?"

"Well, it wasn't easy. I guess I was at the right place at the right time. I met these two scientists on Bourbon Street one night, and we talked."

"You don't just meet people on the street and tell them you want to transmute reptiles," replied Virgil, clearly agitated.

"True, but I'm not at liberty to talk about them," Don explained, becoming hostile. "I can tell you they were experimenting with bio fish."

"Bio fish?"

"These guys are part of a bigger picture that I can't discuss, but I can say they were genetically altering catfish. They somehow made them grow bigger and faster so their fish farms could make much more money in a lot less time. They created a super breed that grew relentlessly," he continued proudly, maybe saying more than he should have.

"What do you mean relentlessly?" Virgil questioned.

Don thought for a moment and realized he had said too much, "Well, Virge, they seemed to become very aggressive. They became territorial and would aggressively attack anything, including each other."

"An aggressive catfish, you must be proud," he replied scathingly. "They did it, not me."

"So where do you fit in with this generically altering picture?" Virgil asked, hoping it wasn't what he thought.

"I was trying to buy a ticket to Easy Street," Don replied defensively. "Go on," Virgil said, standing up and pacing the kitchen.

"I thought that if I could make a superior reptile and sell it as an attraction, people would pay big money to see the thing. Through a mutual friend, I was able to contact these two Chinese scientists who were heavily into biofish research."

"Don, is that monster out there yours?" Virgil cut in flatly.

"Let me finish Virge," Don replied, beginning to sweat. "I wanted to make a big, successful monster attraction, something bigger than King Kong! More dangerous than Jaws! Scarier than..."

"Answer the question," Virgil snapped with a look that could kill.

Don put his head in his hands before answering, "Yes, the damn thing is mine."

The first thing Virgil wanted to do was strangle his old buddy, but that wouldn't help. He needed to know everything about the reptile and, most of all, how to kill it.

"You stupid bastard, you should be hung from the tallest tree in town," he bellowed.

Don knew Virgil wouldn't be happy about the answer, so he tried to ignore the comment and continue his story. Virgil was still pacing and trying to remain calm, but the more he heard, the more he wanted to punch out his former friend. He listened carefully as Don ranted and raved about his work. Finally, he took a deep breath and joined Don at the table. He sat down and poured himself another cup of coffee, refraining from refilling his guest's cup.

Don continued with a dry throat, "These two scientists were making transgenic catfish. They spliced genes of other species into the catfish eggs, somehow causing them to grow faster and much larger. It was quite amazing, to say the least. First, they seemed to…"

"What kind of other species?"

"I'm not sure, but they grew ten times larger and, unfortunately, very aggressive."

"I can't believe what I'm hearing. How aggressive?"

"Enough to make them abandon the project for fear that they would escape and wreak havoc on the entire fish population," Don replied solemnly. "I thought that with a super killer reptile on display, people would flock worldwide to see it feed on large animals."

"You're insane!" Virgil replied acidly.

"God knows I wouldn't have done it if I knew it would escape."

"Where did it escape from?"

Don ignored the question and continued, his voice growing stronger, "A long story short, we spliced genes from a twenty-two-foot saltwater crocodile with eggs from a large alligator and hatched the most dangerous reptile on the planet."

"Where did it escape from?" Virgil asked again.

"They escaped from a place called the Everglades

Sanctuary," Don finally hesitantly answered.

Virgil's eyes grew large as he stood up from the chair, "They? How many of these damn monsters are there?"

"Only three hatched. They broke through the electric fence and climbed out of a steep moat surrounding their pen. The runt of the litter was fifteen feet long and quickly killed by hunters in the Everglades. Another is believed to be headed north. We're still trying to track it, but don't worry about that one. He's in a remote part of the Everglades and will probably never be seen for his entire life. The one we have to worry about is the one you've seen. The damn thing swam straight up the canal leading to the Intracoastal, where it seems to be flourishing."

"I've got to warn Officer Taylor. He just hired some hunters to track it down!" Virgil said hastily, walking to the telephone.

"Chief Bhim already knows about the reptile," replied Don uneasily. "Chief, who?"

"Bhim. Mayor Nick Myers contacted him the minute the reptile escaped."

"Myers knew about that damn thing and didn't warn anybody!?" Virgil shouted, his temper boiling over. He stared at Don like he was going to kill the man before letting out a heavy sigh and collecting his thoughts.

"How big is that monster?" Virgil continued, trying to compose himself.

Don swallowed hard before he answered, "We last measured it at thirty-three feet long, give or take a few inches."

Virgil was speechless. His thoughts went back to the fact that the mayor knew about it and probably could have saved the lives of the victims had he let it be known.

"It's not only the size that's scary," Don continued, breaking the silence, "It's the fact that it's a mix of an alligator and the largest species of crocodile known to man. It's a mutant, having a very wide head with more and extremely larger teeth than the usual reptiles. It is exceptionally aggressive and seems to have a non-stop appetite. We fed it four full-grown pigs and three cows daily."

"That's insane," Virgil replied, his stomach feeling like it was being tied in knots.

"Not only that, but it's almost indestructible," Don continued, becoming more and more enthusiastic. "Alligators have little whisker-like stubble on their head area; crocodiles have them everywhere. They are called integument sense organs. This mutant reptile has these organs everywhere, except they're twice as long and work ten times better, meaning AlliCroc can sense a pressure drop in the water from nearly a mile away."

"AlliCroc? You mean it's got a name?" asked Virgil, taken aback.

"The Indians named it. Every prominent monster has a name," Don continued. "The skin on AlliCroc is an inch thick and, like I said, practically bulletproof because of the armored plates on its back called scutes. The average gator and croc have them, but of course, AlliCroc's are comparable to steel," Don finished in a self-righteous tone.

Virgil sat gazing at the pompous fool, thinking how he should beat the hell out of him before replying, "Well, I've got to agree with you on one thing... every monster has a name, Don Henderson."

"Now wait a minute, I'm not..."

"Congratulations," Virgil cut him off, "You've created a fine predator. Now let's get your ass out of my house and down to Officer Randy Taylor's office so that you can tell him what you just told me."

"No way, I'll be ruined!" Don protested.

"Face the music, mad scientist," Virgil retorted, grabbing Don by the arm and physically pushing him out the door.

9

The sun was intensifying through the dissipating grey clouds that brought an early morning rain shower, and it looked like the beginning of another beautiful day at Sandy Beach Park. The Park Rangers opened the park and were not surprised at the lack of beachgoers. After the reptile attack at the jetties, the few people who entered the park were only interested in taking a picture or getting a glimpse of the devilish monster.

On the back side of the park, Chief Bhim and his son Durjaya were quietly walking through knee-deep water in a narrow creek where the Intracoastal Waterway met the small inlet.

After studying a map of the area in conjunction with the attacks, Chief Bhim determined the creek was probably the best place to find the reptile. It looked like the ideal setting for AlliCroc to amble in and out without being detected. The entrance was too small for boats to enter except for canoes and kayaks but widened to sixty feet along the two miles of the marsh-covered banks in the park. The entire creek had a mixed canopy of Australian pines and palm trees.

The two hunters walked cautiously along the shoreline, searching for any evidence of the reptile. Three-quarters of a mile inside the entrance, they found an unusual mound on the quagmire embankment.

"Hold up Durjaya," Bhim whispered, looking around the surroundings and crouching down.

"I see it father," replied Durjaya, calmly following the chief up the three-foot embankment.

They stopped and stood quietly for a few minutes, scanning the water for small ripples and bubbles, but saw nothing. Durjaya sensed a slight degree of fear in his father's movements, which made him feel a little more apprehensive after spotting the mound. There was no doubt in his mind about what would happen if the vast predator was in the creek and silently hunting them.

Chief Bhim held his hand up, motioning for his son to stay put while he crept closer to the mound. When he reached within five feet of the mass, he knew without a doubt that it was the home of AlliCroc. No other creature was known to create something of that size. It stood six feet high with an oval-shaped circumference of at least thirty feet.

Chief Bhim tried his best to sneak up quietly and observe what was inside, but the sixty-two-year-old bones in his legs creaked with every step. In a different time and setting, Durjaya wouldn't be able to keep from laughing at the thought of his father, Chief of the Seminole tribe, sneaking up on the white man.

He made it to the outlandish mound and took a few deep breaths. Looking back toward his son, he nodded his head and turned to peak over the top. The inside of the mound resembled a mucky swimming pool, except for the fact that it was only about three feet deep. Bits of seaweed, tree branches, and assorted flotsam were nestled together.

Ever so cautious, he looked around the surroundings, anticipating the giant reptile's presence, and jumped inside to look closer. Again, the old bones creaked as he landed hard on his backside with a noisy splash.

Durjaya tensed and wanted to run over and make sure his father was not injured, but relaxed when the Chief stood up and gave him the okay sign. Bhim looked around the rank-smelling nest, making sure that there was no doubt that it belonged to the fierce reptile. All doubts were cast aside when he saw the enormous claw marks in the sand.

Satisfied that he'd found the predator's nest, he leaped out, fell to his knees before regaining his footing, and looked back as if he had gotten snagged on something. He then walked over to Durjaya, who was staying vigilant and watching the surroundings.

"What do you think, father?" he asked hushedly.

"I think we've found our reptile," replied Bhim, walking past his son and heading back to the small skiff they arrived on. "We'll gather the men and come back to set the trap. We'll simply trap it in our net, tranquilize it, and haul it back to the Sanctuary," he continued blissfully.

"Catch it? Nick Meyers wants it killed. It has gotten too large and aggressive for the Sanctuary; we could be liable for the deaths it caused!" Durjaya pleaded.

Chief Bhim turned and gave his son a scathing look, "I don't give a raccoon's ass what that bumbling mayor wants! Don Henderson and I will sell that hideous reptile to the highest bidder overseas!"

Durjaya was defeated. Always respectful of his father's wishes, he nodded and followed Bhim back to the boat. He had an uneasy feeling about the reptile and the overwhelming strength it possessed.

Within a half-hour, the two hunters made it back to the skiff. Durjaya stood behind his father and continued searching for signs of the predator as he waited for him to jump in the boat. Chief Bhim had the remnants of sticks and grass on his back, and Durjaya began brushing them off. Without warning, he jumped back when he saw what was left of a human ear attached to his father's back.

"Hold up, father," he loathed as he tore the ear from the shirt. "I think this validates that we found AlliCroc's nest," he continued, holding back the bile coming up in his mouth. In his hand were earrings attached to the ear that read *Sweet Sixteen*.

"We must catch this reptile quickly," Bhim somberly said after turning to see what Durjaya was holding in his hand.

Later that afternoon, Don Henderson was sitting on the balcony of the Marriot Hotel on the beach. After taking a much-needed shower, he sat overlooking the jetties where the last attack occurred, sipping an ice-cold Heineken when the phone rang.

"Hello," Don answered.

"Don, this is Bhim. We found your reptile's nest," he reported confidently.

"Don't call it MY reptile!" Don spat out. "If this town found out it is mine, they'd kill me!"

Bhim didn't reply immediately. The dead space on the other end seemed to last forever before he continued, "I said I found your reptile," he replied in a sharper tone, ignoring Don's plea.

"Okay, fine. Capture the damn thing, and we'll take it back to the Sanctuary," Don ordered.

"No way," replied Bhim, changing his mind, much to Durjaya's chagrin. "We will kill it and collect the reward. The beast is too big and dangerous to keep in captivity any longer. It has tasted human flesh and knows it is easy prey. We can no longer keep it at the Sanctuary."

Enraged by the conversation, Don slammed the phone down and drained what was left of his beer. He sat back in his chair, contemplating the fact that the Indian was going to kill his beloved monster.

He got up and stormed back to the refrigerator, and pulled out another beer. Somehow, he thought, he would have to stop the chief from killing his creation.

Returning to the balcony, he sat back in his chair and reminisced back to when his reptiles were created. Eight of the eggs were surgically spliced open and injected with crocodile genes, and only three hatched. He didn't know the fine details of how they were created and didn't care. Then he remembered how one of the bio technicians snickered and joked about adding human genes to the mix. He thought they were joking but asked if it were true just to be certain. He remembered the scientists laughed and said it was only to help the reptiles become more intelligent. At the time, Don joined in the laughter and walked away. Now, he hoped to God it wasn't true.

When the three hatchlings survived, he was so proud of his creations that he would boast to his friends on Bourbon Street on more than one drunken occasion. Word got out that he was going to open a small tourist attraction in Louisiana and put his reptiles on display.

One night, in a small dingy bar, he was approached by a shady wildlife officer who claimed the authorities were planning to shut him down and confiscate his freaks of nature when such an attraction was opened.

Feeling the pressure, Don took the first plane to Florida and, through a mutual acquaintance, met with Chief Bhim at a small bar on the outskirts of the Everglades. The two discussed the gruesome reptiles and how Don was looking for a place to raise them without the authorities interfering. The enthusiastic Indian chief mentioned that he had a place in the heart of the Everglades that would be ideal for raising the reptiles. Being a bit of a showman himself, he figured they could become partners and eventually show the awe-inspiring reptiles at his Everglades Sanctuary, which was already a tourist attraction.

They shook hands to seal the deal and set up an area for the creatures.

Within months, the mutants grew twice their size and had a

ferocious appetite. In the back of his mind, Don was always concerned if the scientists were truthful about the injection of human brain cells. It was strikingly apparent that the vicious reptiles seemed to coordinate their attacks like no other predators. It was scary how they carried out their attacks with a well-planned strategy.

The more they ate, the more they craved, and the more they craved, the more aggressive they became until finally, they reached a staggering eighteen feet long in only four years' time. Alarmed at the ever-growing size and aggressiveness, Chief Bhim had no choice but to close down the attraction and seal off the area.

Month by month, the vicious reptiles grew and became more assertive. The Seminole children living at the Sanctuary called them AlliCrocs. Always fascinated at the way they seemed to outwit their prey, the children watched in awe at the endless feeding of wild boar, live deer and sometimes cows.

Don got up and gripped the rail of the balcony. His thoughts drifted toward the day the reptiles escaped.

The tourists arrived in airboats supplied by the Sanctuary and casually walked around the ever-present merchandise booths. The women from the tribe displayed everything from beaded bracelets and necklaces to moccasins and clothing.

The guests enjoyed traditional Indian dances and an alligator wrestling show, where Durjaya would demonstrate his skills of wrestling an eight-foot man-eating alligator.

A lone tourist visiting from Belgium took a walk off the beaten path and wound up behind the arena. Enticed by the twenty-foot high electric fence, he followed a short sandy path to take a look at what was inside when he noticed the lock was not engaged. Taking a quick look behind him, he was pleased to see nobody followed as he quickly entered.

Once inside, he couldn't believe his eyes. He was staring face to face with three horrendous monsters in the act of cornering a couple of petrified cows. He gasped aloud as the ghastly reptiles turned their attention to the unfortunate human. He wet his pants when one of the immense creatures turned in his direction and promptly slid into the moat.

Believing the sheer sides of the moat would shield him from danger, he took a deep breath and tried dreadfully to regain his composure. Looking back toward the gate, he was relieved to see he hadn't closed it all the way as he warily reached for it.

All at once, in the blink of an eye, the repulsive monster rose out of the moat like a never-ending freight train and landed on the terrified tourist before he could utter a single scream.

What Lurks Below

With jaws extended wide open, the ghastly predator clamped down on its prey and shook its head violently to the left and right until the man was torn apart. Chunks of the feeble visitor splashed into the moat, where the other two creatures jumped in and swallowed the scraps. The entire attack was over in less than a minute.

The colossal reptile escaped through the open gate and was followed by the other two. Fortunately, nobody noticed the disappearance of the lone tourist.

Don twitched at the thought of the poor soul and felt sick to his stomach at the thought of how this whole mess he was in could have been avoided if that damn gate had remained locked.

Looking out over the water, he knew he was lucky when Virgil took him to the station, only to find Officer Taylor gone. But for how long?

10

Two kayaks raced through the murky water of the winding Himmarshee River. The river began in the Everglades and flowed east until it entered the Intracoastal Waterway near Port Everglades.

Billy Williams and his buddy Mathew Green had been attending a friend's party. Vince Evert had just turned eighteen, and his well-to-do parents threw him a surprise party at their large estate along the river. Live music filled the otherwise quiet evening air and it seemed everybody Vince knew showed up for the celebration.

Billy and Mathew got their hands on a keg of Pabst Blue Ribbon and snuck it into the party. Although most of the kids were under drinking age, many of them managed to dip a glass or two in the beer. Vince's parents were not so credulous and knew the kids were drinking, but decided to look the other way and let them have their fun. They were aware that most of them drank anyway, so they didn't see any harm if Vince and his friends did it while the grownups could keep an eye on them.

Before long, Billy and Mathew were drinking shots of Crown Royal that they had found in a liquor cabinet. Feeling good, they decided to grab two kayaks sitting on the dock and cruise up the river.

As they dropped the kayaks in the water, Bonnie Walker appeared from the side of the house and promised them a good time if she could come along.

At the tender age of eighteen, she was well-developed in all the right areas and was not shy about flaunting it. She had a dark complexion and big brown eyes, and her long, silky brown hair flowed to her shoulders, framing out her pretty face. Her full lips curled slightly at the ends, giving her a mischievous look.

Bonnie was regarded by most parents as promiscuous. The more they tried to keep their boys from associating with her, the more they gravitated in her direction. It didn't bother her in the least bit that her so-called friends never bothered to include her in their plans because she found it more fun to be around boys.

Billy and Mathew, as drunk as they were, just stood and stared, grinning from ear to ear. God only knew what was going through their minds.

"Well? What's it gonna be, boys?" she rasped, removing her skirt and belly shirt to reveal a bright pink thong bikini that revealed more skin than material.

"Let's go, girl," replied Billy, hardly able to contain himself.

"You just climb your sweet little self on here, and we'll be on our way," Mathew said, using his best smooth-talking Dean Martin impersonation.

The single-seat kayaks were designed for one person, and Billy didn't care for the fact that his buddy was patting the top of the open space above his enclosed seat as he spoke, "Fine...Ride with him," he sulked.

"Come on, Billy, don't be mad...I promised both of you a good time," smiled Bonnie, adjusting her thong.

The two young men looked at each other, grinning like two cats that ate the canary. They couldn't put the kayaks in the water fast enough. Much to Mathew's chagrin, Bonnie changed her mind and climbed on Billy's kayak, straddling the open cockpit with her legs hanging over the sides and her backside hovering over Billy's lap. Billy couldn't help but grin at his friend as he sank lower in the seat. Suddenly, they laughed uncontrollably when Billy whispered to Mathew that if she opened her mouth, he'd be able to see up ahead as he closed one eye and pretended to be looking through a telescope. Bonnie, straddling the kayak like a porn star, smiled and acted like she had no clue as to what they were laughing about.

What Lurks Below

While Billy was discovering just how thin the thong was, Mathew quickly jumped out of the kayak and ran to his car. A minute later, he returned to the dock, strapped a cooler of ice-cold beer to his kayak, and cast off.

"Hurry up! Faster! Faster!" Bonnie shouted, hopping up and down like she was riding a wild bronco while Mathew zipped past them. Billy could barely think straight with Bonnie's naked butt pounding his chest. His first thought was to throw out the paddle and devour her, but he settled on paddling on at a half-hearted pace.

They raced a mile and a half upriver until they reached the Intracoastal Waterway, where they stopped and drifted. Mathew reached inside the cooler, pulled out three cold beers, and handed them out.

The water was calm and smooth as glass. The moon was nowhere to be seen above a cloudless sky as the kayakers sat and looked up at the stars. It was a beautiful night for stargazers, but star gazing was the last thing on their minds.

"Ooh, what a beautiful evening," Bonnie said, sipping her beer. "Cheers!" Mathew retorted, slamming his beer into Billy's and causing both cans to spill the frothy ingredients.

Bonnie felt around in the back of her for a place to set her beer before carefully placing it between Billy's legs. She turned her head and smiled before leaning forward, stretching as far as she could to grab the bow line, then tied the two kayaks together. Billy began hyperventilating as she left nothing to his imagination. When the kayaks were secure, she slowly crawled back as if posing for playboy and gave a seductive smile when she saw Billy staring at her butt as if he were hypnotized.

"Snap out of it, Billy, haven't you ever seen a girl's butt? She teased. Billy didn't reply; he dreamily looked up and smiled when their eyes connected. Mathew couldn't take it anymore. The beer was doing its magic and he wanted Bonnie so bad he could scream. He leaned over to kiss her and lost his balance, falling forward on top of Bonnie and spilling everybody into the river.

"What the hell you doin' man!" Billy shouted.

"Easy for you to say, you're sitting there looking through a telescope...Remember?"

Billy burst out laughing at the comment and splashed his buddy in the face before he replied, "Not true. There seems to be a string blocking the lens."

The two of them burst out laughing and wrestled each other, to the amusement of Bonnie as she swam to the other side of the melee.

"Mmmm...The water feels sooo good," she purred.

Billy and Mathew stopped laughing and looked at each other with a straight face before seeing Bonnie place her bikini top in the kayak.

"The water's kind of cool, guys. Can somebody warm me up?" she grinned, floating on her back and exposing her breasts.

"Damn! We must be dreaming!" Mathew obviously whispered to himself as Billy swam to her faster than a piranha fish. He scooped her up with his left arm and held onto the kayak with his right. They started kissing as Bonnie reached down and pulled off Billy's shorts. With his hand wrapped around her waist like a pair of vise grips, Bonnie called out for Mathew, "Hey Matt! Come over and join the party!" she laughed. There was no answer.

"C'mon Matt! I need some more body heat!" Still, no reply. She stopped smiling and became concerned as she looked around and failed to see him anywhere.

Billy wasn't the least concerned. He was all over her like an octopus until he felt her stiffen with a worried look on her face.

"Matt! Quit foolin' around; she wants both of us...pronto!"

It was quiet, too quiet. All feelings of pleasure quickly

vanished as they searched the water.

"He drank too much; I hope he didn't drown," Bonnie quipped nervously.

"No, he's used to drinking too much...he'll be okay," Billy replied, looking for his shorts and not believing what he just said.

Bonnie worriedly jumped back into the kayak and scrambled for her bikini top as Billy continued searching the area unsuccessfully.

Mathew couldn't hold his laughter or his breath any longer. Hiding parallel under the kayak, he finally sprang up next to Bonnie.

"Hey baby...I'm not here to talk," he whispered, again with his best Dean Martin impersonation.

"You're an ass," a relieved Bonnie replied, acting as if she hadn't noticed him missing. She smacked him playfully on the head with her bikini top and lay back on the kayak, using her top as a pillow.

Billy was seething but didn't want to ruin the mood. He gave his friend a lackadaisical smile along with the finger. To clear his head, he dove underwater, contemplating his next move. He smiled to himself at how lucky they were to have Bonnie with them. He made up his mind to take full advantage of the situation before the night was through. He surfaced and casually took a sip from his beer before taking three big breaths of air and dove underwater.

A quarter-mile from the kayakers, AlliCroc was indolently drifting in the current. Its eyes sprang open when it sensed the radiant splashing in the water. The horrid reptile felt the pressure change and slowly sank to the bottom. Its receptive senses confirmed more than one quarry. The hunger pangs the reptile felt would soon be gone as it aggressively turned and headed toward the unknowing victims at the mouth of the river.

Half swimming and half walking on the sandy bottom, AlliCroc stopped within twenty yards of the kayakers. With its excellent senses, the reptile observed three objects splashing on the surface.

The ravenous monster prepared to attack but stopped short when one of the objects dove deep. Its voracious appetite worsened matters as the beast angrily sprang from the bottom and charged at full speed.

Billy kicked his legs, trying to touch the bottom before resurfacing. Had he not been drinking, he would never have attempted it. Even though the water was pitch black, he opened his eyes slightly. A cold chill streaked up his spine as he suddenly figured he was at least fifteen feet deep, drunk, and almost out of air. He envisioned being attacked by a bullshark and quickly turned to head back to the surface.

Abruptly, he was slammed hard and fast by something that felt like a truck. The soaring pain in his torso caused him to scream out as the air escaped his crushed lungs, and he fought futilely to swim to the surface.

Terrified, he reached down and tried to hit what he thought was a shark in the eyes, hoping against all odds that he'd be released. To his horror, he felt no arm movement and looked down to see his right arm had been torn off.

Blackness fell over him like a blanket as his oxygen-starved brain began to shut down. He suddenly felt no pain and had a warm feeling come over him as he felt a strange sensation of being eaten alive and swallowed.

Mathew and Bonnie were on the verge of intercourse and didn't realize that Billy had not surfaced. Finally, before Mathew attempted to go all the way with Bonnie, he stopped and looked around for Billy.

"Billy!" he called out half-heartedly. "Give me ten minutes, and then you can come back!"

When there was no reply, he figured Billy swam to a dock

and ran back to the party. If he had been thinking clearly, he would have known that they had drifted out to the middle of the Intracoastal, and there was no dock close enough to swim to. Bonnie didn't bat an eye, figuring that Billy was playing the same game Mathew played.

As the two returned to celebrating their bodies, something bumped the kayaks and knocked the beer cooler into the water.

"Jeez Billy!...What the hell!" Mathew shrieked in an irritated tone, jumping up and looking around.

The cooler drifted at arm's length, and Mathew retrieved it. He heaved it onto the kayak and pulled out another beer.

"Where's Billy?" asked Bonnie, stretched out with a look of concern but not attempting to put her top on.

Mathew shrugged his shoulders and finished his beer. "Okay, Billy!... Enough's enough. Come out, come out wherever you are...Bonnie's got a surprise for you!" he bellowed, looking down at Bonnie with a devilish grin. There was no reply from Billy as the two lovers searched around the darkness. The water was still glassy smooth, and Bonnie got a creepy feeling that something was eerily wrong. A creepy feeling she couldn't explain. "Fine, if he doesn't want to participate in the joys of life... I'll just go back for seconds,"

Mathew informed, scooting back over to Bonnie.

"Get off me!" she snapped. "I think something's really wrong this time." She pushed him off her and jumped into the other kayak, reaching into a small compartment and retrieving a flashlight.

"Wow, how did you know there was a flashlight in there?" he asked, dumbfounded.

Bonnie looked over at him and rolled her eyes, "What, you think you're the first one I did this with?"

"Of course not, bimbo," Mathew shot back, reaching over and untying the line holding the kayaks together.

She ruined the mood with her last comment and now Mathew wanted nothing more than to ditch the witch and get back to the party. He felt bad for calling her a bimbo, but it slipped out before he could stop it.

"Matt!" she cried out, scanning the water with her flashlight.

"I know...you're not a bimbo," Matt smirked. "Thanks for the memories, but I'm..."

"Look in the water!" she cut him off with a frightening screech. "What?"

"Look at all that blood in the water!" she cried.

Mathew became rigid from the frightful look on her face and

looked into the water to see what she was talking about. The water was too dark to see anything, "Give me the flashlight," he ordered.

Bonnie tossed him the flashlight as he clumsily fumbled it in his hand and nearly dropped it over the side. He regained his grip and scanned the water.

"Jeez! Look at all that blood!" he gasped. "Billy must have slammed his head into the kayak! I thought he was just playing."

"Oh my God! We have to go get help!" Bonnie cried as Mathew dove into the water and disappeared. He blindly searched under the kayaks with arms extended, feeling around for Billy. When he came up for air, Bonnie shouted for him to get back into the kayak. Ignoring her plead, he took a deep breath and headed for the bottom. He figured that once he hit bottom, he would sweep around the perimeter in a circular motion, hoping against hope that he'd reach his friend.

Bonnie continued scanning the surface while Mathew searched below. Her heart skipped a beat when the flashlight's beam hit on what looked like a pair of enormous red eyes staring back at her from thirty yards away, moving a fraction faster than the slow current and heading for the kayaks.

Mathew came up for air, and Bonnie screamed for him to get out of the water.

"I can't, not until I find Bobby," he replied, panting.

"Get out now! She screamed hysterically. "Something big is coming behind you!"

Mathew looked up and saw her panic-stricken face and wasted no time jumping back into the kayak. He just made it onboard when the colossal object passed underneath, indolently missing him by inches.

"What the hell is that?" Mathew squealed, holding on tight as the wake shook the small vessel. Bonnie was too shaken to reply; she followed the creature with the flashlight until it vanished.

Two minutes passed before Bonnie sat straight up with a horrified look on her face as the flashlight found the two red eyes reappeared. It was hauntingly clear that whatever was out there was leisurely taunting its prey. "It's coming back!" Bonnie cried feverishly. Mathew grabbed the flashlight before it fell into the water and aimed it at the creature.

The reptile returned to the kayaks and dove under once again, but not before what seemed strange to the two horrified people: the beast looked up and studied its prey.

What Lurks Below

The insatiable hunger and newfound desire for human food made it more aggressive than ever. Sensing that the prey in the boat was helplessly terrified and unable to escape, the reptile was content to stir them to a frenzy before going for the kill.

It swam effortlessly under the tiny kayaks and continued out about fifty feet before turning back. This time, the repulsive reptile breached the surface and swam rapidly.

Mathew kept the flashlight trained on the monster as they braced themselves and sat in awe, so alarmed that they couldn't move a muscle. With the devilish red eyes and the size of the wake it was leaving behind, it reminded Mathew of Captain Nemo's Nautilus submarine at ramming speed.

"Oh God... hold on tight," Mathew said with apprehension.

Bonnie screamed at the top of her lungs when AlliCroc slammed into the kayaks, blasting the two through the night air and into the water. They quickly surfaced, regaining their bearings, and looked on in horror as the massive reptile obliterated the kayaks with its enormous jaws. Mathew's heart sank when he realized he was staring at the monster that was in the news, the one he laughed about and thought reporters were exaggerating a story of a typical alligator.

They were now swimming helplessly in the Intracoastal. The

outgoing tide was moving at about one knot, and Mathew spotted the channel marker coming up about fifteen yards away.

"Bonnie! Bonnie, listen to me!" he shouted soberly. "We've got to swim over to that buoy," he continued, pointing at the channel marker. Bonnie was shaking hysterically as she stared at the beast. Never in her wildest nightmares did she ever think she'd see something so hideous and evil.

"Bonnie!... Look at me!" he shouted again. She finally forced herself to look at Mathew and saw him pointing to the buoy. She tried to reply but stopped short when she saw him swimming away like an Olympic swimmer.

She tried to swallow but her throat was so dry it hurt. Her body was completely numb, but she somehow found the strength to follow.

The iron buoy had a base with an eight-foot circumference anchored to the bottom by a massive chain. Steel poles welded to the platform rose diagonally for ten feet with a big red light attached to the top. A small ladder was welded to the side, and Mathew reached for the rusted rung above the water line.

He frantically reached for the ladder but failed to notice the razor sharp barnacles on the rungs beneath the water line and cut his legs and feet, alerting AlliCroc's senses.

The beast became aggressively angry and turned to give chase as it zeroed in on the blood.

When Mathew reached the top of the buoy, he turned to see if Bonnie had reached the ladder. Alarmed that she wasn't there yet, he looked out and saw her splashing twenty feet away, with a large wake trailing not far behind.

"Swim Bonnie!... Swim hard, it's right behind you!" he screamed out. Bonnie was swimming as fast as she could, but like in her worst nightmare, she felt she was getting nowhere. The emotional strain was too much, and she just wanted to give up and scream.

"C'mon Bonnie! Don't give up!"

"God help meee!" she cried, choking on saltwater she regrettably inhaled.

Mathew cautiously stepped down the ladder close enough to give Bonnie a hand. She had made it to the ladder but screamed out in pain as the razor-sharp barnacles sliced through her hands and thighs.

"Bonnie! Reach my hand. I'll help you up!" Mathew insisted as she began drifting past the buoy. He saw the horror in her eyes when she recognized the fact that she was drifting away and wouldn't make it back in time.

"Climb the damn ladder!" he screamed as he dreadfully raced back up the ladder, turning just in time to see the devilish reptile grasp her from below, slicing her in two.

"Aaaaggh!" she screamed. For a brief second, she thought the hideous jaws of the monster clamped down on her lower half. Realizing the pain wasn't so dire, she figured it was the barnacles slicing into her body. *It's no big deal; I'll just get a tetanus shot. But first, I better get my ass out of the water, she reasoned.*

Her head abruptly smashed against the buoy, and she tried to put a foot up on the ladder. Lost in thought, she couldn't figure out why her foot wouldn't go through the rung. She looked up at Mathew with a quizzical look and saw him staring back with wide golf ball-like eyes and mouth wide open in distress as if he were about to shout for her to hurry up for the umpteenth time, only nothing came out.

"Matt, I need your help. Pull me up," she calmly whispered. She couldn't understand why he just stood there and watched. Her eyes remained fixed on Mathew as she slowly sank beneath the surface. The gargantuan creature followed and gulped down her remains.

Mathew stood watching in dismay. He had just witnessed the reptile swim over and bite Bonnie in half. It happened so fast and the bite was so clean that she never knew what happened. She stayed alive long enough to see the horrifying look on Matt's face.

"Oh my God!... No!" he screamed, looking down and seeing more blood than he ever thought possible.

AlliCroc continued devouring his prey before resurfacing and looking up at Mathew through menacing eyes of pure evil.

Mathew quickly scrambled to the top of the buoy and looked down at the giant reptile. From his vantage point, he knew he was in deep trouble. The beast was at least twice the size of the buoy, and he could envision the thing ascending straight up out of the water and reaching him without a problem.

Just when all hope seemed lost, he heard the unmistakable sound of a big boat barreling through the inlet. He turned to see the running lights of an evening fishing charter as it slowed and began its idle-speed cruise up the Intracoastal.

"Ooh la la, check out the naked guy standing at the top of the channel marker," said a slightly inebriated woman on deck as she stood up and flashed her boobs when the boat passed by.

The boat captain was used to seeing the crazy antics of college vacationers who came to town daring each other to do crazy things. He figured the foolish kid was going through some sort of initiation. This one surely won the prize.

With a slight smirk, he reached for his binoculars and focused them on the marker fifty yards away. Viewing the naked figure, he remembered back in the day before things got complicated with bills, mortgages, car payments, and everything else that sapped the life out of people. He envied the kid.

As the forty-five-foot Hatteras cruised by, the first mate blew the air horn at the same time Mathew screamed for help, effectively drowning him out. The captain, still viewing through the binoculars, suddenly became aware that the kid was in trouble.

"Wait a minute! That kid's in danger!" he shouted as he quickly slowed the boat and began turning around.

The first mate ran up to the bridge, "What's going on? Did I hear you say the kid's in some sort of danger?"

"He's covered in blood; the damn fool must've cut himself climbing that rusted derelict," replied the captain, switching on the spotlight.

The laughter aboard the boat abruptly stopped when all eyes followed the spotlight to the young man. His hands and legs were covered in blood, and he nearly slipped off the buoy as he desperately flagged down the boat. The look of terror in his eyes caught everybody by surprise.

"Oh my God...What happened?" screamed one of the ladies, covering her mouth with both hands.

Before anybody on board could reply, something slammed into the buoy, causing it to list nearly ninety degrees before gradually righting itself. The captain quickly showed the spotlight down to the water and gasped, "Son of a bitch! It's that creature that attacked those kids the other day!"

The ladies on board screamed for the kid to hold tight as the captain throttled forward. As he closed the gap, AlliCroc became agitated and turned toward the boat, aggressively guarding its prey from the approaching intruder.

"Shit! It's heading for us!" the captain shouted, turning the boat away.

He dreaded the thought of what the reptile could do to his fiberglass hull if it slammed into it with the same velocity as the steel buoy.

The colossal reptile backed off and returned to the buoy as the charter boat made a wide turn and kept a safe distance away. The startled captain reached for his radio and turned it to channel sixteen.

"Harbor Patrol! Harbor Patrol... This is the charter boat Catchin' Tail, come back." There was no answer.

"Harbor Patrol! This is Catchin' Tail; come back, damnit!"

"This is Harbor Patrol... How can we help you, and please watch your language, over," replied the dispatch calmly.

"I'm at the entrance buoy at the Intracoastal," the captain replied vigorously. "There's an injured young man on the buoy and a very large alligator in the water trying to eat him!"

There was a long pause before the reply, "Repeat that message over."

"You heard correctly! It's that monstrous reptile that attacked those kids on the jetties! Come Quick!"

"I'm on my way. ETA about five minutes," Officer Scott Anderson cut in with a swaggering reply as he heard the call while patrolling in his boat two miles south of the melee.

Officer Anderson was the new rookie at Harbor Patrol. He was twenty-five years old and two years out of the police academy. Before transferring to Harbor Patrol, he was a wildlife officer in the Everglades. Having dealt with his fair share of alligators, he couldn't imagine this one being any different. He was briefed to be on the lookout for the large reptile but hadn't seen the actual size from the video yet. Knowing a thing or two about alligators, he scoffed at the size of the one Randy Taylor had warned him about, believing it to be overly exaggerated.

The officer immediately set the radio down on the console and spun the boat around. He raced off to the scene at full throttle and flashers lighting up the area.

Captain Virgil Goodman also heard the call on the radio. He had just walked up to the tugboat wheelhouse and sat down with a hot cup of coffee when he heard the commotion.

"This is Captain Virgil Goodman of the tugboat Horizon to Officer Anderson; come back," he anxiously called on the radio.

"Come back, Captain," replied the officer in a hurried tone.

"I've seen what that beast can do, it's extremely dangerous," Virgil insisted, realizing the officer had no clue as to what he was dealing with.

"Thanks for the warning, captain. Now let me do my job," the officer replied, shaking his head and wishing the tugboat captain would stay out of his business.

"Where is Officer Randy Taylor?" Virgil shot back. "Did he brief you on this reptile?"

"I know it's a large gator," he replied arrogantly. "I'm sure the big charter boat scared it off. Officer Taylor is off duty tonight... and thanks again for the warning. Out."

Virgil became more and more irritated at the way the officer did not heed his warning, "Listen, jackass, your boat is not big enough for the rescue. I'm on my way with the safety of my tug."

"Negative Captain. I want you to stay clear."

"Get Randy Taylor on the phone and tell him to meet me at the dock when I return. Stay clear of that monster; I'm on my way," Virgil ordered, taking matters into his own hands.

"That's a big negative. Stay put, or I will arrest you for police interference."

Virgil threw the radio down and scrambled to the window, cursing the clueless officer all the way, "Chuck! Crank up the engines! Skip!...Bill! Untie the lines!" he shouted to his crew.

"What's happening, Cap?" Skip asked, poking his head out of the galley door.

"That damn monster's back, and it's trying to make a meal out of somebody trapped on the channel marker near the Himmershee River! Let's go! Grab the stern line!"

It took a few minutes for Chuck to warm up the engine. When ready, Bill and Skip released the lines from the bollards, and the Horizon took off like a bat out of hell.

Almost on the scene, Captain Virgil could see Harbor Patrol was already there, "Damn, only one boat," he grumbled. He cursed under his breath that Randy Taylor wasn't on duty.

Officer Anderson took his boat out of gear and drifted between the charter boat and the buoy. He thanked the bewildered crew of Catchin' Tail for reporting the incident and told them to leave the area for their own protection. The charter boat captain and his passengers were dumbfounded that the officer arrived in a boat smaller than the sadistic reptile and didn't want their help.

"Officer! That alligator is humungous! I've never seen anything so aggressive! Why don't you tie up alongside my boat for safety!" the Captain shouted.

The officer was losing his patience and didn't feel the need to explain to another boat captain that he was experienced with gators and to leave him alone to do his work, "Do not interfere with my rescue!" he shouted brashly. "I will handle this on my own!"

The charter boat captain shook his head, giving up the idea of talking sense to the officer. He put his boat in gear and kept a safe distance from the buoy but close enough to help if the monster returned.

Officer Anderson prepared to secure a line to the buoy. He mistakenly felt little concern about the reptile attacking because he hadn't seen it when he arrived and figured that with all the commotion going on, the reptile most likely had retreated to a safe area.

"Sir, can you hear me?" he shouted to Mathew. "I'm here to help you.

Can you climb down and jump in the boat?"

Mathew had lost a lot of blood and was going into shock. He heard the officer calling out but was unable to respond.

"Sir, look over here... I'm here to help you," he repeated. "I'm going to land my boat next to the buoy so you can climb down and get onboard." Officer Anderson patiently waited to see if the young man would climb down on his own and jump in the boat. It was painfully obvious that Mathew was in no shape to complete the task.

"Hang on, pal, I'm going to shut off the engine and come up and get you," he assured. As he made one last search for the reptile, he looked toward the south end of the Port and noticed the tugboat speeding over, sounding like a runaway locomotive. I'm gonna arrest that tugboat captain, he thought.

After checking one last time for any signs of the predator, he put the spotlight on and directed it toward Mathew. His life jacket was too bulky for climbing, so he unzipped it and threw it to the deck.

What Lurks Below

The *Horizon* was ninety yards from the scene and closing fast.

"Oh no! No, no, no! The Officer is leaning over the side of his boat!" Skip reported, standing outside the wheelhouse and looking through the binoculars.

Virgil grabbed the radio and tried to warn the officer, "Harbor Patrol! Get yourself back in the boat! We'll be there in one minute!" he anxiously shouted into the radio.

When the officer did not observe the warning, Virgil blew the air horn in hopes of diverting the man-eating reptile.

Mathew began making intangible sounds with his mouth with ghastly facial expressions. The officer was relieved to see the kid was coming around but failed to take notice that he was trying to warn him. From the height Mathew was viewing, he could clearly see the fierce monster swimming under the boat towards the officer.

The moment the officer leaped from the boat, the reptile shot up between the boat and the buoy like a rocket. Scott Anderson hastily raised his knees to his chest at the last second, but the massive jaws clamped down on his foot, and he was violently pulled from the buoy and launched into the water twenty feet from the boat.

He surfaced quickly and swam for the boat. Dazed and with

no feeling in his left leg, he suddenly realized that the beast grabbed his foot. Anxiously reaching down, his fear was confirmed: the foot was gone.

"Oh God, no!" he screamed in panic.

The crew on the charter boat was helpless as they looked on in horror. The captain yelled through a loudspeaker for the officer to get out of the water while he put the boat in gear and sped over to rescue him. The first mate hurriedly tied a line to a life preserver and threw it out, but it was too late. AlliCroc surfaced next to the wounded man and clamped down on his torso with its unsightly jaws. Sickening sounds of bones snapping could be heard as the beast went into a death roll.

The voracious reptile spun violently on the surface, shredding Officer Anderson until he was unrecognizable as a human being. The charter boat was unable to get up on a plane at such a short distance and plowed the water towards the reptile before it submerged, missing the collision by seconds.

Holding on for dear life, Mathew let out another bone-chilling scream when he saw the six-foot wake barreling down on the buoy. The buoy rose up over the first wave and went deep into the trough. The next wave buried it completely before it gradually resurfaced, listing to where Mathew was dangling his legs in the water. After a long minute, it slowly righted itself with Mathew barely clinging on.

"Stand clear, Bill!" Virgil shouted, fighting to keep the bile in his throat down after witnessing the slaughter.

"All clear, Cap!" replied Bill, hyperventilating.

"I'm going to put the bow right on top of that damn buoy. When I stop, I want you to grab that kid and throw him on deck, no pussy-footin' around," Virgil commanded.

Captain Virgil began to slow the tugboat, easing it to a stop within inches of the buoy. Bill leaped onto the marker and wasted no time climbing the ladder. He clutched Mathew by the waist, and threw him on his shoulder like a sack of potatoes, and jumped back to the waiting tugboat. As Virgil reversed the tug, Skip covered Mathew with a blanket.

The rescue was over in under a minute and Virgil was headed for the nearest dock to meet the paramedics. Chuck poked his head out of the engine room door and watched as a Coastguard helicopter came into view and hovered over the buoy. *Too late, the heroes*, he thought.

11

Paramedics were waiting for the *Horizon* when it docked. Mathew was hastily whisked off to the hospital in stable condition, and the dock was swarming with reporters.

Captain Virgil was in the galley with a solemn-looking patrol boat officer as the crew was on the dock talking to reporters.

At the time of the attack, Officer Randy Taylor was off-duty and trying to enjoy a rare evening with his wife at a restaurant when he received the call. Even though he had warned Officer Anderson about the reptile known as AlliCroc, he was mad at himself for not showing him the videotape so that he could see for himself how big and aggressive it actually was.

To make matters worse, while talking and getting a statement from Virgil, a call came in about two more kids who were assumed to be with Mathew. The parents were in hysterics and were said to be headed to the hospital to try and get more information on their whereabouts.

"Damn it, there may be more victims," the despondent officer said, getting up from the table. "I'm headed to the hospital to try and talk with the kid; I'll come back in the morning."

"I'll be here," replied Virgil, with a sick feeling.

The officer barely made it off the tug and onto the dock before a television camera was jammed in his face, "Officer, what do you intend to do with this menacing beast lurking in these waters?" asked a feminine-looking man from the channel seven news. The officer grumbled a no comment and pushed the camera out of his face.

Virgil poked his head out of the galley and saw the officer jump in his truck and head off. He speculated what Randy was going to do now that it looked like the Indians were not going to catch the creature quietly.

At eight AM the next morning, Officer Randy Taylor was sitting in the lobby of the mayor's office, waiting for him to arrive. He spent a sleepless night at the hospital trying to get a statement from Mathew. It was true, he found out, that two more kids were with him and they were also killed.

On top of that, he found out that the Indians had reported that they thought they found the nest where the reptile was living, but the elusive reptile had not returned to it as of yet and may have moved on.

At eight-thirty, the mayor came in and walked past Randy with an incredulous look. Randy got up, followed him down the hall to his office, and closed the door behind him. If the mayor thought he could intimidate the officer by coming in late again with the accentuated look on his face, he was wrong; Randy wanted to tear his heart out.

Randy waited impatiently as the mayor leisurely took off his coat. He finally sat down at his oversized oak desk and sighed deeply before looking up, "So, what kind of progress are we making with that damn reptile?" he asked as if he didn't know of the previous night's attack.

Randy couldn't believe how he could act without a care in the world. "First of all... Nick," he replied, practically spitting out the mayor's name, "I want to tell you, since it seems you haven't a clue about what happened last night, that damn monster killed three more people in the Port, including Scott Anderson."

"Scott, who?" he replied, arrogantly picking up his eyebrows.

"Officer Scott Anderson... the new guy," Randy was about to blow up. "Oh yes, I heard he was a good man," he muttered. "Replace him immediately. We need all officers patrolling the Port."

With that, Officer Randy Taylor lost what tiny sliver of respect he had for the mayor, "Excuse me?" he fired back, slamming his fists down on the desk.

The mayor was taken aback by the offensive tone the officer

took and replied cautiously, "Look, Taylor, I'm truly sorry for what happened to Anderson. I will find a replacement while you work on catching that thing before it kills again."

Randy wasn't getting through to him. He walked behind the desk and grabbed the mayor by the scruff of his shirt, "Look here, you heartless bastard, I know you understand what we're dealing with here!"

"Get your hands off me!" he shouted, jumping up and slapping the officers' hands away. "I should fire your crazy ass!" he threatened again.

"Do it! Go ahead and fire me! We'll see how fast your little political career goes down the toilet when I go public and let the whole damn town know all about your dirty dealings with the Everglades Sanctuary and that dumb-ass Chief Bhim that you so happened to hire out of thin air to capture this reptile," Randy snapped, pointing a finger so close to the mayor's nose he could have bit it.

The mayor sat back in his chair defensively. He straightened his shirt and regained his composure, squinting his eyes at Randy, "What the hell are you talking about," he muttered.

"I'm talking about how you knew this reptile was raised at the Sanctuary. You agreed to look the other way as long as you were well compensated, and I'll be a son of a bitch if you didn't know when that beast escaped," replied the officer, playing all his cards and hoping he was right.

Mayor Nick Myers folded his hands together and looked up at the ceiling, letting out a weighty sigh, "Randy Taylor, top cop and extreme pain in my ass, you got me."

Randy was relieved he wasn't wrong. He sat up all night at the hospital, trying to fit the pieces together. He remembered how the trappers didn't seem amazed at the creature's enormous size when shown the video and how Nick Myers' first reaction was to get on the phone to hire Chief Bhim to catch it. Why would he contact the Indian Chief when his name wasn't listed on the list of trappers the city usually called? He also recalled overhearing one of the trappers calling it AlliCroc. It all added up when Randy called the Sanctuary and heard a sigh of relief on the other end of the phone when he informed the lady their reptile had been caught.

"Okay... Now what?" Myers admitted defeat, holding his head in his hands.

Randy was surprised at how quickly the mayor gave up. His detective skills were right on the money. He stood with his hands in his pocket and gave Nick Myers a long, incredulous look before sitting down, "You and I both know what AlliCroc is capable of," he said in a low tone.

"Alli, what?"

"Don't play dumb, Nick. The Indians call it AlliCroc. At first, I was puzzled when I showed them the videotape and watched their reaction. I expected a shaken response, but it didn't even faze them. It looked to me that they were confirming to themselves that I found their reptile."

"Those damn Indians, I should never have gotten myself involved. Look, Randy, if word gets out that I knew about this, this AlliCroc, my career is over," he said solemnly.

"I don't give a damn about you or your career," Randy shot back. "I care about the safety of human lives."

"What do you want to do?"

"First, we keep the Port and surrounding beaches outside the jetties closed to vessels less than forty feet long. That includes swimming and diving. I want nobody at the beach within a mile of the jetties."

"I can't do that! The tourists will pack up and go someplace else; we'll lose millions of dollars!"

"You can and you will," retorted Randy. "And secondly, I got word that another trapper is coming here from Belize, goes by the name Bloodfoot."

"Bloodfoot? What kind of name is that?" Myers asked, scrunching his nose.

"I don't know, and I don't care. He specializes in large creatures and somehow caught wind of AlliCroc."

"Well... I welcome his effort; I'll send somebody to pick him up at the airport."

"That won't be necessary. He's sailing over in a pirate ship," Randy smirked.

"Christ, we'll have every Looney in the world coming over to try to catch that beast. It's going to turn into a circus," Myers erupted, leaning back in his chair.

"Yeah, well, for what it's worth, I heard he's got an impressive track record," replied Randy, walking over to the window and running a hand over his unshaven face. "He should arrive sometime next week. We will keep him and your damn Indian friends on the hunt until AlliCroc is captured and killed. I repeat... killed," Randy continued, turning toward the mayor with an unforgiving look.

Mayor Nick Myers was in no position to argue. He sat and listened, feeling the blood drain from his face.

*****

Sixty feet below the surface, just inside the jetties leading into the Port, AlliCroc rested on the sandy bottom. What little remained of Officer Scott Anderson's body swayed to and fro in the mild current beside the reptile. Scavenger fish happily nibbled on the gory, fleshy parts, keeping a safe distance from the monsters' hideous jaws.

All at once, AlliCroc detected the presence of another large predator circling in close. Its eyes sprang open, scaring off the small scrap-feeding fish as they continued nibbling on the officer. Whatever was out there was coming closer, just beyond the wall of sight. AlliCroc became rigid, slowly opened its enormous jaws like a bear trap, and waited for the intruder to enter his realm.

Several minutes passed before a large shape came into view, swimming over the docile reptile and the officer's remains. The twelve-foot bullshark swam closer to what it thought was the remnants of an easy meal. The scavenger slowly circled the humungous reptile before diving down to bite off a chunk of the drifting meat.

Still sitting quietly, the hideous reptile blended in with the sandy bottom, looking more like a reef than a predator.

When the shark was content, there was no threat in the area; it charged in to take a chunk. At that instant, the aggressive monster sprang up and snapped its crushing jaws down on the shark, causing the startled prowler to twist and turn violently in defense. It was no match for the reptile as it viciously shook its head from side to side, severing the shark in half just below the dorsal fin. The disemboweled predator tried in vain to return the attack but got nowhere without its hind section. In its final act, the shark turned to bite, but the massive reptile burst forward and chomped down on its entire head, killing it instantly.

12

Bob Jackson felt somewhat responsible for what had happened to the Manditto family. If he hadn't sent the kid out on that fateful call, he and his amorous family would still be alive today.

It was just after midnight, and the waters in the Port were smooth. The reflection of the lights on the docks reflected in the water, and a slow, cool breeze was in the air. There were still a few fishing boats coming back in for the night, but otherwise, things were quiet.

Bob cautiously cruised through the Port basin at slow speed on one of his towboats. Making the turn and heading out to the end of the jetties, he was always amazed at how quiet the area was late at night. Hundreds of boaters pass through the jetties during the day but at night, it was almost eerie how quiet it was.

Nearing the end of the jetties, he slowed and put the boat in neutral. He gazed over to the rocks where the kids were attacked earlier in the week and let out a heavy sigh as he contemplated ditching his ghastly plans and heading home.

He decided to stick to what he thought needed to be done, let the boat drift to the end of the jetties, and dropped the anchor.

Turning off the motor, he opened the small compartment under the steering wheel and retrieved a flask containing Johnny Walker Red.

As he took a big swig of the contents, he looked around to make sure he was the only one out there. Satisfied that he was alone, he took another swig from the flask and called for the stray dog he picked up earlier that evening behind the Anchor bar, as it sat half buried in a garbage can eating a hot dog.

After a few minutes of whistling and pleading for the dog to come out, the poor flea-bitten, seasick dog crawled out from inside the console. With her ears drooping over her eyes and the tail between her legs, it was obvious the middle-aged Labrador was a landlubber.

"Gatorbait... come here, Gatorbait," he called out as the poor dog he appropriately named began wagging her tail and hopping playfully in his direction.

Bob sighed heavily, scratched the dog on the head, and, against his better judgment, attached a harness to her. The dog became excited and wagged her tail faster, looking up at him with loving big brown eyes, unaware of his dubious intentions.

He secured the harness and walked the dog to the back of the boat. As he stood looking over the water, he wondered how he could stoop so low as to take a deprived stray dog and use it for bait.

The dog sat on his foot, wagging her tail as if she and her new master were going somewhere.

"Sorry, sport, but I need to use you to catch that monster before it attacks again," he said as if the dog knew what he was saying.

If only the dog could understand what he was saying, now would have been the best time to bite the bad man, but instead, she wagged her tail faster and gave him a big smooch on the cheek.

Bob's eyes began to water as he promptly tied a thirty-foot line with a super large hook to the harness and tossed the dog over the side. The tide slowly took the dog away from the boat until the line became taut.

Gatorbait swam around at the end of the line, splashing and looking back to see if her new master would join her. After a few minutes, when she realized he wasn't going to join her, she began barking and frantically tried to come back to the boat, but the current was too strong. Bob reached for a bucket of fish blood and emptied it over the side as the dog began to tire from trying to swim back to the boat. Bob saw that she stopped wagging her tail as she swam halfway back before losing the battle with the current and drifted away until the line became taut again.

Bob took another swig from the flask as he fought with his emotions to haul the dog back into the boat. As he sat in his chair, waiting for the reptile to take the bait, a fifty-six-foot sailboat slowly turned toward the inlet. It was still a mile out when Bob noticed it. He scrambled for his binoculars and looked at the flag lazily blowing in the breeze at the top of the mast. It read P.E.T.A.

He knew damn well that it wasn't the flag that stood for People Eating Tasty Animals as he had read on novelty t-shirts. No, that would be no problem; the sailboat coming into the port was from the People for the Ethical Treatment of Animals.

"Son of a bitch!" he cursed out loud, "Wouldn't you know it... Of all the bad luck..." He leaped to his feet and began to whistle for the dog to come back to the boat. He grabbed the line and began pulling the dog in, but the exhausted girl sank underwater with every pull of the line.

The sailboat seemed to have picked up speed once it found the entrance buoy and turned on all the deck lights. Now, less than a quarter mile away, Bob spotted a person walk out to the bow and, through his binoculars, noticed the curious look on the man's well lit face.

Bob had a worried look as he decided to act like his dog fell overboard. He gently pulled the line in and called out for his beloved dog, which he now called Rosy.

"Come on Rosy... Come on, girl, you can make it!" he shouted.

"Ahoy matey!" a voice yelled over. You shouldn't let your dog swim in the inlet... It's too dangerous!"

Bob looked up and waved as the boat was now within thirty yards of the inlet, "Mind your own damn business, you long-haired freak," he muttered as the sailboat passed by the dog and began to slow. Fantastic... they must have seen the giant hook sticking out of the harness, Bob thought.

Sitting on the gunwale and reeling in the dog, he wondered what the odds were for a whacked-out PETA group to cruise by a boat in the middle of the night with a dog floating on a line for bait. It was almost funny, he thought as he let out a snicker.

The snicker quickly vanished when the sailboat came to a complete stop and launched a small inflatable dinghy over the side. The dog was near the boat when Bob saw how exhausted it was. The poor creature nearly drowned as she fought to keep her head above water.

Feeling remorseful, he wondered if he had lost his mind. He wasted no time heaving her back into the boat. Too tired to stand, Gatorbait, or Rosy as she was now called, fell to the deck like dead weight, and Bob wrapped her in a blanket and gave her a bowl of water. He then walked to the bow to raise the anchor when, out of the corner of his eye, he saw the dinghy speeding over.

Now what? His first thought was to continue raising the anchor and getting the hell out of dodge. On second thought, he figured, to hell with them. He stood up and waited for their arrival with his hands on his hips.

The inflatable boat slowed and cut its motor as it came alongside and mildly bumped the towboat. The two men in the dinghy looked like rejects from a carnival sideshow. One looked like a Captain Hook wannabee from Neverland and the other like Harry Potter in a Speedo bathing suit. Bob had to turn his head to keep from laughing.

"Permission to board, Captain," asked the pirate-looking one, exasperation in his tone.

"Denied," Bob growled.

The two looked at each other with a startled look and shrugged, "We will come aboard anyway," they replied in unison.

Bob shook his head but didn't say a word, figuring words weren't enough for these animal saviors. He simply stepped forward and offered a hand to help them aboard.

The larger man dressed as a pirate stepped up and grabbed Bob's hand. As he leaped up to the gunwale, Bob threw a punch square in his face, sending the flamboyant pirate flailing back to the dinghy.

Sprawled out on the deck with disbelieving eyes and a look of distress, the pirate covered his nose with both hands and cried out that his nose was broken.

Bob stood his ground with a slight grin and wondered if the two freaks had ever been in a fight before. He'd probably have broken up laughing if he wasn't so annoyed.

"Now get the hell out of here before I do the same to you, ya little shit!" he bellowed.

The Speedo man gave his buddy a towel to wipe his nose before returning the stare toward Bob, "You should have simply let us board your vessel and save the dog. You don't think we saw that big shiny hook sticking out of the harness?" he said, sounding like a resilient preacher. "Now we've got to do it the hard way, and afterward... I hope you will have learned a lesson or two about your fellow creatures."

Bob had heard enough. He began to release the line and

ignore the boy wonder until he took off his shirt and jumped on the gunwale. Crouching in a martial arts stance, the Speedo man was ready to kick ass or have an extended stay in the hospital.

"Get off my boat, or I'll break your nose as well," Bob demanded, his patience wearing thin.

"Not until I save the dog and teach you a little respect," Speedo retorted unwaveringly.

Bob took a step forward and threw a punch before he was met with a foot to the groin and a fist smashing into his nose. He fell to his knees, gasping for air when out of nowhere, a foot came crashing into the side of his head. Before falling flat out on the deck, Bob was hit with another foot to the opposite side of his head, sending him reeling with pain to the deck.

As he lay sprawled out on his back, seeing stars, the martial arts Speedo man grabbed him by the hair and raised his head before throwing four more punches to his face.

A shroud of darkness set in as Bob tried to get up. Another kick to the ribs sent him crashing into the center console, rendering him unconscious.

The Speedo man stood up straight and ran his fingers through his hair. Satisfied with his work, he grabbed hold of the frightened dog and returned to the dinghy. Looking back to the battered man passed out under the console, he said to the dog, "See, that bad man should have cooperated when we came to save you."

He took the harness off and threw it back in the towboat while his pirate buddy cranked the dinghy's motor and made their way back to the sailboat, where the rest of the crew welcomed them like conquering heroes.

*****

The sun faintly rose through the dark clouds that promised a rainy morning. A light drizzle made the Horizon a slippery mess as Skip jumped from the dock to the tugboat.

Returning for another week-long shift, the mood was anything but good as the crew arrived, knowing that the ravenous reptile had not been caught.

The Indian trappers were still staked out in the creek behind Sandy Beach Park. Mayor Myers and Chief Officer Randy Taylor were anxiously waiting for Bloodfoot to turn up.

Arriving early for his shift, Skip relieved the other deckhand early, sat at the stern of the tugboat with an expired loaf of bread, and fed the seagulls.

With his legs blissfully dangling off the back of the tug, Skip's mind began to wonder as he watched the seagulls flying overhead. He was tempted to grab his fishing pole when he spotted a large tarpon joining the bread feast but was too lazy to get up. As he aimlessly threw the bread into the water, he failed to notice the small wake heading in his direction.

For the past five days, AlliCroc sat in a small cove overrun by sea grapes just outside the mouth of the creek at Sandy Beach Park. Sensing the Indian trackers, it managed to keep a low profile instead of returning to its nest.

It felt protected hunting at night, returning in the early morning hours. But on this dreary morning, its sensory organs tingled from the agitating water caused by the tarpon. It glided through the basin like a submarine, just below the surface, toward an easy meal.

Captain Virgil Goodman pulled up to the dock, got out of his Ford van, and pulled his duffel bag out of the trunk. He glanced over at Skip and nearly choked on his bagel at the grave situation that was about to unfold, "Skip! Get out of the way!" he shouted, throwing his bag down and running to the edge of the dock.

Startled, Skip reacted quickly, pulled his feet up, and rolled backwards. AlliCroc sprang out of the water and landed on the flat decking at the stern of the tugboat, snapping its jaws shut like a spring-loaded bear trap, missing Skip by inches before sliding back into the water. Skip thought he was done for as the reptile's weight caused the tug's back end to drop lower in the water and he screamed when he felt the foul air escape the jaws like a pressure hose bursting.

He was still rolling backward and screaming hysterically when he slammed his head on the hydraulic pins, splitting his head open and pouring blood all over the deck.

Virgil stood on the dock awestruck and fearing the worst. With all the blood on the deck, he was sure Skip got bit.

The crew onboard, alarmed at the sudden movement of the tugboat, ran out of the galley where they had been eating breakfast and ran over to Skip. "What the hell happened," Anton Larssen shouted, with a mouth full of pastry.

Anton was another deckhand, waiting for Bill to show up so that he could go home for his week off. He was a fat Norwegian man who had a reputation amongst the tugboat crews as one who broke into other people's business and reported problems to the office staff.

Virgil ignored him and jumped on the tug. Skip was grabbing his chest as the rest of the crew hovered above him.

"Skip! You're alright; it didn't get you," Virgil said, kneeling next to him with blood-soaked knees. He didn't have to be a doctor to see that Skip was having a heart attack. "Call 9-1-1.

He's having a heart attack, and he lost a lot of blood from a gash to the head." Within five minutes, Paramedics ascended with lights flashing and sirens wailing. Television news crews pulled to the dock and set up for live breaking news reports on the creature known as AlliCroc. Mayor Nick Myers was contemplating a bullet in his brain as he watched the news on a television in his office.

Bill and Chuck just arrived when the paramedics were leaving with Skip.

Captain Virgil met them on the dock and told them what happened.

"That damn reptile sounds like it's getting more aggressive," Chuck construed.

"I knew something happened when I was stuck in a traffic line for an hour outside the Port entrance," Bill added.

Virgil looked at him questioningly, "Who caused the traffic jam?"

"Every news station on the planet, I think," replied Bill, "So much for trying to keep AlliCroc out of the news."

After lunch, Captain Virgil, Chuck, and Bill had a couple of hours to kill before the next job and decided to go to the hospital to see how Skip was doing. A somnolent-looking

Anton, who was notified that he had to stay on shift to fill in for Skip, read Virgil the riot act, reminding him that it was against policy to leave the boat while on duty.

"Stuff it, Anton," Virgil replied vulgarly, as he reminded him that he was the captain and there would be dire consequences should the big boss somehow find out.

Skip, as they found out by the doctor before entering the room, suffered a panic attack rather than a heart attack. It was an established fact that he was deathly afraid of the monstrous reptile and clearly spoke out that they shouldn't be working until it was captured. Hoping to surprise him, they slowly opened the door with a smuggled pizza, only to find him looking at them from his bed in the upright position.

"Hey 'ol buddy, how ya doing," Bill asked with a booming voice. "Good as can be expected," Skip mumbled half-heartedly, looking like he had aged ten years overnight. His eyes were red with puffy black circles under them. It almost looked like he was wearing the Lone Rangers' mask. "Sorry about the boat incident, Cap; I lost my mind and freaked out when I saw all that blood. I thought that hideous creature took a chunk out of me... but it didn't, and I screamed like a little girl," he continued, his eyes welling up.

"I think we all would have done the same," replied Virgil.

"I don't think I would have screamed like a little girl," Bill laughed, "Maybe I'd scream like a man, but not a little girl," he continued, trying to get Skip to smile. He didn't; he just gave Bill a blank stare and closed his eyes.

"We'll talk later, Skip. Right now, you need some rest, and we'll come back and get you out of here," Chuck said, retrieving a second slice of pizza and walking toward the window.

Skip knew his crew mates were just trying to cheer him up, but it didn't matter. There was no way in hell he was going to go back to work on the water as long as the reptile was lurking around. He was never so scared in his life until that hideous thing came after him. He would have nightmares for the rest of his life, thinking about how he actually felt its repugnant breath and the brute strength the monster projected. No way, forget going back to the tugboat. His plans were to get out of the hospital and go to Alabama and visit his parents for a while. The three of them sat in the room and finished the pizza while Skip stared out the window. Each of them observed how terrified he was and had doubts about him coming back to work any time soon. As they said their goodbyes, they each got the impression that they'd probably not see Skip again, at least until AlliCroc was captured.

13

The closed-door meeting took place in the mayor's conference room. Chief Bhim, his son Durjaya, Don Henderson, and Officer Randy Taylor were present.

Late as usual, Mayor Nick Myers stormed through the door like a rabid dog. Dressed like a golfer, wearing a dark blue Calloway polo shirt and white pleated microfiber textured slacks, he looked more like a fashion model than a mayor.

Officer Taylor rolled his eyes which caught the attention of Durjaya, causing him to express amusement.

The mayor gave him a malicious look as he seated himself at the head of the oak, oval-shaped table. He snatched a phone from the receiver and dialed a number before the men heard a phone ring from outside the room. His secretary sitting across the hall, could be heard answering the phone as the Mayor told her to hold his calls.

Officer Taylor sighed as he leaned back in his seat and crossed his arms, wishing Nick Myers would get down to business rather than play his childish power games.

"First, I'd like to thank you, gentlemen, for coming," he said, lighting up a Perdomo Habano cigar.

"What do you mean?" Don protested. "Officer Taylor picked me up like a common criminal."

"You are a common criminal," replied Myers, blowing smoke in his face. "You, Chief Bhim, and I are indirectly responsible for that monster out there."

He paused to let it sink in. Randy had a surprised look on his face when he heard the Mayor fess up.

"Our good Officer Randy Taylor here knows about AlliCroc and how it came to be," he continued, holding out his hand and pointing a finger at the officer with a malicious smile.

Don and Chief Bhim glanced at each other like two kids who were caught cheating on a high school exam.

"Obviously, I... like the both of you, do not want this conversation to leave the room. I've worked too hard to get where I am to throw it all away, getting caught up with this damn reptile crap," he continued, turning his eyes to Don and Bhim.

"Hopefully, AlliCroc will return to the creek where my trappers will catch it," Chief Bhim added. "If it does not return within a couple more days, I will continue looking elsewhere."

"Two days is too long," Myers retorted. "I'll give you twenty-four hours. If it doesn't show up, you had better start tracking that reptile the way you people say you do."

"We've been..."

The Mayor cut Bhim off and looked at Don, "I want you and Officer Taylor to put together a team and hunt that reptile up the Himmershee River—track the damn thing all the way to the Everglades if need be."

Once again, he paused for effect, fixing his eyes on the officer.

"What do I know about catching that beast?" Don blurted. "I don't know anybody down here I can trust with my life."

"You know Virgil Goodman," Myers replied indifferently. "Captain Virgil Goodman, I hear, can pilot a boat through anything."

"He'll kill me if I tried to drag him into this!"

"I doubt that," Myers smiled cunningly. "I heard you two were old buddies. He'll gladly help; I've got video footage of him and his crew drinking on the tugboat. I'm sure that if he plans on keeping his job... and Captain's license, he surely wouldn't complain about helping you out."

Don was speechless; he couldn't believe the mayor was actually going to blackmail Virgil. He quickly darted his eyes to Officer Taylor.

"Don't look at me; I didn't give Nick the tape," Taylor shrugged.

"By the way, where is Captain Goodman? I do believe I called for him to be here also," Myers impishly asked the officer.

"He's working... should be docking a ship about now," replied Taylor, holding back his abhorrence toward Myers.

"Fine, we'll wait."

They waited for less than an hour, which seemed a lifetime to Don, who was now trying to fight off an anxiety attack. He sat fidgeting nervously in his chair when Captain Virgil knocked at the door and entered before Myers could answer. He looked around, planted himself in the only empty chair, and made himself comfortable.

"You're late, Captain," Myers said, sounding irritated.

"I was working a ship, sir. I didn't have the luxury of playing golf this morning," Virgil replied dryly, observing the peculiar-looking outfit the mayor was wearing.

Nick Myers despised the fact that Virgil was deliberately mocking him but ignored the comment and continued the meeting.

There was a knock at the door, and a secretary entered the room and placed a freshly brewed pot of coffee on the table.

What Lurks Below

Wearing a red Pima Cotton dress and Gucci high-heeled sandals with embroidered paillettes, she strutted through the room as if modeling down a runway, smiling when all eyes were on her and her shapely tanned legs.

When she left the room, all eyes returned to Mayor Myers with a knowing look that he didn't hire her for her typing skills.

"As we all know, this is a very large and extremely dangerous reptile we're dealing with. Don, why don't you take it from here and tell us about your monster," Myers said, brutally frank.

Don felt his heart pounding in his head as he stood up and walked around the table. He promptly composed himself and took charge of the meeting, "What we are dealing with here is a very dangerous mutant reptile, half alligator and half crocodile, to put it mildly. It is growing larger and more aggressive every day. As you all have probably noticed, it's much smarter than your average reptile, which is probably the reason it hasn't been caught. As we also found out, it can attack anything... including humans. AlliCroc has no natural enemies known to man that can harm it... well, maybe Godzilla," he tried to joke, but nobody acknowledged the humor. He gave a weary smile and continued, "It has razor-sharp teeth, twice the size and amount of an alligator, set in massive jaws that can snap a great white shark in half. The reptile's hide is tough as steel, making it almost impossible to penetrate."

Virgil wanted to jump up and throw him out the window, "Why the hell did you do it?" he spat out.

"You, of all people who know me, should know why I did it, Virge," Don replied, as if surprised he asked. "I accomplished what they said couldn't be done," he paused and looked around the table. "Nature said it couldn't be done, and man made it happen... I made it happen!" he responded like a true mad scientist.

"I hope it eats you, Don," replied Virgil rancorously.

"Why the Everglades?" asked Officer Taylor, wondering why he raised it there.

"It seemed like the best place to raise the hatchlings. I was lucky to meet Chief Bhim, who assured me that it was safe and out of the way," he said, looking to blame the Indian Chief.

"And that it would be a multi-million dollar attraction," Virgil added with a scowl.

"You said hatchlings. Is there more than one?" asked the officer, glaring at Myers.

"No, no, there's only one," Don quickly replied, looking over to Bhim and hoping he would bail him out. Chief Bhim just sat there with his arms folded across his chest and let Don take the heat. When Don was sure he wasn't going to speak, he continued, "Three were raised at the Everglades Sanctuary until they escaped. Poachers quickly killed one, and the other one was ill. It headed north, but I'm sure it's dead."

"Did you find the carcass?" Virgil inquired skeptically.

"We found the first one, minus the head and tail. As I said, the other one took off and headed north. We tracked it for days until we lost the trail... or should I say, the trail suddenly ended. I believe the redneck poachers followed it and killed it."

Virgil and Randy looked over to the Mayor, now fidgeting in his seat. "I hope you're right," Virgil replied, unconvinced, shaking his head. "They escaped four months ago. If it were alive, somebody, somewhere, would have reported it." Don rationalized, beads of sweat running down his forehead.

"Since you said these creatures are nearly indestructible, how do you think the redneck hunters killed it?" The officer questioned.

"At the time of escape, they were nearly eighteen feet long, and those thick plates on their body were not as tough as they are now, meaning they were still susceptible to a man if they had an elephant gun or something of that size," Don lied.

"So, four months later, how big is the reptile that made its way all the way to the Intracoastal?" The officer asked with an infuriating look.

Don let out a heavy sigh and shot a look to Mayor Myers, who nodded his head to continue, "Well, figuring the rate it grew in captivity... I would not be exaggerating to say he is thirty-foot long," Don answered, taking a hard swallow, "Give or take a few feet."

"I can't believe my ears. And you knew about this?" Randy said, pointing a finger at Myers.

"Unfortunately, yes, but I'm as shocked as you are," Mayor Myers replied with a culpable look.

"You son of a..."

"Enough! What's done is done!" Myers cut him off, slamming his fists on the table. "What we need to do now is catch and kill the reptile swiftly before the entire town panics!"

"And you think you can do it with these jokers?" replied Randy, pointing a finger at Chief Bhim and Durjaya.

"We'll catch it, white man... We'll catch it," Chief Bhim replied scornfully as he stood up from his seat along with his son and stormed out of the room.

"That's enough, Taylor!" Myers barked. "Bhim! Get back in here!" he ordered.

There was no reply; Chief Bhim and his son were already in their truck and peeling out of the parking lot.

"Look what you've done; why do you hate those bastards!" Myers grumbled.

"Who needs 'em!" Taylor blasted back.

"You do. You, Captain Goodman, and Don," Myers replied with a crooked grin.

"I want no part of it. What you, Don, and that Indian chief got yourselves into is of no concern of mine. Just kill that damn monster before it eats my goddamn tugboat," Virgil replied, standing up and heading for the door. "Sit down, Captain," said Myers in a low tone. He picked up a video cassette that was sitting at the table and continued, "What I have in my hand is a video of some men having a few drinks on a tugboat. You wouldn't believe who these guys are," he paused, waiting for a reaction.

Virgil stared at Myers with no emotion, "So you've resorted to blackmail. Why am I not surprised," he said calmly, conspicuously looking over to Randy.

"Call it what you will, but if you would like to remain a captain, and if your crew wants to remain employed, I'm going to need your help capturing AlliCroc," he declared, chomping down hard on the end of his cigar.

Virgil closed the door and returned to his seat, "I'm listening."

"I didn't give him the tape, Captain. Somebody gave him the Port security video," the officer was quick to point out.

Virgil ignored Randy and focused on the Mayor while Don sat quietly in his seat with a guilty look.

"Why me? What do I know about hunting that monster?"

"Because your old buddy Don doesn't feel he can trust anybody else to watch his butt on the trip," Myers replied piercingly.

The look Virgil gave Don made him feel like escaping to another country. He stared at him for a full minute before continuing, "I'll do it. I've got a few days left before my shift is over..."

"You'll leave after your shift," Myers cut in. "You guys will begin the hunt in two days."

Virgil sighed and took a deep breath, "As I said, I'll do it, but if my crew refuses, I won't force the issue," he said sternly.

"Fair enough, but I'm sure they'll see the urgency for their services," smiled Myers, pounding his cigar stub in the ashtray.

"Have you got a plan?" Virgil asked Randy.

"I'm hoping we'll find the reptile somewhere between the Intracoastal and the Everglades. We'll drag a sonar until we find it," replied Randy with a weary look.

"Alligators and crocodiles are territorial. With the Indians staking out the creek and us cruising down the river with sonar, I'm sure we'll find it," Meyers added.

"AlliCroc is not your usual reptile," Don added. "What do you suggest?" inquired Randy.

"It's very smart. I just want to suggest that we stay on guard," Don murmured, noticing Virgil become increasingly irritated while he spoke.

"Fine, do it. I want that hideous thing killed swiftly before we lose all the tourists, and try to do it before the media digs deeper and get some crazy idea that I'm involved," replied Myers, as he abruptly got out of his seat and walked out the door. "Remember... if I go down, we all go down," he threatened.

"I never liked that bastard," revealed Randy as Myers walked down the hall.

"Anything else you want to warn us about?" Virgil asked, looking over to Don.

"AlliCroc is a very intelligent creature," Don replied proudly. "It has extremely good integumentary sense organs. They're much more responsive than the usual gator or croc, to put it mildly."

"Speak normally so we can understand," Virgil snapped, detesting the scientific language Don seemed to have picked up.

Don shuddered and wiped the sweat off his brow before continuing, "I'm talking about small sensory pits dotted around the jaw area, which are capable of detecting pressure changes in the water. Of course, gators have them, too, but naturally, AlliCroc's are magnified at least four times more. In other words, besides its incredible eyesight, it can sense movement in the water from a great distance," Don persisted, like a self-righteous father.

"Well, you must be proud," Randy angrily replied, "Is there anything else unusual about your beast you might want to divulge?

"Its head, try to stay clear of the head," he rambled on. "Crocs have a narrow head and a longer muzzle. Gators have a wider head. AlliCroc's head has both these qualities but tends to look more like an Indian Mugger."

"What in God's name is an Indian Mugger," asked Randy, subconsciously thinking of Bhim.

"The Indian Mugger is a Crocodylus Palustris, a crocodile with a round head like an alligator. But as you can see, AlliCroc's head is about four-foot wide," he paused, watching the look of horror on their faces before continuing. "And then the teeth. Crocodiles have a fourth tooth on their lower jaw that you can see protruding out of the side of the jaws when closed. Somehow, with our genetic altercations, AlliCroc has an entire row of teeth protruding."

"Don, if you're still alive when this is over, I'm going to kill you," Virgil promised.

"What are the Indians using to eradicate this thing if it returns to the creek?" Virgil asked Randy.

"Bhim and his outlaw band of trappers set up a trap," Randy answered skeptically. "If the reptile returns, they will be hiding in the trees near and over the water. They will seal off the entrance with a large net so it can't escape. Should they be successful, they'll have plenty of time to kill it with shotguns," he said cynically, repeating what Durjaya told him earlier.

"You don't seem to have much faith in Bhim," said Myers,

returning to the room when nobody followed him out.

"Bhim and his crew are a bunch of lazy-ass Indians that don't have a clue about the brute strength of that genetically altered mutant," Randy quipped. "Oh, I don't know about that," Don hastily replied. "After all, let's not forget that Bhim and those very same Indians raised those reptiles."

"And he underestimated them, and they escaped," Randy was quick to point out. "If they do trap the damn thing, it will be extremely aggressive, not to mention nearly twice the size of when it escaped."

"They plan to shoot it full of diazepam from a tranquilizer gun," Don cajoled.

"They think they can get a dart through that armor-plated hide?" Virgil mused.

"No, not through the skin. That would never work. They will shoot the dart into the jaws," Don elaborated.

Virgil leaned back in his seat with his hands folded over his head, flabbergasted at what he was hearing.

"Okay, so it's set," Myers said, clapping his hands together and looking at the faces around the table. "The trappers are in place at the creek as we speak, and you guys will begin your hunt in two days from now... and remember, the sooner we catch the reptile, the better we'll all be," he continued deliberately.

The meeting was over. Don was completely discounted as Virgil and Randy talked to each other in the parking lot, "It bothers me to see how the big Mayor Nick Myers callously made it clear that he could care less about the danger involved as long as the media doesn't find out he's involved in this mess," Randy said with disgust.

"And it bothers me how my good old friend Don thinks he can get away with giving him a tape of me and my crew," Virgil answered, giving the officer a knowing look.

14

While Chief Bhim met with the Mayor, his trackers had their trap set up and were waiting patiently at the creek inside Sandy Beach Park. It was an extremely hot and humid afternoon, and the mosquitoes were getting worse by the hour.

One of the trappers, a strong-looking, tattoo-armed, eighteen-year-old by the name of Johnny Cougar, couldn't stand it any longer. He had been sitting quietly on a tree branch hanging over the creek all day, waiting for a creature that was probably miles away.

It was getting to be late afternoon, and he doubted that the vicious rep tile would return. Against Chief Bhim's orders, he decided to take a quick dip in the creek. Disregarding the discouraging whispers of his fellow trappers, he stood up on the tree branch and jumped into the brackish water ten feet below.

AlliCroc's eyes sprang open the second the young man plunged into the water. The elusive reptile had quietly returned to the creek a few hours earlier and sensed danger. It slipped undetected below the surface, swimming near the sea grapes and overgrowth near the edge of the creek, blending in with the surroundings as it sank to the bottom and waited until the threat of the trappers was gone.

The ravenous reptile was only sixty yards away when Johnny Cougar splashed into the water. Its insatiable appetite caused him to become agitated as it crawled forward, aggressively stalking its prey.

"Get your ass out of the water, you fool!" one of the other trappers whispered angrily.

Johnny smiled contemptuously and dove under the surface. He sprang up from the bottom and floated on his back, ignoring the hushed shouts from his peers.

Billy Bear, who aptly got his name because he was as big as a bear, standing six-foot-four and weighing two-hundred and eighty pounds, was pure muscle. He was livid as he jumped down from the tree and ran to the water's edge, "If I have to get in the water and drag you out, you're not going to be happy," he said in a low, piercing tone.

Billy was put in charge while Chief Bhim and Durjaya attended the meeting with the mayor. Although he grew up with the other trappers, he was a natural-born leader, and the other men faithfully respected him.

"Lighten up, Bear. AlliCroc hasn't been here in days; he's not coming back. I had to cool off for a few minutes. Don't tell

Durjaya I'm coming out now, and I'll get back on that branch and pretend like I'm waiting for AlliCroc to return... just like the rest of you guys," he reasoned.

He looked at the others, who appeared to be gnashing their teeth, and sluggishly swam over to the embankment until he touched the bottom, where he began walking out. Stopping when he was waist-deep, he leisurely stooped over and looked at his left foot.

"Get out now!" Billy shouted, losing his temper.

"I am!" he snapped back, "Just let me get this crap off my foot." Walking along the bottom, he picked up some gooey tar-like stuff between his toes.

He no sooner put his foot down when he saw the shadow of the reptile ascend on him. Like a deer in the headlights, his muscles refused to perform as the grotesque reptile charged in and compressed its jaws around his mid-section.

The young trapper was terrified as he looked over to Billy and let out an ear-piercing scream before a gut-wrenching gurgling sound replaced it, as blood burst out from his nose and mouth. Johnny tried to grab the reptile and force its mouth open to no avail.

Billy and the others watched helplessly as the reptile violently shook its head, tearing chunks of flesh and bone from their friend.

Out of sheer desperation, Billy jumped on the reptile's back and frantically whacked it with a machete. As sharp as the blade was, it could not penetrate the thick, armor-plated hide. Another trapper jumped in and swam around the reptile, staying clear of the hideous jaws, and began tying a line around the immense girth in hopes of restraining the monster. When finished, he instinctively swam backward in order to stay clear when the massive tail thrashed at him. The first whip of the tail missed him, but as he turned in a panic at the huge splash of water, the tail smashed him head-on, knocking him unconscious.

Billy quickly jumped off the massive beast when it suddenly went into a death roll. The sound of bones crunching and breaking was horrifying while the trappers watched in stunned disbelief.

Billy ran out of the water and grabbed one of the spear guns, "When it stops rolling, hit it with the tranquilizer darts!" he ordered as the others frantically loaded their weapons.

At once, AlliCroc stopped rolling and raised its enormous head out of the water, swallowing the bloody mass that once was Johnny in one gulp. While the jaws were raised, Billy shot a dart inside the jaws, penetrating the soft skin. AlliCroc hissed loudly and became even more violent, aggressively snapping out at the hunters as they fired their weapons in and around the head area, where the darts ineffectively bounced off.

After several minutes of fighting a losing battle, the trappers rushed over and grabbed the line still attached around the monster's enormous girth and fastened it to a tree so it couldn't get away. AlliCroc turned around and dove toward the center of the lagoon and deeper water. The attached line whipped through the water until it became taut, "We got him! He can't escape the…"

The ardent trapper's sentence was cut short when the line snapped and hit the tree like a bullwhip, missing him by inches.

Billy fell to his knees, exhausted and emotionally drained. He sat for a moment, trying hard to regain his composure before getting up and walking over to where the hunters had gathered around the man hit by the enormous tail.

Curled up in the fetal position and straining for air, the men were alarmed to hear a gurgled hissing sound when Tommy Slade exhaled. Billy figured the man had broken a few ribs until he cautiously rolled him over and gasped at the sight of his broken rib cage protruding through flesh.

What Lurks Below

"Adahy, Call 9-1-1!" Billy ordered to his cousin, his voice noticeably shaking. He stood up and walked closer to the water with his hands on his hips, trying to grasp the tragedy that just took place. Looking out toward the creek's entrance, he shuddered at the sight of the sizeable wake exiting. He'd swear the wake came from a small submarine if he hadn't known better.

Billy sluggishly reached into his pants pocket and pulled out his waterproof cell phone. Surprised it was still working, he punched the key and grudgingly waited for an answer.

Chief Bhim answered the call as he drove inside the park en route to the creek. He listened for a couple of minutes before dropping the phone in his lap. His face became pasty white and grief-stricken as he managed to pull the truck off the narrow road and stop. "Father!... What is it?... What happened?" Durjaya erupted, anxiously grabbing his father's arm.

Chief Bhim was unable to speak as he opened the door and fell to his knees onto the sandy ground. Durjaya jumped out of the passenger side and rushed to his father's side, "Father! Talk to me!" he raised his voice with apprehension.

The Chief remained silent on his knees, his fists clenched tight and tears pouring out of his red, swollen eyes. Durjaya helped his emaciated father up as a paramedic truck passed by with sirens blaring and lights flashing. Durjaya felt a lump in his throat as he realized something must have gone terribly wrong with his friends in the creek.

He quickly led his father to the truck's passenger side and helped him in.

"Johnny's dead... Your cousin Johnny is dead, and Tommy Slade is badly injured," Bhim mumbled as his son drove like a madman.

Durjaya sat in stunned disbelief. It was he who practically begged his father to let his younger cousin come along for the hunt. Growing up in the Everglades, Johnny had absolutely no fear of the animals and reptiles he'd encountered. Now that he was eighteen years old, he wanted to prove to everybody that he was a man. Finally, against his better judgment, the Chief let him come along and join the other hunters, promising his sister that he would be protected.

Durjaya felt the pain of one hundred spears in his heart as he pulled the truck off the road and headed toward the creek. He threw caution to the wind as he tore through the picnic area and sped past the pedestrians.

Within minutes, Durjaya and the Chief arrived just in time to see the paramedics load the injured trapper into the ambulance. Durjaya hit the brakes, screeching to a stop, and jumped out of the truck. The remorseful Paramedics were about to close the back door when Durjaya bumped past them and jumped into the vehicle. Before he could utter a single word to his wounded friend, he was hastily pulled out of the truck.

"Step aside, please, let us do our job," the medic said, releasing his firm grip on Durjaya's arm.

"How bad is he?"

"He's heavily sedated right now. He'll live if we get him to the hospital pronto," the medic replied hurriedly.

Durjaya stepped to the side as the Paramedic shut the door behind him. As the ambulance sped off to the hospital, his eyes followed the flashing lights until they stopped on Billy. His fists clenched in rage, he stormed over to confront the man who was left in charge.

"I'm sorry for what happened to Johnny," he said as Durjaya hastily walked closer and threw a punch at Billy's face.

Billy saw it coming and, with lightning speed, blocked the punch with his left arm and grabbed Durjaya's throat by the other, "Don't be silly, son. Just because you are the son of Chief Bhim doesn't mean I won't think twice about ripping your throat out," he angrily whispered, before letting go and throwing the powerless Durjaya to the ground.

"My father left you in charge for one afternoon, and you got his nephew killed!" Durjaya said angrily, rubbing his throat.

"Johnny got bored and jumped into the creek," Billy replied, helping Durjaya to his feet. "Everybody told him to get out, but he wouldn't listen." "The fool, he never listened to anybody... and now look where it got him," Durjaya muttered, his eyes welling up.

"It was quick. I don't think he felt pain," Billy lied.

Durjaya gave him a knowing glare as they walked over to the Chief.

It wasn't long before the news media got wind of the attack and ascended on the scene in full force. Channels Four, Seven, and Ten parked their vans alongside the road, extending their long antennas from the roof while the reporters emerged like vultures at a road kill.

Acting on the orders from Chief Bhim, the Indian trappers declined to answer all questions asked of them by the news teams.

Durjaya ignored the entire melee and climbed out on the branch where Johnny jumped into the creek. He quietly studied the water, checking every ripple, hoping to find the hideous reptile. Billy informed him that they hit AlliCroc inside the jaws with at least five tranquilizer darts, which should have been enough to knock out the creature for a week. Still, he found no evidence of the monster in the creek.

15

Officer Randy Taylor parked his patrol truck next to the emergency room entrance and walked inside the hospital. It was nearly ten o'clock in the evening, and visiting hours were over. He knew it would have been a waste of time to try talking to Bhim and his crew about the attack, so he thought he'd try the next best thing: get the news directly from the source.

"Good evening. I'd like to know what room Tom Slade is in," he politely inquired to the front desk nurse. "He's the Indian trapper transported here this afternoon," he continued when the nurse gave him a curious look.

"I know who he is, Officer, but visiting hours are over, and besides, he's in no condition to talk right now," she said in an uncompromising tone. "I'm here on business, lady; what room?" he demanded, causing the lady to jump.

"Two-sixty-three," she blurted.

Randy gave her a look that could freeze hell as he walked towards the elevator. After a long day listening to the mayor's cock and bull stories about how he wanted the reptile handled, he was in no mood to take any lip from the nurse.

He was stopped short of the elevator by a portly police officer who came running when he heard the commotion. The overweight cop hesitated when he saw Randy in uniform, "Uh, what kind of business do you have here, Officer Taylor?" he asked, reading his nameplate.

"I'm going up to see the Indian who was attacked earlier," replied Randy with a stern look.

He waited impatiently as the man nervously looked around, "Okay, make it quick; I don't want any trouble around here."

"Don't you worry," Randy said as he stepped into the elevator, "I won't be long."

The elevator doors opened on the second floor, and Randy stepped out. He looked left and right before walking down the hall a short distance until he stopped at a large roundabout where four nurses sitting at a monitoring station gave him the evil eye. Apparently, the bimbo downstairs called ahead to warn them he was on his way. He thought.

"Well, well, well. I thought it would be you, Officer Taylor," a shapely blonde nurse said, grinning as she stepped out of the ladies' room and opened her arms to hug him.

"My, oh my, look at you," Randy responded with a wide grin as he hugged her. "Nice to see somebody up here with a pleasant face," he added, looking back at the hostile-looking nurses.

"Now, now," she said, grabbing his hand and walking down the hall. "They're just doing their job," she smiled.

Kathy Vandenberg had worked at the hospital for the past two years. She and Randy had met in the emergency room on more than a dozen occasions and became fast friends. They dated quite a few times but never became too serious because she didn't want to get intimately involved with a police officer and all the danger involved with his line of work. But that didn't mean she wouldn't fool around when they wanted to share some body heat.

"The lady downstairs must be new," Randy assumed. "You got it. She means well, but she plays by the book."

"Yeah, well, I'm not here on a social call. I need to ask Slade some questions, and I'll be on my way," Randy said in his defense.

"I know, I know. You don't have to give me the details," she replied, still smiling as she led him down the hall like a mischievous schoolgirl.

They stopped at the entrance to Slade's room and waited for a nurse to finish reading his vital signs.

"Okay, I'll leave you to your business, but don't rough him up any," she said, the smile leaving her face, "He's in a lot of pain."

The nurse inside the room turned and gave Kathy an inquisitive look, "Why would he rough up that poor man?" she asked as she led Kathy out of the room.

"Let's just say that the good officer doesn't care much for the red man," Kathy replied, walking away and avoiding a full explanation on the subject of how Officer Randy Taylor thought that most of the Indians living in the Everglades were either running or hiding from one thing or another.

Randy removed his cap and pulled a chair next to the bed. He sat in the chair and leaned closer to Slade. He studied the wounded man for a full minute and came to the conclusion that he was really sleeping.

"Hello, Tommy, can you hear me?" he whispered gruffly, squeezing his arm.

"Ugh, who are you?" he mumbled, flexing his arm from the painful grip. "My name is Taylor, Officer Randy Taylor."

Slade's eyes popped open when he heard the name. "Chief Bhim says you're a bad man. I will answer no questions you ask," he said, with fear in his voice.

"Oh, but you will," Randy retorted with an evil grin. "It's because you and your half-assed tribe can't catch your unsightly pet that I have to put my ass on the line and do it for you."

"AlliCroc is too big and strong," Slade gasped in pain as Randy flicked him on the forehead.

"Were you guys able to shoot the tranquilizer inside its jaws?"

"The reptile is too big and aggressive. It's unstoppable!" Slade shouted. "Answer the question," Randy continued, squeezing the bandage on Slade's arm.

No answer. The patient worked himself into a sweat and passed out. "Let him be Randy," Kathy intervened as she stopped him from what looked like the beginnings of the Vulcan death grip. "He's out. We've got him hooked up to so many meds, it's a wonder he even opened his eyes."

"I need to know if that monster is lying at the bottom of that creek or not," Randy retorted, irritated.

"Well, you won't hear it from him, not tonight anyway," she said sternly.

"Useless piece of sh..."

"Randy! What's gotten into you," Kathy cut him off, exasperated. Officer Taylor let out a heavy sigh and turned to face her, "I'm sorry, Kathy, but I needed to know if that beast is knocked out and lying at the bottom of the creek."

"Why? Why do you need to know tonight? It's quite obvious

this man won't be able to tell you anything."

"Because my boss is sending me out to kill that thing," Randy replied, storming out of the room.

Early the next morning, Captain Virgil, Chuck, and Bill sat in the galley of the Horizon, waiting for the new deckhand to arrive. Anton, feeling tired and unappreciated by the crew, sat on the dock eating a bagel.

The word from the office was received the following evening that Skip had no desire to return to work at this time and took a leave of absence. His immediate plans were to get out of the hospital and visit his parents.

"You know," said Bill, chomping on bacon and eggs, "I really thought those Indian trappers were going to catch that damn reptile."

"Yeah, well, I think Chief Bhim underestimated the power of a thirty-three-foot mutation," replied Chuck, pouring himself a cup of coffee with a shot of apricot brandy.

"Mutation, I can't believe dumbass Don created the damn monster," added Virgil, studying a picture of the beast.

"Whew," Bill whistled, taking a look at the picture. "Bhim sure miscalculated when he thought he could just throw a net on this thing. Sometimes, I think that maybe those Indians smoke too much of the peace pipe," he added for effect.

At that moment, the new deckhand poked his head through the galley door, "Not all Indians smoke the peace pipe, and I know I don't. Especially when I must work," he grinned.

The three crewmen were startled as they looked at the replacement.

They couldn't believe the man was an Indian. "Open mouth, insert foot," Chuck whispered.

Captain Virgil walked over and shook hands with the new deckhand, "Welcome aboard, I'm Captain Virgil Goodman. This is my engineer, Chuck McClouski, and deckhand, Bill Brighton," he said, pointing to the crew. "The fat lazy guy on the dock is Anton," he continued, "He's not a part of this crew."

As Virgil had hoped, Anton heard the jab and made a note to report it to the office.

"My name is Tom Powhatan, and I have no relation to Chief Powhatan of the Pocahontas and John Smith story," he replied with a slight smile.

"Aye, so you are an American Indian?"

Bill replied, stating the obvious. "Yes, I am Bill. But don't worry, I don't smoke the peace pipe," verifying that the little remark by Bill wouldn't be forgotten.

"I was joking about a group of Indian trackers working around here trying to catch an alligator," Bill said flatly.

"Yes, I heard they're tracking some sort of monster reptile," Tom replied, seemingly well-informed. "Don't worry, I'm not one of them. I'm from Virginia," he smiled.

"Oh?" said Bill, pretending to be interested.

"I am a Mattaponi Indian. My people live on over one hundred and fifty acres of land on the banks of the Mattaponi River."

"Wow... sounds interesting," replied Bill, lying through his teeth.

The crew sat in the galley for the next hour boat talking and getting to know Tom. Chuck offered him a shot of brandy, but he declined and retrieved a can of grape-flavored cool-aid from his duffel bag, "No thanks, Chuck, I'll stick to my cool-aid," he said, "I love this stuff."

"Whatever floats your boat," replied Chuck disparagingly, walking out of the galley for some fresh air.

"It would probably taste a little better mixed with rum," Bill mused. "No thanks, I like it just fine the way it is intended," Tom quipped.

The sunrise tried poking out of the gloomy clouds, but the sound of thunder from the west assured it was going to be a decadent morning.

Virgil excused himself from the galley and casually walked up to the wheelhouse just as a light drizzle began. He sat in his chair and looked out over the basin. To his surprise, he caught sight of a small seventeen-foot dusky open fisherman sneaking out past the jetties. He quickly grabbed his binoculars and focused on the vessel.

So much for keeping small craft out of harm's way, Virgil thought to himself.

The two brothers in the small craft somehow managed to slip past the single patrol boat cruising around the Port. Erwin and Eric Norse were diehard fishermen who had no desire to keep their boat out of the water just because the authorities closed the Port. They heard the fishing would be good today, and there was no stopping them.

Cruising slowly through the jetties, Erwin looked up at the sky toward the west, "Looks like the storm's heading this way. Maybe we shouldn't go out too far," he said to his younger brother.

"What, you afraid of a little water?" Eric replied, ducking down low and lighting a cigar.

The small vessel continued toward the open sea as Eric prepared the bait.

Erwin didn't say anything; he just shook his head and continued navigating the boat through the jetties. When they cleared the jetties, Eric got up, set two fishing poles over the side, and spaced the lines out for trolling. When finished, he took the steering wheel, and Erwin repeated the process on the other side of the boat.

They trolled past the mile-marker buoy and opened two beers. Eric looked at the depth finder and saw they were just passing the one-hundred-foot depth mark, which was time for him to set the downrigger.

As Eric set the bait about eighty feet down, Erwin watched the black storm clouds building up and heading out to sea.

"Damn, that storm's heading out right behind us," he said with concern. "No worries, it'll probably rain itself out by the time it comes over our heads. We'll just stay out here until it's over," Eric answered, thinking about the dozens of other times when they stayed clear of storms.

But all was not well when they were three miles offshore. All hell broke loose when the storm erupted. The choppy two to four-foot seas were now a raging debacle as six-foot waves pounded the small boat. Erwin kept the bow heading into the waves, but they were getting swamped every few minutes when they went down in a trough and couldn't get out before the next wave crashed over the bow.

"We've got to turn and head for shore before we sink!" Eric screamed, bailing water with a bucket and holding on for dear life.

"Gotta wait 'til the time is right, or we'll capsize!" replied Erwin, anxiously looking for a break in the waves so he could turn the boat around.

Knee-deep in water and struggling to stay afloat, they finally saw the break they sought.

"Looks clear after this next wave!" Erwin yelled.

Eric peered over the gunwale as he took a break from bailing the water, "Shiiiiitt! Look at the size of that one!"

The wave looked like a good ten-footer. It would have broken right on top of them if they had continued at the same speed. Erwin goosed the throttle and climbed the wave before shooting over the top and free-falling back down. As they splashed down, the boat felt like it hit rock bottom. Trying to keep his wits about him, Erwin turned the wheel and gunned the throttle simultaneously, effectively turning the boat toward shore. Relieved they were able to turn successfully without capsizing. They crossed their fingers and set their sights on shore. The rain was coming down so hard that they couldn't see five feet beyond the bow. Erwin gave up trying to spot the shoreline and focused on the compass bolted to the console. As long as it pointed west, they'd hit shore if they didn't sink first.

The boat was now surfing down the bigger waves. Eric gave up bailing water and took the two plugs out of the lower transom, hoping the water would run out.

"I think I should get a couple of life preservers," Eric solemnly said, realizing the boat was still taking on water.

"Good idea," replied Erwin, with a somber look.

They prepared for the worst, but nothing could prepare them for what they were about to experience. As they stood side by side, squatting down low and holding onto the console, Erwin caught something huge out of the corner of his eye. *Why the hell is a submarine coming up under the boat? It's going to sink us,* he thought.

But when he turned his head to look at the object, his heart sank to the pit of his stomach as he stared in awe. He was looking eye to eye with the largest monster he'd ever seen. He turned and looked at his brother, who stood like a statue, mouth wide open and eyes bulging out.

They stood motionless, staring at the hideous-looking

monster for what seemed forever as it peered back at them through alarmingly evil eyes. It was so close to Erwin that he could feel the heat from its breath.

Finally, after getting a close-up look at the boat's occupants, the monster veered off and fell back behind the sinking boat. As it swam off, Erwin and Eric got a perfect eye view of the creature's immense size.

"What the..." they said in unison as they watched the beast trailing behind.

All bets were off. There was no way they were going to live to tell about it. The thought of them dying on this stormy morning never occurred to them. All hope was lost as they knew in their hearts they were doomed.

"Look... Eric, when that thing comes back and sinks the boat, try to stay between the boat and that monster."

"We might have a better chance if we take off the life jackets," Eric replied, sounding hollow.

"Okay, good idea," said Erwin, unbuckling his jacket.

They watched the beast follow them as they tried to keep the boat afloat as long as possible. As they surfed down the bigger waves, they kept the boat on course the best they could, careful to turn when needed so that the boat wouldn't take an unexpected dive straight for the bottom.

"Oh no!" Eric suddenly realized. "That monster must be that alligator thing that's been attacking people around the Port!"

"Yeah, I thought about that, too," Erwin replied, failing miserably at trying to sound calm.

"Wish we could have said goodbye to the family," Eric mumbled.

The longest twenty minutes of their lives went by, with neither of them saying a word. As they rode up and down the waves, hoping against hope that they'd make it back, they thought to themselves about how sad the family would be when they found out they had died a terrifying death.

"I don't see it anymore," Eric abruptly said, taking a quick look behind the wake.

"Stay alert, it could be under the boat and ready to slam us," Erwin replied, gripping the wheel as hard as he could.

Another twenty minutes went by when the rain eased up a little, and they were able to see the shoreline.

"Look! I see the buildings!" Erwin cried out.

"We're about a half-mile out!" Eric pointed out.

"Wow, that storm pushed us pretty far north," Erwin said, pointing to the lighthouse in front of them. "We're headed for the inlet in the next county.”

“Head for it. I sure don’t want to go back into Port Everglades with that monster around,” Eric said in a crackling tone.

Eric took the wheel and headed straight for the lighthouse inlet. Erwin grabbed a bucket and continued bailing water out of the boat. The waves were bigger as the water became shallower. Eric waited for the next big set of waves and gunned the throttle, practically surfing straight through the inlet.

“We made it!” Eric screamed out as they both grabbed each other and hugged like only brothers could get away with.

The storm blew itself out as the little fishing boat cruised down the Intracoastal Waterway with two of the luckiest people around.

“Oh man, so good to be alive,” Erwin grinned, grabbing two beers out of the cooler.

“I just want to get home and take a hot shower,” Eric replied, cutting the tips off two celebratory cigars.

“Here’s to you, bro, best bros forever,” they toasted. They were so tired they could barely raise the cans above their heads.

“I wonder why that monster didn’t attack?” Erwin pondered. “It was probably as seasick as we were,” Eric beamed.

16

Don Henderson and Chief Bhim met at the Anchor Bar and sat on a couple of stools at the end of the bar. Don noticed the Chief looked angry and was in a combative mood as he ordered a double Jim Beam on the rocks.

Don raised the glass to his lips and quickly drained it, then ordered another beer before speaking.

"Look Bhim, I'm sorry for what happened to your trapper. I mean that sincerely. I know he was a good…"

"You know nothing!" the Chief erupted, stopping him in mid-sentence. He grabbed his glass and chugged the contents before slamming it down hard on the bar. "You know nothing!" he repeated, leaning into Don to where their foreheads almost touched. "You knew damn well those reptiles would eventually escape the sanctuary! You knew they were growing too fast and getting stronger and stronger, and yet, you insisted on keeping them. I can't imagine how vicious that damn thing is now."

"Now, wait a minute Bhim! Don't pin this crap on me. You knew just as well as I did that the risk of keeping those reptiles was uncertain."

The Indian Chief backed off and put his head in his hands. When he finally looked up at Don, tears were rolling down his face.

"The trapper, the damn fool trapper was my nephew," he murmured. "Awe Christ Chief... was it Johnny? I had no idea," he said genuinely. "Durjaya asked me to let him come along. I said no because it was too dangerous, but he insisted. Johnny said he was a man, and a young man had to prove he was credible. He begged me, and I gave in. I told his mother I would personally keep him out of danger. And now... now he is dead."

Don didn't have to be a doctor to see that the Chief was a broken man. He signaled the bartender to bring another round. Carlos kept half an ear on the two as he worked behind the bar, hoping to hear firsthand about the sadistic reptile, since the news stations seemed to dramatize the story so much to where it became nearly unbelievable.

But when he heard about Chief Bhim's nephew, he gave them the rest of the bottle, "Here, Chief... it's on the house."

Don gave Carlos a nod and poured Bhim and himself a refill. He quickly drank it down and poured another. Watching Bhim gradually degrade from a fearless leader to a frightened old man was disheartening. He knew, right then and there, that the Chief was in no state of mind to continue hunting the reptile.

They drank in silence until the bottle was empty. Finally, Chief Bhim was ready to leave. He looked over to Don, slurred some intangible words, and stood up, looking like a lost kid in the supermarket as he tried to locate the exit door. Carlos came from behind the bar and took Chief Bhim by the arm. He led him outside to a waiting taxi.

"Jump in Chief. I called you a cab," Carlos said with concern while opening the door.

"My truck's here, I'm driving it home," Bhim slurred incoherently. "You take the cab or I call the cops," Carlos retorted and the smile vanished.

"You're too drunk to drive; you'll kill someone."

Bhim stuck out his chest in an attempt to intimidate the bartender, but Carlos just rolled his eyes and put his hand on the Chief's forehead, pushing him into the cab, where he fell on his back in the backseat.

He rolled him on his side so that he wouldn't choke on his own vomit and shut the door, "Here's his address," he said to the driver, handing him a piece of paper and a fifty-dollar bill.

Carlos walked back in and strolled behind the bar. He looked over and saw that Don was still there. Pouring a glass of Budweiser from the tap, he walked over and gave it to him.

"What was the Indian talking about? What killed his nephew?" He asked, trying to get information on the reptile.

"I'd rather not talk about it," Don tersely replied, moving from the bar to a small table in the corner.

As he sipped his beer and got lost in his thoughts, he didn't notice the tall, burly man walk in and head in his direction. The patrons stopped doing what they were doing and cleared out of the way as the intimidating man dressed in black made his way to the table. He wore black leather boots with an arrangement of what looked like shark, alligator, and human teeth attached to a buckle around the ankle area. Attached to a thick leather belt was a hunting knife that would make Crocodile Dundee's look like a butter knife. He wore a silk button-down, sleeveless shirt that exposed his arms - the size of a regular man's thighs. Standing six-foot-five, with blonde shoulder-length hair in dreadlocks, he looked every bit the rogue pirate that would make Blackbeard feel uneasy in another place and time.

He walked over to Don and stood at the table, peering down at the man sitting with his thoughts in his glass, and spoke with a deep commanding tone, "Don Henderson." It was more an acknowledgement than a question. Don broke away from his thoughts and looked up. He gasped and nearly peed his pants where he sat, "Who wants to know?" he replied, trying to sound casual but couldn't stop the palpitation in his voice.

"My name is Bloodfoot, Captain Bloodfoot," he thundered, taking a seat across the table.

The patrons looked on in apprehension and admiration as they couldn't decide what to make of the pirate-looking hulk, but they quickly went about their business when Bloodfoot looked up and glared at the onlookers.

Carlos worked up the nerve to leave the safety of the bar, and walked over to ask what the man was having.

"Give me your finest rum in a large glass, no ice," he rumbled, then turned his attention to Don.

"Look mister... I don't want trouble," Don said in panic. "I'm sorry, but I think you're looking for somebody else."

"Don't apologize. It's a sign of weakness," Bloodfoot sneered, draining the glass in one swallow.

Don was beside himself. He looked over at the entrance door and pondered the idea of jumping up and running for his life. No good, he concluded. Bloodfoot didn't have an ounce of fat on what looked like a three-hundred-pound frame and would probably catch him before he left the table. He had no intention of having his teeth displayed on the pirate's boots.

"How do you know my name," he asked timidly.

Bloodfoot let out a belly laugh that shook the entire bar, "Not only do I know your name, but I know what you've created, you and your bio-chemist, fiendish friends in Louisiana," he replied with a glare that made Don melt in his chair.

The menacing look on Bloodfoot's face made Don aware of the fact that if there truly was a devil, he was sitting at the table. He sat for a minute, wondering with his inebriated mind if he was going to die at the hands of the Grim Reaper or maybe, just maybe, the oversized pirate just wanted to be friends. He took another drink and opted for the first thought.

"Listen, I don't want any trouble. I just..."

"Relax," Bloodfoot snarled as he cut him off. "I'm not going to hurt a squirrel like you; I'm here to kill your reptile."

"What makes you think I know anything about that monster? It's out of my hands; I hadn't seen it in years."

Bloodfoot leaned across the table and grabbed Don by the throat. "I don't have the time or patience for your feeble games, Don Henderson. I know exactly how you are directly involved with the reptile."

Carlos and a barback saw the pirate grab Don and quickly pick up a couple of baseball bats, and grudgingly headed for the table. One glare from Bloodfoot stopped them in their tracks as they froze where they stood.

"Alright, you win," Don gasped when he was convinced that the Calvary was not coming to the rescue. "I certainly don't want to get on your bad side. How can I help you?"

"You're a smart man," Bloodfoot replied, releasing his grip on Don's throat. "First of all, I want you to tell me everything I should know about your mutated reptile."

Don breathed a heavy sigh and decided it would be in his best interest to spill his guts. Bloodfoot was straightforward and meant business. He was going to get the answers he needed one way or another. He ordered another round of drinks, noticing the patrons slipping out little by little until it was just Bloodfoot and himself in the empty bar.

An hour passed, and Bloodfoot figured he had heard everything he needed to know. "Okay Don, for your sake, I hope you told me everything," he said, standing up and walking towards the bar, drinking the last ounce of liquid from his glass.

"By the way, what makes you think you can kill that thing?" Don asked, slurring his words.

"Funny you should ask," he replied, ordering more rum.

"That vicious beast is thirty-five feet long for cryin' out loud!" Don blurted, losing his fear of the pirate with every swallow of his drink. "It's hide is at least an inch thick, and even so... you still have to get past the armor plates on its back!"

Bloodfoot slowly turned and faced Don, "You told me it was twenty-three feet long," he snarled.

"I'm not really sure how big it is, I hadn't seen it in a while," Don vacillated.

Carlos stood behind the bar, unable to comprehend what he was hearing, "I thought the news said it was just a big alligator?" He whispered to no one. He wanted to hear more, but Don was getting so drunk that he had to intervene. He respectfully walked over to Bloodfoot without the rum bottle, "Uh, Mr. Bloodfoot... Don's had it, one more drink and he'll have to be resuscitated."

"No kidding," he growled, looking back at Don, who was now passed out on the table. "Thanks for the lousy information, Don Henderson, I'll be in touch," he continued, walking to the front door.

Before he could reach for the handle, the door flew open, and he was quickly surrounded by police officers.

"Hold it right there big fella," one of the officers said, trying to subdue Bloodfoot and get his hands behind his back.

"What the hell! Get off me, I've done nothing wrong!" he bellowed. "Calm down, big guy, don't make it hard for yourself," replied the officer as he fought to put a handcuff on one of the massive wrists.

The handcuff barely clicked on his wrist when Bloodfoot swung his arm around with the officer holding on, hurling him through the air like a rag doll and sending him crashing behind the bar and into a shelf displaying liquor bottles of every brand. Another officer jumped on Bloodfoot's back and was violently thrown into a table, smashing it to pieces. At the same time, Carlos rushed over with a baseball bat and prepared to strike when the angry pirate stopped him with one point of a finger, "Don't start something I know you can't finish," he thundered.

Carlo's eyes bulged out of their sockets as he froze and dropped the bat. Holding his hands out, he cautiously scrambled back to the safety behind the bar.

Before Bloodfoot could make his getaway, three more squad cars pulled up in the parking lot with sirens blaring. Unable to escape through the front door, he made his way to the rear exit. Stopping to unlock the door, he failed to notice the woman come out of the restroom and walk up behind him. He quickly unlocked the door and kicked it open when his lights went out. The woman behind him produced a brand new, unopened bottle of Makers Mark and swung it like a major league slugger to the back of his head, knocking him out cold.

"Ah, my lady, you never cease to amaze me at how you can stop a man in his tracks," Carlos smiled as he stepped out of his hiding spot.

"Yeah, I'm a real knockout," she replied with a satisfied look.

Captain Bloodfoot woke up with a splitting headache. He sat up and rubbed the back of his head as he looked around and found he was sitting in a jail cell.

"Well, good morning, Prince Charming. Didn't your mother ever teach you not to turn your back on a lady?" A jail guard snickered, holding a freshly brewed coffee in one hand and a donut with pink frosting in the other.

"Mother? Hell, he was probably hatched," replied an officer with his right arm in a sling.

"What happened?" Bloodfoot grumbled, well aware of what had taken place, but wanted to hear their side of the story.

"Well, my friend, while resisting me and my fellow officers at the Anchor Bar last night, a little tramp knocked your lights out with a whiskey bottle," Sergeant Joe Reilly explained with a tight smile.

Joe Reilly was an ex-marine. His no-nonsense attitude toward police work allowed him to quickly climb the ranks. Now, at age forty-eight, he was grudgingly sent to street patrol after ripping a man's ear off in a drug bust that had gone bad.

"You must be the candy-ass that tried to arrest me," Bloodfoot sneered, looking at the officer's arm in the sling.

"I'm an ex-marine," he retorted angrily, unable to control his rage.

"I bet your mommy's proud," Bloodfoot continued, fueling the flames of the Sergeant's temper.

Joe didn't answer, he realized the pirate was amused at the way he seemed to push his buttons.

"Why was I arrested?" Bloodfoot asked flatly, standing up and walking toward the cell door.

"Our intent was not to arrest you," Joe replied. "We merely wanted to talk."

"Then was it my imagination that you handcuffed me faster than pigs on slop?"

"Easy son. I don't like the way you're talking."

Bloodfoot glared at the Sergeant for a long minute, then

returned to the tiny bed and took a seat, "So, here I am… what would you like to talk about?"

"I don't want to talk to you about anything," Reilly barked, "But in about twenty minutes, the mayor and another officer will arrive and have a word with you."

Bloodfoot watched the sergeant walk out of the room with his tough-guy swagger and made a mental note to revisit him at a later time. He waited impatiently for his meeting, pacing back and forth in the ten-by-fifteen-foot cell like a caged bear.

An hour later, Mayor Myers and Officer Randy Taylor walked through the door. They casually said hello to the sergeant and guard, not taking notice of the bulky man in black standing in the cell staring at them. They exchanged small talk and niceties for a few minutes, testing the pirate's patience.

When the sergeant asked how Myers' golf game was, Bloodfoot finally exploded, "Who the hell are you, and why am I locked up in this goddamn cage!"

Nick Myers jumped up with a startled look on his face while Randy grinned and wondered to himself why it took so long to rattle the man. Nick quickly composed himself, folding his hands behind his back and casually walked over to the jail cell. He stopped at a safe distance and studied the man before speaking, "My name is Nick Myers. I am the Mayor of this town," he said with authority.

Captain Bloodfoot took a step forward, sizing up the little man before replying, "Why am I locked up in your jail cell? I have done nothing unlawful."

"You are in here for our own good," Officer Taylor replied, walking over to the pirate. "It seems your reputation precedes you."

"I don't know what the hell you're talking about, I only arrived last night," Bloodfoot spat.

"Yes, I know exactly when you arrived. I was alerted by the authorities in Belize that you were coming," the officer said with a slight grin. "The minute you anchored that unsightly sailboat off my beach, I knew it was you."

Bloodfoot let out a heavy sigh and glared at the men like a trapped animal ready to attack. The ominous look on his face made the Mayor's hair on the back of his neck stand.

"I did not come here to start trouble, but should trouble come looking for me, I am more than ready to deal with it," he stated in a low, deliberate tone.

Officer Taylor liked the man. There was nothing fake about him, and he truly believed Bloodfoot was prepared for anything that would get in his way.

"Well then, suppose you tell me exactly why you are here, Mr. Bloodfoot," Randy said as Nick took a step back and observed the conversation.

"Call me Captain Bloodfoot," he insisted. "I am here on business. If you must know, the mayor and I have a mutual friend," he paused to let the words sink in. "His name is Chief Bhim."

Nick Myers almost choked. He wondered how a pirate from Belize could possibly know about the dealings he had with the Indian chief.

"He's an acquaintance, not a friend. I hired him to take care of a little business for me," the Mayor stammered.

Bloodfoot tilted his head past Randy and frowned at the mayor, "So… a thirty-three-foot reptile is a little business?"

Myers ignored the question as the sergeant and guard gave a quizzical look and quickly changed the subject. "I know who you are, but I don't know what you are," beads of sweat dripping from his forehead. "Are you a smuggler? A thief? Hell son, you look like a damn pirate! Are you here to pillage and plunder? You're a dangerous man, and I want to know why you came to my t…"

"Shut the hell up! You pencil pushin' pussy!" Bloodfoot roared, cutting him off. "You know why I'm here!"

Bloodfoot saw it coming from the corner of his eye, but it was too late.

Sergeant Reilly withdrew his club and smashed it against his head. "Show some respect for the mayor, you smelly pig!"

Bloodfoot didn't twitch a muscle as the club made contact with his head. "You speak to the mayor like that again, and I'll make you wish you've never been born," the sergeant promised.

If looks could kill, Reilly would be dead and buried. Bloodfoot wiped the blood trickling down his face with the palm of his hand and spat on the floor before replying, "Hit me again with that toothpick, and I'll knock you out in front of your girlfriends."

It was clearly not the meeting Randy expected. He tried to intervene in another assault by the ex-marine but was pushed out of the way. Sergeant Joe Reilly was no stranger to fights and leaped forward to give Bloodfoot another whack, but this time, the pirate was ready. He caught the club in midflight and pulled in one quick motion, catching Joe off balance. As he fell forward into the cell bars, Bloodfoot grabbed him by the hair and lifted his face before smashing three powerful punches to the nose, mouth and forehead, knocking him out cold.

"That's enough!" Officer Taylor yelled as he grabbed Bloodfoot's arm with two hands. "He's out!"

Bloodfoot released his grip on Joe's hair and the sergeant fell to the floor with a thud. "He started it... Not me," Bloodfoot snarled.

Officer Taylor and the astounded guard picked the sergeant off the floor and carried him to a couch in the next room.

"That man's an animal," Myers said, following them in and closing the door.

"You think? Nick, don't act surprised," Taylor replied as he gave the immobilized sergeant a smelling salt.

"Yeah, but I also know that he's just the right man we need to capture that monster."

"I can't trust him."

"So what? He's probably my only hope to get out of this mess," Myers retorted, looking through the small window in the door only to find Bloodfoot staring down at him. "That guy gives me the creeps."

"You don't care about the safety of anybody as long as you clear your fat ass," Taylor replied with a nasty look.

"Watch it Taylor, don't push me," Myers replied, pointing a

finger in the officer's face.

"It's my search party. What I say, goes. If he gives me any trouble, I will shoot him," Taylor promised.

"You do whatever needs to be done. Just kill that godforsaken reptile," Myers said as he walked out the door.

17

The sun looked like a fading light bulb in the grey, decadent sky while the rain fell all morning long. A strong wind was blowing from the northeast, and the seas near shore were choppy, with waves of three to five feet higher offshore.

Had the beaches not been closed due to what the news reported as dangerous bacteria in the water, it would be a beautiful day for surfing and kiteboarding.

Stella Stevens arrived on the beach just in time to watch her friends get chased out of the water by police officers. Finding a place to park her Volkswagen van was easy since the only people crazy enough to be at the beach on such a dismal-looking day were a couple dozen surfers and spectators.

Earlier in the morning, the lifeguards were busy trying to keep the surfers out of the water but gave up when it became futile. The overwhelmed lifeguards would no sooner turn their back than the angry surfers were back in the water.

Stella was a California girl. Born and raised in Malibu, the twenty-two year-old learned to surf at the tender age of five. By the time she was fifteen, she was one of the top surfers on the West Coast.

What Lurks Below

No stranger to the dangers of sharing the water with sharks, she was amazed on more than one occasion to see Great Whites actually swimming inside the very waves that she and others had surfed on, and miraculously, nobody had been bitten. They would simply get out of the water and wait until the curious predators moved on.

Stella felt perfectly safe to go surfing on this day. She had seen the news that depicted the warnings about some larger-than-usual reptile terrorizing the area, but that was a couple miles South of where the action was today. Besides, she hadn't seen the actual size of the reptile. After all, she was accustomed to sharing the water with man-eating sharks, much more dangerous than some oversized alligator that was undoubtedly overexaggerated by the news media.

After a quick check on the direction of the wind and waves, she decided that the waves were too choppy for surfing and chose to go kiteboarding instead. The waves were too choppy to get a good ride and they were crashing down on a sandbar about twenty yards off the beach. She laughed at the surfers who were barely able to catch a wave before it crashed down and tumbled them to shore in the whitewash. It was nothing compared to the beautiful swells in California.

She ran back to her van and stripped out of her tee shirt and shorts. Modesty was not one of her fine points as she left the doors wide open, causing a middle-aged man to walk straight on into a parked car.

She smiled to herself as she slipped into her new flesh-tone colored thong bikini and stepped out of the van. Standing five-foot-eight and weighing one-hundred and five pounds, she had all the nice curves in the right places that enabled her to wear such a bikini. No sooner than she closed the van door, three guys came running over in the rain. Wearing polo shirts, white baggy shorts and brand new Ocean Pacific sandals, Stella politely greeted the tourists as they braved the bad weather and asked her if she needed a hand carrying her kiteboard and gear down to the water.

She answered affirmatively and gave them each a hug before leaving the equipment behind and running down to her waiting friends.

"Jeez Stella! We thought you were streaking down here!" said one of her friends, wearing a bright fluorescent green, one-piece suit with nothing but a thread in the back, laughing with the others as they noticed all eyes on the beach were on them. Stella smiled and modeled the new suit to her friends. When she noticed the entire beach watching, she took off her red baseball cap, revealing thick blonde hair that flowed down her shoulders.

"You're such a tramp!" the friend laughed.

"Oh funny! Look at you!" Stella laughed and pulled the concealed string on her friend's suit, giving her a slight wedge.

"Who're those guys walking over with your kiteboard?" asked another friend, fully clothed in blue jeans and raincoat, looking over Stella's shoulder.

Stella turned and acknowledged, "Tourist perves... I think they saw me naked when I was changing."

"You think?"

The three guys walked up and dropped the gear next to the girls. They took off their water-logged shirts, revealing pinkish-white skin and what looked like the beginning of their beer bellies. Stella's friend in the green bathing suit smirked at the sight of one of the guy's apparent man-boobs that were despondently bigger than hers.

Stella thanked them again with a hug and began strapping on the harness. The tourists, still eager to please her and hoping to get another hug, helped straighten out the kite lines as her friends watched with amusement at the guys' enthusiastic kindness.

Stella finished attaching the harness and walked backwards until the lines pulled straight between her and the kite. When the wind filled the kite, she guided it straight up into the overcast sky, pulling it to the left and right until she was satisfied everything was in working order.

"Hey, you're not going out there by yourself, are you?" a concerned mother walked up and asked.

"Sure am," replied Stella, focused on the kite.

"You're nuts! They're chasing everybody out of the water."

"I'll be fine… fine and dandy," she replied, placing her feet in the kiteboard straps.

"Maybe she's right, it looks pretty bad out there," her fully clothed friend stated, "Not to mention that alligator or whatever it is."

"Well… If you girls lost the nerve to be out here with good 'ol mother nature, sit on the beach and watch me have all the fun," Stella replied in a lofty tone. "I've surfed with Great White sharks the size of jaws in California, and I do believe they are more dangerous than a sleepy old alligator… or whatever it is. Besides, have you ever heard of an alligator running around in the ocean in this kind of weather?"

"Fine, don't say we didn't warn you."

Stella ignored the warning and began to move out. She waited for a wave to crash on shore and jumped over it, sailing five feet through the air. "Uh oh, don't look now," said one of the girls as a beach patrol jeep pulled up.

Stella glanced back and smiled, "See ya girls. Tell the lifeguards I'll be back in about half an hour!" she shouted as the wind took her out to sea.

The girls, along with the beach patrol, watched as she raced out in a southeasterly direction, jumping and surfing on every wave the ocean could offer.

The unsightly reptile was aggressively hungry, and the waves and current aggravated the monster ferociously. Since the attack the previous day by the Indian trappers, the reptile experienced sluggish movement and intense pain in its jaws. It remained at Hammerhead Reef, where it recuperated and felt safe from the attack.

Now, with the rough seas and inclement weather, it slowly swam across the sandy bottom, heading back to the comfort inside the Port basin.

As the creature cruised along, it abruptly stopped when it sensed vibrations approaching from the north. The rough seas and large waves crashing on the jetties made it difficult for the reptile to substantiate what it was, but the hunger pangs in its stomach made it turn to investigate.

Stella was skimming across the water at a speedy clip. The

five to eight foot swells were wearing her legs out, but she was having too much fun blasting off the waves and getting airborne twenty feet through the dismal air.

She was having so much fun showing off for the spectators on shore that she forgot that she wanted to stay clear of the mouth of the inlet until she found herself soaring past it. A chill went up her spine as she glanced over near the jetties where the three kids were attacked by the vicious predator.

Nervous tension swept through her as she began to speculate that maybe the monstrous reptile might be in the area, watching her, waiting for her to fall. She reasoned that since she was at least a quarter mile offshore, and if the reptile was near the jetties, it would never come out this far, even on a good day. But, just to ease her mind, she turned out to sea and returned North.

A lifeguard sitting in his station picked up his binoculars and focused on Stella the minute she left the beach. At first sight, he thought she was completely naked, but quickly realized that she was wearing a flesh-colored bathing suit. He whistled to himself and thought she was the most beautiful girl he'd seen in a long time. He gave up trying to chase kids off the beach all morning and now sat in the warm confines of his warm-up suit and dry tennis shoes. There was no way he was going to try to stop her and get soaked through to the bone again.

He kept his binoculars trained on her the whole time, admiring her skills and flexibility, along with her swimsuit that left nothing to the imagination. He decided he would leave the comfort of his dry station, walk down, and have a conversation with her when she returned.

When she sailed past the warning buoys on the South end of the beach, he became concerned for her safety and called a patrol boat officer to go out and get her.

Officer Randy Taylor was on duty and took the call. He was amazed about the stupidity of the kiteboarder but then realized that the surfer probably didn't know the extent of the danger she was in, as the mayor didn't want all the facts about the reptile made public. He zipped up his foul-weather gear, turned on the flashing blue lights and cautiously headed out through the jetties.

Stella successfully completed her turn before getting slammed head-on into a breaking wave. She quickly recovered as she shot through the white foam and felt the left side of her bikini bottoms become untied. Most girls would have ditched into the water to fix it, but not Stella. She knew that if she ditched, she would never get the kite untangled from the lines and back in the air.

She nonchalantly looked down and noticed the tiny suit flapping on her right leg like a flag. Damn, I'll never hear the end of this one. Oh well, so they can see my booty! Who's gonna care in a hundred years... Nobody can see anything in this weather anyway, she thought.

She was wrong. She caught the air on a rogue wave and shot straight up, suspended twenty feet high as the unmistakable sounds of whistles and cat-calls flooded her ears from shore. When she landed, she balanced the control bar with one hand in the middle and reached for her bikini bottoms only to find they were completely gone. Oh goody, this'll be interesting to see how I get out of the water.

And then she saw it coming, coming straight for her. Her eyes grew larger as she prepared to meet a set of huge swells heading her way. She crouched down low and pulled the kite into the wind to make her go faster. She surfed to the top of the first swell and skyrocketed through the air again, revealing more than the average man's fantasy. At the same instant, the monstrous reptile exploded out of the waves where Stella had been, snapping its colossal jaws shut and missing her by inches. Still airborne, she let out a ghastly scream when she looked back and saw the creature soar out of the water and close the gap between them. She tried to keep her senses and pulled the left side of the kite lines, sending her gliding back toward shore and landing a good thirty yards from where the reptile splashed down.

Stella landed where a wave broke and violently covered her with white foam and spray. She quickly recovered and looked up at the kite to make sure it was still flying strong. Anxiously shaking her head and clearing her eyes, she desperately looked over to where the reptile landed and was now gone. Her stomach felt like it was knotted up in her throat as she fought to maneuver the kite-board toward shore. The adrenaline was pumping through her arms and legs, and she felt her heartbeat pulsating in her head.

Stay on top, one bad move and I've had it. Breathe, gotta stay calm and keep my wits... I can't believe this is happening!

Her friends and everybody watching on the beach screamed out in horror as they watched the surreal nightmare unfold. Her friend in the green bikini was the first to cry out and point when she witnessed the dreadful reptile shoot out of the water and snap its immense jaws at the kiteboard, twisting its massive trunk toward Stella before splashing down and giving chase. The loud pop of the jaws snapping shut could be heard from shore as the spectators screamed.

The lifeguard admiring Stella through binoculars dropped

them and frantically picked up his walkie-talkie, and screamed for the patrol boat to hurry up.

Stella kept her sights on shore. She was beginning to get her poise back and felt that she could make it back alive. Hitting every swell perfectly, she tried to stay airborne as much as possible. While sailing through the air, she kept glancing back to see if the reptile was close behind. *Okay girl... Almost here... Stay in the air and you'll be fine.*

Seventy yards from shore, she began to worry about getting caught up in a crashing wave. As long as she could keep the kiteboard in the air and if she didn't get caught in the maelstrom when landing, there was no way the beast was going to reach her.

Good going kid... looks like you're gonna make it... Just keep your wits about you and land this bird one more time... Hope I don't see my naked butt on youtube this afternoon...

The kiteboard made a smooth landing between the waves. Stella turned parallel to the shore and set up to catch what she hoped would be the last wave that would launch her on the beach.

Okay... Once more in the air and I'll crash land right on top of those tourist guys...Oops, never mind, forgot I'm naked...Maybe I'll ju... "OH SHIII!" she screamed, her thoughts broken.

She was preparing to shoot off another wave when the insatiable reptile shot through it like a torpedo, slamming into the board like a freight train as the hideous jaws snapped shut.

Stella screamed at the top of her lungs as she was hurtled through the air, crashing in the surf twenty yards away. The slack line attached to the harness wrapped around her neck, and she gasped for air when a wave dragged the kite through the water and tightened the lines.

Panic-stricken and on the verge of passing out from the lack of oxygen, she somehow managed to untangle the line from her neck while trying to stay afloat. Completely overcome by the turn of events, she unwittingly tried to get the kite in the air again, but it was completely submerged.

As she struggled to get the kite going, she caught sight of her left foot still strapped to the front of the board. She quickly tried to secure her right foot on the board again, but when she couldn't feel anything, she looked down in the water and cried hysterically when she noticed the back half of the board was missing, along with her leg.

Her leg had been sliced clean below the knee. Gasping in disbelief, she screamed out for help as she felt herself getting weaker. A shroud of blackness swept over her as she fought to keep her head above the crashing waves.

Officer Randy Taylor was past the jetties and gunning the boat through the raging seas when he witnessed the attack. He threw caution to the wind and pushed the twenty-five-foot Whaler with twin Yamaha motors dangerously close to capsizing in an effort to save the kiteboarder.

Minutes later, the awestruck officer pulled up alongside Stella. She was now floating just outside of where the waves were breaking, as he thought she might have gotten caught up in an undertow.

For a brief second, he wondered why some brave-hearted lifeguard didn't swim out to her rescue until he saw the larger-than-life reptile swimming in the surf between the horrified crowd and Stella, guarding its prey like a rabid dog.

There was no way in hell he was going to jump in and rescue Stella like a knight in shining armor, he thought. Instead, he grabbed a ten-foot gaff and reached into the water, snagging the harness attached to her.

Stella was bleeding profusely and was unconscious when he finally grabbed hold of her and pulled her into the boat. No sooner did they collapse on deck when the reptile shot out of the water, missing the side of the boat by inches.

"Damn!" Randy gasped; his eyes nearly bulged out of his

head as he was overcome by the sheer terror of watching the immense girth splash down so close. Watching the reptile on the Port security camera was nothing compared to being so close that he could feel the ferocious power it commanded. The hideous creature surfaced twenty feet off the port bow. Its massive head was at least four-foot wide with big eyes that seemed to glare at him with menacing evil. The overwhelming brute strength and enormity of the evil-looking beast was too much for Randy to comprehend. His head was spinning as he fought to keep his sanity.

The predator slowly swam closer toward the boat until it got tangled in the kite lines dangling in the water and quickly descended.

To make matters worse, Stella was still attached to the harness. The slack lines swiftly pulled taut and dragged her across the deck like a rag doll and nearly dragged her over the side of the boat. With Randy's quick thinking, he hastily jammed the lines under a cleat and wrapped them around it several times, preventing Stella from being pulled to her death.

As the reptile continued descending, the Whaler's stern dipped below the surface and water gushed in at an alarming rate. Randy drew his pistol and prepared to shoot the lines, but just as he was ready to pull the trigger, the cleat snapped off, and the stern shot back above the waterline.

He quickly stripped off the harness and glanced down at Stella and gently propped her head up with a boat cushion to keep her from drowning in the two feet of water sloshing around the deck. Her face was extremely pale and her lips were blue. She had lost a good deal of blood, and Randy realized she was near death.

A wave crashed over the bow and swamped the boat while he fretfully stripped off his shirt and tied a tourniquet above Stella's knee. When finished, he stood up and reached for the throttle. His hopes of a getaway were dashed when the creature rammed the starboard side of the boat and continued to push against the current and through the waves, taking them out to deeper water.

The ill-fated vessel was taking in more water as the waves crashed over the port side. A thought raced through Randy's mind as he remembered an old Boston Whaler commercial on television when the boat was cut in half and still floating. That was the selling point. No matter what happened to this kind of boat, it would never sink. He hoped to God it was true.

He quickly reached for the throttles and pushed them forward. The twin engines roared, but the waterlogged vessel was sluggish. There was too much water in the boat.

Sensing its prey trying to escape, the reptile became more aggressive and to Randy's horror, it grabbed the boat with its immense jaws and began tearing it apart. The dismayed officer had seconds to react as he grabbed his Sid Sauer 9mm pistol and unloaded the clip at point-blank range at the reptile's head.

He was dumbfounded when he saw the bullets bounce off the creature's head as if they were fired from a kid's toy gun. He fell back and hit his head on the gunwales and noticed the flare gun case strapped to the side of the console.

As a last resort, he ripped the case off the straps and opened it. He quickly loaded the flare gun and fired directly into the gruesome jaws. The flare exploded in a fireball as Randy covered Stella with his body. The startled reptile roared like a prehistoric dinosaur and turned away, retreating underwater.

Randy jumped up and stood at the controls of the flooded vessel. He set his sights toward shore as the lethargic boat scarcely remained above the water line and came about facing the beach. He contemplated gunning the motors but decided the boat would sink if he tried.

As the sinking boat headed towards the beach, another rain storm hit, and Randy could barely see the shoreline. He was still at least fifty-yards from shore when a rogue wave crashed over the stern and stalled the motors. With all hope dwindling, he put a life vest on and waited for the inevitable. He crawled over to Stella and tried to make her comfortable when he suddenly heard a small outboard motor.

He got up on his knees and searched the water in hopes of finding its location, praying that it would find them before it was too late. To his dismay, it sounded like the boat was coming up on them, then passing them by. The rain was coming down hard in sheets, and he couldn't see five feet in front of him.

"Help… Over here!" he shouted. "We're over here!" His heart raced faster as he thought he heard the small boat turn and head in his direction.

When the rescue boat finally poked out through the gray wall of rain, Randy was disheartened to see a ten-foot Zodiac inflatable boat heading over. He could only envision the huge reptile bursting from the depths and annihilating the inflatable like a pit bull ravaging a balloon.

The small boat fought the crashing waves impressively well as it speedily raced over and came alongside the lifeless Whaler. Randy was surprised to see the lifeguard throw the boat in neutral and put one leg in the boat to keep it from drifting off.

What Lurks Below

Kim Rutner was the lifeguard on the beach, watching Stella through the binoculars. After he saw the attack and called for help, he ran to the lifeguard shack and pulled out the Zodiac. It sat on two plastic balloon wheels and was ready for any emergency that required more than a rescuer on a surfboard.

"Hello Officer, let's get the two of you aboard and beat feet," he said with a rigid smile and a look of determination.

"You must be out of your mind!" Randy quipped as he picked Stella up in his arms and placed her in the Zodiac.

"No sir, just thought I'd cruise out here and save your arse!" he shouted above the squall.

Randy barely made it in the inflatable when the lifeguard threw the boat in gear. The Zodiac jumped to life and careened back toward the beach.

"You're a brave man for coming out here in this little raft!"

"Believe it or not, this Zodiac can go through a hurricane! Let's hope we make it back before that croc comes back!"

"It's no croc! It's a thirty-three-foot freak of nature!"

"Seen 'em before when I worked in Australia; those saltwater crocs are relentless!"

Randy didn't reply, he warily kept an eye around the surroundings and hoped the mammoth reptile would not return. He looked down at Stella when he felt her hand grab his ankle. She was awake and murmuring incoherently as the rough seas shook her all over the fibreglass deck.

"Hang on kid," he whispered in her ear.

"Hold on! We're almost there!" Kim grinned as he eased off the throttle to avoid ramming the crest of a large wave.

Twenty yards from shore, Randy became fearful of getting slammed into the sandbar by the persistent waves. Just as he thought he convinced himself that things would work out, a large wave scooped up the small boat and slammed it down on the sandbar.

All aboard were violently thrown into the crashing surf, flipping head over heels in different directions. Randy tried his best to hold on to Stella but lost her when his shoulder slammed into the gritty sand.

The lifeguard was the first to surface and feverishly searched for the other two. At last, he caught sight of Stella drifting ten yards away. He took off running on the three-foot-deep sandbar when Randy's head popped up closer to Stella.

"Behind you, the girl's behind you!" Kim shouted before he dove through a wave that was beginning to crash.

Disorientated and on the verge of complete exhaustion,

What Lurks Below

Randy shook the sand off his head and turned to see Stella floating on her back just a few feet away. He trudged over and scooped her in his arms before another wave crashed on top of them, driving them into the sandbar once again. Randy recovered quickly and regained a strong hold on Stella. He noticed Kim fighting the waves and trying to catch up.

The closer they got to shore, the deeper the water became as they left the sandbar. The waves were not breaking on them anymore, but Randy had to fight the undercurrent as the water rushed back out to sea. At last, he came to the point where he could no longer touch the bottom. He quickly re-arranged Stella and let her float on her back while he swam with one arm and held her tight with the other.

Finally, Kim made it over and relieved Randy of the wounded girl. Randy saw people gathered on the beach filming them while others stayed clear of the water and screamed for them to hurry up. Stella's friends were crying hysterically as the three tourists who helped her with her gear earlier were knee-deep in the water and wanted to jump in to help, but the current became so strong that they were afraid of being dragged out to sea.

As they raced to shore, they became deftly aware that they were being pulled parallel to the beach. Kim was horrified when he recognized that the sandbar had opened somewhere to the South of them and at the rate they were moving, he hoped they wouldn't be dragged out to sea in the undertow.

"Swim harder... a little to the North or we'll get swept out with the undertow!" he shouted to Randy as he fought to keep his head up.

Their hearts raced, and their thoughts were on the gargantuan reptile when, only ten yards from shore, they were swept out beyond the sandbar in the relentless undertow current. There was no point in trying to fight it, so they tried to relax their pulsating muscles until the current played out. The powerful undertow finally ended, releasing them ninety yards from shore. Randy resignedly looked over at the sudden disheartened look on Kim's face. "We've had it, mate," Kim grunted in a low, inaudible tone. "There's nobody around that can save us."

They were beyond worn out, but the thought of giving up never crossed Randy's mind, "Don't give up... We're going to make it."

"No... I mean, look behind you," Kim replied in a wobbly tone.

Randy was too tired to turn and look; he didn't need to. He knew by the look on the man's face that the reptile was behind him. After a long minute, Randy slowly turned and saw the aberrant monster cruising slowly through the swells like a guided missile in slow motion.

Too tired to swim or fight, Randy and Kim sat idle in the water and looked on in dread as they awaited a horrific ending.

In the distance, Randy heard what sounded like the unmistakable sound of a train engine at full speed, and it was eerily getting closer. While the sound got louder, the reptile circled its prey as if choosing who it would eat first.

"Hey Officer, you hear an engine?" Kim asked as the sound was nearly on top of them.

Before Randy could answer, a large tugboat crashed through the swells and blinding rain and stopped between the reptile and the swimmers. The flow of backwater from the propeller being thrown in reverse nearly flushed them away from the tugboat.

Randy heard Captain Virgil Goodman shouting out orders to his crew as they scrambled on deck and threw a life ring to him with a line attached. Randy was about to shout over and tell Kim to grab the ring, but he was already reaching for it. Kim grabbed the ring, then swam over to Randy and helped him hold on to Stella as shotgun blasts could be heard from the other side of the tug. Randy saw Bill and a new crewmember haul in the line with intense speed. When they reached the side of the tugboat, they were too weak to climb the tire bumpers, so Bill reached over the side and pulled them on deck one at a time with his massive arms.

They were quickly whisked aboard like a Special Forces mission to rescue hostages as the deafening shotgun blasts continued. Captain Virgil threw the tug in reverse and headed back out to sea as the repulsive beast rose out of the water and landed on the bow of the tugboat. Chuck held his position and continued blasting as the bow of the tug dipped low before the creature was blasted back into the water.

"Get off my boat!" Virgil shouted like a crazed demon. He continued backing for fifty-yards before moving the throttle forward and heading for Port.

Bill gently picked Stella up from the steel deck and took her to his bunk. He changed the tourniquet and covered her with a flannel blanket. Tom guided Randy and Kim to the galley and gave them blankets and water.

Randy found his sea legs and climbed the stairs leading to the wheelhouse, where he met with Captain Virgil and Chuck.

"The girl is bad. She's got to get to the hospital fast," he wheezed.

"I've already called. The paramedics will meet us at the

dock," Virgil responded, steering the tugboat along the coast through another heavy squall.

"You guys saved our lives. That beast was ten seconds from another feast," Randy said, squeezing Virgil's shoulder.

"Lucky for you that I was monitoring the radio and saw you speeding out of the inlet," Virgil replied.

"Where'd you guys get all that firepower? It sounded like a war zone." "After what happened to Skip, we're not taking any chances. But even so, I don't think one damn shot had penetrated that damn thing," Chuck added in an irritated tone.

Randy didn't reply. He was tired and worn out. He sat back in the chair and reviewed what happened in his mind. He was amazed at the strength and aggressiveness of the reptile. It was creepy to see how well the thing seemed to plan its attacks; it was definitely not like any other reptile he'd ever seen.

As the *Horizon* cruised through the inlet and docked, the news media seemed to come out of the woodwork and scrambled to interview the rain-soaked crew.

Police had to clear a path for the ambulance to race to the hospital with Stella, who had lost a lot of blood but seemed like she would pull through. After a threatening call from the mayor about leaking too much information on the reptile, Officer Randy Taylor reluctantly told the reporters that his boat sank in rough seas while attempting to rescue the kiteboarder and that it just so happened that the poor, frightened, wayward alligator was also in the area. He smiled to himself when none of the reporters believed him and wondered what Nick Meyers would say when the people who witnessed the attack on the beach released their videos.

When the media circus finally thinned out, Kim Rutner emerged from the galley and leapt to the dock. Randy spotted him walking away and called him over.

"Kim, you saved our lives," he said genuinely, shaking his hand. "But for a big, strong lifeguard like yourself, what's with the name Kim?"

"Kim is the name my parents gave me. And like you said, I'm a big, strong lifeguard and anybody that's ever ragged about it received a mouthful of knuckles," he replied in a husky tone and a slight smirk.

"So, you say you've seen these reptiles in Australia, eh?" Randy changed the subject.

"No, definitely not. I've tangled with some good-sized crocs, but never a big bastard like this one," he answered as a taxi cab pulled up. He opened the door and turned to face the officer with a serious look, "If I were you, I'd close the entire town until that creature is killed."

Randy stood there and watched the taxi cab drive away and thought how easy it sounded to close down the town, but with a mayor who was worried about scaring away tourists, he knew it would never happen.

His cell phone rang as he walked back to the tugboat. It was the mayor, "Nick, we've got to talk," he answered.

"Are you watching the breaking news on channel seven!?" The Mayor screamed. He went on ranting and raving for ten minutes. Randy did all he could to stay calm until it was his turn to talk.

"Now you listen to me, you fat ass loudmouth! None, I repeat, none of this would have happened if it wasn't for you and Bhim!"

"Damnit Randy! I'm going to have your badge!"

"Like hell you are Nick! Take my badge, and you'll be flushed down the toilet like the useless piece of crap that you are. I will tell the entire story of how you, Bhim and Don Henderson raised that damn monster and even knew about it when it escaped the Sanctuary!"

There was a long pause before he replied, "Now hold on a

minute Randy. I thought we already went over this. Let's not do something we're going to regret," he said coolly.

"The only thing I regret is how I let you sucker me into this thing."

"I need to know that you and your guys are still going to hunt that thing tomorrow."

"We meet at one tomorrow afternoon. But let me make myself clear, I'm not doing it for you; you can go to hell for all I care. I'm doing this because I want to make sure that monster is killed before it attacks anybody else,"Randy spat out.

"You're a good man, Randy, I'll see to it that..."

Randy slammed the phone down on the receiver before listening to another one of the Mayor's phony stories.

18

The calm water mirrored the reflection of the half-moon in the pre-dawn hours where the tugboats were docked. The rain and nasty weather of the previous day were gone as the sun began to poke out of the east and greet the busy Port with a new day.

Seagulls sleeping on the pilings were harshly awakened from their slumber when a loud diesel engine suddenly cranked up and disturbed the peaceful quiet. It revved up, disgorging a large cloud of black smoke.

Don Henderson quickly pulled to the dock area with his rented Grand Prix and tried to catch the Horizon just as it cast off.

"Hey Virge! I need to talk to you before we meet the hunting party!" he shouted desperately.

Captain Virgil looked out of the wheelhouse window and gave Don a spiteful look before replying, "Back in one hour, got to bring in a ship! We'll meet at the house at one o' clock."

Don could see the irritated look on his former friend's face. He knew Virgil wanted to kill him for involving him with the malevolent reptile, but Virgil was the only one he could trust to get him back in one piece.

Don was scared. He didn't want to go on the hunt with the crew that Officer Randy Taylor put together. He was petrified of going on a boat with the imperious pirate whom he met last night and an old degenerate Vietnam vet whom he had yet to meet.

He nervously chain-smoked as he leaned on his car and waited for the tugboat to return. The mosquitoes and no-see-ums were eating him alive as he checked his watch for the fifth time in five minutes.

In less than five hours, he was to meet with the rest of the crew at the old Vietnam war heroes' house and prepare for the hunt. He learned that the man had brought back what they called a fast-boat from the war and kept it docked on the river behind his house.

He wanted to talk to Virgil about something that didn't sound right to him. Why would the mayor want these guys to hunt such a terrifying monster? There was no doubt in his mind that they didn't have the resources to capture or kill the reptile. He concluded that maybe the mayor wanted them all dead so that the only people who knew he was involved would conveniently vanish.

Fidgeting to find his keys, he walked over to open the door

while pulling out a handkerchief to wipe the sweat from his brow. He just stuck the key in the door when he looked up to see a Harbor Patrol jeep turning into the parking lot.

The jeep pulled in next to Don, and Officer Randy Taylor stepped out. "Officer Taylor, you're up early," he grudgingly said, sensing trouble. "Screw you," replied Randy as he grabbed Don by the arm and practically pushed him inside an empty storage shed. Slamming the door behind him, he shoved Don to the middle of the small space.

"As you damn well know, I was nearly eaten alive by your goddamn reptile the other day. I was close enough to count its malformed teeth. In fact, I was close enough to realize that it can't be killed by blasting it with shotguns."

"That's why I'm here right now, trying to talk to Virgil. This whole thing sounds strange about Nick wanting amateurs like us to kill it. It just doesn't make sense," Don replied, fidgeting with his hands in his pant pockets.

"Nick's a dumbass and I'm his fall guy. He's blackmailed Virgil, his crew, and me to do the damn job quietly. If he hired anybody else, the media would make a circus out of it, and they would eventually find out how he's involved," Randy replied angrily, kicking an empty lobster trap across the floor.

"There's a way to kill it using shotguns," Don carefully said.

"Those armored plates are not on the reptile's underbelly. If we can shoot its underbelly and head area, preferably into the jaws, it can be killed."

Randy stood staring at Don with his hands on his hips, thinking. After a long minute, he replied, "When you leave here, I want you to go to Sandy Beach Park and go to the creek where you'll find your dumb-ass Indian friend. Tell him what you just told me. I'm going to get some bigger firepower and meet you at the dock by one."

"I can't do that," Don anxiously replied. "Chief Bhim and his men quit last night and headed back to the Everglades Sanctuary."

"The bastard, he had a contract."

"The reptile killed his nephew, Bhim fell apart and Durjaya thought it was best to quit the hunt."

Randy gave Don a malicious look, "I've said it before, and I'll say it again, those free-loading-good-for-nothing Indians can't be trusted, and here's another prime example of what I knew would happen."

The frustrated officer kicked the door open and walked out. Don slowly followed, drenched in sweat and on the verge of a breakdown.

Randy turned and pointed a finger in Don's face, "You make sure you make it by one o'clock," he said in a threatening tone. "I'll be there as soon as I can, with some bigger guns," he continued, climbing into his jeep.

"Oh, uh, by the way... how'd you know I was here," Don asked. "I didn't, I came here to talk to Virgil and his crew."

"They'll be back in an hour," Don replied timidly.

Officer Randy Taylor drove through the early morning traffic as the sun was rising from the east like a glowing inferno. The street lights had just turned off and street sweepers were slowing traffic along US1.

After driving for an hour and a half, Randy finally pulled into the driveway of an old friend's house.

Walter Bronson was a weapons buff whom Randy had met during the Gulf War. The man had lost a leg when his Hummer truck was hit by a rocket launcher during an ambush. Randy scrambled from the vehicle behind and rushed over, dragging him to safety.

Walter spent the next four months in the hospital, and Randy checked in on him from time to time. They soon found that they both grew up in Florida and lived one county away from each other. They pledged to stay in touch when they returned but soon lost contact.

Walter was a likable man with a funny sense of humor before he lost his leg. Now, he was one of the many casualties that had to go through life feeling handicapped. Where some people took the bull by the horns and made an effort to carry on, others would blame the world for their misgivings and retreat from society. Walter was the latter.

Randy got out of his truck and walked up the neglected path to the house. He rang the doorbell and took a look around the tattered yard.

"Go the hell away!" a voice barked from inside the house.

"I'm looking for Walter, Private Walter Bronson," replied Randy.

After a long pause, he replied, "Who the hell are you, and what do you want!"

"My name is Taylor, Randy Taylor. We met in the ..."

Before Randy could finish his sentence, the door swung open, and Walter sprang from the other side.

"Holy crap! If it isn't the man who saved my goddamn life!" Walter said as he lost his balance and nearly tumbled out onto the walkway.

Randy grabbed his flabby arm until he regained his balance, "Careful buddy, take it easy."

"Come in Taylor, what're you drinkin'?" he said as he hopped on one leg toward the kitchen.

"Nothing Walt, I'm in a rush. I need your help."

"Hadn't seen you in years and you're in a hurry? What the hell?" he replied with a world-weary look.

Randy started to say something but tripped on a box of clothes strewn out on the floor.

"This place is a pig sty... Watch your step," Walter said with embarrassment.

"Who am I to say?" Randy struggled to say as he made his way to the kitchen.

"I've been feeling like hell since I got back," explained Walter. "I think I've kicked my ass long enough. I'm trying to clean this place up and straighten out my life."

"That's good news Walt, I'll stop back here in a week or two and help you out."

"Yeah right, it's only been what... six or seven years since I've seen your ugly mug."

"Damn! It's been a while, hasn't it? But you hadn't contacted me either," Randy retorted, looking at his watch.

"Okay, we're even. So what brings you here today in such a hurry?"

"I need guns. Big guns," Randy cut to the chase. "I'm sure you heard about that giant reptile attacking people down by Sandy Beach Park."

"Indeed I did," he replied with a frown.

"Yeah, well you hadn't heard the worst of it. The damn thing is like a prehistoric monster. It's over thirty feet long and shotguns won't kill it. I need bigger guns and you are the only person I know who might have them." "Oh? And what makes you think I might have illegal armaments

Officer?" he said in a swaggering tone.

"Cut the crap, I'm not here to bust you. I need something to kill that beast before it kills again," Randy exploded.

"Walk this way," Walter replied, hopping toward a bedroom. "You saved my life, and I'm indebted."

Randy followed behind Walter as he hobbled to the room and opened the accordion doors where a closet used to be. In its place was a safe that would rival any bank vault. He politely asked Randy to turn his head while he thumbed the combination dial. The safe clicked open and Walter disappeared inside for a couple minutes. He returned with two cases in his hands, one large and one small, and placed them on a table.

Walter opened the large case and pulled out what looked like a space-age shotgun from a B-rated science fiction movie.

"This, my friend, will stop Godzilla dead in its tracks," he smugly said, placing it on the bed.

"I've seen something like it on Star Wars; what the hell is it?" asked Randy with a confounded look.

"This little beauty is a Pancor Jackhammer shotgun," Walter said, looking like a proud parent showing off his baby. He picked it up and continued, "It is seven-hundred and eighty-seven millimeters in length. It carries a rotary cylinder magazine that cycles through conventional twelve-gauge shells at a rate of four rounds per second. It also features what is called a bear-trap device that can blow its full load at once; just be careful, it has a nasty kick," he grinned.

"Whew! What is considered a full load?" Randy asked, amazed that he'd never heard of such a weapon.

"This beauty holds ten rounds, but watch your ass 'cause it'll knock you on it."

He passed it over to Randy and tottered over to the smaller case. He blew the dust off the cover, slowly opened it like a kid on Christmas morning, and pulled out the largest pistol Randy had ever seen.

He held it up near his face and admired it before he continued, "Unlike Dirty Harry's little forty-four magnum, which used to be... I repeat, used to be the largest handgun ever made. This little monster has a ten-and-a-half-inch barrel. Be careful, as this thing also has a jarring recoil," he boasted. "If you're not careful, it'll snap your wrist like a matchstick."

"I'm not even going to ask where you got these things," Randy said with stunned relief.

"I actually picked up the Smith and Wesson at a gun show in Miami. But the Pancor, the Pancor I got lucky with. These things are extremely rare; they never actually went into production. I was lucky enough to run into this old lady who was getting rid of it. Her old man had died, and she had no idea how rare this thing was. I practically got it for free," he laughed and then broke into a two-minute smoker's cough.

"I owe you one, Walt," Randy said as he looked at his watch and hurriedly packed the guns in their cases.

"No, we're even. Just bring them back in one piece."

"You bet I will, if I live through this," he despairingly replied. "I just have one request," Walter coyly said.

Randy knew what he was going to ask before he said it. "Include me in the hunt," he said flatly.

"Sorry Walt, the boat's full," replied Randy, picking up the cases and making a beeline for the door.

"Ah bull shit, you don't want me in on it because I only have one leg.

You're just like everybody else; you see me as a cripple."

"Don't pull that shit with me, Walter. That hideous creature is the nastiest thing I've ever seen. It's extremely vicious and an aggressive killer. You know as well as I that we might have to run like hell at any given time," Randy candidly retorted.

Walter leaned against the front porch like a jaded dog and watched as Randy placed the guns in his jeep and hopped in. He cranked the engine and pulled out of the driveway. Before speeding off, he slowed and stuck his head out of the window, "I'll see you in a week or two," he shouted.

"Make sure you bring my guns back in one piece," Walter shouted back with a revolting look.

19

Dieter Heilbronner unloaded the dive gear from his van and walked through the backyard of the large four-bedroom, three-bath house located two miles up the Himmershee River.

Suffering a small hangover, Dieter carried the gear to a beautiful fifty-two-foot Amel Super Maramu sailboat. He stopped and admired the yacht before making a look of disgust at the thought of the cleaning job ahead.

His boat hull cleaning business was extremely busy seven days a week, but his hired help was not dependable. After countless complaints and having to follow up with his workers, he finally had to let them go. Lucky for him, his son Bjorn had recently finished high school and happily gave his old man a hand for the summer.

Dieter, born in Hamburg, Germany, was the son of a sea captain who had spent the better part of his life at sea. When Dieter had breaks from school, he was able to travel with his father and sail across the Atlantic on a large container ship his father captained.

At one point, he marveled that he had stopped in nearly every Port along the East Coast of the United States. The city where he had the fondest memories during the spring break was Fort Lauderdale, Florida.

He was the envy of all his friends when he returned to Germany with loads of records from rock bands that were next to impossible to find at home.

He would boast to his friends about the nights when he would sail into Port Everglades, walk across the Intracoastal bridge, and drink at a place called the Elbo Room, where the movie '*Where the boys are*' had been filmed.

At the age of twenty-one, he packed his bags and left Germany for the only place in the world he'd rather be, Fort Lauderdale.

Lacking a college degree, it was hard for him to make any real money, so he decided to start his own little business of cleaning boat hulls. A couple years later, he met an attractive young lady working in a restaurant whom he soon married.

His hard work started paying off when word of mouth spread amongst the boat people that *Heilbronner Hull Cleaners* was a highly reputable company, and his small business has soared ever since. Soon after, Dieter and his wife were blessed with a healthy son they named Bjorn.

Looking at his watch, it was half past eight in the morning. He assured the yacht owner that he would be finished before noon so that his client could sail to the Bahamas that same afternoon.

He walked over to Bjorn, who was busy readying the air tanks and shook his head. *It will take a miracle to get this finished on time,* he thought.

"Tanks are full dad, what side do you want me to start from?" Bjorn asked as he finished checking the gauges.

"The yacht is fifty-two feet long with a fifteen-foot beam. We'll start at the bow and take a break and refill the tanks," Dieter replied impatiently, a bit peeved that his son didn't realize they would need at least twice as much air to do the job.

"I should have brought the other tanks," Bjorn said, rolling his eyes and slipping into the wetsuit.

Dieter said nothing as he sat on the dock next to Bjorn and spat in his mask. He noticed the gross look his son gave him and continued rubbing the spit around on the glass.

"Want to use some of my fog-resistant spray?" Bjorn asked scornfully. "Nope, just finished," Dieter replied with a cheeky smile.

"You know dad, if you ever feel like joining the twenty-first century, you'll notice that people don't spit in their masks anymore; they use this stuff," Bjorn lectured, holding up his bottle of mask cleaner. "And another thing, why don't you get a wetsuit instead of diving in those ragged cut-off jeans?"

Before answering, Dieter bit his tongue and sat there smiling until his nitpicking son was finished, "I guess I'm what you fancy guys call old school. And to me, old school is good school. And I certainly know as a fact that us old school men would have been smart enough to bring enough air tanks to complete this job."

Bjorn suddenly felt like an idiot for trying to lecture his dad. Without another word, he watched as his dad flipped the tank over his head and fastened the tank straps. He followed suit and buckled his BC vest.

Dieter adjusted his mask and looked over to his son. He gave him a wink and jumped into the river, disappearing under the sailboat. He swam from bow to stern, inspecting the buildup of barnacles and algae attached to the hull, then returned to the surface.

"It doesn't look too bad," he said, spitting water from his mouth. "Okay, let's do this."

"There's an ebb tide, so be careful you don't get stuck under the boat." Ignoring the jab, Bjorn slipped his mask on and jumped into the murky river. He quickly realized his father wasn't kidding about getting stuck under the boat as he noticed the keel was about one-foot from the mucky bottom. Dieter would normally have arranged to clean the hull during high tide where it would be safer. Since this was a rush job, he figured he would scrape off what he could before the hull settled into the muck.

Visibility was next to nil. Bjorn could only see about three-foot in front of him and couldn't help getting an eerie feeling that a bull shark might come by and take a bite out of him.

As a little kid, his father told him a story of a time when he was cleaning a boat hull more than ten miles inland on a river that connected to the Intracoastal Waterway. While he was busy cleaning the hull of a small boat, an eight-foot bullshark suddenly came out of nowhere and bumped his air tank. Staggered from the collision, he turned and caught the tail end of the shark as it disappeared through the murky brown wall of vision. Startled at the sight of the size of the tail fin, he dropped his tools and quickly swam over to the other side of the boat where his co-worker was and motioned for him to get out of the water. As they hurriedly climbed a ladder attached to the dock, the shark came back and took a chunk out of his dive fin.

He tried to block the thought of that happening to him as he continued scraping and cleaning. Luck was on their side. The hull was well kept and properly maintained which made the work much easier. After working at a steady pace for nearly an hour, the starboard side was finished.

Dieter came from behind and grabbed Bjorn's fin and laughed through his apparatus as he knew his son was probably thinking about his shark story. Bjorn pulled his leg free and turned at lightning speed to see the ebullient face of his father, pointing a finger toward the surface and going up.

Bjorn met his father at the surface, and they removed their masks. Bjorn had an irritated look on his face as Dieter fought an uncontrollable laugh, "Kinda spooky down there, eh son?"

"Not funny dad, you scared the crap out of me," Bjorn said scornfully. "Sorry kid, just wanted to see how you'd react," he beamed.

"Anyway, are we done with this side?"

"Yes we are. Let's get out of the water and take a break while you refill the tanks," replied Dieter, swimming over to the aluminum dock ladder.

"I'll stop at McDonalds on the way back."

"That junk will kill you. Stop at a market and pick up a couple of real sandwiches," Dieter said, stepping on the dock and looking at his watch. "Better yet, just hurry back with the air and we'll finish the job, then we'll stop at the Anchor Bar."

"Whatever pops," Bjorn replied as he loaded the tanks on a little cart and wheeled them away to the van.

Thirty-five minutes later, Bjorn returned with full tanks. His father noticed the special cheese sauce from a Big Mac sandwich on the corner of Bjorn's mouth but didn't say anything.

"This has got to be one of the easiest cleaning jobs I've ever done. The algae are coming off like butter," Bjorn informed, strapping his tank to the BC.

"And now, the tough part," Dieter replied deliberately, standing up and flipping the tank over his head and onto his back. "The keel is now resting on the bottom and the yacht is listing to starboard. It's too risky for you to go back down and take a chance of the hull shifting to port and crushing you."

"Oh, but you're going down? What are you, Superman?"

"Far from it, I'll go down and start cleaning the port side. If a boat passes, I want you to slap the water with your dive fin and I'll stay clear until the boat goes by," replied Dieter, testing his regulator.

"Sounds a little risky," Bjorn burped uneasily.

"I should be alright. I've never seen a yacht this size shift under a no-wake zone. Just relax and digest your Big Mac. Let me know if a boat approaches," he said slipping the mask on and walking down the ladder.

"Damn, how'd he know?" Bjorn asked himself.

Dieter grabbed his tools and disappeared under the hull. Against his better judgment, he slipped his tank off so that he could squeeze between the hull and riverbed to clean the area by the keel. Resting on his back, he gradually crawled under the boat, dragging his tank by his side and continued scraping the algae.

Twenty minutes into it, Bjorn was bored. Sitting at the end of the dock with his feet dangling over the side, he kept looking at his watch and wondered if it stopped. He kept a watchful eye on the river, but no boats could be seen or heard. His mind began to wander as he began planning his afternoon. After a while, his butt was sore, and he got up and paced back and forth on the dock.

Suddenly, a school of tarpon crashed the surface, breaking his thoughts. He counted five racing downriver like they were being chased. *What the hell? Must be a good size barracuda chasing 'em,* he thought. He shielded his eyes from the sun and searched the water for any predators, but didn't see anything.

As he turned to take another stroll down the dock, he was

greeted by the homeowner's pet dog. The big, one-hundred-pound Labrador nearly bowled Bjorn to the ground, wagging his tail and giving him sloppy kisses. "Whoa boy! Take it easy! Who let you out?... Tell me, c'mon boy!" he said as he playfully fought the dog. He looked over toward the back of the house and noticed the gaping hole in the patio screen.

"Oo-wee, your momma's going to get you when she sees that!"

The dog was unyielding. He ran around the yard, each time circling back and jumping on Bjorn as he slowly began packing up his gear. Enough was enough. He gave the dog a diminutive kick in the butt to make it clear that he wasn't playing any longer. The dog gave a little yelp and scrambled to the other end of the dock, where he sat and licked his wound.

Bjorn gave another look up and down the river, and since he hadn't seen a boat pass by while his father was in the water, he decided to haul his gear up to the truck and save time. He no sooner made it to the front of the house when he heard the dog barking and growling aggressively.

He figured that his father had finished the job and was climbing up the dock ladder, startling the dog. He smiled and threw his tank into the van, and another thought entered his mind - *maybe a boat was passing by, and the dog was barking at it.* Whatever the reason, Bjorn stowed his equipment and jogged back down toward the dock.

The Labrador was barking viciously with his head down low near the water and his back end high in the air. Bjorn snickered and couldn't keep the grin off his face at the thought of dear 'ol dad being held at bay by the neighborhood's most playful pooch.

"Hey killer! Calm down," he said in a playful manner. The dog didn't flinch as he kept barking. Bjorn felt guilty for the little kick he gave the dog earlier and got down on all fours.

"Come here boy! I'm comin' to getcha!" he shouted lightheartedly, crawling over to the pain-in-the-butt dog.

He was just feet away from reaching over to grab the dog's tail when the humungous reptile's head slowly came up out of the water and up the side of the dock. It was like a monster movie in slow motion as the horrific jaws opened and snapped shut with an enormous popping sound just inches away from the anxious dog.

The terrifyingly large reptile continued rising out of the water and onto the dock, splintering the boards as they bent under the massive weight. The jaws opened again and let out a daunting hissing sound as the reptile climbed past the crumbling dock and onto the seawall.

Bjorn stood straight up and looked in awe at the unbelievable sight. Never in his wildest nightmares would he believe such a monster could exist. Too stunned to move, he marveled at the incredible size of the monster's head. It looked as big as a small car, with teeth the size of a man's hand. Instead of the teeth being conical like an alligator, they were jagged like a hunting knife.

As the reptile continued its slow move toward the frightened dog, Bjorn became aware of something stuck between its teeth. His heart sank when he realized it was his father's scraping tool.

"Oh no! No, no, no!... Dad!" he screamed.

He began sobbing uncontrollably at the thought of his father being eaten. His legs still refused to move until the reptile turned its ghastly head and glared at him. At that moment, the dog turned and ran like a Greyhound back to the house.

Bjorn felt the bile in his throat rise when the reptile turned its attention to him. He had to think fast; there was nowhere to run. He looked over towards the side gate leading to the front of the house, but it was a good thirty yards away and he'd never make it.

He looked at the yacht. He could take two giant leaps and jump in the boat if his legs didn't fail him and then jump on the radio for help. *But what if it followed? That damn thing can eat the boat,* he thought.

Before he could make up his mind, the malevolent creature leaped forward and snapped its massive jaws at the same instant Bjorn took charge of his senses and leaped onto the bow of the sailboat. With his heart pounding in his ears, he crash-landed on the deck and rolled toward the other side, where he thought he'd be out of danger. Looking back at the monster through his eyes as big as a golf ball, he was clearly petrified at the speed the creature chased him and leaped onto the boat, causing it to slam down on the river's bottom.

Bjorn heard a loud crack as the hull crushed and nearly broke apart. He got up and quickly ran to the stern, where he thought he could jump back to the dock.

Just as fast, the reptile turned to give chase, but the deckhouse gave way, and the reptile fell through the cabin.

"Help! Somebody help!" he screamed as the boat splintered apart.

The hideous reptile began to crawl out of the hull as the boat shuddered under the weight. The once beautiful sailboat was being torn apart and was now half submerged and listing away from the dock.

Bjorn was so scared he wanted to curl up in a corner and give up, but instead, he managed to get the courage to take a leap for the dock. He jumped at the same instant that the dock lines snapped, causing the yacht to roll over, away from the dock.

Bjorn lost his balance and was tossed backward into the wreckage, landing on the reptile's back. He let out a blood-curdling scream when the armored plates on its back sliced into his shoulder. Out of sheer terror, he tried to grab onto its back and stay clear of the snapping jaws.

Sensing the prey on its back, the reptile quickly went into a death roll. Bjorn could do nothing more but hang on as the unbelievably tough and rigid plates on the monster ripped through the flesh of his arms and legs, finally causing him to lose his grip and let go.

The beast was wildly rolling on top of Bjorn as he lay trapped on his back, stuck in the mud. Almost out of breath and with no way possible to free himself, Bjorn knew the end was near as he began to see stars and felt the blackness set in when you lose consciousness.

Suddenly, the reptile stopped spinning and moved forward, allowing Bjorn to escape. Easier said than done, he quickly found out. His back was suctioned to the muck, and he was too exhausted to free himself.

Out of nowhere, a hand grabbed Bjorn by the shoulder and

yanked him off the bottom, thrusting him briskly to the surface. Standing waist-deep in the water, Dieter heaved his son with all his might over toward the dock ladder.

"Get the hell out of the water... Fast!" he shouted.

Bjorn was weak and disorientated and didn't know which way was up or down. His father wasted no time dragging him through the water and nearly flung him up the ladder as the beast swam back toward them to finish the attack.

Dieter had one foot on the bottom rung of the ladder and Bjorn sandwiched between his arms when he turned to see the reptile coming up behind. With one last ditch effort to save his son, he let go of the ladder and grabbed Bjorn with both hands, practically throwing him through the air.

As Dieter fell back into the water, he was relieved to see his son land on the lawn and out of harm's way. With seconds to live, he closed his eyes and tucked his arms and legs closer to his body in hopes of a miracle.

To his welcomed surprise, he heard the sound of loud gunshots coming from the dock. He opened his eyes and saw three neighbors standing on the crumbled dock with shotguns blazing.

The irate reptile was still coming and only feet away. Its enormous jaws were wide open and ready to strike while the men continued blasting at it. At the last second, a lucky shot hit inside the jaws, causing the reptile to snap its jaws shut and retreat under the murky water.

Dieter, surprised to be alive, righted himself and made it up the ladder faster than humanly possible.

By now, with what sounded like a war going on in the quiet neighborhood, more neighbors came running out of their houses and toward the river to try and get a glimpse of the monstrous reptile they'd seen on the news.

Dieter was bleeding and dead tired. He was helped to his feet by one of the men with the shotguns.

"What in god's name was that?... You're lucky to be alive," he said as the other two men came up with looks of bewilderment.

"Buddy... You and your friends couldn't have come soon enough; thanks for saving my son and me," he sincerely replied between deep breaths.

"Just glad to be at the right place at the right time," he replied with a pat on Dieter's back.

"I'm just glad we had shotguns handy," said another.

"Yeah well, I don't think these damn twelve-gauges could kill that thing. I don't know how many just bounced off that thing's back. Jim here got lucky with a shot inside the jaws," the third man said, pointing to his buddy. Dieter looked over and saw a crowd of people hovering over Bjorn. He dropped the towel that was draped over his shoulders and ran over to his son.

"Dad, I thought it got you," Bjorn whispered with a faint breath.

"What, and leave you with all the work?" Dieter joked, trying to hide his feelings of distress.

Bjorn gave a little smile and continued, "I saw your scraping tool stuck between that monster's teeth and thought he ate you,"

"No, I luckily saw it coming. At first, it looked like a submarine. I wondered to myself what a submarine was doing cruising in this river until it opened its jaws. At that instant, I nearly dug a tunnel to the other side of the boat. Lucky for me, there was a little valley where I was able to squeeze through. I waited on the other side to see what it was going to do. When I swam back to the rudder, I heard the dog barking like mad and saw the reptile climbing out of the water."

"It nearly got the dog," Bjorn added.

"When it was completely out, I waited a few more minutes until I was going to surface and make sure you were out by the street where I hoped you would have gone. All of a sudden, the boat slammed down on the bottom and cracked like an eggshell. Before I could get over the shock of that happening, the whole damn boat rolled over and fell apart."

"I'll fill you in on what happened topside later," Bjorn replied as he passed out.

A crowd gathered on the usually quiet street when word got out about the giant reptile attack. News reporters seemed to come out of nowhere and blocked the street with their news vans while the police and paramedics tried to get through. Channels four, seven and ten were set up in the middle of the street, while channel six was involved with a fisticuff with a Latin news truck.

"Get the hell out of my way!" screamed the paramedic as he zigzagged down the street, trying not to hit pedestrians milling around. His partner was riding shotgun and was turning the siren on and off, making it sound like a video game gone berserk, "I bet they'd move if it were their mother needing our help," he said with a look of disgust.

Thanks to the news trucks blocking the road, it took nearly fifteen minutes before they finally pulled up on the scene. Three paramedics jumped out of the truck, grabbed their gear and headed through the side gate leading to what was left of the dock.

The news media was set up in the grass along the dock with cameras rolling inches away from Bjorn's face while others were scrambling for an interview with Dieter.

Unable to control his anger, a veteran paramedic named Chris lunged forward and pulled the plug on a camera, effectively cutting off the newscast.

"Hey! What gives you the right to..."

"Stay out of my way!" Chris cut the news lady off in mid-sentence.

A group of police officers rushed over and stopped the melee before it could escalate, "Stay back Judy," an officer said, recognizing Judy Bailey from the Channel Seven news. He took her by the arm and gently removed her from the dock.

The other officers scoffed at his kindness as they knew that Officer Jack Stevens secretly had a crush on her. He would never miss the evening news and comment on her beauty. He told them that if he ever ran into her in public, he'd bedazzle her and ask her out.

"Get your hands off me, you animal!" she shouted.

The other officers cracked up when they saw the look on his face. He looked like a heartbroken school kid who just lost his prom date.

"Look Judy, I want you and your crew to back off so that these paramedics can do their job," he retorted sternly.

"And I need to do MY job!"

"The boat sank and the kid was trapped under it, end of story!" Jack replied, his temper rising. With so many sightings of the monstrous reptile, he felt like an idiot denying the truth, but word was out that the mayor distinctly advised to say nothing about the creature.

"You must be out of your mind to think I'll believe that crap!" Judy spat out in dismay.

"That's it, everybody out!" another officer announced with a bullhorn as he received orders from his superiors to clear the area.

"We have the right to be here!" a Channel Ten reporter shouted.

"You have the right to go directly to jail if I have to tell you again," replied the officer with the bullhorn.

"This is madness! What is the mayor trying to cover up?" a cameraman shouted as he hastily packed up his equipment.

Mayor Nick Meyers sat brooding in his office as he watched the news break on television. The whole thing with the mutant reptile had gotten out of hand, and there was no way he could keep a lid on it any longer. Sooner or later, the townspeople were going to find out that he was a part of it, and his career would be down the toilet.

He couldn't trust Officer Taylor to not spill his guts out at the first chance he got. Someway, somehow, he had to make sure Taylor couldn't tell anybody how he was involved with the reptile. He reached for his phone and dialed someone who could ease his weary mind. The business card simply read *Wolf*.

20

Officer Taylor drove into the gravel parking lot of the Patrol Boat station. He quickly looked at his watch as he climbed out of the jeep and dashed inside. It was eleven-forty-five, which gave him a little more than an hour before he was due to meet the hunting party.

"Get the mayor on the phone, will you Cathy," he said to his secretary as he breezed by her and into his office.

"Mr. Myers had called earlier looking for you," she replied, following him down the hall.

"I had to make a pit stop and see an old friend; did Nick say what he wanted?" "He didn't say, but he was really peeved and wants to see you ASAP." "What's the word on the latest attack?"

"Looks like the two lucky boat cleaners are going to make it," replied Cathy, keeping pace with Randy and talking faster than a lady who drank a full pot of Cuban coffee. "But it looks like we have another problem on our hands."

"Oh? And what can that be?" he replied without batting an eye as he raced out the door and jumped in his jeep.

"The news media aren't buying the Myers story anymore,"

she said, huff ing and puffing as she chased after Randy.

He started the jeep and gave her a smile, "I knew that bullshit story would never fly. How gullible did he think they were, telling them that the reptile was just a big alligator that lost its way."

"Yeah, well... when he called, I got the impression that he still wants news of that creature to be limited." Cathy replied bluntly.

"That's his problem. I'll stop by his office and see what he wants before I meet up with some guys that are going to help me hunt and kill that beast," he said, revving the engine and putting it in gear. "I'll be back in a few days; hold the fort until I return." He gave her a wink and pulled out of the parking lot.

"You just be careful!" she shouted as the jeep sped off in a cloud of dust. Ten minutes later, Officer Randy Taylor pulled into the nicely manicured parking lot of the mayor's office. He jumped out of the jeep and half jogged through the front door and was stopped at the front desk by Mayor Myers' secretary.

"Hello Officer Taylor. Are you here to see Mr. Myers?" "Yes I am, Donna," he said with a tight smile.

"I'll let him know you're here," she replied, picking up the phone. "Please do, and let him know I'm a little pressed for time," he added politely but with an edgy tone.

Randy paced back and forth, looking at his watch with irritation as it was now twelve-twenty. Five minutes later, as Randy was ready to leave, the phone rang, and the secretary stuck her pointer finger up at him, telling him to hold on. She picked up the phone and after a couple "yes sirs," hung up and told the officer that the Mayor will see him now. Randy resented the way Nick Myers played his little waiting games, thinking it gave him leverage.

He gave the secretary a disparaging look and took a deep breath before walking down the hall. Myers opened his door before Randy could knock on it. He greeted Randy as if they were old buddies and gave him a pat on the back.

"Randy, I'm glad you could stop by," he said in his usual irritating, condescending voice.

"Hello Nick," Randy replied resolutely. "Let's make this quick, as you're aware, I've got to meet up with my hunting party shortly.

"Change of plans," he replied flatly. "I want you to cancel the hunt for the reptile."

Randy was not in the mood for Myer's ever-changing games, "What the hell are you talking about?"

"The reptile is dead... or at least mortally wounded."

"And what brings you to that conclusion?" Randy impatiently replied. "The latest attack, I have witnesses saying the reptile moved like a slug after it was nearly blown to pieces by high-powered shotguns. Oh, by the way, I want you to find out if those fellas have a license to carry such high-powered weaponry," he continued, with a smug look, casually taking a half-smoked cigar out of his breast pocket.

"You've lost it Nick, I think you've finally lost your mind," Randy spat out, smacking the unlit cigar out of his mouth in a fit of rage.

Nick gave Randy a look like he wanted to shoot him where he stood; instead, he cleared his throat and said, "Look Randy, I know all this stuff with the reptile has got you on edge; you're not thinking straight," he patronized. "Why don't you take the week off and get some rest."

Randy was beside himself with anger. He grabbed the report of the hideous reptile and threw it at Nick, "Sit your fat ass down and read this report!" he said, gritting his teeth. "I want you to read carefully where it says shotgun blasts appear to ricochet off the armor-plated hide of the reptile!"

"I'll tell you one more time," Nick retorted. "Take some time off or I'll fire your stupid ass here and now."

"Fire me? You sure you want to go down that road again?"

"Randy, listen to me," he quickly changed the subject. "The reptile has got to be dead. After those guys unleashed their shotgun assault, nobody's seen or heard from the damn thing."

"Well then, if that's the case, my team and I will take a pleasure cruise up the river just to make sure it's dead."

"It's not in the budget," said Myers, trying a different tactic.

Randy shook his head and smiled, "So that's how you want to play it. I should be surprised, but I know how your dubious mind works. You want to tell everybody that the reptile is dead and gone, bury the fact that this reptile has anything to do with you and move on before the press finds out the truth," he smirked.

"The reptile was blasted to smithereens," Myers insisted. "So, where's the body?"

"It hasn't surfaced yet. The current probably took it miles upriver and every fish from here to the Everglades feasted on it," he lectured.

"I guess a big shot like you doesn't know what an ebb tide is. That means the tide was outgoing. If your gigantic reptile was dead, somebody would have spotted the carcass."

"This is not a debate, I'm telling you, the reptile is dead."

What little patience Randy had was now gone, "Okay... enough of your bullshit. I'm going to hunt down your monster come hell or high water. I will kill that thing before it kills again," Randy said as he started for the door.

"Wait a minute Randy, hear me out," Myers sighed. "You go ahead and do what has to be done," he changed his tone. "Report to me, and only me, on any developments pertaining to this matter...agreed?"

Randy stood for a long moment, squinting his eyes at the mayor, trying to figure out why he changed his tone again before replying, "Sure Nick," he said with a sarcastic grin and walked out the door.

He walked to the window and grudgingly watched through a window as the officer climbed in his jeep and peeled out of the parking lot before he picked up the phone and dialed Chief Bhim's number.

"Bhim... we've got problems," he said in a menacing tone when the Indian Chief picked up the phone. "I gave a statement to the media that the reptile was dead and gone. I thought that would be the end of it, but now, Officer Randy Taylor is still going after that thing."

"So what? I've got nothing to do with that creature anymore," Bhim replied tersely.

"Forget the reptile. If it's not dead, I'm sure it's gone back to the Everglades, never to be seen again... or at least, not while I'm in office."

"So what's the problem?" Bhim asked warily.

"Officer Randy Taylor," Myers answered blatantly. "I want him eliminated. He knows too much. I know that sooner or later, he will inform the media that I was involved with this whole mess."

"That's your problem, not mine," replied Bhim, coldly.

"No, it's our problem, mine and yours. If I go down, you and your god damn Sanctuary go down with me," he assured in a threatening manner.

Chief Bhim didn't like what he was hearing. "You think I'm an assassin?

You want me to kill Taylor for you?" Bhim shouted resentfully.

"No, I don't want you to do it, but I want it done. I don't want Randy Taylor to make it out of the Everglades alive. I called your buddy Wolf a day or two ago and told him I might need his services."

"You're out of your mind. I will take no part in it!"

"If you don't, I'll have your ratty Sanctuary closed down by this time tomorrow," Myers threatened.

After a long pause, Bhim murmured, "Okay, what do you ask of me?" "All I want you to do is be the go-between man. Wolf will track Taylor's boat when it gets to the 'glades. He shouldn't need your help, but if he gets lost or loses them, he'll need your help to find them."

"You are a coward," Bhim said disdainfully and slammed the receiver down.

"And you're a red-blooded whiner who never would have made it without me," smiled Myers as he replied to himself, gently returning the receiver to the phone and sitting back in his chair with a satisfied look.

Chief Bhim sat in his office with a look of disgust. He didn't like Officer Randy Taylor any more than the officer loathed him, but his animosity toward him was no reason to have him killed.

Wolf was a hired assassin. His fastidious manners and good looks concealed the fact that he was a cold-blooded killer. He marveled at how he had more political clients than he had of the mob, but it didn't matter the least; a job was a job, and he was good at it.

He finished packing a duffel bag of camouflage clothing and set out to the Denver Airport to take a flight to Florida for his hit in the Everglades. This particular assignment seemed a piece of cake. Ordinarily, he would have to track his victims for a week and find the least conspicuous place to carry out his work, but this time, there'd be nobody but him and his intended victim for miles around.

21

Skip Long was visiting his parents in Dothan, Georgia. Known as the peanut capital of the world, nearly half the peanuts grown in the United States are grown within a one-hundred-mile radius of the city.

His parents lived in a ranch-style home on fifty acres of farmland just outside the city limits. Born and raised on the farm, Skip didn't share his father's excitement in peanut farming and couldn't wait to leave the area and move to Florida. Much to the chagrin of his father, Skip's mother kept his bedroom just the way it was when he and his estranged wife left, hoping that he'd return one day.

After the near-fatal attack from the vicious reptile, Skip decided to take time off and go back to the farm and try to mend his relationship with his hard-nosed father. If things went well between the two, maybe he would stay and never return to Florida and all the man-eating creatures that lurked in the water.

It was nearly one o' clock in the afternoon when he dragged himself out of bed and leisurely strolled downstairs. The house was quiet, and he saw his father sitting at the kitchen table.

"G'morning Pop," he garbled, his face showing three days' worth of stubble.

"Good afternoon, son," he replied austerely, eating a salami sandwich, with his head buried in a John Deere tractor magazine.

One could slice the tension in the kitchen with a knife as Skip sat across from his father.

His father, retired Captain Ken S. Long of the U.S. Naval Destroyer *Shogun*, was a highly decorated captain in the Vietnam War. His no-nonsense approach and relentless quest for perfection amongst his crew finally caused him to suffer a mild heart attack, rendering him unfit for duty. He had grudgingly taken the honorable discharge and went back to the farm, where he expected the same hard work from his farm hands as he did with his crew. Hard work was rewarded with hardy paychecks, and slackers were quickly fired.

"So, what's on your agenda today, son?" he inquired patiently.

"Hmm, I think after breakfast, I'll take a stroll down to the hardware store and pick up some parts to fix mom's birdhouse," he yawned.

"For Christ's sake, son, is that what your life has whittled down to?"

"C'mon, Dad, don't start," he replied, getting up from his chair and walking to the living room turning on the television.

"You've been here nearly a week, and you're acting like a miserable retiree," he shouted, slamming the magazine down on the table. "Get over it! The damn alligator didn't eat you... quit acting like a damn sissy and accept some responsibility!"

Ignoring the continuous ranting of his father, he scanned the paper, paged through to the national news section and gasped out loud when he read the headlines: *Two men escape death when enormous reptile strikes again!*

"I see you found the alligator article," his father said with a cold stare, walking into the living room.

"That monster is no alligator, Pops," Skip replied with a quiver. "I've seen it up close; it's got to be over thirty-foot long, and its head... its head looks like it came out of a Japanese horror movie."

"Really," the senior said with disgust. "If you read the article, the mayor gave a statement saying it was just a large alligator that lost its way from the Everglades and has since been killed."

"Dad, the mayor's full of crap. It tried to attack me, remember? It's a freak of nature. It has what looks like armor-plating covering its back. It is some kind of a mutation, I met the maniac who created it. I don't know why, but the mayor is trying to keep it quiet. I don't even care anymore 'cause there's no way I'm going back down there to find out," Skip replied, his voice trembling.

The disapproving look on his father's face exploded in rage, "Damnit, son! When are you going to grow up?"

Skip stood up, walked back to the kitchen, and was ready to walk out the back door. He stopped, punched his fist at the doorknob and turned, "Okay, Dad, let's have it. You hate that I came here because you think I'm running scared, and guess what? You're right again. I'm scared to death of that beast," he shouted, the tears flowing down his face. "When that thing leaped out of the water, I swear I looked into the eyes of pure evil. I can't explain it, but something about the way it..."

"Listen to you!" his dad cut him off. "You sound like one of the wimps I had to babysit in Vietnam!"

Skip stood there in disbelief, looking at his angry father with contempt. Finally, after staring each other down for a long minute, Skip threw his arms up and stormed out the back door.

Trying to get his father to understand what he was going through was futile. After all, his father took on more challenges and risks during the war than most men would do in a lifetime. His superiors had a nickname for him; they called him Captain Iron-balls. He smiled to himself and wondered how he could ever compete with that.

Feeling sorry for himself and tired of arguing with his father, Skip sat down on the porch swing and quietly reflected on the day of the attack. A few minutes later, he heard the door open and looked up to see his father walk over and sit next to him.

"Look, son," he said in an apologetic tone. "You're a grown man, and I want to support your decisions. I know that gator attack shook you up pretty good, but if you don't put it behind you and move on, it will eventually kill you."

Skip gave him a puzzled look and started to reply before he was cut off again.

"I hear you screaming in the middle of the night and tearing at the sheets as if you're fighting that thing in your dreams," he continued awkwardly.

"I know, Dad, I know. I've got to get it out of my mind and move on, but I've never been this scared in my life. I made eye contact with that creature, and it glared at me as if it... as if it were trying to read my mind, anticipating my next move," Skip replied with certainty.

The senior Long got up from the double swing and leaned on a wood post. He took a deep breath and turned toward Skip,

"Well, son, sometimes you've got to get the courage and find your way."

"What do you mean by that?" Skip asked with a confounded look. "What I'm saying is, sometimes you have to go and face your fears." "You think I should go back down there and face that hideous creature again?

"No, no. I just want you to know that the crew you worked with is getting ready to hunt the reptile today," he replied prudently before walking back into the house.

Skip watched his father enter the house and close the door behind him. He sat and wondered what he meant with that little piece of information. Does he really think his only son should go back and join the crew? He jumped up and ran through the door.

"How do you know Captain Virgil and the crew are going to hunt that reptile?"

"Captain Goodman called earlier this morning while you were sleeping. He wanted to know how you're doing. I relayed the nightmares to him, and he seemed a little disappointed. He then told me that he and the crew were going to hunt that thing and kill it," he continued, looking up at the clock and reading one-thirty. "As we sit here chatting, your crew is out there hunting the reptile," he replied in a staged-manner.

What Lurks Below

Approximately five-hundred and fifty miles south, Captain Virgil, Chuck and Bill sat at a table near the back of the Anchor Bar. They sipped from a pitcher of Beck's beer and talked about the upcoming hunt for the reptile.

Tom Powhatan heard the talk about what the crew was in for and was disappointed when his request to come along was denied. Captain Virgil saw no reason to risk the life of the newly arrived deckhand.

They had just ordered another pitcher of beer when the front door opened, and Don Henderson came strolling in like a lost child. He stood in the doorway until his eyes adjusted from the bright tropical sun to the din inside, finally focusing on the table in the back. He watchfully made his way over and stopped at an empty chair.

"Good afternoon, fellas. Aren't we late for our appointment?"

Nobody replied as Virgil motioned with his hand to take a seat. He gave his old friend a peculiar look before saying, "What brings you here? I thought I told you to meet us at one o' clock at the Vietnam Vets house."

"Look, I know you guys don't have much use for me and with good reason. If I would have known that damn reptile..."

"Save it, Donald," Virgil cut him off. "What's done is done, and you, Bhim and Myers will have to live with it, but why you dragged me and my crew into this nightmare is beyond me."

"Because you're the only one I thought I could trust, and I'm sorry. But now, things have gotten completely out of hand. I'm not going on that boat to hunt the reptile; I just want you to know I'm getting the hell out of here before more people find out that I created that hideous monster and string me up to the nearest tree," he said fearfully.

"Like hell you are," Virgil shot back. "You're going to come along with us on this little outing. You included us in this mess, and I'll be damned if I don't see you on that boat."

"Look Virge, if I go out there with those guys, I'm pretty sure I won't be coming back alive."

"Randy Taylor's a cop. He won't let us feed you to the reptile," Chuck declared without a hint of joking.

"Officer Taylor," Don glared at Chuck. "He met me at the docks this morning. I tell you what, the man has it in for me. I don't think he'd think twice about wasting me out there."

"Randy's a good man," Virgil added, pleased to see Dons' uneasiness. "Oh yeah? I thought he was going to do me in at the docks. Right after the *Horizon* left the dock, the officer pulled up and dragged me into an old abandoned shed and started drilling me with questions about the reptile."

"Can you blame him after what he went through," said Bill, speaking through his beer mug.

"Yes, yes, I understand that. But you know what he did next?" his wavering voice getting louder. "He took out his gun and threatened to shoot me!" he shouted as all conversation in the bar came to an abrupt stop, and people gazed over to the table.

"I can see why he'd be a little pissed at you, Don. Your vicious reptile nearly had him for lunch," Virgil grinned.

"Yeah, well... That's why I've got to get the hell out of here. If I go on the boat with Taylor and the other cut-throats, I might as well just put a bullet in my head."

"Speaking of the devil," Chuck smiled as he eyed the opened front door. Officer Taylor stood at the entrance for a minute, making his presence known before walking into the bar like he owned the place. Captain Virgil and his crew watched as Don nervously squirmed in his chair.

The officer stood at the bar, ordered a shot of tequila and quickly downed it before ordering another with a Budweiser. He slowly turned and walked over to the table, "Hello, boys," he said, checking his dive watch. "I figured I'd find you here."

"Just having a drink to get the edge off before meeting your friend Bobby," Virgil said, gesturing for Randy to have a seat.

"Me too," replied Randy, sliding a chair from another table over and taking a seat.

"Nick says he believes the reptile is either dead or headed back to the Everglades," Randy said, referring to the mayor and pointing a thumb in Don's direction without looking at him.

"And Nick Myers, with his infinite wisdom, wants us to track it and kill it in the 'glades," Virgil added, lighting a non-filtered camel cigarette.

"In so many words," answered Randy, bumming a cigarette from the pack. "Bobby's getting the boat ready, said it should be ready to go when we get there."

"It's too dangerous," Don murmured.

"What?" replied Randy in mock surprise. "Isn't capturing the reptile the reason why you came down here in the first place?"

"I tried to capture that thing before all hell broke loose." "Sure you did... Too late now," Randy replied callously.

"And since you know more about that monster than anybody, I'm sure you'll find the best way for us to catch it," added Virgil.

"You have no idea what you're up against... that vile reptile tasted human," Don snapped.

"Yes, we know that," said Bill, rolling his eyes.

"Which means the reptile is more dangerous than ever before. If the first attack was merely a mistake, there wouldn't have been the others," Don reasoned. "But no, the reptile has found a new and easy prey."

"You and I both know it, and that is why we have got to hunt and destroy that menace," said Randy. "Unless you'd rather have some more half-assed trappers get killed while thinking they're just hunting a large alligator."

Don sat in silence, mulling over his options as if he had any, before looking up and seeing everybody staring at him. He inhaled deeply, "Okay, I'll be on that boat," he murmured, sounding like he was doing the others a favor.

"No shit," Randy replied. "You thought you had a choice?"

Everybody at the table, excluding Don, broke out laughing and stood up. Don sat nursing his beer and wondered if he'd be alive this time tomorrow.

"Okay, I'll see you guys at Bobby's house in about half an hour," said Randy, giving a tight smile to Don as he walked away.

Captain Virgil and his crew were going to leave with the officer but decided to have one more pitcher for good luck.

"I'm a dead man," Don stated flatly.

"We're all dead men if you don't tell us every little detail about your reptile," Virgil replied.

"I already told Captain Bloodfoot everything, what else can..." "Bloodfoot? Who the hell is Captain Bloodfoot?" Virgil cut in.

"You mean your buddy Randy Taylor didn't tell you about that maniac?"

"No," Virgil looked over to Chuck and Bill with contempt.

"Probably thought you'd change your mind if you knew about him,"

Don speculated.

"Who is Bloodfoot?" Chuck asked.

"The guy came here from Belize and looks like a pirate, and I'm not talking the Jack Sparrow type. This guy is more like Blackbeard times ten," Don explained with enthusiasm. "He hunts all kinds of killer beasts anywhere on the planet, the big bastard sails the world like an eighteenth-century pirate, and I wouldn't put it past him to pillage, plunder and rape either."

"That explains the strange-looking sailboat we spotted anchored offshore," Said Bill.

"Damn right, it is. It looks like a damn pirate ship. I tell you, the guy scares the hell out of me. If I didn't know better, I'd swear he's the reincarnation of Blackbeard himself," Don said uneasily.

"Okay, enough with the Blackbeard crap," Virgil said with a slight grin. "This trip is getting better all the time, Pirates, giant reptiles, Vietnam war heroes. Let's go meet the circus," he continued as he stood up and walked toward the door. Chuck and Bill gave Don a menacing look and followed the Captain out, "You can pay the tab," Chuck said.

22

Officer Randy Taylor left the Anchor Bar and drove directly to the jailhouse where Captain Bloodfoot was sitting in the small cell, finishing his lunch. Randy walked in the front door and was greeted by two officers. They exchanged small talk until they saw that Randy was in a hurry as he asked to open the cell door with the pirate in it.

"Careful, that is one nasty son of a gun," said the officer with the keys, pointing a finger at Bloodfoot.

"I'll be fine George, do me a favor and gather his belongings, he'll be leaving with me," Randy replied, giving him a squeeze on the shoulder.

"I'll trust your judgment Randall, but I'll be right here and ready to shoot if he tries anything," George assured, with a tight grin.

Randy appreciated his concern and wished there were more caring officers like him, but George was the last of a dying breed. At seventy-five years of age, the old man loved his job so much that retirement had never crossed his mind.

George carefully opened the cell door and stepped aside as Randy walked through. He was hesitant to close the door until

Randy gave him a nod. Captain Bloodfoot didn't say a word as he sat on the bunk and watched with curiosity to see what the windswept-looking officer was going to do next.

Randy didn't allow the cold stare from the pirate to intimidate him as he returned the look.

"Captain Bloodfoot, tell me what you know and how you found out about this depraved reptile lurking in my waters," said Randy, bypassing the niceties and getting straight to the point. He tossed his baseball cap on the bed and put a leg up, waiting for a reply.

"Piss off," grumbled Bloodfoot.

"Fine, have it your way. You can stay in this cell until you turn green, or you can help me catch that damn reptile; it's up to you," Randy replied with a withering stare.

Bloodfoot glared back at the officer, not sure what to make of the man, admiring the way he carried himself and the fact that he wasn't easily intimidated. After a long minute, he stood up, walked closer to him and growled, "You're hunting a mutant reptile. It's a cross between an alligator and a crocodile. From what I've heard, it's at least twenty-three feet long with a head about four-foot wide, if you can believe that."

"I believe it because I've already encountered the monster," Randy said, pleased to see the look of surprise on the pirate's face, "And I've got to say that you're about ten-foot short on the actual size."

Bloodfoot was at a loss for words as he stared into Randy's face with a puckered brow, "You encountered the reptile?"

"Sure did, and it's nothing short of a miracle that I'm sitting here to talk about it," replied Randy in an austere tone.

From that moment on, Captain Bloodfoot treated the officer with utmost respect. He reached out and put a big, calloused hand on Randy's shoulder and said, "I see by the look in your eyes that you speak the truth. I've got to admit that it's very rare that a man with no experience with a reptile like this has lived to tell about it. I'll try to answer any questions you have."

"How did you hear about this monster?"

"I was in Belize when I received a call on my satellite phone by a man sounding very anxious for me to come hunt the reptile," Bloodfoot proclaimed regally.

"Who and when did he contact you?"

"I won't tell you the name. I was contacted one week after the reptile escaped from the Everglades Sanctuary."

Randy looked sideways as if trying to see through the pirate, then finally said, "Bhim contacted you."

"Hmm, very astute officer," Bloodfoot smiled, scratching his chin.

"He knows how to contact me because I've done some work for him a while back, but why would he hire me to catch that menace when he gathered up his own hunting party to catch it himself?"

Again, Randy was silent as his mind went over the scenario. "It was Myers... Mayor Nick Myers, the rat bastard!"

"Congratulations, you win," Bloodfoot replied with fervor. "He will pay extra if I do it quickly and quietly without the townspeople getting antsy."

"It's too late for that," Randy grunted, "The entire town is in a panic. That bastard, Myers should get an award for acting like he didn't know about you when we came here earlier,"

Officer Randy Taylor wasn't totally in the dark about the presence of Bloodfoot. When he heard the illustrious pirate was headed to his town, he did his homework, contacted the law enforcement in Belize and requested information on him. Within an hour, Randy had a file two-inches thick faxed over.

Reading the file was like reading an old swashbuckling novel. He scanned through the reports of Bloodfoot's bar fights and illegal smuggling activities. He was like a modern-day pirate born two-hundred years too late. He stopped and thoroughly read the files on his amazing hunting conquests. Captain

Bloodfoot may have done a lot of things legal and illegal for money, but he made the lion's share of his income by hunting large predatorial creatures that no ordinary man would dare encounter. If a client needed something, or in rare cases, somebody out of the way, they could rest assured that Captain Bloodfoot would eliminate the threat, as it was his trademark to bring back the head of his prey to verify the kill. Although it was never proven that he killed a man, the telltale signs showed otherwise as he would always take a tooth of his prey, which he kept as a souvenir or trophy and attached to a leather strap on his boots.

One story caught Randy's eye which seemed too bizarre to believe. He read the report with fervor, which took place eight months ago where Bloodfoot was anchored off the coast of Africa. There had been a fifteen-foot great white shark spotted near a popular swimming beach that didn't want to leave the area. After weeks of eluding capture by local fishermen, area hotels anteed up and hired the renegade to rid the problem.

The fearless pirate jumped in the water with nothing but his trusty hunting bowie knife and a mask. After twenty minutes of splashing around, his crew spotted the large dorsal fin slice through the water and alerted him of the approaching menace.

Most men would have come to their senses and made a

beeline back to the boat, but not Bloodfoot. He grinned impishly and pulled the knife out of its sheath, and dove ten-foot below the swells. Within seconds, he spotted the missile-shaped predator swim past him, curiously checking out its prey. He watched as the giant tail-fin disappeared beyond the blue curtain of vision. He slowly turned in a circular motion and waited for its return. Just as he anticipated, the beast came back from behind and headed straight for him.

Bloodfoot timed it just right and was able to swim below it and plunge his knife deep inside its belly. The startled Great White became enraged and spun around to attack, but with the shark jerking away and the knife buried in its stomach, Bloodfoot was able to slice open the belly, spilling out the contents.

Bloodfoot lost his hold on the shark as his knife came out of its belly and watched with satisfaction as the shark swam away in spasms. He surfaced for another breath of air and returned for the finale. Sure enough, the ill-fated predator returned to get revenge. Again, Bloodfoot escaped the snapping jaws and plunged his knife into the gills, savagely slicing them to shreds.

Standing in the small jail cell with the hulking, rogue pirate left Officer Randy Taylor with little doubt the story was fabricated.

"I've got a crew together and we're heading out to destroy the reptile," Randy said, looking for a reaction.

"Good luck," Bloodfoot responded with a withering stare. "I want you to join me."

"I work alone."

"You'll work with me or not at all," Randy pledged.

Bloodfoot stood quietly with his arms crossed against his chest and his right-hand fingers curling his beard, mulling over his situation. Finally, after several moments, he spoke, "What boat will we be using?"

"A Vietnam Swift boat," Randy replied with a throaty voice.

Bloodfoot's eyes lit up as he recalled the effigy, "A PCF. I believe those relics are about fifty-foot long, made with quarter-inch aluminum alloy construction," he said, cocksure of himself.

"You know the type?"

"Sure do. I acquired one a few years back," replied Bloodfoot with a tight smile. "I commandeered it on the Mekong River when I…"

"Save it Bloodfoot, I'm a law officer. I don't want to hear how you wound up with it," Randy cut him off with a sordid look. "What is a PCF?" "Stands for Patrol Craft Fast," Bloodfoot grumbled caustically, looking offended by the officer's rude interruption. "Anyway, it's a strong boat and should be adequate for the job."

"So, you in or do you want to rot in this cell?" Randy asked with a complacent look.

"Who's coming along for this little adventure?"

"I've got Captain Virgil Goodman, a straight-forward, no-nonsense Tugboat captain, his engineer Chuck McClowski, deckhand Bill Brighton, who's got arms nearly the size of yours, Don Henderson, whom you've already met, Bobby Reynolds, a roughneck from the Vietnam War and owner of the PCF and me."

Bloodfoot sat and considered the list before replying, "Henderson's a pussy; the only good he could do is if we use him for bait."

"I hope you're joking, but since he created this monster, it's only fitting that he comes along for the ride. The rest of the guys are tough as nails. Captain Virgil and his crew came to the rescue twice when the reptile appeared, and there's no way I'd even consider doing this without them."

"Okay, things are beginning to sound a little better. Everybody is aware of what they're getting into."

"All except Reynolds, he's the only one that's never seen it," replied Randy, with a dead-serious look.

"Well then, let's go hunt that beast," said Bloodfoot as he smacked Randy on the shoulder and proceeded to collect his belongings.

"Good," said Randy, rubbing his shoulder and signaling for the guardto unlock the cell door.

Within twenty-minutes, Officer Randy Taylor, along with Captain Bloodfoot parked the jeep at the patrol boat station. Randy called Bobby Reynolds on his cell phone as he jumped in the patrol boat and let him know that he'd be a half-hour late.

He untied the dock lines as Captain Bloodfoot stepped aboard and started the motor. The secretary Cathy, saw the unsightly buccaneer follow in Randy's footsteps and came running out of the office with a worried look, "Officer Taylor! Is everything alright?" she shouted with concern.

Randy put the boat in neutral as it drifted off the dock, "Everything's okay Cathy. This is Captain Bloodfoot and he's coming along with me on the hunt!" he shouted back with a smile. Bloodfoot didn't look at her. He just walked to the center console, shaking his head, wondering what she could possibly due if the officer was truly in danger.

What Lurks Below

When they cleared the dock, Randy pushed the throttle forward and they cruised out through the jetties to where Bloodfoot moored his horrid-looking sailboat.

As they approached, Randy stood with an incredulous look at the sight of the vessel. It looked straight out of an old pirate movie. He was both astonished and amazed at what looked like a replica of an old ninety-foot brig. In a different time and place, it was the preferred ship used by pirates. Looking up at the two square rigged masts, he was at a loss for words.

"What the hell Bloodfoot, where'd you get this... Neverland?"

Bloodfoot never tired of the reactions he got when people first set eyes on the relic, "I found her off the coast of Haiti a while back. Long story short, I had a run-in with some dreadful people and wound up commandeering this ship as well," he replied with a trivial smirk on his face.

The flabbergasted officer was sorry he asked. He didn't want to know how Captain Bloodfoot battled pirates in the Caribbean and ended up withtheir ship. He began to wonder if Bloodfoot was a ghost of days gone past. He swallowed hard and couldn't help but ask one more question,

"Where's your crew? Surely you can't sail this ship by yourself."

"Now you're getting personal Taylor," Bloodfoot grinned.

"But now that you've asked, I've got a crew of twelve onboard," his smile vanished and was replaced with a foreboding stare.

Just as Bloodfoot answered the question, Randy caught sight of a beautiful young lady in a string bikini sunning on deck.

"Women? You've got a crew of women?" Randy was beside himself. "Tahitian," he replied with a devil-may-care grin. "I've got a crew of ten beautiful women from the island and two males for ballast."

"Damnit, the plot thickens," replied Randy. "And don't tell me they're here illegally, and I don't want to see them off this ship," Randy said in a pragmatic tone.

"Don't you worry," Bloodfoot replied as he leaped onto the pirate ship and disappeared below deck.

The officer waited patiently for Bloodfoot to return. He slowly cruised around the massive ship with his patrol boat, amazed at the number of sails wrapped around the masts. He began counting them out loud when Bloodfoot finally poked his head out of the companionway. He barked orders at one of his crew before stepping out on deck and threw a large duffel bag to the deck of the patrol boat.

Randy was still counting the sails when Bloodfoot jumped aboard, "Six sails on the main mast," he said, pointing a finger at each sail as he named them. "The big one is the main sail;

above it is the top sail. The smaller one above it is the top gallant, and the little one on top is the royal," he said proudly.

"Isn't that where you would normally display the Jolly Roger?" Randy mused.

Captain Bloodfoot ignored the pun and continued, "On the backside of the mast, you'll see the trysail, on top of that, a spanker," he concluded.

"That explains the crew of twelve. It would be literally impossible for one man to sail this substantial ship," Randy added for good measure.

Captain Bloodfoot smiled to himself and came to the conclusion that the good officer didn't know much about sailing ships.

Randy stretched his neck one last time for a peek at the bathing beauty before turning the patrol boat toward the inlet and pushing the throttles all the way forward. The boat responded with a throaty roar as it leaped forward and quickly sped off to meet the hunting party at Bobby Reynolds' dock.

Captain Virgil Goodman and his two crew members arrived at Bobby's house an hour behind schedule but were still the first ones there. Surprised that nobody was there yet, they knocked on the enormous front door. When nobody answered, Bill and Chuck followed the captain through a side gate leading to the back yard.

The well-manicured lawn wrapped around a large swimming pool with a waterfall flowing near the deep end. Palm trees swayed freely with the breeze as the men walked further down a pathway leading to a large cement dock, complete with a fully stocked tiki bar.

They made their way to the dock and spotted the old Swift Boat. The well-kept PCF looked brand new.

"Well, well, well," a smiling Bill said as he clasped his hands together. "I see we're going to hunt that reptile in style," he continued, pointing to the twin fifty-caliber cannons sitting in a large guntub behind the wheelhouse. "Don't get your hopes up," came a voice from inside the wheelhouse. A short, muscular figure appeared in the doorway, wiping his hands with a rag. "Those cannons won't roar. They hadn't been used in over thirty-five years. I'm Virgil Goodman. This is Chuck McClouski and Bill Brighton, my humble crew," Virgil said, extending a hand toward his crew as he made the introductions.

The man who looked like an older version of Rambo jumped to the dock and extended a hand, "I'm Bobby Reynolds."

"You've got quite a place here Bob," Bill said, as he tried to spark up some small talk.

Bobby gazed over to Bill and replied in a relatively short manner that killed all hopes of a conversation, "It'll do."

Chuck smiled impishly when he saw the shocked look on Bill's face from the short reply and walked toward the stern of the old boat to conceal his face.

Bobby Reynolds grew up in the luxurious mansion that sat overlooking the Intracoastal Waterway, and reluctantly inherited it when his parents were tragically killed in an automobile accident ten years earlier.

On the fateful evening, Bobby had planned to take his parents out to dinner to celebrate their fiftieth wedding anniversary. They were just heading out the door when the phone rang. Bobby met the disappointed look in his mother's eyes as he answered the call. Being a career soldier, his presence was needed at an emergency meeting, which only made matters worse when he couldn't tell his parents the details.

Bobby insisted the two go out as planned and enjoy a nice evening without him. He remembered hustling them out the door as he ignored their plea to wait for another day.

The next morning, when he arrived back home, he was greeted by the local police who gave him the tragic news of how his parents were killed in a head-on collision with a massive eighteen-wheeler. The police reported that the bright lights of the oncoming truck apparently frightened the elder driver, causing him to steer the car straight-on into its path.

Bobby never forgave himself for insisting they go out without him. If he was with them, he'd have been driving and there'd be no accident. After a while, he found the only way to relieve the pain and guilt was through a bottle of Jack Daniels every night. Before he knew it, he drank himself into a forced retirement from the Marines.

Now, at the age of sixty-one and alone in the big, empty house, the only thing that kept him busy and his mind from wandering was tinkering with his Vietnam Swift Boat that he somehow acquired from the armed forces.

As the men stood on the dock getting acquainted, a loud police siren sounded for a brief second, enough to make everybody jump but Captain Virgil, who casually turned his head to see Officer Randy Taylor and a large figure that looked like a pirate idle up to the dock.

Captain Bloodfoot leaped to the dock; his eyes took in the beautiful, luxurious scenery. He smiled to himself with approval at the beautiful green lawn with luscious plants and flowers placed in all the right places. A large statue of a naked lady pouring water from a jug sat in the middle of a circular fountain with a circumference of twenty-five-feet.

Randy turned off the motor and stood with his hands on his waist, marveling at the beautiful property. He wondered how guys like Bobby Reynolds could possibly care about beautiful greenery and flowers and still keep their to-hell-with-the-world reputations.

The introductions were made, and Bloodfoot quickly realized he was completely wrong in sizing up Bobby. After viewing the man's back-yard floral abilities, he pictured Bobby to be one of those rich, soft-palmed, spoiled momma's boy types. And since his parents obviously had money, he imagined Bobby's stint in Vietnam came with a silver spoon and that he probably never had to risk his life in a Swift Boat like the one sitting at his dock.

"You like this boat. I see the way you're checking her out," Bobby said with a cocky grin to Bloodfoot.

"I used to own a similar one, not in this shape, though," replied Bloodfoot, with a nod of approval.

"I picked this beauty up in 'nam while serving in the MRF, Mobile Rivereen Force. A young guy like you probably never heard of it," he laughed and gave him a smug look.

"The Brown Water Navy," Bloodfoot acknowledged, returning the stare.

"You got it kid, you're not as dumb as you look," replied Bobby, giving Bloodfoot a friendly slap on the back.

Virgil, Chuck and Randy saw what was going on and sort of froze on the dock, waiting to see what Bloodfoot was going to do about the lack of respect he was getting from the old veteran.

Bobby continued, "Yessiree, me and the boys ran this boat all through the dirty waters that permeated the rivers and canals on the Mekong Delta." "I'm impressed," replied Bloodfoot, deciding to let the old man have his fun and not beat him to a pulp. He liked the old guy. The vet still had some piss-n-vinegar and Bloodfoot felt he'd fit in perfectly with this oddball hunting outfit he was stuck with.

Don Henderson finally showed up and made his way through the backyard. He nearly tripped and fell into the swimming pool as he nervously eyed the dock, hoping the officer or pirate changed their mind and decided not to go. No such luck; everybody was there, and nobody greeted him at the dock. The men were gathered around the dull green Swiftboat with black camouflage patterns as Bobby thoroughly reviewed the vessel's specifications.

"This boat is fifty feet long with a beam of thirteen and a half feet. The draft is about four feet, which should be our only downside on this mission, especially if we end up as far back as the Everglades," he paused, anticipating that somebody would ask why they needed such a large and powerful boat to catch an alligator. When nobody said anything, he continued. "This boat is constructed in seven sections. There's the forepeak, which is used for storage and you can enter through this hatch," he said, pointing to a small hatch just forward of the pilothouse. "Over here, we have the crew quarters. Unfortunately it has only three bunks and a head.

"Where the hell are the rest of us going to bunk?" Don complained as nobody listened or acknowledged.

"The pilothouse is where I will be in total control. It has nine fixed windows all around, meaning they don't open and I'll be sweating my ass off," he said dourly.

"Don't you worry about getting sweaty Bob. I'm the captain of this party," Virgil said flatly.

"He's right Bobby. Like you agreed on when I called, we need your boat, not you. Virgil is the captain," Officer Taylor stated firmly.

"It's my goddamn boat!" Bobby shrieked.

"It's your boat, my party. Captain Virgil will be the man in control of this vessel," Randy repeated, a little surprised that Bobby had completely forgotten what they had talked about when he asked for his help days earlier. He chalked it up to the many years of drugs and alcohol as the reason he forgot important details.

Bobby recovered and continued in a low, somber tone, "Here's the deckhouse. Two more of you pragmatic ruffians can bunk in there, so don't get your panties in a bundle," he said, glaring at Don with a balled fist. "It also has a galley with a refrigerator and sink; any questions?" he asked, losing his ambition to carry on with the tour.

"What kind of propulsion does she have," asked Chuck.

Bobby's eyes lit up again, and everybody followed him to the engine room. "Two General Motors, Detroit Marine diesel, starboard mode equipped with two big-ass blowers. It has four-hundred and eighty horsepower, using the N-Seventy type injectors, SM-One-Eighteen Hydraulic Marine Gear Clutch with 1.15:1 reduction gears and driving two counter-rotating screws," he proudly answered like a kid bragging about his toys on Christmas morning.

Nobody except Chuck knew what Bobby was talking about but still shook their heads and whistled with approval.

"You've done a great job taking care of this boat," Chuck said as he admired the cleanest engine room he'd ever seen on a boat this age.

"Much thanks, coming from an engineer," Bobby replied.

Once everybody stowed their duffel bags, Virgil called the men to order, "Okay, before we get this party started, I want to go over a few things and make sure we all know our place on this trip," he said, enforcing authority. "First thing, I'm the captain and what I say goes...Clear?"

As expected, Bloodfoot spoke up. "What makes you think you're qualified to be captain?"

"The simple fact that I'm probably the only boat captain here with an actual license, for one. And because I'm being blackmailed into this trip and I'll be damned if one of you runs this boat into trouble while I'm on it," Virgil replied intensely.

"Captain Virgil has seen this creature and has demonstrated nerves of steel when confronted by it. I don't believe there is another captain anywhere who I'd rather have for this trip."

"I'll trust your praise for the captain and hope he's as good as you say," replied Bloodfoot, taking a seat on the gunwale.

He watched Virgil as he dismissed the crew and made his way to the pilothouse. He liked him. He decided they both were cut from the same mold; how tough he actually is, is what remained to be seen.

The rest of the crew pretty much knew what was expected of

them, all except for Don. His nerves were shot and the thought of the reptile becoming more ferocious than ever before made him wonder if it was too late to even attempt to kill it. He was also well aware that if the monster didn't kill him, the crew might.

An hour later, the Swift Boat was stocked with enough provisions, booze, fuel and ammo to last a week. Chuck accompanied Bobby to the engine room where he fired up the twin diesels. Bill took a quick check to see if anything was left on the dock and cast off the lines as Captain Virgil engaged the engines and began to cruise up the Himmershee River.

As they crept slowly up river, half of the crew was in the pilothouse conversing and keeping a sharp eye out for the reptile while Bill, Don and Randy dropped a Dibson DH model sonar off the side of the boat, tethered by a twenty-foot line to monitor below the surface.

They vigilantly cruised up the river and came upon the area of the latest attack, "Wow! The damn thing shredded both the sailboat and the dock," Virgil said as he surveyed the damage.

The once beautiful sailboat sat on its side, facing away from what was once the dock. Three-quarters of the yacht was under water, and there was a yellow barrier around the hull to contain the spilled fuel and oil. The area looked like a ghost town except for the dog sitting near the broken dock wagging its tail and watching the old relic cruise by.

"I bet that dog could tell us a story," Bloodfoot murmured to Virgil as they both stared at the dog, knowing the poor mutt must have gone through hell with the reptile.

They continued their slow and uneventful cruise up the river for the rest of the afternoon. At one time or another, everybody but Bloodfoot made it known that they thought maybe the creature went back to Sandy Beach park instead of the Everglades. Only Bloodfoot seemed to know they were tracking in the right direction.

The sun was descending in the west when the old boat came to a stop near a clump of saw grass at the beginning of the Everglades. Bobby threw the anchor out in the center of the river and dragged it until it snagged the bottom. At that point, Virgil shutdown the engine and did a visual check around the boat, making sure all was in order.

Chuck watched as Bobby grabbed a beer out of a small cooler and made his way to the engine room. He curiously followed slowly behind. Sure enough, just as he thought, Bobby was wiping down the engine and checking the vital parts for wear and tear.

"Now here's a man who loves his boat," Chuck stated with a

smile.

"Just want to make sure she keeps performing like a Vegas Showgirl," replied Bobby, chewing on an unlit cigar.

Chuck grabbed a seat on the gunwale and shot the bull with Bobby until the sun was dead and gone.

For the first time since they left Bobby's dock, Virgil was glad the windows surrounding the pilothouse were closed. The mosquitoes and no-see-ums were deadly in the Everglades when the sun went down.

Bloodfoot exited the pilothouse as Virgil made an entry in his logbook. Before he was finished, the door opened and Bloodfoot returned with a couple beers.

"Cheers Captain," he said, tossing a Budweiser to Virgil as he crashed down in a chair.

"Tell me Bloodfoot, what makes you so sure the reptile is headed back for the Everglades?" asked Virgil, taking a liberal gulp from the bottle.

"I follow instinct," he replied furtively. "Did you see the look on that dog's face when we passed by earlier? At first, I thought maybe it was still scared from the attack, but then I noticed strange things further up river."

"Go on."

"There were no ducks in the water. Never in my travels did I see so many ducks along the bank of a river that are too afraid to get in the water unless they are afraid of something," he said with a look of conviction.

Virgil finished his beer and sat looking at the pirate for a minute as if mulling over what he said. In conclusion, he stood up and gave Bloodfoot a friendly slap on the back, "Okay, I'll buy that. We'll continue the hunt at first light."

"First light it is then," replied Bloodfoot, following Virgil out the door and into the galley where Don just finished preparing a dinner for the crew.

23

White Egrets and Ibis birds were staked out along the stunning wetlands and cypress hammocks of the Everglades. The yellowish-orange glow of the morning sun rose peacefully as the hungry marauders sought after breakfast. What they didn't notice was the hideous-looking reptile as it sat motionless on a grassy bank of the river with its mouth open, waiting for the unsuspecting deer or wild boar to venture too close.

Suddenly, its lucid eyes opened as it sensed something large moving in the river not far away. With its vibratory senses tingling, it became progressively eager when it felt the presence of not one but two objects in the water. The mammoth creature slowly closed its mouth and silently crept closer to the water's edge.

"C'mon Linda, get your butt in gear!" said her friend Janis.

"Why don't you chill out for a minute and enjoy this beautiful morning," replied Linda, as she snapped pictures of every bird and plant that materialized in her viewfinder.

"Look at you girl, you think you're another Clyde Butcher," Janis teased, referring to the well-known nature photographer.

"Well, you never know sweetie. Maybe one day I'll actually publish these pictures," Linda retorted with a lazy smile as she lagged behind her friend by a good twenty yards.

Friends since childhood, the two girlfriends were in their early fifties. They were taking their once-a-month kayak trip through the eastern side of the Everglades.

Children of the sixties; they fell in with the wrong group of kids and eventually dabbled in drugs. Janis was smart enough to quit before she would eventually follow the flock of hippies and get into the hard drugs. Soon after, their friendship was tested when Linda took LSD at a rock concert and never quite recovered.

Janis tried to reason with her friend, and her parents were at wit's end trying to regain their daughter, but Linda eventually ran away from home to join a commune. A few months later, after giving away everything she owned, Janis intervened for one last ditch effort to save her estranged friend and snatched her away from the degenerates.

Linda's parents turned their back on her when they saw how withdrawn she looked. They were horrified to see how their little girl had turned into a drugged-out vegetable of a person.

With nowhere else to go and no prospects of having a normal life anytime soon, she accepted the invitation to live with Janis until she could take control of her life again.

Janis bought Linda a camera in hopes that she might take up an interest in photography and get her mind focused again. To the exhilaration of her parents and best friend, Linda began her lifelong amateur career of taking wildlife photos.

As an added step to regain her health and stay fit, Janis suggested they purchase a couple of kayaks and travel through the Everglades at least once a month.

"C'mon Linda, you're lagging again. I've got to go to work in a couple hours, remember?" Janis pleaded.

"Okay, here I come," replied Linda, stowing her camera in her backpack and reaching for the paddle.

Janis drifted slowly ahead, waiting for her friend to catch up. She set the paddle across her legs and reached in her backpack for a bottled water. With one foot dangling in the water, she unscrewed the bottle cap and tilted her head back to take a sip, and then she saw it.

Startled and excited at the same time, she couldn't believe what she was looking at. Crawling down the river bank just forty yards behind Linda was the biggest monstrosity she had ever seen. She slowly put the bottle down and slipped her foot back in the kayak.

The perilous reptile seemed to come out of nowhere and crept closer to the water. Janis became alarmed when she noticed that when she pulled her foot out of the water, the creature seemed to stop and look in her direction.

She swallowed hard as she watched the reptile rest on the riverbank with its enormous head just touching the water. Its mouth cracked open just enough to make it look like it had an evil grin as it stared at the kayaks.

Linda finally caught up to her friend and observed the queer look on her face, "Thanks for waiting speedy. What's with the look on your..."

"Shhh," Janis cut in, trying to remain calm while pointing at the gargantuan reptile.

Linda had a perplexed look on her face as she followed her friend's finger and instantly panicked when she saw what Janis was pointing at. With her eyes bulging, she opened her mouth as if to scream, but the only audible sound came out like a terrified squeak from a rat.

"Linda! It's okay, stay calm," Janis tried to whisper. "Alligators aren't known to attack people in kayaks... so chill out," she forged a smile and gave a reassuring wink as she grabbed her paddle tightly like a vise grip.

"Oh my God! Don't you watch the news?" Linda replied with

what she thought was a whisper but could be heard even fifty-feet away.

"Not lately, why?"

"Look at the size of that thing! It's the monster!" Linda screamed uncontrollably as she burst out crying.

"Shhhh, calm down, it's just a big, ugly alligator. Relax and enjoy nature. It's not often you can get face to face with these beauties," Janis replied with an Australian accent, imitating the phrase used by Steve Erwin on the crocodile shows she'd seen on television.

As Janis was talking to Linda and trying to calm her down, she got a closer look at the gargantuan reptile. The hideous-looking head was wider than anything she thought possible and had the most horrible, jagged teeth she'd ever seen on an alligator, or any animal for that matter. Its girth looked big enough to swallow both kayaks whole and the claws were more than a foot long with dagger-like nails.

All of a sudden, it dawned on her. She felt her heart sink to the pit of her stomach, and she could feel her heartbeat pounding in her ears as she became aware that she and her friend were in grave danger.

It hit her like a ton of bricks, but it was too late. When she realized they were face to face with the monstrous reptile, she'd heard in the news when it attacked the kite-boarder. Being out of town for the last couple of days, she only heard of the reptile while having the television on in the background and didn't pay much attention to the details, especially when the mayor himself was heard saying the news media was trying to make a big story out of nothing. Even so, the attack she heard about was in the ocean, not over twenty miles away in the Everglades.

Janis took a deep breath and tried to remain calm as she looked over to Linda. She knew they had to get out of there fast and didn't like what she saw when she observed her friend hyperventilating and trembling uncontrollably.

"Linda," she whispered. "Do you think you can paddle quietly out of here?"

Linda tried to answer, but nothing came out.

"Linda! Can you paddle out of here?" she repeated in a more forceful tone.

"Yes, let's go," she squeaked out, her arms trembling so hard that the paddle vibrated on the side of the kayak.

Janis cautiously adjusted herself in the seat and slipped the paddle in the water. She gave two long strokes and the kayak gracefully moved downriver. Linda felt abandoned as she watched her friend paddle away, but quickly dismissed the thought in her mind and took a long, deep breath and attempted to follow.

She grasped the paddle with her trembling hands, and it splashed awkwardly into the water. The reptile responded to the splash by opening its large jaws and emitting a guttural hissing sound while it turned its hideous head toward the terrified quarry, seemingly enjoying the torment.

Linda felt paralyzed as she tried to regain control of herself and paddle away. Janis looked in awe at the mind-boggling size of the beast and tried to remain calm and not tell her friend that the grotesque reptile was now in the water with only its massive tail on the bank. She thought it eerie to see how the reptile sat there watching, waiting to see what its quarry was going to do next. She tried to convince herself that the repulsive reptile was just a huge, misfit creature on this beautiful planet, but something deep down in the pit of her stomach told her the creature lurking in the water was pure evil. The way it seemed to take pleasure in terrifying Linda sent shivers up her spine.

"Let's go Linda... move smoothly, try not to splash and stay focused on me, don't look behind you," she persisted, her voice cracking as she held back tears.

Linda couldn't reply, she could feel the bile rising up in her throat and tried to fight it off by swallowing. She looked at her friend in the eye and nodded her head as Janis returned the nod and gave her a reassuring wink. Linda could see the fear in her friend's eyes as she began to paddle toward her, but she was too scared to turn around and see what the creature was doing.

She finally caught up to Janis and they continued their escape downriver. They quickly paddled around a bend when they heard a loud splash where the reptile had been. Never in their wildest nightmares would they have thought the reptile would give chase.

"Oh my God, Linda! I think it's chasing after us!" Janis cried out, her calm reserve gone astray. "We've got to paddle faster!"

Linda was on the verge of a breakdown. In a panic, she dropped the paddle and looked over to Janis as the distance grew between them. She dreadfully looked back at the paddle drifting away and knew there was no way she could retrieve it. She screamed out in horror when the kayak slowly came to a stop and started drifting sideways near the river bank, "Janis!... Help me!... God help meeee!"

Janis had no idea that Linda had fallen behind and quickly turned her kayak around. Her heart sank when she saw that

Linda's paddle was in the water. She wanted to help, but there was no way that she was going to go back towards the dreadful reptile.

"Linda! Listen to me. You've got to get out of the kayak and swim to the river bank!"

"I can't do it Janis! I'm scared!"

"Get to the river bank or that monster will get you!" Janis cried out, screaming and crying at the top of her lungs.

Linda thought about it for another minute before she flipped out of the kayak and swam ten feet to the grassy bank. Janis was relieved for a brief moment to see Linda crawling out of the water. No sooner did she stand up to walk out, when she came to a complete stop.

"Oh, my God! I'm stuck in the mud!" she cried out, looking over to Janis with an incredulous look.

Linda was stuck up to her knees in the mud. The loose silt and sediment felt like quicksand as she tried unsuccessfully to free herself.

Janis gasped as she saw what looked like a submarine come around the bend just below the surface, leaving a large wake behind.

"Oh my God Linda! Here it comes!... Get out of the water!"

Janis squealed.

Linda's nerves were shot as her body gave up trying to pull herself free. She balled her fists in her hair and started pulling as she screamed for somebody to help her.

"Linda! Get your ass out of the water now!" Janis screamed at the topof her lungs, tearfully watching the creature closing in.

"I can't, I'm stuck in this mud!" She screamed morbidly, pulling a lock of hair out of her head.

"Linda, please!" Janis pleaded before she witnessed the mammoth reptile leap out of the water and clamp its massive jaws around her best friend, dragging her back like a rag doll below the surface. The brackish water turned a dark cherry red as it erupted in an explosion of vehemence.

All went quiet for a long moment until Linda's head surfaced and her blood-curdling screams seemed to echo for miles. The reptile swam through the muck with Linda in its hideous mouth. Janis vomited as she watched the macabre scene unfold and fought the urge to pass out when she heard a loud crunch as the reptile chomped down on Linda and caused blood to erupt through her nose and mouth. When Janis thought she witnessed the worst thing possible, the sinister creature shook its head violently from side to side, slicing through flesh and bone as it continued chomping. Linda's lifeless body seemed to explode as arms and mutilated legs detached and flew through the air.

Janis felt completely numb and removed from her body as her mind couldn't comprehend what just happened to her best friend. She looked on in dreadfulness, fighting to regain her senses and escape.

The reptile was nearly finished eating Linda when Janis finally was able to take control of herself. She knew she had to get out of there quickly before the beast turned on her.

Janis turned the kayak away from the monster and paddled as fast as she could. Her plan was to find a place to come ashore and run for her life, but she began to cry hysterically when she noticed there was no place to land her kayak, as it was low tide with at least ten feet of muck between her and dry land.

The menacing reptile lifted its head and swallowed the remains of Linda before turning to see where its other quarry had gone.

Janis had the kayak moving through the river so fast she was nearly a quarter-mile downstream by the time the beast gave chase. She rounded another bend and was out of sight when she heard the unmistakable splash from behind.

What Lurks Below

Oh my God! This can't be happening! Since when do alligators just keep eating? She thought. She knew better than to look behind to see how close the reptile was. Instead, she chose to keep paddling as hard as she could while she was able.

I hope I can beat that thing... Maybe it'll get tired of chasing me and just go away since it already ate... Linda. Sure wish I knew more about alligators... Doesn't matter, that thing chasing me is no ordinary gator anyway.

All those thoughts were going through her mind as she quickly rounded another bend in the river and was relieved to see two men fishing on the banks with cane poles.

Wilbur Jenkins and Todd Johnson were self-proclaimed outdoors men who prided themselves with living off the land. They hunted, fished and gathered everything they needed to survive off the land, all except for their cooler of beer, which they were able to trade their much sought after, homemade wild-boar-jerky for the continuous flow.

Both were divorced with children and chose to escape the confines of society and live in the Everglades rather than live by the social order of the city.

Janis was exhausted and about to scream for help when she spotted a small clearing just past the two men. It looked like hardened sand instead of the muck her friend got stuck in, and would make for a good spot to land the kayak on.

Her arms felt like they were about to explode. The lactic acid shot through her veins as she raced past the men before turning toward the landing spot. She expertly maneuvered the kayak between patches of saw grass and continued paddling for the race of her life.

The fishermen gave an approving whistle as she passed by, exposing her tanned, muscular body through Daisy-Duke cutoffs and tank top.

The Kayak skidded to a stop twenty yards past the men as Janis dropped the paddle and sprang out of her seat in one hurried motion. She landed on her knees and rolled a couple times before getting to her feet and making a mad dash up the embankment.

Wilbur and Todd grinned at each other, dropping their fishing poles and scurrying over to see what kind of crazy lady would be racing a kayak through the Everglades by herself.

"Hey, hey... Slow down young lady, you won the race," Todd said with a light-hearted chuckle.

Wilbur smiled as he killed off another beer and smashed the empty can flat before putting it in his back pocket.

Janis ignored the banter while she scratched and clawed her way to the top of the fifteen-foot embankment. When at the top, she turned and searched the water and was about to say something before collapsing from exhaustion.

Wilbur and Todd followed her up the mound with their eyes and came to the conclusion that the lady was on some kind of drug, "What the hell's she on?" Todd asked, as he slowly began to climb up the hill. "Why don't you secure the kayak and we'll bring the little lady to camp and get her some help," he continued, grunting and wheezing up the steep embankment.

When Wilbur didn't answer, he stopped climbing and looked down to his buddy. "Hey Will, you alright?"

Todd turned and sat down as he watched Wilbur near the water's edge, staring wide-eyed upriver with his mouth agape.

"Wilbur, you drunk bastard! What are you lookin' at? Is your fishin' pole doin' a dance? You got a fish on?"

Todd's joking was cut short when he saw the look of horror on his friend's face. He stood up and looked upriver to see what was so dreadful.

"What the..."

The fishermen stood staring at the large anomaly in the water heading in their direction. As it came closer, the men became sickened to see two sinister eyes and a hideous snout poking just above the surface.

"OH Sheeeiiit!" they said in unison, before Wilbur bolted up the embankment, hoping it didn't see them.

"What the hell is that!?" he shouted anxiously, trying to catch his breath. "Never in all my years had I ever set eyes on such a demonic reptile," replied Todd, his heart beating so hard that the side of his neck was pulsating.

Janis regained consciousness at the same time the gruesome reptile surfaced and slowly crawled out of the water beside the kayak. The sadistic eyes were fixed on the three objects of prey on the embankment as the reptile nudged the kayak with its enormous snout.

The two fishermen stood at the top of the hill, hoping they were reasonably safe when Janis began to shout, "You stupid alligator! I'm up here!" she laughed hysterically.

Todd tried to stay as calm as possible when he put his hand on her shoulder and squeezed, "You had better quiet down because if that monster comes up here, we've got no place to run."

"That son of a bitch couldn't make it up here," she hissed, obviously delusional.

What Lurks Below

Wilbur gave the thirty-plus foot reptile a timid look and disagreed, "On the contrary lady, this mound we're standing on is only about fifteen-foot high and that prehistoric monster can easily snatch us up in a flash, so keep quiet and don't move," he ordered.

The reptile crawled further out of the water, sending goose bumps up the fishermen's spines. Janis turned to see what was on the other side of the embankment in hopes of a clear getaway, but there was nothing but swamp.

Paralyzed with fear, the three held their breath and stared eye to eye with the beast for over an hour, waiting to see what it would do next. When the mid-morning sun began to heat the swampy area, the grotesque reptile retreated to the water. The malicious eyes never left its prey as it sank below the surface.

Janis and the fishermen warily watched the reptile swim upriver and disappear around the bend.

"Why is it going back the way it came?" Wilbur wondered out loud. "It probably has a specific area where it lives, I think they're territorial creatures," Todd answered, "One thing for sure though, we can't go back to our campsite," he said flatly, as it was in the same direction as the reptile.

"Well, let's get the hell out of here before it comes back," said

Wilbur, in a shaky tone.

The three of them walked the length of the embankment for about one hundred yards until it ended and gradually sloped down near the water. They took turns watching behind them to see if the creature would return while they walked another two miles in ankle deep marsh.

It was early afternoon when they came upon a dirt road and found a campsite with hunters that agreed to drive them to Janis' car, but when warned about the vicious predator, they laughed and promised to invite them to a gator-tail barbeque.

24

Randy Taylor was sitting in a lounge chair, smoking a large Perdomo Habano cigar under a shady umbrella on the bow of the swift boat while the morning sun baked him like a roast. It was his turn for lookout as he watched every splash and ripple in the water through binoculars.

The rest of the men were huddled at the small table in the galley, looking over various maps of the Everglades before continuing their search for the monster.

Bill stood up and stretched while Bloodfoot pinpointed some areas on the map where he thought the reptile may be. He looked out of a porthole and shook his head before stepping out and joining Randy.

"Find anything interesting?" Bill asked, inviting a conversation. "Found some good fishing holes, but no luck in locating the creature." Randy replied as a two-inch ash broke from the cigar and crashed to the deck.

Bill took a seat on the gunwale, squinting his eyes, he looked over toward a boat ramp sixty-yards away, "Who else knows about this hunting trip?"

"Nobody to my knowledge. Myers wants to keep this as quiet

as possible," replied Randy, blowing a smoke ring.

"Hmm, interesting," Bill responded with a hint of doubt. "I wonder what that guy at the boat ramp is looking at."

Randy turned to see what Bill was talking about. Sure enough, there was a man watching them through binoculars. At first, he thought it might be a tourist checking out the Everglades, but when the man became aware of them watching him, he jumped in his dark colored Lincoln Continental and sped off.

"News media?" Bill inquired.

"Too rugged looking," replied Randy, smacking a mosquito off his neck and tossing the binoculars to Bill. "It's your turn to stand watch," he continued, tossing him the binoculars and moving toward the galley.

Little did they know the assassin simply known as Wolf was tracking them since they left Bobby's dock.

Don was busy cooking chili in the small galley when Bobby bumped his arm while reaching for a bottle of apricot brandy, "Excuse me," he murmured.

"Excused," Don replied with a smile, happy that somebody on the boat spoke to him. "By the way, why do they call this a Swift Boat?"

Bobby acted as if he hadn't heard him and walked away. He didn't like Don. He thought of himself as a good judge of character and as far as he was concerned, Don had none.

"As Bobby explained earlier, this boat was used to run around the rivers in Vietnam. It was small enough and maneuverable, enabling it to work well in a tight situation," Randy explained, before grabbing Don by the shoulder and whispering, "Let me give you some free advice. Stay out of Bobby's way; you seem to get on his nerves worse than mine. But unlike me, I think he'd actually kill you if he knew that you were the cause of that sadistic reptile."

Before he could continue making Don feel as unwanted as a leper, he sped off to the pilothouse when Captain Virgil shouted his name.

"You've got a radio call," said Virgil, handing him the mic as he walked through the door.

"This is Officer Taylor to dispatch, come back over."

"Sorry to bother you, but I thought you'd want to know that I've been inundated with calls about a pirate ship entering the Port."

Randy's face went rigid as he held the mic in one hand and stepped out of the pilothouse, placing his foot on the gunwale. He listened with a disdainful glare toward Bloodfoot until the dispatcher was finished, and then calmly replaced the mic on the radio.

"Bloodfoot! We need to talk!" he shouted at the top of his lungs.

Less than a minute later, Bloodfoot walked into the pilothouse with a serene look, "What do you want Taylor," he said with a low, throaty voice, lacking any respect he once showed the officer.

"What did I tell you about your ship!" he continued shouting, the veins pulsating on his forehead and neck. "You can't bring that pirate ship into the Port!"

"It's the least you and Mayor Myers can do for me," Bloodfoot retorted, looking Randy dead in the eye.

"Now look here Bloodfoot," Randy said in a calmer tone, "There's going to be a big problem with your pirate ship docking in Port."

As the officer discussed his disapproval of the pirate ship, Bloodfoot's second in command slowly guided the old ship straight to a berth normally used for big cargo ships.

Most of the boats in the Port seemed to stop what they were doing and looked in amazement as the relic from a different age cruised through and prepared to dock.

Immediately after the pirate ship stopped, a patrol boat with sirens wailing and flashing blue lights descended on the ship.

"Well Bloodfoot, looks like your ship has docked and all hell is breaking loose," Randy said rancorously, raising his hands to the sky and giving the pirate a look of ill-will while listening to the scene unfold on the radio.

He grabbed the mic and called to the officer at the scene, "This is Officer Randy Taylor, can I get a ten-forty-three on the pirate ship docked in berth eight, over," he said, requesting information.

Officer Terry Johansen was quick to respond, "You're not going to believe this!"

"What's your twenty," Randy spat out, his irritation growing.

"I've pulled up alongside what appears to be a pirate ship illegally docked at berth eight," he replied anxiously.

Randy cursed under his breath before continuing, "Do not pursue the crew and stay clear of the vessel."

"Stay clear?" the confused officer asked.

"Stay clear. The captain of the vessel is working with me and I'll take full responsibility for his ship, over," Randy brusquely replied, slamming the mic down on the radio. He paced back and forth a few steps before speaking to Bloodfoot, "I thought

I made it clear for you to keep your damn ship out of the Port," he growled.

"I heard you loud and clear Taylor, I just didn't think it was a good idea," replied Bloodfoot.

"You can't dock your damn pirate ship in berth eight. It's for large container ships, besides, do you know what kind of attention that thing is going to draw?"

"If you don't like it," he answered condescendingly, "I can always leave and you and your boy scouts here can hunt the reptile without me."

"You hunt this thing with us or go back to jail, Bloodfoot," Randy replied acidly.

"Blackmail, I like that... Builds character," Bloodfoot said, spitting out a huge wad of Redman chewing tobacco.

"That's right, you've been blackmailed the same as the rest of us on this wonderful cruise," Randy shot back sadistically.

"You want my help, my ship stays put," Bloodfoot affirmed. "If that greedy little cunning mayor expects me to risk my life and kill the beast so that he can continue counting tourist money, the very least he can do is let me dock my ship in the Port."

"You came here on your own free will to catch that

godforsaken reptile," replied Randy.

"To hunt alone, not with this crew," Bloodfoot grumbled explicitly.

Bloodfoot had him on the spot and he knew it. The pirate radiated a winning sneer because he knew Randy needed him.

After pondering the idea to dig out more information on the pirate, Randy decided to let it go and replied, "Fine, the ship stays in the Port. But I want you and that ship out of here when this is over."

"Agreed," Bloodfoot replied.

"Fantastic, now let's quit squabbling like old hens and get the show on the road," Randy said, turning and walking toward the stern and wondering if it would have been easier just to shoot the ravenous pirate.

Bloodfoot leaned on the gunwale and watched Randy walk away and wondered the same.

"Bill, hoist the anchor, prepare to move on!" Virgil shouted out of the wheelhouse door as he cranked the engine. "Bloodfoot spotted some areas on the chart that look like a good place to start hunting."

Bill pulled the anchor up and took a position on the bow where he could act as a lookout. As he scanned the area, his eyes drifted toward the boat ramp where he caught a glimpse of the black car as it returned and followed on a dirt road. He was thinking about telling Randy until he saw Bloodfoot standing with a foot on the gunwale, watching the car with a fierce look.

Before Bill could get his attention and opinion about the car, a call came in on the radio, "Harbor Patrol to Officer Taylor, come back."

Randy was standing next to the receiver and quickly responded before the call was repeated, "This is Officer Taylor, what's on your mind Jackie?" "I've got heart-wrenching news about the reptile," she replied dolefully.

Jackie Caldwell was one of two dispatchers at Harbor Patrol. Married to her high school sweetheart at age eighteen and a mother of two at twenty, she never had a chance to pursue her lifelong dream of becoming a police officer like her father and two brothers had done. When offered the dispatcher job, she readily accepted, as a way to get her foot in the door where she could work her way up the ladder.

"Go ahead Jackie, what have you got?"

"The reptile was last seen by the Tommy Tiger camp near the preserve. It attacked two kayakers."

"Damn, are they alright," Randy asked with trepidation.

After a short pause, she took a deep breath and continued, "One dead, the other in shock."

"Damnit, okay Jackie, keep me posted. We'll head over and see what we can find, over and out," Randy replied, looking at Virgil through vexed eyes. "Where is the Tommy Tiger camp?" asked Virgil, preparing to throttle up the engine.

"It's a hunting campsite about two miles from here," replied Randy, removing his holstered forty-four magnum and checking to see that it was fully loaded. "Right now it will look abandoned, but during hunting season, you'll find every redneck hunter in the state there."

Captain Virgil mashed the throttle forward and the old relic responded with a deep tone as the well-maintained boat headed toward the scene of the attack. Randy and Bobby walked into the galley where they grabbed their shotguns and prepared to fight the sadistic beast.

Bill remained at the bow of the boat, watching Bloodfoot as he stood outside the galley door with a pair of binoculars trained on the mysterious black car that reappeared for a moment until they rounded a bend and lost sight of it again.

25

Bob Jackson sat in a wheelchair while being checked out of the hospital. His broken nose caused him to have two black eyes which made him look like a bandit. His right arm was set in a sling and itched worse than he had imagined, adding to the discomfort of the punctured lung and two broken ribs.

Being laid up in the hospital for nearly a week drove him crazy, as all he could think about was how he single-handedly destroyed the Manditto family.

As a nurse wheeled him through the hallway, he was met by his secretary, Margaret.

"Hello Marge, what's with the funny look?" he tried to joke when he saw the worried look on her face.

"Bob, you can't go out through the front. The ASPCA is waiting outside along with all the major news channels," she said while breathing heavily.

"What the hell is ASPCA?"

Margaret rolled her eyes and wondered if he ever got through high school, "It's the American Society of the Prevention of Cruelty to Animals," she replied in a huff, grabbing the wheelchair out of the nurse's hands and wheeling him down a different hall.

"Ah Christ! More PETA crap!" he cursed.

The elevator door opened at the end of the hall and Margaret practically ran to meet it as Bob held on for dear life.

"Easy Marge, I don't want you to crash this thing into the elevator wall."

"That would be the least of your problems," she replied, wheeling him inside and mashing the buttons. The elevator opened to the main lobby and she continued running with the wheelchair through the emergency exit and to her parked car before the hostile animals group knew of the escape. She wasted no time getting her boss in the car and tossing the wheelchair back to the agitated nurse who followed behind, and jumped into her car, speeding away like a renegade.

"Good to be out of there Marge, thanks for picking me up," Bob said casually when the coast was clear, "How's business been?"

"Busy, Johnny and Vince are working eighteen hour shifts," she said, referring to the two towboat captains that remained on the payroll.

"Wow, How come so busy?"

"Nobody up the river wants to work on their boats ever since that monster attacked the Heilbronner Hull Cleaners. We've been working day and night towing yachts upriver to be cleaned in the marinas.

"Deiter and his son?" Bob asked, surprised and shocked at the same time.

"The very same, luckily they're alive to talk about it," she replied, calming down a bit.

Bob was quiet for a few moments as he let it all sink in. Then, "Well, good business for us, but I hope the Indians capture or kill that reptile soon. Chief Bhim and his trappers quit, but there's another group hunting it."

"Damn quitters, who've they got hunting it now?" Bob grumbled, losing all deference he had for Bhim.

"From what I've heard, it's Captain Virgil Goodman and his crew, Officer Randy Taylor and some pirate looking guy named Captain Bloodfoot and a couple of other guys," She replied, stopping at a red light and checking her rear-view mirror for the ASPCA.

Bob's eyes grew twice their size, "What the hell? How come nobody told me?" he asked, sounding like a hurt kid who was not invited on the baseball team.

"Because you've been in the hosp…"

"Take me to the office," he demanded, cutting her off as he removed his arm sling and threw it in the back seat.

"Bob, the nurse said that you should keep that sling on and rest for a couple of weeks," she pleaded on deaf ears.

Bob ignored her as he reached into his pocket and pulled out his cell phone. He painfully punched out the number of the Patrol Boat office and waited impatiently for an answer. Finally, after five rings, an officer picked up.

"Patrol Boat office, how can I help you?"

"This is Bob Jackson, I'm a friend of Officer Randy Taylor. I need to know where he and his charter are located."

"It's confidential sir, he will be out for about a week and ..."

Slam! Bob became enraged and threw his phone against the dashboard, "Bastards won't tell me where they're at!" he shouted.

"Calm down, they're in the Everglades," Margaret said with a look of repugnance.

"Why didn't you tell me?" he asked as he froze and looked across the console.

"You didn't ask."

She quickly pulled into the driveway of Bob's house and parked in the garage in hopes of hiding the car.

"The Everglades is a big place, would you happen to know about where they are?" he asked graciously, amazed at how it seemed she knew everything about everything.

"Last I heard, they were near a place called the Tiger Preserve... or something like that."

"You never cease to amaze me Marge; what would I do without you?" he joked, affectionately tapping her arm.

"You'd probably live a little longer, since I told you where they're at and knowing you, you're probably going to catch up with them," she replied contritely, walking to the passenger side to help her boss out.

Bob crawled out of the car and walked up three steps and fidgeted with his keys, feeling every aching bone in his body. "Look Marge, I appreciate you caring for me like this, but you don't understand... I need to be out there to help kill that reptile. That damn thing killed my best friends' son."

"It wasn't your fault," she retorted.

"I sent him out there, he wasn't even on shift."

"He was doing what he got paid to do."

"No, I should have been out there. I was too damn lazy and called Rick instead."

"How were you to know there'd be a man-eating reptile

waiting for him?"

"Look Marge, I don't expect you to understand. It's because of my actions that the entire Manditto family is destroyed."

"You're wrong and you know it," Marge said, her eyes welling up. "Thanks for everything Marge," he said with a warm smile. "One more thing, ask John and Vince if they can keep up the overtime for a few more days."

Knowing there was nothing she could do to change his mind; Margaret peeked out of the garage door to see if they were followed and turned to Bob, "I'll ask them Bob, I'm sure they'll do it."

"Thanks Marge," he said, sincerely.

"Please be careful, don't take unnecessary chances." "Don't worry, I'll..."

"Do I look worried?" she retorted angrily, as she got in her car and cranked the engine. "You just come back alive and in one piece," she tearfully said as she put the car in reverse, pulled out onto the street and drove away.

Bob stood on the steps leading into the house and watched her drive off. Scratching his head, he gave up trying to understand what was going on in her head. He dragged himself into the house and took a long, hot shower.

After being in the hospital for so long with little more than a daily sponge bath, the hot water felt good.

Afterward, he made himself a ham and cheese sandwich and checked his telephone messages. There were eighteen messages, far too many for him to answer any time soon.

He packed a duffel bag and painfully walked out to the dock in his back yard. Tied to the dock was his seventeen-foot Boston Whaler where he proceeded to throw his bag into, narrowly missing the boat completely if not for the dock post that he hit, ricocheting the bag into the boat.

He gritted his teeth as he climbed into the boat and checked the gas tank, making sure it was full while he prepared to take it upriver to join the others in their search for the gargantuan reptile.

Being a die-hard fisherman, he kept his little boat in tip top shape. Since he spent most of his working hours offshore or in the harbor area, he couldn't imagine the idea of spending his free time fishing the same waters. Instead, he preferred doing his fishing on the back waters and the flats in the Keys.

It was late afternoon, and time was not on his side when he untied the bow and stern lines from the dock and cranked the engine. It was four-thirty, plenty of time to catch up with the hunting party before the sun went down.

What Lurks Below

Two hours after reaching the spot where the kayakers were attacked, Bloodfoot was growing impatient waiting for the elusive reptile to surface or show any sign of being in the area. Captain Virgil had shut off the engine and quietly drifted with all hands looking for any signs of the monster.

"Hey Virgil, crank up and continue upriver; our reptile is not here," Bloodfoot declared.

Virgil trusted that Bloodfoot was the only one onboard that knew what he was talking about when it came to hunting the reptile and cranked the engine.

The old boat slowly continued up the river as Bobby walked to the bow and proceeded to open a hatch in the floorboard. The others watched with amusement as he carefully pulled out a small arsenal of hand-grenades and what looked like an old bazooka.

"Have you got any more surprises Bobby?" Randy asked, walking over to him with his hands on his hips.

"No, no. This is all I've got," he replied with a malicious grin.

"I should ask where you got this stuff, but I don't think I want to know," replied the officer, shaking his head with a satisfied look.

"Good, because I don't think you'd believe me anyway."

"Bobby, come in here," Virgil ordered.

The grin left Bobby's face as he looked over to Virgil. He looked at Randy before replying, "Aye Captain."

He walked into the small wheelhouse where Captain Virgil gave him a menacing glare.

"I don't like surprises, tell me where you got the grenades," he said matter-of-factly.

"Take it easy Virgil," Randy said as he followed Bobby inside. "I'm still the cop."

"You're a Harbor Patrol Police Officer, I'm well aware of that. But I'm captain on this boat and I run the show," Virgil replied in an imposing tone.

Randy was taken aback by the tenacity of the captain but understood where he was coming from and half-heartedly agreed.

"The grenades, where did you get them," Virgil grilled.

"I don't have to tell you squat, Captain. Hell, I don't even know you. Get off my back or you just might find a grenade go off right where you stand," Bobby threatened.

"Is that a threat?" Virgil asked as he put the boat in neutral.

"Take it how you want tough guy," Bobby replied just before a hard and heavy punch landed square on his jaw.

Bobby fell back and landed in Bill's massive arms.

"Any problems Captain?" Bill asked with a disturbing look at Bobby as he propped him up on his feet again.

"None I can't handle Bill," replied Virgil. "Now, where did the grenades come from?"

Bobby shook himself out of Bill's arms and ran a hand over his throbbing jaw, "Okay, okay. Damn, you didn't have to hit me."

"I won't ask you again," threatened Virgil.

Bobby was well aware that the captain meant business, "I brought them back from 'Nam, are you happy?"

"Just what I figured," Virgil smirked, putting the boat in gear once again. "You Navy Squabs stash away old explosives and wonder why they blow your ass off when you touch them thirty years later."

With a look of surprise, Randy added, "You stashed those things since Vietnam? What are you... Nuts!"

Bobby swallowed hard and looked over to Randy, "Yes, I must be. First, I lend you my prized specialty boat and volunteer to hunt for this oversized alligator. And now, I've got the reincarnation of Captain Ahab on my ass! I must be crazy as hell!" he shouted defiantly.

"What makes you think those grenades are still good?" Virgil ranted. "Well, I didn't bury them in the backyard or anything. I stored them under my bed in an air-conditioned room," Bobby replied proudly. "You should have told me before we left the dock," Virgil retorted.

Bobby sat in a chair in the corner of the wheelhouse, looking at the two men with empathy, "I'm sorry, you're right and it won't happen again."

Virgil didn't say anything as he turned and focused on steering the boat. Randy remained in the wheelhouse for a few minutes to make sure Bobby wouldn't say anything stupid before exiting and returning to his lookout.

As the boat cruised further into the Everglades, dirt roads and hunting cottages gave way to mosquitoes and marshes. The low tide couldn't have come at a worse time; the old boat slowly turned around a bend in the river and got stuck in the mud. Virgil shouted obscenities at what he thought was a working depth finder before cutting the engine.

All eyes were on the captain as he walked past Bobby and out of the wheelhouse, "Well fellas, might as well make ourselves comfortable for the next few hours," he said, throwing his hands in the air. "It's low tide and we're stuck on the bottom."

"Of all the rotten luck," a voice came from the head, as Don stumbled out with a wet pant leg. Chuck and Bill looked at Don and tried not to laugh as Bloodfoot let out a hearty chuckle.

"So who's hungry?" asked Bill, reaching for his fishing pole.

"Good idea. We might as well break here until the tide comes in," replied Chuck, reaching into a cooler and grabbing an ice-cold Heineken.

Bill walked to the galley and retrieved a couple slices of bologna for bait and jumped over the side of the boat. He leisurely walked through knee-deep water until he reached the bank and climbed out of the water.

"Why the hell are you fishing over there?" Don asked.

"Because it's quiet," replied Bill, as he sat on a tree stump and baited the hook.

Don seemed a little put-off, but he just shook his head and joined the others for a beer, "So really, who's hungry?" he asked.

"Don't worry Donald, Bobby has packed all kinds of food," replied Virgil, keeping a watchful eye on Bill as he cast his line.

"You want to eat mercury laden bass? That's your choice. I've got pork ribs and steaks in the box," Bobby retorted, wiping his brow.

"You'd never make it living off the land," Bloodfoot continued, giving Bobby a nasty glare and walking toward the stern. He reached into his shirt pocket and pulled out a big, fat Diamond Crown cigar. Looking out over the water, he began to relax as the sun slowly fell below the trees. Smiling to himself, he thought back at how he couldn't stand Bobby's war hero types who thought they were tough as nails, he ate people like that for lunch.

Captain Virgil and Chuck followed the pirate and joined him for a smoke as they watched Bill fish. As Chuck leaned against the gunwale, he was ready to shout over to him that fish don't like bologna when Bill suddenly let out a loud cheer and pulled back on the fishing rod, "Oh yeah! I think I've hooked a nice one," he proudly boasted.

While Virgil and Chuck cheered him on, Bloodfoot stood motionless as he caught sight of an unusual wake heading in Bill's direction. He quickly backed up to his duffel bag and retrieved a high-powered rifle.

Virgil turned in time to see him taking aim, but before he could utter a single word, he shot off two rounds within ten-foot of the startled fisherman. "What the hell are you doing!?" Bill screamed out, as he jumped for cover.

Don, Randy and Bobby bolted to the stern of the boat and

prepared to grab the pirate before realizing what he'd shot. Floating next to the abandoned fishing pole was a fifteen-foot, headless python.

"What the hell was that?" a bewildered Don asked.

"That my friend is a python," Bloodfoot cooly replied. "Now put those hot dogs away and I'll cook a real dinner."

Still visibly shaken, Bill walked over and grabbed the snake along with his fishing pole and returned to the boat, "Somebody want to give me a hand with this thing?" Bill asked, heaving the huge snake into the boat.

"I'm not eating that thing," Don said testily, with a repugnant look. "Fine, more for me," Bloodfoot replied, pulling the gargantuan snake into the boat.

As Don returned to the galley to prepare his hot dogs, the rest of the crew helped lay the snake out along the starboard side of the boat as Bloodfoot sharpened his bowie knife.

Virgil and Chuck grabbed a couple more beers from the cooler and stepped ashore to gather firewood and prepare a campfire for the feast.

As the sun disappeared behind the trees, everybody but Don huddled around the campfire, watching as Bloodfoot expertly skinned and sliced fillets of meat from the dead snake. As they drank apricot brandy and beer, Don heard the hearty reaction from the crew as they tasted python for the first time. A few minutes went by before he self-consciously grabbed his burnt hot dogs and joined them.

"About time you joined us city boy," Bloodfoot taunted. "I didn't want to miss all the comradely."

"Well, have some brandy 'ol boy," Bobby slurred as he poured another round.

As they drank and talked, exchanging wild stories in which Bloodfoot's were so amazing they were hard to believe, they decided to not search for the reptile until morning.

After a few more rounds of brandy, Don thought he was brave enough to try some python, "Hey big guy, you want to slice me off a piece of that snake?" Don asked, putting on his best drunken tough-guy voice.

Bloodfoot stopped chewing and grinned, "Well, well. See what a little grog can do for a man?"

The crew fell back laughing as Don tried to keep his tough-guy impression in check. Suddenly, all was quiet while they waited for Don's reaction. Bloodfoot sliced off some meat and passed it to him.

Don cautiously bit into the meat and his sour expression

quickly vanished when he realized it tasted good.

"Well goddamn! It tastes like chicken."

"I knew you'd say that," Bobby said, clearly annoyed. "If something doesn't taste like beef or pork, you Americans say it tastes like chicken."

The crew gave a puzzling look toward Bobby, "Well, you're American too, aren't you Bobby?" Randy asked.

"That's not the point Randy!" Bobby retorted. "Take for instance, when I was hiding out in the rat-infested waters in Vietnam, we didn't have cans of spam or hot dogs and hamburgers. No, we ate off the land," he lectured.

Bloodfoot looked over to Virgil and Randy, rolling his eyes and shaking his head, hoping not to hear another war-hero story. When he stood up, Bill thought for sure that he would start something with Bobby, so he jumped up and stood between the two. Bloodfoot gave him a bewildering look, turned and walked away.

While the others sat in relief that a feud didn't start, Bloodfoot turned his attention to what looked like a small campfire in the distance. He found it odd that somebody would be camping in this part of the Everglades and decided to walk closer and have a look without alarming everyone.

"Take it easy with the war stories. I think Bloodfoot's had his fill," Randy cautioned.

"Forget that pirate, I'll kick his ass."

"Yeah, okay... I'd like to see that," Chuck laughed.

"What do you mean you ate off the land?" Don asked, like a confused boy scout.

"We ate rats, beetles, you name it; we ate it to survive," Bobby continued, glad to have somebody's attention.

"You ate it raw?" an amused Don asked, egging on the old burnout. "Sometimes... Oh yeah, sometimes we ate maggots when we were in a pinch," Bobby grinned.

Forty minutes later, Bloodfoot returned and sat by the fire. The crew watched with fascination as he whipped out his knife and peeled the skin off a freshly killed iguana, and took a bite. His eyes turned to Bobby as he chewed on a gristly section, "Want some?" he mumbled, handing the grotesque cadaver over to Bobby.

Without warning, Bobby vomited violently into his brandy cup and ran for the boat. Bloodfoot spat out the rest of the meat and threw the rest of the carcass in the river. The crew looked at the pirate as if he'd lost his mind.

"What the hell was that all about?" Randy asked.

Bloodfoot grabbed a beer and gulped it down completely in one long swallow before belching out loud and replying, "That my friend, is proof positive that Bobby, the fearless Vietnam warrior is full of shit."

Looking wide-eyed with his mouth agape, Don affirmed what the others were thinking, "Damn... That's a hell of a way to prove a point."

"Yeah, well sometimes you've got to either put up or shut up," Bloodfoot responded, in a surprisingly sober tone.

At ten-thirty, only Virgil, Randy and Bloodfoot were still talking and sipping brandy by the campfire while the rest of the crew retreated to the boat to get some much-needed sleep, for the next day they were fretfully hoping to meet the gargantuan reptile and kill it.

"So Bloodfoot, what's your story?" Virgil asked. "Why do you ask,"

"It seems you live an interesting life. Besides, I've never met a pirate before."

Bloodfoot gave the captain a cold, hard stare before continuing, "Well if you'd like to hear about my interesting life, pour me another brandy and I shall start from the beginning," he grinned.

"I actually ended up being who I am today, courtesy of Her Majesty, the Queen of England."

"Excuse me?" Randy gagged, coughing up his drink.

'That's right officer. I was in the Third Commando Brigade Royal Marines. After a stint in the Falklands and several other places that would give you nightmares, they sent me to Belize where I was more or less forced to become an instructor at a jungle warfare training camp. I immediately fell in love with the place and vowed to start a new life there. Belize was practically created by pirates and frankly, I don't think much has changed."

"That's why you stayed in Belize, to become a pirate?" Virgil quizzed. "No, not quite. The reason I stayed was because of the weather,"

Bloodfoot smiled, wondering if he sounded believable. "The weather?" Virgil replied, skeptically.

"That's correct, you live half your life in balmy England, thinking that's the way life is, and then you travel to Belize and find out there's a whole different world out there. There was no way in hell I was going to return to stuffy, old England."

"After you left the Royal Marines, what did you do for work," Virgil asked, pouring another round and listening intently.

"I became a hunter," he answered, looking for a reaction. "I hunted anything and everything with a price on its head."

"What's with the assortment of teeth dangling on your boots?" Don asked, as he seemed to come out of nowhere to eavesdrop.

Bloodfoot turned and glared at Don as if he were an unwanted guest before replying, "After an unusual hunt, I will take a tooth from the subject and attach it to my boot, sort of like a trophy, if you will."

He paused for effect. Virgil and Randy looked at each other and nodded in agreement as Don turned pale, hoping he wasn't on the list to become hunted prey by the pirate.

"Makes sense to me," Virgil said, raising his cup and toasting in agreement.

"Take for instance, this one," Bloodfoot said, pointing to a very large shark tooth. "A couple years back, I was on a small boat off the coast of Africa when this big, enormous Mako shark comes up and decides to attack my outboard motor."

"I think I'd of had heart-failure," Randy alleged.

"That's right, but she didn't stop there. After the motor, she proceeded to eat the damn boat. I don't know what pissed her off, but I'd never seen a fish so angry in my life."

"You must have thought you were done for," Virgil added.

"Hell no, it was going to be a challenge… a challenge to see who'd be the predator," Bloodfoot grinned, flexing his muscles.

"What size was the boat," Don asked, trying to fit in the conversation.

Bloodfoot looked at Don and took a long swig of his brandy before replying, "It was a seventeen-foot, no-name, open fisherman with a ninety-horse Evinrude."

"What were you doing out there… fishing?" asked Randy.

"It's probably best that I don't say," Bloodfoot responded with a wicked grin.

"Did you try to get away or did you welcome the challenge?" Randy jeered, unable to believe two shark stories with similar outcomes.

"Like I said, she ate the motor. It happened so fast, I thought I got hit by a submarine," he continued, "The boat was beginning to take on water, so I knew I had to act quickly."

"So what did you do, jump on her back?" Virgil sarcastically asked. "That's exactly what I did Captain," detecting the mockery. "I had no other choice, the only weapon I had was my trusty knife," he said, giving the captain a look that could cut steel as he patted his knife. I leaped at her and landed just ahead of the dorsal fin. Before she could shake me off, I grasped the gills on her left side like a vise and plunged my knife deep into her nose area, it felt like cutting through three-inches of leather.”

“Right… Now I’ve heard it all,” Virgil said, standing up and returning Bloodfoot’s creepy look as he was about to call him a no-good, lying son of a bitch.

They watched Virgil stagger back to the boat before continuing, “So what happened next?” Don inquired like a boy scout at a campout.

“The damn shark began shaking her head violently, trying to throw me off. I knew if I let go, it would surely be the end for me. I kept stabbing the nose area, hoping to destroy all of its sensory glands. Once I thought I’d inflicted enough damage, I plunged my knife into the gills. I sliced and diced, trying to cut the gills away so it would suffocate. The skin was equal to rough sandpaper; I don’t know who lost more blood, me or the shark. My body was completely raw as I fought to hold on.

“You’re damn lucky to be alive,” Randy said as he tried to pour more brandy out of the empty bottle.

“And then it happened,” Bloodfoot paused, waiting for a reaction. “What? What happened… Super pirate?” Virgil scoffed, staggering back over with a brand new bottle of brandy.

Randy and Don looked at each other with uneasiness as they anticipated trouble about to erupt. "What happened next?" Randy quickly countered. "She went down... The damn shark had one more trick up her sleeve and dove down to the depths. I knew damn well that if I let go and swam back toward the surface, she'd be on me before I could suck in a breath of air. I continued stabbing through the gills until I began to lose consciousness. I was about to give up and let go when the shark suddenly turned and torpedoed straight for the surface."

"Good thing you were able to hold on super pirate," Virgil continued taunting.

Bloodfoot gave the captain a look like he wanted to tear him apart, but instead, continued his story. "I was able to hold on because my left arm was practically jammed inside the sharks gills and there was no way in hell that I was going to fall off. I reached around and had a clear shot of her belly and plunged my knife as deep as it would go. We broke the surface and shot through the air like a guided missile."

"What? I didn't know they leaped out of the water," Randy stated. "They surely do, my friend. It is a terrible misconception that people think of the mako shark as being too big and heavy to jump out of the water. But in the waters near Africa, witnesses have seen these monsters jump even higher out of the water. They are extremely fast. But anyway… where was I?"

"You and the shark were airborne," Virgil affirmed, rolling his eyes.

"Right, I let go of the shark when we left the water, but I kept a firm grip on my knife as it slid down and sliced the belly wide open.

"Then what happened?" Don asked, nearly idolizing the pirate.

"It started quivering and swam in circles. I just floated in the water and kept an eye on the shark, but by then I was relieved to know I had become the predator. There was quite a lot of blood in the water, so I figured I'd better head for shore before more sharks arrived. As it made another pass around me, I grabbed the dorsal fin and held on tight. I stabbed the shark in the eyes and it finally rolled over and died. As it sank, I cut out a tooth and swam for shore."

"You're the craziest man I've ever met," Randy declared.

Bloodfoot beamed with a grin and replied, "I like a good challenge."

"That is one hell of a story Bloodfoot. If there's anyone more qualified to catch this reptile, I know it's you," Virgil said, standing up and stretching. "Then why are you riding me, you don't think my story is true," Bloodfoot asked, in a menacing tone.

"You help me kill this reptile, and I'll believe in the tooth fairy," Virgil drunkenly replied.

Bloodfoot was man enough to know not to press the issue, as everybody was belligerently drunk and probably wouldn't remember anything in the morning. They finished their drinks and headed back aboard the boat and fell fast asleep. All accept Bloodfoot, he leaned against the gunwales and looked out over the calm water. He was surprisingly sober and had the feeling that he was being watched by the man he'd spied on at his campsite, the same man he spotted at the boat ramp earlier, the man with the black car.

26

Skip Long paid the cab driver and walked into the American Airlines terminal at the airport in Atlanta. He hated this airport because no matter how many times he'd been there, it seemed he always got lost and nearly missed his flight. Always thinking it was a dirty trick; he couldn't understand why he bought a ticket at one end and had to sprint to the opposite end to catch the flight. This time was different, after checking his baggage in, he looked at his watch and smiled to himself at the thought of having a couple hours to kill before his departure.

With the weight of the world on his shoulders, he strolled into the airport bar and ordered a beer. Sipping his drink, he couldn't stop thinking about the way his father provoked him about the reptile, telling him to man up and not run away from his troubles. What did he know about the vicious creature? He felt mortified the way his father made him out to be some kind of sissy for running scared and not wanting to return to work.

His thoughts of going home and staying with mom and dad were quickly abandoned. Skip knew his dad would be hard on him but he wanted to make him proud, he knew the only way to make that happen would be to return to the crew and help kill the reptile, at all costs.

He ordered a shot of Jack Daniels to take the edge off and sipped his beer as he waited for his flight to depart.

The plane touched down at Fort Lauderdale airport later that afternoon. Skip hitched a ride to the Anchor bar where he knew he'd get the latest information on where the hunting party would be located. He grudgingly stepped into the dimly lit room and took a seat at the bar. Looking around, he didn't see any friendly faces, "Where can I get a beer around here?" he joked when he saw Carlos tending bar.

"Where the hell have you been?" asked Carlos, pouring a cold Budweiser from the tap.

"I went home to see the folks for a few days."

"Damn... I hadn't seen you since I kicked you and your buddy out of here," Carlos said with a slight grin.

"Much has happened since then," Skip nodded.

Carlos felt like he was dragging every word out of Skip as he pumped him for information about the horrific reptile until he finally told him he was going to catch up with his crew and hunt the beast.

"You're going after that thing?" Carlos asked, a look of surprise in his eyes.

"That's right," Skip replied with a courageous face, taking a vast swig from the glass.

"Well then you should meet up with the rest of the suicide crew that thinks they can kill it," Carlos sneered, with a disenchanted look.

Skip's eyes widened, "What crew are you talking about?" he questioned, wondering how much the bartender really knew.

"I heard the crew consisted of a cop and his lunatic Vietnam War hero friend, a big pirate looking guy named Captain Bloodfoot, and the captain and crew from your tugboat. Oh yeah, one more. Bob Jackson left yesterday afternoon with his little skiff. He plans to catch up with the others in the Everglades."

"How do you know all of this? I heard they were trying to do this quietly."

"I'm a bartender. I hear everything," Carlos replied with a pompous tone. "Besides, Vince the towboat captain popped in here last night complaining about overtime and spilled his guts."

"Call me a cab Carlos... and give me a shot of Jack; make that a double," Skip ordered as he jumped up and ran for the restroom.

A half-hour later, the taxi cab pulled into the gravel parking lot of the towboat building. Skip quickly paid the cab fare and headed inside the small office.

"Can I help you?" Marge asked, with a startled look.

"Hi, my name is Skip Long. I understand that Bob is out looking for that perilous reptile."

Marge stood up from her desk and put her hands over her face. Tears began to well in her eyes as she replied, "He hasn't called. He said he would call when he caught up with the others."

"Hold on miss, I know Bob, he's a tough guy and I'm sure he's alright," replied Skip as he walked around the desk and held her.

"No, something's wrong. He said he'd call when he found the others and I can't get him on the radio," she cried.

Skip held her by the shoulders and guided her to a leather sofa, "How long ago did he leave?"

She tried to compose herself as she grabbed her purse and retrieved a handkerchief. They sat and talked for twenty minutes as she filled Skip in on the plans to kill the monster. She also warned him about the latest attacks on the river leading into the Everglades.

"Okay," he said, as he stood up. "I will find him and the crew and give you a call on my cell phone, sometimes when you're so far in the 'glades, the radio reception is bad. I'm going to need to borrow one of the towboats."

Marge looked into his eyes as if deciding, "Okay, take the one at the end of the dock," she said, pointing out through the window, "The tank has just been filled."

She made her way back to the desk and reached inside a drawer, retrieving a key attached to a floating key ring, "Please be careful."

Skip took the key and put his hand on her shoulder, "Don't worry, I'll find him," he assured her, giving her a wink and a weak smile.

He grabbed his suitcase and trotted down to the dock. Throwing his baggage into the boat, he quickly untied the stern and bow lines without realizing Vince getting out of the boat next to him.

"So where do you think you're going, buddy?"

Startled while he leaped onto the boat, Skip sprung up and hit his head on the T-top, "Ouch!... Son of a ...Who the hell are you?" Skip screeched, holding his injured head.

"I was just about to ask you the same thing," Vince replied, cracking the knuckles of his fist and looking ready to attack.

"Look, I don't want any trouble. My name is Sk..."

"Trouble? You don't want trouble?" Vince cut in before Skip could finish. "I'd say you're in deep trouble unless you've got a good explanation as to why you're stealing this vessel."

Just when it seemed things were coming to a head, Marge stuck her head out of the office door and shouted, "Vince! Leave him be, he's not stealing the boat!"

Vince, who was now standing on the gunwale of the drifting boat, gave Marge a menacing look before dropping onto the deck and starting the motor. Without saying a word to Skip, he expertly returned the boat to the dock and tied the lines. Marge met them at the dock and explained the situation to Vince.

After a long moment with Vince giving Skip an ominous glare, he reached out and shook his hand, "Thought you were a thieving bastard, I apologize. I will run you out to meet with the boss."

"No Vince, Bob needs you and John to work the business while he's out," Marge replied with authority.

Vince took a deep breath and sighed before storming off, "Fine."

Skip thanked Margaret for saving him from a brutal beating and jumped into the boat. Within minutes, he was speeding up river at a perilous pace. NO WAKE signs seemed to pop up around every bend as Skip failed to comply, wreaking havoc on the private boats tied to docks.

Within two hours, Skip found himself slowing down as he passed a boat ramp at the mouth of the Everglades.

He laughed to himself at the sight of a dark, luxurious Lincoln with an empty boat trailer near the ramp, "Now I've seen it all; even redneck-wanna-be lawyers fish in the 'glades," he said to himself.

He continued cruising through the swampland until he came upon a partially submerged kayak. He put the boat in neutral and drifted past the eerie sight, looking and hoping not to find human remains. Goose bumps ran up his spine as he tried to imagine the horror that took place. He looked around and found himself amazed at how he was just in the busy city and how after cruising twenty miles or so, he was all alone in no-man's land.

A splash coming from a grassy bank broke his thoughts as he turned to see an eight-foot alligator swimming in his direction. His first thought was to put the boat in gear and put as much distance between him and the gator as possible, but decided to stay put. He knew he had better get used to seeing them around or turn the boat and head for home.

He sat watching the reptile as it swam up to the boat and looked at him through looming eyes. He thought twice about taking his old shotgun out of the bag and trying it out to see if it still fired.

He hastily put the boat in gear and headed upriver. As the afternoon sun started descending behind the trees, Skip tried to decide whether or not to keep going. He surely didn't want to spend the night by himself in the swamp if he couldn't find the others. He decided it would be best to turn around and start again at sun up. He wondered what his fearless father would do in his situation while he impulsively turned the boat around. Before he could push the throttles forward, he heard a faint sound of somebody crying for help.

"Help! Over here... I'm over here!"

"What the hell?" Skip asked himself while putting the boat in neutral and walking to the stern to make sure he wasn't hearing things.

Looking over near the sodden banks, he was shocked to see none other than Bob Jackson climbing out of a tree.

"Bob? Bob Jackson?"

"Yes, it's me," he gasped with a look of relief on his mosquito-bitten face.

Skip quickly threw the boat in reverse and idled as close as possible to the tree without running aground. Bob looked like he'd been through the ringer. His face looked haggard and there was blood and dirt all over his body. The cast on his arm was completely soaked and he was gasping for air. As the boat got closer, Skip was amazed to see the multitudes of mosquito bites all over him.

When the boat was as close as it was going to get, Bob took a long look in the murky water before stepping in. Skip gave him a hand as he climbed the transom and fell flat on the deck.

He remained flat on his back with eyes closed for a good minute before attempting to stand.

"Bob, it's okay, you're gonna be alright," Skip encouraged, helping him to his feet. Bob made it up far enough to sit on the gunwale and catch his breath. He began taking off his muddy shoes and looked up to see the man who saved him from another night in the mosquito-infested hell. His movement became rigid as he took a double-take of the man standing there, "Hey... you're not Vince or John. What the hell are you doing on my towboat?" Bob demanded.

"I'm Skip Long. I worked on the tugboat Horizon," a startled

Skip answered.

"After a long, strange look, Bob replied, "Ah yes, you do look familiar, Captain Goodman's deckhand."

"I was also attacked by that monstrous reptile," Skip informed him, to some how make him feel at ease.

"I heard about that. The damn thing snuck right up on you," Bob beamed, his broken ribs causing him to recoil.

"Sure did. I nearly had a heart attack."

"So what brings you out here?"

"It's a long story. I don't want to bore you with details, but I'm out here to find the crew and help hunt that monster."

"Who gave you the authority to take my towboat out here?" Bob questioned.

"Your secretary, Margaret. When I got back into town, I heard my buddies were out here to kill the beast and she said you followed shortly after. When she didn't hear from you, she thought the worst. Long story short, I told her I needed a boat and that I would find you."

Bob walked to the center console, shaking his head in agreement and picked up the VHS mic. Turning to channel seventy-two, he called to the towboat office. He took a quick glance at his watch and waited for Marge to respond. Within seconds, Margaret's' voice replied, and he immediately described the situation.

After explaining that his radio fell out of the boat and shorted out, he hung up the mic and turned to Skip, "I think she bought my story."

"So what really happened," Skip asked, with a concerned look, as his boat was nowhere to be found.

"Well... Just like you, that damn thing snuck up on me too. If I didn't know better, I'd say that reptile had a well-thought-out plan to trap me... the way it... Ah, forget it," he said, not wanting to continue, fearing that Skip would think he'd lost his mind.

"Sneaky thing, isn't it," Skip replied, handing Bob a bottled water.

"It sure as hell is. I was making good time heading through here, trying to catch up with the crew, when that monster took me by surprise. One minute I'm cruising along and the next, I'm swimming for my life and hauling my ass up a damn tree with a gigantic reptile in hot pursuit."

"Damn, you didn't even see it coming?"

"Nope, no warning at all. The reptile must have heard me coming and went underwater. It waited until I was right on top of it before it shot up and rammed the motor. It hit so hard, the engine bracket snapped right off the transom," Bob explained, with his arms waving to demonstrate the blast.

"Must have been terrifying," Skip acknowledged.

"Once I caught my breath and realized what had happened, I looked over and saw the beast heading straight for me like a torpedo. It practically leaped into the boat, jaws snapping like crazy at everything. The boat was instantly crushed and sunk while I tumbled into the water and thought I was going to be chopped sushi."

"It's amazing that you made it out alive."

"Now that's the freaky part," Bob replied, wide-eyed and beginning to shudder. "That devilish monster could have easily gotten me. It swam faster than I could ever imagine for a reptile of that size. When I was surprised that I made it to shore with this broken arm, I climbed the tree and turned to see where the beast was," he continued, his voice beginning to tremble audibly.

"It disappeared under the surface?" Skip asked cautiously, realizing the poor guy was working himself up with emotion.

"Hell no! It sat in the water where I had been, watching me... watching me through the most hideous eyes I'd ever seen. It looked like it took pleasure in the fact that I was so frightened

I nearly died of a heart attack. It could have easily gotten me, but with that devilish look on its mug, it thrived on my fear, knowing it'd get me later."

Skip was sitting on the gunwales while Bob explained the story. A shiver went up his spine and he promptly stood up, took a quick look around the murky water and moved to the center of the boat.

"You're lucky to be alive," Skip mumbled, "Let's get the hell out of here."

"Okay, with that being said, let's decide what we're going to do," Bob said with vigor. "Should we keep going and catch up to the crew or turn tail and run for home?"

Skip was taken aback by the sudden change of tone in Bob's voice. While telling his story, Bob looked like he was about to go into shock. Now, the guy sounded like a brawny outdoorsman. He didn't have the heart to tell him he'd like to turn tail and run for home, "Let's keep moving. I think we can catch up with the crew before it gets too dark."

27

Day two was less eventful than the day before. The crew woke up early, all suffering hangovers except for Bloodfoot. They continued their search for the elusive reptile and came up with nothing more than dozens of ordinary alligators lurking in the waters. Randy and Bill became so frustrated with the sonar getting caught up in the weeds that they nearly cut the dragline and shot the sonar.

The last rays of sunlight disappeared with striking orange and red colors when Captain Virgil cut the engine and ordered Bill to drop anchor. The frustrated crew was tired and hungry; Don was beside himself with the thought of the sun going down with only half a can of mosquito repellant remaining.

Once again, Bill took out his fishing pole and began casting his line at every ripple he saw, this time from the back of the boat. Bobby tried to keep the spirits going by preparing dinner while Virgil, Chuck and Bloodfoot filled their first brandy glasses of the day. They sat in the small galley, reviewing charts and making plans for the next day while Don stomped off to his bunk with a book, hoping to stay away from the mosquitoes.

"Ah, now that's nice," Chuck said after taking a long sip from his glass. "Make it last. We're not having another night like the last," Virgil replied.

Bloodfoot and Chuck looked over at each other but said nothing. In the back of his mind, Chuck knew it was the best decision, but only a decision the captain had the guts to make. Bloodfoot just shrugged and figured he'd go along with it for the sake of the crew.

They were now deep in the immense swamp, and the mosquitoes and no-see-ums were a continuous problem as they seemed to show aggression like vampires in a bad movie.

"That's it damn it! I'm completely out of repellant," Don griped, smacking his face and storming out of his bunk when he felt yet another bite on his cheek.

Randy gave a hearty laugh before replying, "Here, you can use some of this," he said, tossing him a full can of Off. "Sorry, I forgot to tell you we have a full case of the stuff."

Don gave the officer a pathetic look, "You forgot," he murmured, grabbing the can and quickly applying the contents.

Before they could taunt the mosquito-bitten man further, Bloodfoot held up his hands and motioned for quiet as he peered through some brush just ahead of the boat, "Something's out there," he whispered.

The crew stood quietly and looked over to see what Bloodfoot was talking about. Just beyond the bow of the boat, they heard footsteps plowing through the sawgrass. Finally, as it got closer, Virgil pointed toward something breaking out of the foliage, "Would you look at the size of that!"

"It's a wild boar," Chuck said eagerly.

Bloodfoot smiled to himself, debating if he should stalk the animal as it gingerly walked to the water's edge to take a drink. At the same instant, its tongue poked at the water, a tremendous blast erupted when the vicious reptile blasted out of the water and grabbed the boar with incredible strength and just as quickly disappeared below the surface with its meal.

The crew stood motionless as they witnessed the violent display while Bloodfoot reached into his duffel bag and pulled out four sticks of dynamite.

"Get out of the way!" he shouted, running to the bow.

Everybody on deck leaped out of the way and ducked for cover at the sight of the ruthless pirate running while lighting the fuses at the same time. The dynamite landed in the water where the beast had submerged and sank a few feet before blowing up, shaking the ground and the boat like an earthquake.

Bloodfoot was hoping that if the explosions didn't kill the monster, then maybe the concussion would damage its senses or at least maim the terrifying creature. The crew waited eagerly for the smoke to clear. All eyes searched the water for any sign of the reptile when Bloodfoot threw four more sticks of dynamite. The explosions rocked the boat and threw mud on the crew as they warily scanned the area.

When the smoke cleared and the swamp became still, you could hear a pin drop. Randy was the first to stand up and walk over to the pirate while he kept a watchful eye on the water.

"You think we got it?" he whispered.

"I don't see anything to validate that claim," Bloodfoot snarled.

The rest of the crew stood up and brushed the sand and muck off their clothing without saying a word, for each of them knew the creature was long gone and most likely planning its next attack.

"Don, it's your watch; you stay out here and keep your eyes peeled for that reptile. Everybody else, meet me in the galley," Virgil ordered.

Bloodfoot stowed his duffel bag with the dynamite and joined the others in the undersized galley while Don sprayed a coat of mosquito repellant all over himself and took a seat at the bow of the boat. He couldn't remember the last time he was so scared as he watched for the reptile's return. There was no doubt in his mind that the fierce monster was toying with them. Why else would it attack a boar instead of the hunting party? It sensed the fright in each individual and found it irresistible, he thought. It terrified him to know the reptile took great pleasure in frightening its prey before going in for the kill.

Skip and Bob were about to give up hope on finding the crew. As the sun faded in the western sky, Bob looked on with dread at the thought of spending another night alone in the swamp without food and water. After a full day of trying to find the fast boat, they began to squabble over who should have brought the provisions, but before matters could escalate, they heard the explosions coming from about a half-mile upriver.

"What the hell's going on over there?" Skip shouted in a vexed tone. "We must be getting close. What kind of weapons did you bring?" Bob replied excitedly.

Skip swallowed hard as he turned and pointed to his bag, "I've got my dad's old shotgun, what did you bring?"

"I brought a shotgun too, only it went down with my boat,"

Bob replied with a regretful look.

"Great, you operate the boat while I grab my gun."

Skip walked to the front of the center console, grabbed his duffel bag and gently pulled out his father's old two-barrel shotgun.

"What the hell?" Bob said, beaming. "That thing looks like an elephant gun."

"Probably is. I don't know too much about guns, but the kick from this thing will knock you on your butt," Skip replied with a slight grin.

"Have you ever fired that cannon?"

"Nope, never in my life, but I'm sure I will be using it shortly," Skip answered, feeling a lump in his throat.

Bob wiped the grin off his face and put the boat in gear while Skip took his time wiping down the shotgun with an old rag and hoping it still fired. When he was finished, he nervously put two enormous shells in the barrels and admired the power in his hands.

"We'd better find those guys, 'cause I sure as hell don't plan on spending another night out here alone with that monster," Skip informed.

"My thoughts exactly," said Bob, pushing the throttle down

further as the boat gained speed upriver.

For the next few minutes, they cruised as quickly as possible in the dark until they finally spotted the old Vietnam relic.

"What the hell is that?" Skip said, pointing his finger toward the fast boat. "It looks like the boat from that movie Apocalypse Now."

Bob slowed the boat to an idle as they watched the old war boat come into view. His first thought was that they'd run into some redneck hunters blasting at everything that moved. Skip slowly cocked the old shotgun and prepared to fire while he kept his eyes on the old relic.

Don was looking miserable as he stood watching. He heard the wake from the towboat and the water washing over the sawgrass in the distance and first thought that the reptile was charging from behind. "Hey Virge, looks like we've got company!" he shouted aloud.

The crew rushed out of the galley at the same moment the towboat rounded a bend.

"It's another boat!" Bill cried out with relief, pointing over to the vessel closing in.

Randy, Virgil and Chuck ran to the stern with guns drawn, thinking it could be drug dealers fending off their territory,

"Stop right there!" Randy shouted, shooting three rounds into the air.

"Hey Captain! Don't shoot! It's me... Skip Long," he shouted back while Bob threw the throttle in neutral and looked down to make sure he didn't soil his shorts.

"Hold your fire! It's Skip Long and Bob Jackson from the towboat company," Skip continued, desperately waving his hands in the blackened swamp.

Virgil waved a hand at the crew and ordered Randy to stop shooting as the towboat grew near, "What the hell are you doing out here? I thought you went to visit your parents in Georgia," he shouted over.

"I did. Long story short, I'm back to help you cowboys kill the reptile!" Skip smiled with relief as he coiled up the bow line and prepared to toss it over.

Without saying another word, Virgil helped Bill toss a couple of fenders over the starboard side and waited for the towboat to idle over. Bloodfoot stood at the stern with his hands on his hips and watched the towboat come alongside, pleased it wasn't the stranger following them.

The crew waited patiently and helped Skip and Bob onto the fast-boat. Once onboard, Virgil led the two tired men into the galley while Chuck made another pot of coffee.

"I'd like to say I'm glad to see you two, but Bob... You look like hell. What can you do with a broken arm and ribs except get in our way?" Virgil asked bluntly.

"Look Captain. I know how it looks, but I've got to be out here. I need to be here to help kill that sadistic monster; it wiped out my best friend and his family."

Virgil stood and listened as if he were trying to figure him out. Finally, he gave a nod with his head and looked at Skip, "What about you? How can you possibly help this crew? When that reptile attacked you on the back of the tugboat, you nearly died of a heart attack."

Skip stared back at the captain with a determined look, "It's personal, but this time, I'm damn sure that I will not turn and run."

"That's all well and good. But in our situation, I can't just leave you at the next stop, so... welcome aboard," Virgil responded. "I believe some introductions are needed. First I'd like you to meet Bobby. He was kind enough to let us take his fast-boat on this trip."

Skip and Bob extended a friendly hand to the old Vietnam warrior, and their eyes suddenly grew large when Bloodfoot walked in.

The name's Bloodfoot... Captain Bloodfoot," the pirate

rumbled, extending his right hand and nearly crushing Skip's hand with a handshake.

"Ouch! Let go!" he screamed in pain.

Bloodfoot let go and gave a disdainful look toward Bob and shook his hand in the same manner, "At least one of you seems fit for this trip," he said, acknowledging Bob's firm grip.

"Thank God he's on our side," Skip winced, nursing his mashed hand.

The sun was long gone, and if not for the three-quarter moon rising over the treetops, it would be pitch-black in the mosquito-infested swamp.

The crew sat in the diminutive galley and filled Skip and Bob in on the latest events of the indefinable reptile. Don proudly presented some kind of mystery stew made from the fish Bill had caught earlier and the leftover snake meat.

As the hungry crew ate, Bloodfoot explained that alligators were usually active at night and thought it might be a good idea to hunt the predator when they finished their meal.

The crew sat and considered what Bloodfoot had said before Bob cleared his throat and spoke, "Well, we all know that beast is no ordinary gator, and half the attacks happened during daylight hours."

"He's got a point Bloodfoot," Bill continued, uneasily. "I don't know if it's such a good idea hunting that killer in the darkness."

"It's not a good idea to hunt that thing at all," replied Bloodfoot, "But here we are in the middle of the Everglades, and for two days we've struck out in the daylight. I'm only suggesting we try it tonight."

Virgil sat patiently and finished his bowl of stew before sliding it to the side and looking around the table. All eyes were on him when he stood up and spoke, "Okay, we're going to hunt tonight. Bloodfoot might have a point and the faster we kill this thing, the better the chances that it won't escape. We'll hunt until one 'o clock, if we don't find it we'll stop and continue at sun-up."

"Don't forget that AlliCroc is very intelligent. It might be hunting us as well," Don said, fidgeting in his chair.

"Alli what?" Bob asked, with the same surprised look as the others had as they looked over to Don.

Feeling all eyes on him, Don swallowed the lump he felt in his throat and continued, "AlliCroc. Chief Bhim and the Indians at the Sanctuary named it AlliCroc," he said, placing his head in his hands.

"Well... We had to give it a name for the attraction," Don

continued.

"You never cease to amaze me Donald," Virgil leered, shaking his head. "Okay, besides the Pancor shotgun and the shotguns we're carrying, let's see what other arsenal we have," Virgil intervened.

The crew got up from the table and retreated to grab their armaments. A few minutes went by before they returned to display their contents on the table. Bloodfoot was the first to empty his duffel bag. He still had enough sticks of dynamite to blow apart the entire swamp, along with a pistol-gripped twelve-gauge shotgun, his trusty over-sized hunting knife and an ax. The crew took a double-take at the ax but said nothing. Bill was next to empty his bag. The contents included his gear, along with Virgil and Chuck's. It consisted of three twelve-gauge shotguns and three pistols of various sizes. Skip displayed his father's old shotgun while Randy took his pistol out of its holster and placed it on the table along with a shotgun of the same caliber as the others.

Don just stood at the table with his hands in his pockets and whistled at all the guns. With all eyes on him, he finally shrugged his shoulders and confessed that he never shot or owned a single gun in his life.

Finally, everybody turned to Bobby as he sat watching with

a childish grin on his mosquito bitten face.

"Well boys," he said, clasping his hands together. "Let me show you my little cache."

Randy didn't bother looking up but gradually directed his eyes on the psychotic war veteran, knowing that he would not be outdone, "By all means, show us what you've got."

Swollen with pride, Bobby walked over to the small refrigerator and lifted the hatch to a hidden compartment on the floor. In it were five cases of old Vietnam-era hand grenades, one rocket-launcher with more than enough rockets, an AK-47 and a BB gun.

"A BB gun?" Don sighed. "Sure is, I'll use it to..."

"No, no," Randy quickly cut him off. "We don't want to know. "Okay, it looks like we have enough fire-power to kill AlliCroc," said Virgil. "Let's turn on some spotlights and start hunting."

Bob stood with an intimidated look on his face, "Sorry guys, my weapon went down with my boat."

"No worries, you just rest those broken bones and keep a lookout for that monster. If you see it, feel free to toss my grenades at it," Bobby smiled sarcastically, as he walked out the door and headed for the bridge to turn on the spotlights.

28

Chief Bhim was still fuming at the way he and his tribe had been treated by the mayor and Chief Officer Randy Taylor. Even with the death of his nephew, he was heart-broken and surprised at the little sympathy he and his tribe received.

Now, back on his own land on the Everglades Sanctuary, Mayor Nick Myers called to tell him that AlliCroc was back in his area. As expected, he told the mayor to go to hell when asked if he could assist in the kill, and ordered the tribe's women and children to stay clear of the water and shoreline until the reptile was captured and killed.

Bhim had no intensions of letting AlliCroc live. He hastily assembled his best hunters and prepared to track the reptile straight to hell if he had to.

While the chief was making last-minute adjustments with the boats along his dock, Durjaya cautiously walked up to his father and put a hand on his shoulder, "Father, it is time to come home for supper."

Bhim cleared what looked like a tear from his eye and looked at his son, "Tell your mother I will be there shortly. And son, Listen to me and stay clear of the water."

"Yes father, I know… Everybody knows to stay…"

"Listen to me!" Bhim cut in, grabbing his son by the arm. "Stay clear of these waters until AlliCroc is dead and gone!"

Taken off guard, Durjaya was fearful of what he saw in his father's eyes. For the first time in his life, he saw fear in the chief and had a bad feeling about him going after the reptile.

"You have my word. I will not go near the water," he replied anxiously as he turned and ran home.

Later that evening, Chief Bhim was sitting at the table smoking a pipe, his wife of thirty-five years finished the dishes and joined him.

"We're all worried about you Bhim," she said quietly, taking his hand. "We're worried about your health. You're in no condition to go out and hunt that killer."

"Stop worrying, I've never felt stronger in my life," he insisted.

"Let it go; let somebody else risk their lives and kill that reptile. You have too much to lose," she pleaded.

"No! Can't you see it's my responsibility?" he shouted, standing up and walking toward the back door.

"Why is it your responsibility? Is it because you're the chief of this diminishing tribe? Or do you have to prove that you're still a strong warrior!" she shouted back, holding her hands over her mouth when she realized she may have gone too far.

He took a deep breath and pounded his fist into the door before turning to face his wife, "Woman, I don't need to hear that from you; how dare you speak to me in that tone?"

She broke down crying and begged for him to stay but his mind was set on vengeance.

It was one-thirty in the morning when Captain Virgil and his crew called it quits. After spending nearly an hour stomping through the wetlands with halogen spotlights, AlliCroc had evaded capture once again.

At the suggestion of Bloodfoot, they decided to leave the safety of the boat and walk along the bank when the water became too shallow to cruise further with the fast-boat. Unfortunately for a few nosy alligators, the crew had no other choice than to blow their heads off when they wandered in too close.

"Okay fellas, let's call it a night. We'll backtrack to the boat and get some rest before we continue at dawn," said Virgil, raising his shotgun toward another set of big red eyes of an alligator sneaking in from the sawgrass. He was about to pull the trigger when it suddenly spooked and shot off underwater.

"Good call," replied Skip. "Any longer and these bloodsucking mosquitoes will sap out what little blood I still have."

Bloodfoot in his usual pissed-off mode replied, "You should have stayed in the boat with the other city boys," he said, referring to Bob and Bill, who stayed behind to guard the boat.

"That's enough Bloodfoot. Bob is too broken up to be walking around out here and I wanted Bill to stay and secure the boat," Virgil smirked, knowing the pirate was just trying to get a rise out of Skip.

They took their time and stayed vigilant as they backtracked to the boat, sloshing through ankle-deep water that hadn't been there before, and hoped they'd make it back before the water rose any higher.

Don, never one to hide his feelings, continued complaining that he should have stayed on the boat, as he seemed to stumble and fall at every fourth step. They continued in a single-file order, spaced about ten-feet apart so that nobody would get poked with a gun-barrel or get jabbed by Skip who was so frightened that he would all but climb a tree every time he heard a frog croak.

Three-quarters of the way back to the boat, Randy saw Virgil stop suddenly and wave a hand for everybody to look ahead.

"Oh my God!" Skip hysterically tried to whisper. "There it is! Right in front of us...Blocking our path to the boat!"

What Lurks Below

"Okay boys, it's show-time," Bloodfoot whispered, slowly making his way to the front of the unmoving line as if he were somehow able to protect the crew.

He slowly reached into his bag and pulled out three sticks of dynamite. Looking at the size of the reptile, then looking at what he was holding in his hand, he made a wise decision and reached for an additional three sticks.

Virgil remained calm and slowly began to walk backward and was floored when the vicious reptile followed his pace, as if taunting its prey. AlliCroc was now less than thirty-yards away.

Bloodfoot carefully stood his ground as the rest of the crew scrambled back and found cover behind some trees, but Virgil wasn't so lucky. Being ahead of the crew, the monster seemed to single him out.

"Virgil! Get the hell out of there!" Chuck shouted abruptly.

Virgil recognized that to make any sudden move would entice the reptile to attack. He turned to see a gumbo-limbo tree standing twenty-feet away and decided he'd have to make a break for it. He then looked over to Bloodfoot who was now puffing on a large cigar and preparing to ignite the dynamite. Running out of time, he knew the gumbo-limbo tree was slippery and hard to climb, so he unsheathed his bowie-knife and took several deep breaths.

"On the count of three, I'll break for the tree while you guys blast that son of a bitch," Virgil said in a low, calm tone.

"Run like hell and don't look back," Bloodfoot replied, blowing the ambers of the cigar, before lighting the fuse. "On my count...One... Two... Three!"

Virgil dropped his backpack and sprinted to the tree while AlliCroc appeared to know what was going to happen and gave chase before Bloodfoot reached the three-count. The crew blasted their shotguns and the dynamite exploded directly on the creatures back, but AlliCroc gave chase like a speeding locomotive. With shotguns blaring, the swamp looked like a Japanese fireworks display as Virgil leaped onto the tree, burying his knife deep into the trunk. He used the knife to quickly pull himself up as the gargantuan reptile rushed in, missing him by inches.

To the amazement of the crew, the dynamite and shotgun blasts seemed to bounce off the armored plated menace and only succeeded to make the reptile retreat as it let out an incredibly loud, ear-numbing hiss before escaping to the deeper, brackish water and disappeared.

"Everybody up the tree!" Bloodfoot shouted, "The damn thing went under!"

Virgil made room as the crew scrambled up the tree and Bloodfoot quickly shimmied up a nearby palm tree. Everybody was safe with the exception of Bobby, who couldn't climb a tree even when his life depended on it.

"Bobby, give me your hand, I'll pull you up!" Randy insisted, extending his hand.

"Too late 'ol buddy," he replied gravely, turning his attention to the hellacious shadow rising out of the water and moving towards him.

His composure remained as he dropped his empty shotgun and took the safety off his AK-47.

"Get behind the tree!" Bloodfoot yelled out, knowing it was too late.

Before the crew could reload their shotguns, AlliCroc emerged out of the water and was barreling through the muck toward its prey. Surprisingly, Bobby held steady until the mammoth's mouth opened and he was able to get a clear shot inside its mouth.

He crotched in a low combat stance and leveled the gun at the hideous jaws before squeezing the trigger. The crew watched in horror as half the rounds missed their mark completely and only a few found their way inside the vulnerable flesh of its mouth.

Bobby squeezed his eyes shut tight, waiting for the inevitable, when he heard the crew firing their shotguns.

"Bobby! Get your ass out now!" he heard Randy shout. Surprised he was still breathing, he opened one eye and saw that the reptile stopped charging and snapped its jaws shut before turning back towards the water. When he opened the other eye, he caught a brief glimpse of the enormous tail come around before it smacked him in the chest with full force.

Bobby was thrown like a rag doll through the air, landing with a sickening, bone-crushing thud against an old tree stump.

Once again, AlliCroc retreated into the water and disappeared. The stunned crew remained in the tree with their spotlights canvassing the water while Bloodfoot jumped down and ran over to Bobby.

A few minutes went by when the crew cautiously climbed out of the tree and ran over. Bobby looked like a rumpled sack of potatoes as Bloodfoot put a hand on his neck and felt for a pulse. He was alive but his breathing was shallow with a labored gurgling sound. Lying face down, it was hard to tell if he was paralyzed or unconscious.

"Alive?" Virgil asked, as he and the others walked up.

"He's alive but not well," Bloodfoot replied as he backed off so that Chuck and Randy could carefully turn him over on his back.

Blood was oozing out of his nose, mouth and ears while Chuck tried to remember what little he knew about internal injuries, "I'm no doctor, but it looks like he's got a concussion and some broken ribs," he construed.

"Okay, let's pick him up carefully and get back to the boat," Virgil ordered, taking a quick look around to make sure the reptile did not return. "We can't move him," Skip protested. "His neck looks like it may be broken. If we move him, he might die."

Randy looked at him as if he were from another planet, "Do you suggest we leave him here and go back to the boat to call the paramedics?" he scoffed. "Did you forget we're in the middle of the Everglades and nobody knows where the hell we are? By the time they finally find us, we'll be in that reptile's belly."

Without another word being said, Randy and Chuck picked Bobby up by the arms and walked side by side with their arms around his waist for support. Bloodfoot led the way with Virgil not far behind. Don and Skip trailed behind the captain while Bill searched the water with a spotlight from the boat, hoping to spot the crew.

They were painfully aware of the fact that high-tide was continuing to creep in, as they were now walking through knee-deep water. Skip and Don were nervously spotting and pointing out all the curious alligators while Bloodfoot systematically blew them away with his shotgun.

"Maybe we should try to be a little quieter," Chuck suggested.

"What's the point? Don says AlliCroc has extra-special senses and most likely knows exactly where we are," Randy replied.

"Not to mention that if we don't shoot those ten-foot gators, they'll eat you alive as well," Bloodfoot grinned.

"Damn! I didn't realize the boat was so far away, are you guys sure we're going in the right direction?" Don complained to nobody in particular.

"Keep moving, we're almost there," Virgil replied, eyeing the glow from the boats' spotlights in the distance.

Ten minutes later, Bloodfoot crouched down and signaled everybody to stop, "I see the boat. Everybody break and check their ammo. Skip, I suggest you make sure the safety switch is off this time."

"You check the ammo, I'm exhausted and I just want to get back to the boat," Don retorted.

"Stay put," Virgil ordered, "We'll move as a team."

The crew checked their weapons as Bloodfoot quietly pulled a pair of infrared binoculars from his rucksack. Virgil watched incisively as Bloodfoot took a couple steps forward and crouched down, peering through the binoculars intently.

"Don't tell me you spotted that monster near the boat," Virgil whispered.

After a long moment, Bloodfoot let the binoculars drift off his eyes and exhaled deeply, "The damn thing is at the boat. Its eyes and snout are just out of the water enough to keep an eye on the two aboard while waiting for our return."

"Smart animal... Too smart," Virgil replied, gnashing his teeth.

The two sat silently while the crew reloaded their shotguns and sloshed over, "All set, let's break for the boat," Chuck said with gusto.

"Not so fast," Virgil warned, holding out an arm to stop the engineer. "What the hell are we waiting for? Let's break for the boat!" Skip retorted, anxiously.

"We've got company waiting to greet us," Bloodfoot replied in a calm, calculated tone.

"What!?" Skip squealed, feeling his heart drop out of his

chest. "Should we alert Bill and Bob?" Don suggested spinelessly.

"No, Bob's too crippled and Bill will probably get himself killed if he aggravates that thing. It's sitting right off the bow," replied Virgil.

"What about us? We're gonna get killed either way!" Skip ranted.

In the blink of an eye, Bloodfoot grabbed Skip by the throat hard enough to make his eyes bulge, "I can do without the pessimistic ramblings. Maybe I should put you out of your miseries right now," he growled.

Bloodfoot abruptly felt a hard metal object on the back of his head as he heard the unmistakable sound of a gun's hammer clicking back, "Release my deckhand or I'll pull the trigger," Virgil advised in a low ominous tone.

Bloodfoot slowly turned his head and locked eyes with Virgil. Deep down, he knew without a doubt that Virgil wasn't bluffing and would do anything to save his crew. He turned his head back to Skip before releasing his grip and warned, "Don't say another word."

"Okay, now let's focus on the reptile before he comes charging," Randy said angrily, relieved that he wouldn't have to drop his hold on Bobby to break up a fight.

Virgil reholstered his gun and focused on the life-threatening monster, "Who's got a plan," he asked.

"I do," replied Bloodfoot, reaching for his rucksack. "The reptile is hurt. Bobby was able to shoot a few rounds into its mouth, which seemed to do some damage," he continued, pulling five sticks of dynamite out and wrapping the fuses. "If I can get close enough, with a little luck I can throw this bundle down its throat and blow its head off," he explained, in a sudden dry and troubled voice.

"How close are you going to get?" Chuck asked, uneasily. "As close as it takes."

"That's suicide," claimed Don.

"I'll have the element of surprise. I'll slowly walk over and get as close as possible until it makes its move."

"Okay, let's do it," Virgil replied quickly, surprising the crew at how fast he seemed to seal the pirate's fate. "But you're going to need some help... I'm going with you," he added.

Bloodfoot looked at Virgil for a long minute, trying to size him up. He couldn't figure out what made him tick, brave or foolish, he knew he could count on him to watch his back, "Very well, I could use the help," Bloodfoot responded, digging in his bag and retrieving more dynamite and another cigar.

"Whatever happens, make sure you keep this cigar dry so that you can light that fuse," he continued, handing Virgil the cigar.

The captain took his time lighting the cheap Dutch Master and gave the pirate an offensive look.

"What's with the face?" asked Bloodfoot. "I'm not going to squander my good cigars until we're sitting on the boat drinking your apricot brandy."

"Just make sure your throwing arm is in working order."

The two men puffed on their cigars and walked closer to the overwhelming reptile. Skip and Don relieved Randy and Chuck from the hold they had on Bobby and searched for a safe area to retreat to when all hell broke loose. Randy and Chuck quietly moved forward with their shotguns at the ready.

Chills went up Virgil's spine when they were within twenty-yards of the reptile and it leisurely moved its head in their direction. Suddenly a spotlight from the boat turned on and pointed in their direction with a blinding light.

"Ahoy Captain! I was getting a little concerned about..."

"Turn the spotlight off!" Virgil and Bloodfoot blurted to Bill, trying to shield their eyes and see where the monster was.

Bill quickly turned the spotlight off and ran to the

wheelhouse while Virgil was ready to leap out of his skin when he saw that AlliCroc was gone. "Hold steady Virgil!" Bloodfoot shouted. "The reptile submerged. The water's too shallow for him to take us by surprise... We'd see the wake!"

Virgil couldn't remember the last time he was so scared. He stood still and kept a watchful eye on the water, ready to bolt out of there at any second, "Any suggestions?"

"I believe AlliCroc just submerged. Bill! Put the spotlight on about ten-feet off the starboard side," Bloodfoot ordered, unruffled.

Bill's eyes widened at the thought of the gruesome behemoth so close to the boat and turned the spotlight where directed. At that instant, the vicious beast shot out of the water, snapping its enormous jaws toward the spotlight before splashing down and missing the wheelhouse by inches. Bob went running toward the bow and began blasting at the foamy water as the reptile changed direction and took off straight for Virgil and Bloodfoot.

"Here it comes!" Chuck shouted, as he and Randy joined the fight with shotguns blazing.

Virgil and Bloodfoot wasted no time lighting the dynamite and shouting for the others to take what little cover they had. The short fuse was timed perfectly as the explosion hit the beast's enormous back, causing AlliCroc to roar like a dinosaur as it continued racing forward. Bloodfoot waited until the deadly creature bore down on him with only thirty-feet to spare. As AlliCroc opened its mouth, the pirate threw the dynamite and dove under water. Just before the blast, the monster turned its head and veered off to escape, but the explosion seemed to stun the reptile as it rolled over on its back and sank.

When the smoke cleared, the crew cheered as they looked over and saw the reptile's belly sticking out of the water.

"We did it!" Virgil bellowed, his ears ringing from the blast. "I don't see blood," Bloodfoot was quick to point out.

Virgil stopped smiling and looked over to see if Bloodfoot was just being trivial, "Well... Why don't you swim over and rip a tooth out?"

"I probably would, if it were still there," he replied, inert faced.

Bill quickly flashed the spotlight to where the reptile had been and to the incredulous look from the crew, it was gone.

Bill felt the lump in his throat and searched the water with the spotlight, "I see the wake! It's moving away; it's swimming behind the bend sixty-yards on the port side," he continued anxiously, following the large flow of water. "Everybody get back to the boat... fast!" Virgil shouted, waving the crew on.

The crew made a bee-line for the boat. Bill helped Virgil and Bloodfoot as they quickly climbed out of the water and rushed to turn on every spotlight on the boat. The swampy area lit up like a used car lot as they stood guard with shotguns in hand, shouting for the others to hurry. Virgil ran to the galley and retrieved the pancor before returning to scout the water.

To pick up the pace, Skip flipped Bobby on his back and started to drag him through the water, only to see Don leave them behind and rush toward the boat.

"Hey! Get back here and give me a hand with Bobby," Skip shouted.

There was no way Don was going to help, he was beyond terrified. The only thing he could hear was the noisy splashing from his spineless retreat and the thumping of his heartbeat inside his head.

"You damn fool! You'll get us all killed!" Randy barked, as Don splashed by him with nothing more but to save himself.

Bloodfoot pushed Bill out of the way and grabbed Don by the scruff of his neck as he pulled him on deck, "Run and hide, coward!" he snarled, throwing Don to the side.

Randy made it to the boat and threw his shotgun on deck

before scrambling back to help Skip.

"Let's pick it up Skip," he encouraged, as he grabbed Bobby and helped drag him through the water.

"Almost there! Keep going, we're almost there!" Skip chanted, his eyes fixed on the boat.

As Bill and Bloodfoot continued to pull the crew out of the water, Chuck felt a sigh of relief when he watched Bobby being carefully pulled on deck.

Skip was still in the water, fretfully pushing the wounded veteran aboard when Virgil's heart felt like it squeezed tight in his chest. As he vigilantly searched the water with a spotlight, he saw a large wake emerge just beyond the stern, thirty-feet away and closing fast.

"Get Skip out of the water! It's back and swimming fast!" Virgil shouted, as he jumped out of the wheelhouse with the pancor shotgun and expertly moved the switch to engage all the shots to fire at once.

In a panic, Skip swam over and jumped into the smaller towboat tied to the fast-boat and leaped onboard. Virgil ran to the gunwale on the opposite side and blasted the reptile as it swam with tremendous power under the boat. The recoil knocked Virgil to the deck as the rest of the crew shuddered from the blast. They quickly recovered to witness the creature spring up from the bottom and explode through the side of the towboat, snapping the tie-line and sending it flying through the air. Skip could be heard screaming out of control as the crumbled boat landed a few yards away and quickly sank in the shallow bog.

Skip's head popped to the surface with a frenzied look as the crew shouted for him to find cover, "Get out of the water!" they shouted simultaneously.

Dazed and confused, Skip shook his head quickly and was about to make a swim for the boat when AlliCroc appeared in the path. The vile creature made no effort to attack its prey, it just floated on the surface with a devilish looking grin as it stared at Skip.

"No!" Skip screeched, as he froze in shock. In a panic, he lost his bearings and swam out to deeper water until he heard a shotgun blast and looked to see Bloodfoot firing shots at another predator swimming towards him. The pirate's aim was dead-on as the head exploded from what looked like a ten-foot gator. For a brief moment, he thought he was safe until he heard the crew shouting for him again while more shotgun blasts were hitting the water behind him. He turned to see AlliCroc unhurriedly swimming toward him.

"Don't look Skip! Swim fast to the boat!" Bill shouted, the

apprehension in his voice prevailing.

Don was paralyzed with fear as he broke down and fell to his knees, letting out a repulsive scream while the crew continued to open fire at the pursuing creature. As the shotgun blasts appeared to bounce off the armored plating, Virgil finished reloading the pancor and blasted a single shot, hitting the monster in the back of the head.

AlliCroc contorted and roared violently as it retreated underwater and swam like a torpedo toward Skip, leaving a small trail of blood.

"Give me your hand!" Randy shouted, as he reached over the gunwale next to Bill, who looked like he was debating whether or not to jump in and throw Skip on deck.

"Hurry up!" Skip screamed, as he finally made it to the boat and held out a hand.

Randy locked eyes with Skip as their hands met. The look of determination was staggering for a fleeting moment, and then suddenly replaced with terror as Skip let out a petrifying scream and was brutally slammed into the side of the boat. Startled, Randy jumped back and opened his eyes just in time to see AlliCroc's jaws chomping Skip from the waist down. Skip's ear-piercing screams became muffled by the gurgling sound of blood bursting through his nose and mouth while the monster continued to gulp down its prey. The rest of the crew continued shooting at the reptile to no avail, as the blasts continued to bounce off its hide. There was nothing they could do, with only Skip's upper body sticking out of the creature's massive jaws; it began tossing its head up and gulping down in gory abandon while Skip had the surprised look on his face of one who couldn't believe he was being eaten alive.

Finally, with one quick shake of its head, AlliCroc swallowed the horrified deckhand and submerged. The attack only lasted about a half-minute, but seemed forever to the horrified crew who now stood silently, trying to comprehend what just took place.

29

Chief Bhim sprung up from his sweat-soaked bed and sat with a look of dismay as he stared out of the window. His wife, awake all night and keeping a watchful eye on her husband's deteriorating health, worriedly jumped up after him.

"What's wrong Bhim? Is it a nightmare?" she asked.

The chief didn't reply as he rushed out of bed and stood by the window. Daybreak was still a couple hours away and the surrounding area looked calm and peaceful.

"Come back to bed and we'll talk about it," she continued.

"The monster is close... It must be killed before it returns to the Sanctuary," he admonished in a whisper.

Bhim quickly got dressed and charged out of the house and hastily walked down by the water. His wife ran to the phone and called his best friend and senior tracker, Billy Boggs.

Boggs was the tribe's most dependable hunter/tracker. He grew up in the Everglades along with Bhim and helped catch most of the animals at the Sanctuary. A long-time silent partner, he preferred to stay out of the lime-light and let Bhim take credit for the successful tourist attraction. At a height of six-foot-five-inches, and built like an Olympic body-builder, his commandeering presence was a big contrast to his mild, courteous demeanor. His soft-spoken voice was a major misconception to those who didn't know him and thought he was a softy.

"Billy! I'm worried about Bhim, he's gotten worse!" she cried. "What is it?" replied Billy, wiping the sleep out of his eyes.

"He's still talking about AlliCroc and just got up and walked down by the water."

"I'll find and talk sense to him while you make some coffee," he replied lazily, sliding the window curtains over to peer down by the docks.

Minutes later, barefoot and wearing a camouflaged warm-up suit, Billy walked down to where his old friend stood and threw a rock in the quiet waters.

"It came back. I can feel it," Bhim said eerily, his eyes fixed on the docile river.

"Impossible. AlliCroc is haunting your dreams. It is being hunted far to the east from here, it will never..."

"They said it swam upriver," Bhim cut him off. "But I didn't think the reptile was this quick, or smart."

Billy didn't say a word. He squatted down and stuck a hand in the muddy water as if to feel the vibrations. After a long, quiet minute, he stood up and turned to face his friend, "What do you want to do?"

"We must kill that horrific beast," he replied, his mouth a tight, grim line.

"The white man turned his back on you, let them deal with it," Billy retorted.

"No!" he shouted angrily, confirming that he was still the leader. "It killed too many people, including my nephew. It will kill again unless we stop it."

"Stop it with what? It's a monster! It can't be stopped with the weapons we have!" Billy shot back, raising his voice to the chief for the first time ever. Bhim looked at Billy with dismay, "We must kill AlliCroc. It tasted human flesh and will keep killing until we stop it!" he ordered, becoming irritated that his friend saw him as fragile and incapable of thinking clearly.

Billy threw another rock into the river and let out a heavy sigh, "Let's kill the menace, have you got a plan?"

"I have a plan," the chief nodded. "When the sun rises, we gather our best hunters down here by the dock; we'll rid this land of that mutated reptile once and for all."

Billy waited patiently for Bhim to explain the plan and was surprised to see him turn and walk away, "So be it," he murmured to himself, hoping his fearless leader turned fragile friend was doing the right thing and not leading his men to their death.

Officer Randy Taylor was the first to emerge from the galley. The shock of what he and the crew went through a few hours earlier had sapped the will they had to carry on with the hunt.

The dismal sun was trying to poke out of the overcast sky as a light rain drizzled on the hot and muggy swamp. Randy leaned over the side rail and put the hood up on his rain jacket while sipping his coffee, and watched the wildlife awaken from its slumber, searching for breakfast. It was hard to imagine the tranquility of the swamp was accommodating the most ferocious reptile known to mankind since the dinosaur-age. Somewhere below the surface of the calm waters lurked the devil's reptile, and its creator was on the boat. He wished Don was killed instead of Skip.

Captain Virgil slowly walked out on deck along with Chuck and stood at the bow with Randy. The death of his deckhand weighed heavy on him as he leaned over the side and scanned the area.

"We're pulling anchor and heading for the Everglades Sanctuary where we'll drop Bobby off before continuing," he informed.

Chuck and Randy gave each other a surprised look and saw the unwavering face of the captain. "Agreed," replied Randy.

Bill stepped out of the galley a minute later with a troubled look, "He's still unconscious. I think his neck is broken but I'm no doctor."

"We're taking him to the Sanctuary," Virgil replied calmly as he headed for the wheelhouse.

Bill turned and watched with a puzzled look as Virgil entered the wheelhouse, "Why don't we just take him back with us?" he asked.

"Because we're not going back," Chuck replied sourly.

Don was nowhere to be seen. After he frantically made it back to the boat and witnessed Skip's grisly death, he locked himself in the head and refused to come out. With the porthole open, he heard the conversation and stumbled out, "We can't fight AlliCroc by ourselves! Where the hell is Bloodfoot?" he ranted.

"Hadn't seen him," Randy replied dryly.

"He took off on his own after the attack," Bill added.

"Well that's just great! Why didn't anybody stop him?" Don fluttered anxiously.

"Why didn't you get your damn head out of the toilet and

stop him yourself," Randy disdainfully replied.

The crew waited an hour for Bloodfoot to return. When it was clear he wasn't coming back, Bill pulled up the anchor as Virgil cranked up the engine and put the boat in gear.

Don walked into the wheelhouse on the verge of tears and practically begged to stop the hunt.

"For God's sake Virge, can we at least radio in for some help out here?" he pleaded.

"Take a look at the radio," Virgil calmly replied.

With a perplexed look, Don turned to see the radio sitting in pieces as if it had exploded, "What the hell happened to the radio?"

"I'd say somebody shot it," Virgil shot back in an annoyed tone.

Don collapsed in a chair and put his hands on his head. Bill heard the commotion and promptly entered, "What's this I hear?"

"Somebody shot the radio," Virgil coolly replied.

Where Virgil thought one of the crew got caught up in the fire-fight with the reptile and accidentally shot the radio, Bill thought right away of the man who seemed to be secretly following them.

"It wasn't any of us Captain. There's somebody out here watching us," Bill counteracted.

Virgil looked at him as if he'd lost his mind before replying, "Let's hear it."

"When we passed by the boat ramp at the mouth of the swamp, Bloodfoot and I spotted a strange black car that looked out of place. There was a man watching us through binoculars. When Bloodfoot picked up his binoculars and peered back, the man got up and ran."

"I think you're paranoid."

"I thought so too, until I spotted that campfire close to ours. That's when Bloodfoot disappeared for a while, He told me not to tell you guys and get your mind off the hunt, I think he went over to check it out."

"I also saw a boat Virgil, it was following along behind the sawgrass, about fifty-yards behind us," Randy added, hearing the conversation and stepping inside the wheelhouse.

"Maybe Bloodfoot saw the flash from the rifle that hit the radio and gave chase," Don said, picking his head up out of his hands.

Virgil didn't like what he was hearing. Who would possibly spy on them while hunting the monster? Finally, he looked over to Randy and caught his eyes staring back… "Meyers, Mayor Nick Meyers, the rat bastard," Randy acknowledged.

"Okay, stay vigilant. If somebody wants us dead, it won't happen until after AlliCroc is killed," Virgil presumed.

Chief Bhim and twenty of his best hunters gathered near the water at sunrise. He explained in great detail how they would be split up into five groups, closing off access canals to the area AlliCroc is believed to be in with large, thick nets. The nets would be weighted on the bottom and stretched across the surface where the reptile would be driven into and tangled. While tangled in the netting, the hunters will blast at its head with twelve-gauge shotguns until dead.

When the chief finished explaining the plan to his men, he looked up at the sky with discontent as it rained harder, feeling cursed that even the heavens were against him.

The hunters made their way to the boat dock where five eighteen-foot skiffs and an airboat were waiting.

The Chief's son, Durjaya and a couple of his friends had already loaded four skiffs with the heavy nets, "I think your father is being overly cautious Durjaya. Why don't we hunt that gator the way we always hunt?" asked his younger, cocky friend who remembered AlliCroc when it was a caged attraction.

"You have no idea what that reptile has done. It's no ordinary gator," replied Durjaya, taking offense at the way his friend sounded towards the chief.

"Sure it's big, but when it was caged in the pit, it was so passive that I stood on its head and nothing happened, remember?"

"It's done a lot of killing since then," Durjaya retorted, deciding not to carry on with the useless conversation. He shook his head and continued to drag the last net into a skiff. When finished, he climbed into one of the five boats and cranked the engine before looking up and seeing his father walk over.

"We're fueled up and ready to go father," he said with a smile.

Bhim looked down and saw himself as a young man as he reached down and put a hand on his son's shoulder, "I want you to stay behind," he said, flatly.

The disappointed look on his son's face said it all, "Why? Besides you and Billy Boggs, I'm the best hunter here," he argued.

"You know what that reptile can do. If something bad happens to me, I'll need you to carry on in my name," he grudgingly replied.

"But you need me out there," he protested angrily.

"I need you alive," Bhim insisted, growing tired of arguing with his son. Durjaya felt rejected as he shut down the motor and stormed off the skiff. He knew deep down that his father was right, but he was more concerned about his father's health and well-being ever since his cousin was killed and the mayor treated him like dirt when they returned to the Sanctuary. His father had become somewhat detached from his people and a bit confused, AlliCroc had become a personal threat to the chief and he knew damn well that he had to kill it to preserve his sanity.

Captain Bloodfoot fought and killed many large animals in his time. He fought hand-in-hand with some of the largest sharks in the world. He kept teeth as souvenirs of all his conquests, including the biggest crocodiles from Australia and attached them to his boots. He jumped on the backs of menacing orcas off the coast of Costa Rica and gutted them to death with his bare hands and trusty hunting knife. He killed bigger boar with his bare hands that would make the world record seem a joke and there wasn't a man in the world he wouldn't stand up to.

The challenge of killing AlliCroc was the only thing that kept him in the mosquito-infested swamp, hunting the mutant reptile as it was hunting him until now.

Now there was another problem facing him and the crew, as he clearly saw the flash of a gun deep in the thicket of the swamp while he and the crew were fighting the reptile. All reservations about the strange man with the black car had vanished when he saw the radio explode after the flash from what he knew was a rifle.

He jumped on the muddy bank when the reptile disappeared and made his way to the mysterious flash. Upon arrival, he wasn't surprised to see the tell-tale sign of a hitman. A tripod stand was set up between two bushes and only one spent shell from a high-powered rifle was lying next to it. He sat and wandered why the hitman didn't finish the job and kill the crew, or did he hit his target, the radio. Who would hire a professional killer to come out here and just watch what the hunting crew was doing and why would he just shoot out the radio?

He turned back toward the boat and decided it would be foolish to try to return to the boat with AlliCroc lurking around, so he found a gumbo-limbo tree and climbed to the thickest branch. He tied himself to the branch which hung fifteen-feet over the water and tried to figure out the predicament he was now facing.

He thought Captain Virgil and his crew were stand-up guys who worked hard and couldn't figure they'd have any enemies trying to kill them. Randy was a cop in the Port and probably made some enemies, but none that would go through these drastic measures to kill him. Don was nothing more than a trouble-making coward who probably had more enemies than friends, and Bloodfoot could probably take the side of the men who wanted him dead, but it didn't make sense; they could kill him anywhere.

Bloodfoot continued down the list as he tried to make sense of the situation when it suddenly dawned on him. Mayor Nick Myers had the most to lose if one of the crew talked about his dealings with AlliCroc. The reason the hitman took out the radio was so that all communication would be gone. He wouldn't have to worry about one of the crew accidently blurting over the radio that Meyers was involved, but what next? Bloodfoot became uneasy with the feeling he got when he figured the hitman will finish the job after the crew killed AlliCroc.

He planned to get back to the fast boat and warn the captain and crew, but not before he got some rest. The safest place for him to get some shut-eye was in the tree, so he made sure the line he tied himself with was secure before he nodded off.

At first light, he was suddenly awakened by the rain and a painful feeling of his chest caving in. Looking down past his chin, he found himself wrapped up with a giant python that looked to be at least eighteen feet long. Bugger! was the only thing he could think of as he heard the fast-boat engine come to life in the distance. He held his breath, careful not to exhale, as he struggled to reach for his hunting knife strapped to his waist. Too late, the damn thing's got me good. His mind was racing as he gave up trying to snatch his hunting knife. With every slight move he made, the snake squeezed harder as he tried to calmly reach his boot where he kept a smaller knife.

He frantically felt for the handle of the smaller knife with his increasingly numbing hand and pulled it out of the scabbard. If he dropped the knife, he knew it would be over, so he carefully wrapped his fingers around the handle and began stabbing and slicing into the mid-section of the python.

The snake responded swiftly by squeezing harder and inching closer to Bloodfoot's neck. For a minute or two, Bloodfoot thought he had finally met his match. He felt his eyes bulging out of his head and could no longer breathe as he struggled to keep stabbing and twisting the blade to cause maximum damage.

Suddenly, the snake's head slammed into his shoulder and bit down hard. Bloodfoot let out a vicious shriek that sounded more like a Viking attacking, than a cry of pain and plunged the knife deeper and deeper. He suddenly could feel the snake's palpitations with every thrust of the blade and knew the predator was in great pain. He also knew that he was seeing a wave of black shadowing over him as death came knocking, but he refused to give in.

Bloodfoot's stabbing motions slowed as his brain was starved for oxygen when the snake impulsively convulsed and loosened its death grip. He fought back the urge to pass out and was able to un-wrap the snake from his body. He plunged the small knife deep into the convulsing snake and quickly drew his bowie knife, cutting his lifeline to the tree and falling to the muddy bank. The snake was quick to react as it fell on Bloodfoot and swiftly wrapped itself around him. This time, the giant python had no chance. Bloodfoot instinctively grabbed the snake behind the head with his powerful hand and sliced its head off in one quick motion.

"Aaaarrgh!" he shouted, holding the snake's lifeless head in the air like a conquering hero. Worn out and relieved his ribs weren't broken, the pirate had the unmistakable look of the proud, victorious hunter after the fight of his life. One minute, he thought he would succumb to the Grim Reaper and the next, he had yet to see another adventurous day and add another trophy of a man-eating reptile to add to his list of conquests.

He washed off in the river and bandaged the bleeding snake-bite on his shoulder in addition to carefully putting the snake's head in his duffel bag. Ten minutes later, he was refreshed and full of life. With a triumphant grin on his weathered face, he once again set his sights on AlliCroc and the new threat, the hitman.

30

The Vietnam fast-boat plowed a wake through the overcast swamp, searching for the Everglades Sanctuary. Captain Virgil grew increasingly agitated as it seemed they had become completely lost. Nobody on the boat except for Don had ever been there and it appeared he had no idea where they were, as every side canal they entered turned out to be a dead end.

Bill attended to Bobby as the rest of the crew eagerly watched for signs of the biggest tourist attraction in the Everglades. Finally, after an hour and a half of searching, Virgil rounded a bend and nearly hit the dock to the Indians money maker.

"Whoa!" Virgil gasped, as he cut the throttle and eased away from the dock, "About goddamn time we found this hell-hole."

Randy and Bill stood portside with dock lines as the captain turned toward the waterfront and idled up. He eased up to the dock and gently tapped it with the boat as Bill jumped off and quickly tied the lines.

Before the engine was shut down, six Indians met them at the dock and patiently waited for Virgil to exit the wheelhouse.

"Hey fellas, it's me, Don Henderson," Don said with a smile as he leaped off the boat.

"Get back on your boat and get the hell out of here," one of the Indians replied with a no-nonsense look.

Don stopped in his tracks and erased the smile, "Who the hell are you and where's Chief Bhim?"

Bhim's wife walked over and stopped in front of Don, "You and your men are not welcomed here, please leave."

Not surprised that the tribe felt ill-will towards Don, Randy stepped off the boat and walked over, "I'm Officer Randy Taylor. We have a hurt man aboard and we're dropping him off here. You will call the paramedics to pick him up," he ordered, before stepping aside and walking past the six Indians, toward the souvenir shop.

An Indian turned to stop him when Bhim's wife said, "Let him go. These men are here to unload a wounded man, they won't be long."

Virgil stood in the wheelhouse watching the incident unfurl while lighting a cigarette. The look on his face showed no sign of compassion as he stepped out and leaned on the gunwale, "Call the paramedics now," he ordered.

Before Randy made it to the small shack, a giant swamp buggy strolled up with ten happy tourists aboard and Durjaya at the wheel. He took a double take at the site of the familiar officer and quickly jumped out and ran over, "Why are you here?" he said with a concerned look.

"We're hunting your damn reptile and one of my men is hurt. Paramedics are on the way and we're leaving soon after," Randy replied flatly.

"My father is also hunting AlliCroc. He and twenty hunters left earlier and headed up that canal," he said, pointing his finger to a passageway that looked like it wrapped around to the back of the Sanctuary.

"What makes him think the reptile's in that direction?"

"He thinks it's coming back home," replied Durjaya, as he turned and ran down to the dock to tell the others not to start trouble with the crew.

Randy didn't know if he felt better or worse knowing Bhim was still hunting the beast. He shook his head and walked inside the shop to get out of the rain.

Nearly an hour went by before the paramedics arrived and loaded Bobby into the helicopter. He finally woke up screaming in pain as the medics performed their routine checks and balances. Afterword, they stabilized him and prepared to take off.

"I had better go with Bobby to make sure he's alright," Don told Virgil. "Take one step off this boat and I'll shoot you," replied Virgil, as he cranked up the engine.

The crew huddled in the wheelhouse to get out of another downpour as the captain pulled away from the dock and headed for the foggy, sawgrass-ridden path Durjaya said his father took. The crew had a bad feeling as they entered the river and the Sanctuary disappeared from view in the gray wall of rain.

Chief Bhim and his hunters reached the area where he thought AlliCroc would be headed and positioned their heavy nets. The dreary rain turned into a steady drizzle as they feverishly set their nets around a wide open basin lined with sawgrass and brush. Four small tributaries, one from each direction, gingerly snaked their way into the area, and Bhim had the uncanny intuition that the reptile would come through one unless it crawled over land, but they would have seen the tell-tale signs.

When the weighted nets were connected as one, the hunters sat quietly and waited for the chief to give them the word to start closing in. Bhim and one of his men traveled with the airboat, but switched to a canoe as they cruised around the area equipped with a sonar and depth finder, hoping to find the massive reptile hiding on the murky bottom. The deepest part was thirty-two feet in the center, which gave AlliCroc plenty of room to hide, should it be already in the area.

What Lurks Below

Between the misty rain and the heat in the swamp, an eerie fog loomed as the men sat soaked to the bone, hoping AlliCroc was nowhere near. Billy Boggs noticed that one of the hunters involved with the attack in Sandy Beach Park was so frightened and cold; he sat shaking with blue lips quivering, undeniably in no shape for this hunt.

"Let's pack it in chief, we'll do it again tomorrow when the weather's more agreeable," he called from a portable walkie-talkie.

"Sit tight, AlliCroc will be here," Bhim responded.

Billy had a bad feeling about sending the hunters out, especially in this weather. Most of them saw the aggressiveness of the reptile and wanted no part of it, but to say no to the chief would put them in exile.

"I see nothing Chief," said the hunter staring at the small green screen. "Keep watching," said Bhim. "I know AlliCroc is here."

Suddenly, two hunters saw a large wake coming out of the tributary from the south, "Chief! It's here!" they shouted in a panic, pointing toward the wake that caromed off the banks.

"All boats close in!" Bhim bellowed as his canoe-mate dug through the water with his paddle back to the airboat.

The wake disappeared as quickly as it arrived, meaning the gargantuan reptile had gone deep, sending fear throughout the hunters as they wondered where it would attack. They slowly closed in with the net and hoped AlliCroc would quickly get caught up in it to ease their reservations, but they had no idea what was about to take place.

"There it is!" cried another hunter, pointing at the re-established wake. "It's going back the way it came."

Bhim was quick to realize that the two boats rushing to close the net and block its escape were moving to slow, "Hurry up, close the net!" he screamed into the walkie-talkie.

The big wake disappeared once again and Bhim was relieved to think the reptile abandoned its escape, "It's gone down again! Hold your positions and slowly close in!" he continued to bark into the walkie-talkie.

The net was finally connected in a huge circle as the boats slowly moved inward. The hunters kept a wary eye as they retrieved their shotguns and anticipated the reptile's next move.

Without warning, one of the boats shuddered as if something slammed into it and was dragged backwards at an alarming speed. Water was flooding over the transom as the five hunters aboard anxiously fired their shotguns into the water.

"We caught the reptile in the net!" a grinning hunter cried out. His grin turned to terror as the boat continued backwards and began to take on water.

The boat next to the one being dragged also began to draw water. The panicked operator tried to compensate by slamming the throttle forward, but it was too late. The livid reptile was caught up in the net and went wild as it tried to escape. The two boats collided and quickly submerged, dumping all ten hunters into the water. One man was tangled in the net and was quickly dragged under and drowned.

"Fire!" Bhim shouted as the reptile's hideous head breached the surface. The hunters blasted away at the creature as it snapped its jaws at the netting and tried to get free. Another hunter in the water got tangled in the net when AlliCroc rolled and became wrapped tight against the reptile's lower jaw. His screams of panic stopped when the beast turned its head and quickly decapitated him while the horrified others swam to the muddy bank and ran for cover.

As the shotguns continued blasting, AlliCroc stopped spinning and tried to head for the bottom, pulling the remaining two boats closer together as they struggled to remain afloat. Chief Bhim was now in his airboat and promptly pulled up alongside the feeble boats. Billy Boggs jumped aboard and hastily grabbed a section of the net and wrapped it around a cleat. AlliCroc roared like a dinosaur and plunged toward the bottom, dragging another boat with it. Half the hunters in the water swam for shore while the others climbed aboard the remaining skiff and the airboat. They reloaded their shotguns when a great force pulled the bow of the airboat below the surface.

"I can't believe it! It's pulling us under!" Billy shouted, amazed at the tremendous strength.

The front of the airboat submerged three-feet before the cleat snapped and the aluminum hull shot back to the surface.

"Damn, cleat snapped off!" Bhim shrieked, reaching into the water and grabbing more netting. He quickly tied the net to a stern cleat and jumped back in the seat, "Hold on!" he shouted as he gunned the airboat, hoping to drag the reptile back to the surface.

After a couple minutes of what felt like a tug-of-war match, AlliCroc shot out of the water, twisting and snapping at everything in sight. The hunters continued blasting at it relentlessly.

Two miles away, Virgil and the crew heard the turmoil and gunned the boat full throttle in the direction of the melee.

"Jeez!" Bill said. "Sounds like a war zone over there!"

"It is a war zone... man against beast!" replied Virgil. "Everybody grab your weapons and get ready!"

Randy ran to the galley and grabbed the case containing the Pancor Jackhammer shotgun. He anxiously threw the case open and grabbed the fully loaded drum before sprinting off to the bow of the boat. Virgil expressed amusement when he saw Randy standing at the bow, earnestly connecting the heavy drum to the shotgun and standing like Rambo; if he had spread his legs any further apart, he'd do a split.

As the old relic practically flew through the water, Bloodfoot, who also heard the blasting, ran toward the excitement. He was amazed at his good fortune that he'd walked in the right direction.

Running through the swampy banks in ankle-deep muck, Bloodfoot was nearly engulfed by the wake of the fast boat as it careened around a bend.

"Hey Captain! That was Bloodfoot we just passed!" Chuck shouted. "We'll pick him up later!"

"We might need him!"

"No time to stop, get your shotgun ready!" Virgil shouted, giving the engineer a defiant stare.

Chuck through his arms up in defeat and walked toward the

stern, "God help us," he murmured under his breath as he watched the soaked pirate standing with a confounded look on his face.

Chief Bhim and his men were recklessly blasting away at the creature when it finally stopped moving. The tension on the net eased and Bhim ordered to cease fire. The worn hunters sat in the remaining boats and looked on in awe at the bulk of the massive reptile as it floated on the surface. The airboat was running dead slow, just enough to keep tension on the nets in order to keep AlliCroc's flaccid body from sinking.

"It sure looks a lot bigger in the wild than it did at the sanctuary," Billy said, wiping water off his brow.

"It is bigger, much bigger. It's been eating well," replied Bhim, patting his longtime friend on the back. "Now let's tie a line to its tail and drag it back to the sanctuary. Tonight, we celebrate like never before," he smiled wearily.

Billy shook his head in agreement while keeping a watchful eye on the reptile. He wasn't going to celebrate until the beast was hauled out of the water and cut to pieces.

As the hunters tied a line to AlliCroc's tail, they heard the unmistakable sound of a diesel engine roaring toward them. Bhim looked to the south as the fast-boat turned another bend and came into view. Captain Virgil could be seen in the wheelhouse as he eased up on the throttle and slowly made his way toward the airboat.

"They did it!" Bill shouted, "Bhim and his men killed the beast!"

"And not a second too soon," replied Virgil with a sigh of relief.

Virgil eased the old relic along the port side of the overcrowded airboat with precision and cut the engine, allowing it to drift the final few feet. Bill threw Bhim the line, but he refused to take it.

"Go away. You men are not welcomed here," Bhim said in a disgruntled tone.

Standing in the wheelhouse, Virgil shot him a look like he wanted to rip his heart out before replying, "Don't be a fool Bhim. Let the officer shoot the reptile in the head with that thing and make sure it's dead," he said, pointing at the Pancor shotgun.

"The white man thinks I'm a fool," Bhim scornfully shouted to his men. "I don't think you're a fool Chief," Virgil replied in a diplomatic manner. "We both know how thick those plates on its back are... they're like armored plates. All we want to do is blow its goddamn head off to make sure it stays dead."

The Chief's men stood on edge when Virgil began to shout near the end of his speech.

"Leave now, while you still can," Bhim threatened as he and his men trained their weapons on the crew.

Randy held an itchy finger on the trigger of the fierce Pancor Jackhammer shotgun. He wanted to blow a hole in the airboat so bad he could taste it, but Virgil shrugged in defeat and ordered Bill to retrieve the dock line. Cranking up the noisy diesel engine, the captain slowly backed away from the Indians.

"What the hell Virgil," Randy protested under his breath.

"Stay calm," he coolly replied. "I'm going to back off about twenty yards. When we're clear, I want you guys to crouch below the gunwale. Randy, when you get a clear shot, I want you to blow AlliCroc's head off."

While Don scurried away and hid in the galley, Bill and Chuck looked at each other and slowly crouched down below the side rail.

"Randy, make sure you use that Pancor at full maximum, shoot the full load at once," Virgil grinned, knowing damn well that the officer intended to do just that.

Randy looked up toward the wheelhouse with a slight grin

and replied just above a whisper, "With this gun, it might blast the chief and his men out of the water as well."

"Bhim wants to play hardball and we want to know damn well that the beast is dead, aim for the head and try not to miss," Virgil boldly replied.

The hunters secured a line to the monster's enormous tail, linking it to the one remaining skiff and cranked up the engine. The small boat was seriously overloaded, so Chief Bhim ordered a few of the hunters to swim to the mucky bank and wait for another boat to come back and pick them up.

As Bhim started the engine on the airboat, he noticed Billy flinch and stare at the behemoth reptile with concern. Billy wasn't positive, but he thought he saw AlliCroc's head turn slightly in his direction.

"I think we should make sure it's dead Bhim," he finally said, with a hint of alarm in his deep voice.

"The white man has you second guessing eh?" Bhim smirked, putting the airboat in gear.

"No no, I just think..."

"I'll do the thinking," Bhim interrupted. "You just keep an eye on AlliCroc and make sure that line stays secure."

Chief Bhim grew impatient with what he saw as the lack of

confidence his hunters were showing towards him. He reminded himself to bring this matter up later after the AlliCroc ordeal was over.

Captain Virgil backed the fast-boat away and put it in idle when he was fairly sure his crew was out of harm's way. He gave Randy the nod as the officer vigilantly aimed at the monster's head. Beads of sweat began to run down his face as the Indians gradually made a wide turn around a bend and headed towards the Sanctuary. The misty rain broke into a heavy downpour once again as Randy found his target.

"I've got a clear shot. The Indians just rounded the bend and with luck, they should be clear of the blast," Randy said.

"Wait... almost there. Fire when the airboat is behind the trees," replied Virgil, putting the boat in gear and slowly trailing behind.

Randy quickly wiped the rain and sweat out of his eyes, "It doesn't matter, there's no doubt they're going to feel the blast. The reptile is being towed ten yards behind them. I'm sure they're going to feel it. But if it's still alive, they'll surely die."

Virgil put the throttle forward and sped up to the behemoth, hoping to keep the blast away from the hunters, "Fire at will," he shouted.

Nobody was prepared for the nightmare that was about to

unravel. Without warning, the gargantuan reptile jumped back to life and thrashed like never before. The line tied to the skiff was jerked back when AlliCroc swung his massive tail and the small skiff shot back like a child's toy, throwing the two hunters onboard into the murky water.

The reptile was hurt, angry and threatened, which made it probably the most aggressive creature on earth. The two terrified hunters in the water didn't stand a chance as AlliCroc turned on them and released its full fury. Too paralyzed with fear to move, all they could do was scream as the revolting reptile swam over and engulfed the closest swimmer while the other found the adrenalin to swim for the bank.

Chief Bhim and his men on the airboat could do nothing but watch as the monster tore through the two men. The first man was quickly ripped apart and swallowed before the reptile chased after the next at lightning speed. With just several feet to go until he could pull himself up on the bank, AlliCroc leaped at the man and snapped its massive jaws around his waist. He let out a repulsive, blood-gurgling scream before the reptile went into a death roll, turning the river into a red, blood-soaked slaughterhouse.

"Fire!" Virgil shouted at the top of his lungs.

Randy pulled the trigger on the Pancor Jackhammer

shotgun before the captain could utter the word. The blast missed the reptile and hit the bank like a meteor, blasting sawgrass and muck fifty-feet in the air. AlliCroc turned toward the fast-boat while chomping on the fleshy remains of the dead hunter and charged.

With a look of horror, Virgil had no other choice than to gun the throttle and ram the monster head on, "Brace yourselves for impact!"

The old relic jumped up to a hydroplane and headed for AlliCroc with full power. A second before impact, the gargantuan reptile appeared to try to leap out of the water. The fast boat slammed head-on into the creature and all hands on deck were violently thrown through the air. Before impact, Virgil leaped out of the door and skimmed across the surface, missing the reptile by inches.

Chief Bhim and his men watched with fascination as the bow of the boat seemed to disappear on impact while the creature let out a gut-wrenching roar and turned belly-up before sinking.

Bill was the first to surface and survey the situation. Except for a large gash on his left thigh, he was surprised he survived with nothing broken. Virgil was slowly crawling out of the muck in a thicket of sawgrass near shore when he saw Chuck,

Randy, Bill and Bob surface and swim like a racing team toward the bank, where they quickly scuttled out of the water. All accounted for but Don.

"Where's Don?" Virgil hollered.

"He must be in the boat!" Randy grunted, trying to catch his breath.

The crew looked to where the fast-boat should have been and saw the radio antenna sticking out of the water like a mile-marker. The boat was sitting on the bottom about fifteen feet and the only thing marking its watery grave was the roof-mounted antenna.

Without saying another word, Virgil dove in the water and swam toward the antenna. He took a deep breath and disappeared below the surface in search of his former friend. As the crew anxiously waited for the captain to resurface, Chuck and Randy all of a sudden looked at each other and realized Bhim and his buddy were all too quiet. They looked over to where they were last seen and saw the airboat flipped over and Bhim and Billy sitting on the overturned hull with dire expressions.

Minutes later, Don's head splashed up, and he made a bee-line to the shore.

"Where's the captain?" Randy asked, as he grabbed Don's

arm and helped him out of the muck.

"He's looking for that big-ass shotgun you had," Don panted.

"Why the hell did you stay down there?" Chuck added.

"There's an air pocket in the head, I was afraid AlliCroc would get me if I swam to shore. I was going to wait as long as I could until Virgil opened the door and drug me out by my leg."

Bill and Randy took a quick search of the water and prepared to jump in after Virgil, but his head finally breached the murky surface, "Lost the damn Pancor shotgun," he grunted, spitting out a mouthful of water and doing the backstroke to shore, keeping an eye behind him.

The crew gathered around the mucky bank as the rain continued. They took count of their injuries and were glad to see nobody had broken any bones. When finished, they looked over and saw the two Indians still sitting on top of the overturned airboat and waved them over.

"Swim to the shore Bhim, let's get the hell out of here!" Virgil shouted. The chief slowly looked up and seemed to take forever before slapping Billy on the back. They both got to their feet in a crouching stance and jumped into the river.

The crew helped pull them out of the muck and huddled

under a small tree as if to get out of the driving rain.

"So, what happened to your airboat Chief?" asked Bob.

"I tried to get out of your daredevil captain's way and hit a tree," he murmured with an agitated look.

"What's done is done," Virgil added before anyone else could add to Bhim's deteriorating demeanor. "Now, before we do anything, I think we have to do a little diving," he continued, taking off his soaked shirt.

31

"Diving? You think we should go diving? Don asked, his eyes the size of golf balls.

Virgil flashed him a cynical look, "Unless you shoved the weapons up your you-know-what, they're lying somewhere down there," he said, pointing toward the sunken boat's antenna. "All the weapons are sitting somewhere on the bottom. I'd say it's about fifteen to twenty feet deep."

"And if that monster's still alive?" Randy asked, but he already knew the answer.

"We'll need your Pancor shotgun to finish it off," Virgil grimaced. "Sorry guys, but I'd rather quit while I'm still breathing and head back.

If that beast is still alive, it's got to be mad as hell and waiting for us to get within the striking distance," Bob Jackson added with a worrisome look.

Chief Bhim took a step closer to Bob and looked around, "We're at least five miles from the sanctuary and way too far from civilization. We're standing on a marsh-encircled island no bigger than fifty yards. I'd say we're in striking distance."

To attempt to walk back, the men would have to walk through

the wild sawgrass from island to island, sometimes swimming through deep areas infested with alligators and large pythons, not to mention the thought of AlliCroc stalking them. The only weapons they had were the two twelve-gauge shotguns that Bhim and Billy clutched in their hands. To make matters worse, the skies opened up with torrential rain as a thunderstorm hampered their vision.

"Well, I'm in no shape to go diving, so I'll have to sit this one out and stand guard," Bob said, lifting his arm as if reminding them of his injury.

"Look around Bob, the captain's right. If we don't retrieve those weapons, we're as good as dead."

Bob cursed his bad luck, realizing the Indian chief was right. His bruised body felt like it was on fire as he let out a heavy sigh and put his hands on his hips, "So, what's the game plan?"

"I'll need a volunteer to dive with me while the rest of you keep a look out for hungry alligators. I don't think we have to worry about AlliCroc because I believe the fast-boat crushed its skull."

"Then why are you diving for the weapons?" Randy asked. "What if I'm wrong?" Virgil retorted with tenacity.

"I will dive with you," Billy said, walking over to Virgil's side. "I can hold my breath for two minutes and I'm the strongest swimmer here."

Nobody protested as the Indian began hyperventilating in preparation. Virgil and Billy sized each other up and walked to the water, "Okay, let's do this," said Virgil.

The two men quietly entered the murky water and swam out to the sunken fast-boat. Virgil took one last look at the crew and saw them despairingly watching the area. He laughed to himself when Chuck gave him a thumbs-up, as he knew that nobody could see clearly through the rain storm. He turned to Billy and nodded as they took a deep breath and disappeared below the surface.

Visibility was non-existent when they reached the boat. Feeling his way around, Virgil found his way to the crushed bow. Just when he was about to return to the surface for another breath of air, he felt the hard barrel of a shotgun resting on the deck. He quickly picked it up and sprang to the surface.

He breached the surface and shouted for someone to swim over and retrieve the shotgun. Without hesitation, Bill scrambled into the water and swam over, "Good job, Captain. Take that gun to the shore. I'll go down and find another one."

"Thanks, but no thanks Bill. You can't hold your breath for fifteen-seconds. Here, take this back," Virgil replied, handing the shotgun to Bill and slapping his back before taking a breath and heading back to the wreckage. Feeling around, he found another shotgun near the wheelhouse.

Suddenly, there was a loud crack near the stern, and the boat shook and tilted to the port side. Virgil froze, anticipating the monster's large jaws to close in and snap him to pieces. When nothing happened, he figured the old boat was just settling in its final resting place.

His head barely broke the surface when he heard Chief Bhim's booming voice, "Where is Billy?" he shouted.

"He didn't come up?" replied Virgil, fearful of the answer.

"He never came up for air!" Bhim and Chuck answered in unison.

At that time, Virgil put his head down and swam like a speed boat to shore. Randy and Bill pulled him out of the muck while the rest of the men stood around searching for Billy.

A school of fish abruptly jumped out of the water as if avoiding capture and swam upriver for their safety as an eerie calm crept in. The hard rain continued pelting the river as the men struggled to hear each other speak.

They fanned out and desperately searched for Billy. After twenty minutes, the relentless downpour stopped to a light drizzle, and they gave up searching. Soaked to the bone and completely worn out, Randy insisted they stop and regroup.

"I think he's had it Chief," Virgil said, referring to Billy. "On my last dive, I think AlliCroc slammed into the fast boat and got Billy."

"What are you saying?"

"The boat was hit by something big and turned on its side. I thought the boat was settling, but now I think it's obvious that the reptile is alive and killed your friend," Virgil replied uneasily.

Without a word, Chief Bhim shook his head and acknowledged the captain. The rest of the crew held their heads low and coolly looked into the water. They were at a loss for words as it sank in that they were more or less doomed. Virgil and Randy looked dismally at each other and cautiously walked to the water's edge.

"Well men," Virgil finally said, "Looks like we have two choices. We can call it quits and wait for that son of a bitch to return and eat us... or we can turn it around and kill that beast once and for all."

"With what? Randy lost the Pancor shotgun. All we have is these three shotguns," Don blurted on the edge of total panic.

Randy was on edge. The last thing he needed to hear was Don blaming him for losing the immense shotgun. "Why you whining, yellow-bellied bastard," he shouted, walking swiftly over to Don with his fists clenched in rage, "When I'm through with you…"

"Take it easy!" Virgil cut in, stepping in front of the fuming officer with one hand on Randy's shoulder so that he couldn't take another step.

"The last thing I need is you guys fighting out here!" Virgil lectured.

"And the last thing I need is a civilian telling me what to do. Now get your hand off me before I…" He didn't see it coming; Virgil decked him with a right punch to the jaw and knocked him out cold. Before the officer could hit the ground, Bill and Chuck ran up behind him and grabbed his arms, gently placing him on the ground.

"Oh boy, somebody's not going to be too happy when he wakes up," Bill said with a fretful look.

"Couldn't be helped," Virgil retorted, "We've got enough problems to contend with."

Virgil paced back and forth, contemplating their next plan and noticed all eyes were on him. He looked up and saw the men standing over Randy like lost children in the land of the lost. "Okay, the sun's going down in a couple hours. I need one of you to gather firewood and the rest to find something to eat," he said in a composed manner.

"What the hell Virge, there's no market out here? What the hell do you think we're going to eat?" Don uttered.

Virgil stopped and looked dead-on into Don's eyes, "I don't expect you to find anything; I'll leave that up to the men who want to survive. As for you, I want you to get your fat ass out of here and bring back something to start a fire. We're staying put here tonight because the odds are against us to walk around here in the dark. We'll eat and get some rest, we'll switch off standing guard until sunlight," he spat out.

Without another word, Don followed Bob toward the other end of the swamp and gathered what little branches weren't soaked to the core while Bhim and the others sported bowie knives and a single shotgun and quietly trekked off to hunt. Chuck stayed behind to see what kind of mood Randy would be in when he woke up.

He strolled over to Virgil with his hands in his pant pockets and stopped. Before he could utter a word, Virgil smiled and stuck a hand in his pocket, retrieving a plastic baggy with dry matches, "Thought I was nuts, huh Chucky?"

"Nope, who am I to say you're nuts? I'm standing right by

your side in the middle of the Everglades with a monster stalking us... and the sun's going down."

They both smiled uneasily for a second or two before they heard Randy groan and sit up. Chuck hurried over and knelt down beside him, hoping he wouldn't retaliate.

"Where the hell's Virgil?" Randy asked, massaging his sore jaw.

"I'm right here Randy," replied Virgil, casually walking over. "I didn't want to hit you, but you left me no choice."

"Understood, but when this is over, you and I are gonna settle up," Randy promised.

"I'll look forward to it," Virgil scowled, making sure he got the last word. "Sit tight; the others are collecting firewood and should be back shortly."

"Firewood? It's been storming all day. How do you think you're gonna start a ..."

Virgil threw the bag of matches at Randy's feet. "...Fire," Randy grinned.

A half-hour later, a fire was burning, and Chief Bhim arrived with a dead alligator that looked to be about two feet long.

"Oh, that's just great!" Randy stood up and complained, "Are we going to eat that damn thing?"

Taken aback, the chief tossed the gator by the fire and looked at Randy with disappointment. Randy stared back with an imprudent look, as he himself was surprised at what he had just said, and leisurely walked to the edge of the water and opened a fresh can of Copenhagen, "Sorry fellas, it's been a long day."

At once, everybody turned in unison when they heard something shuffling through the sawgrass toward their makeshift camp. Chief Bhim jumped up, expecting to see Billy pop through, when Bloodfoot appeared through the thicket.

"Greetings from hell!" Bloodfoot shouted derisively. He walked over like a stormtrooper, carrying a freshly gutted boar over his substantial shoulders and dropped it next to the fire. "Gator is good, but boar is better!" he proclaimed in a deep, beaming voice.

"Where the hell did you come from!" Virgil blurted with welcomed relief, jumping up and practically giving the pirate a smack on the back.

"You mean, before or after you nearly drowned me in your wake?"

Virgil dismissed the jab and gave Bloodfoot a stern look, "You jumped ship, remember? We waited far too long for you to get back to the boat, but you never showed."

"The Captain's right," Chuck continued, "We figured you've had it until we saw you in our wake earlier."

"Nevertheless, the boat is gone and we're in deep *you-know-what*," Virgil said.

"Yep, and now we have an additional problem," Bloodfoot stated. "We're also being stalked by a hitman."

"What?" Bob asked.

"That's right. While AlliCroc was chewing on Skip, I saw a flash deep in the swamp at the same time that the radio exploded."

"If somebody wanted us dead, he'd have killed us by now instead of shooting our radio," Bob assured, looking cynical.

"Not if he's waiting for us to kill the reptile first," Virgil figured.

"Do you think it's the same guy we saw at the boat ramp at the mouth of the swamp?" Bill asked.

"The same," Bloodfoot agreed.

"And most likely the same guy that had a campfire the other night, just upriver of where we camped," Randy ventured to say.

"Same footprints," Bloodfoot growled.

"What do you mean?" Don asked, looking like a hunted rat. "How do you know it's the same footprints?"

"I checked his campsite that very same night, and I also checked the area where I saw the flash when AlliCroc attacked. That's the reason I left the boat," Bloodfoot grinned, amused at the looks he was getting from the crew.

"Who would order a hit on us?" Chuck asked.

"There's only one person who knows what we're doing and has the most to lose if we ever talked," Randy said, becoming livid the more he talked about it.

"Myers, Mayor Nick Myers," Virgil spat. "That bastard ordered the hit. He's waiting for us to kill the reptile before his hitman kills us. All because he's afraid we'll talk and drag his name in connection with that murderous reptile," he confirmed for the last time so everyone heard it.

"When I get out of here, I'm going to choke the life out of him," Bhim assured.

"Well, we have to figure a way out of here first," Bill added, squatting slightly and looking around as if trying to locate the hitman.

Virgil and Bloodfoot looked over at each other without saying a word, for they knew deep down that it would take a miracle for the entire crew to make it out alive.

32

Durjaya was lying awake in bed, staring out of the window as the rain fell in a light mist. It was cool and damp outside and he knew something must have gone terribly wrong when his father and the hunters had not yet returned after a full day. He tried to ease his weary mind by thinking that maybe they had no luck finding AlliCroc and continued their pursuit deeper in the swamp.

But the worst case scenario kept nagging in the back of his mind, *maybe they did find the reptile and were in grave danger.* So, before he could change his mind, he climbed out of bed and decided to gather a couple of men and search for the hunting party.

He quickly dressed and looked at his watch, five-forty. The sun would rise soon and he wanted to be well under way by then. Stepping outside his front door, Durjaya took a quick survey of the area. The river was quiet except for the sound of croaking frogs and the occasional chirp of birds waking up to another rainy morning.

He bent down and tied the laces of what looked like combat boots and proceeded to walk toward the cabin next door, where he knocked quietly on his long-time friend's door. He was startled when the door sprung open and his buddy walked out.

"What took you so long?"

"What do you mean?" said Durjaya, looking startled.

"Chief and the others are not home yet. Something must be wrong, and you came over here to get me so we can search for them," Johnny replied.

Durjaya and Johnny had been friends since kindergarten, where their parents made an attempt to put them through the public school system. Johnny had the misfortune of relentless teasing since his last name was Jumper. The kids would tease him on the playground, calling him Johnny Jumper the Indian thumper, and thump him in the ears with their fingers until he cried. Durjaya felt inclined to help a fellow Indian and would chase the bullies and beat them up.

After many meetings with the principal and school counselors, it was decided that in the best interest of the boys, they would be home schooled on the Seminole reservation.

Even though the Jumper family was Miccosukee Indians with a different culture than that of the Seminoles, the two families became fast friends. At the same time that Chief Bhim was getting his tribe settled in the newly founded Everglades Sanctuary, Johnny's parents were tragically killed in an automobile accident on I-75, also known as Alligator Alley. Bhim took Johnny in as one of the family.

"You're right Johnny; I think my father is in trouble. Let's take a skiff out and find them."

"But he left strict orders to sit tight and guard the Sanctuary," Johnny added.

"I've made up my mind, I'm going to search for them. If I'm wrong, I will take the blame," replied Durjaya, growing edgier by the minute.

"Okay, count me in. Let me get my shotgun and I'll meet you at the dock."

Durjaya turned and quietly trotted over to the dock. He checked to make sure the fuel tank was full and untied the dock lines. Within five minutes, Johnny climbed in the boat and Durjaya pushed away from the dock. They rowed until they were far enough where the engine wouldn't wake anybody and pulled the cord on the twenty-five horsepower Evinrude. As it sputtered to life and they were on their way, Johnny settled on the bench and gave Durjaya a withering look, "Great, I forgot the raincoats," he muttered. They cruised through the darkness of the wet, foreboding swamp, slowing at every junction and searched with a single, hand-held spotlight at every splash or ripple in the water.

The nerve-wracking tension shown on their faces was in complete contrast to the beseeching posture the two young men projected. A creeping disquiet came through them as they heard what sounded like a waterfall in the distance, heading straight for them. A minute later, they were engulfed by torrential rain.

"Stop over there and we'll wait it out!" Johnny shouted over the roar of the downpour, pointing to a small canopy of trees hanging over the water.

Durjaya slowly steered the boat over and cut the engine. Without a word, Johnny grabbed an old Styrofoam coffee cup lying on the deck and began bailing water.

"Damn! If this keeps up, this little boat is going to sink," he stated, half-heartedly with a thin smile to mask his nervousness.

"It will pass," Durjaya replied with a dry lump in his throat.

Forty minutes later, the torrential rain subsided to a drizzle and they resumed their search. It was now seven o' clock and the sun refused to shine. Instead, it looked like a dull light bulb on the verge of fading out. The air was thick with moisture and they felt all alone on a different planet as the morning birds and wildlife refused to stir.

Within the hour, the small boat reached the area where the

hunters set the large nets in hopes of catching the reptile. Durjaya cut the engine and drifted to the center of the large area where they searched with trepidation at the carnage that must have taken place.

Two skiffs from the Sanctuary were sunk and floating just beneath the surface and they shuttered when they saw a section of the transom on one boat had been torn off.

"Look, here's the net!" Johnny said, as he leaned over and grabbed it. "Careful, it looks like there's something caught up in it," Durjaya replied, as he sat on the opposite side of the boat for ballast, watching the slack tighten as Johnny pulled the net.

"Here it comes," Johnny replied, watching the shadow of what was in the net rise to the surface. "It's probably the motor."

The words barely left his mouth when the object surfaced. Johnny gasped in horror and dropped the net, falling back as he tried in vain to hold back the vomit exploding through his nose and mouth.

"What is it!" Durjaya shrieked, looking over the side.

Words could not explain the grotesque object drifting toward the bottom. It was a tribesman's upper torso, just below the chest and up to the head. There were pieces of flesh, gore and intestines trailing from the chest cavity with small fish and crabs feasting on it. Before the dreadful sight disappeared into the depths, a four-foot alligator swam up and snatched the remains.

They sat in stunned silence for what seemed forever, each one reviewing the horror in their minds. Finally, Durjaya crawled over and started the motor, "We'll go further upriver until I find my Father's airboat," he said, in a numbing tone.

Johnny didn't dare say what was on his mind. He was sure that, without a doubt, the entire hunting party was dead. He sat low on the bench seat and just nodded to Durjaya.

All hope of finding his father and the remaining hunters vanished when he rounded a bend and saw the antenna of the fast boat sticking out of the water. It's serene, quiet calm made it look like a grave marker, he thought. Then, to deliver the final deadly blow to his dreadful nightmare, he looked a few yards upstream and saw his father's upturned airboat as it sat stuck in the muck.

"Ah no, no father..." Durjaya cried out. Again, he killed the engine and let the boat drift to the bank where it stopped two feet short in the muck. He held his head in his hands and wept openly. Johnny tried his best to keep his composure, but the tears welled up in his eyes, blurring his vision as he looked around the area.

As Durjaya's demeanor crashed in sorrow, Johnny suddenly spotted what looked like the remains of a campfire, "Durjaya, look!" he said, pointing toward the campfire, "They made it to shore!"

With a rapturous look, Durjaya jumped out of the boat and ran to the campfire, "They made it! Look, it's my father's footprint!" he said, pointing to the big, wide footprint that only his father could own.

"I see seven different footprints!" Johnny pointed out, "Looks like they're going to walk back to the Sanctuary."

"Make that eight," a deep voice added from behind the foliage. "I followed behind Chief Bhim and the others... for backup," he lied.

Durjaya and Johnny turned toward the man casually walking over. "Who are you?" Durjaya asked, trying to get a glimpse of the massive rifle slung behind his back.

"The name's not important. I'm here to help kill AlliCroc," he smiled, keeping the rifle out of view.

"Then why aren't you with my father and the rest of the hunters?" Durjaya asked with suspicion in his eyes.

"I became separated when AlliCroc attacked. I ran clear and

thought the others followed me," he explained. "I want you two to stay here while I rescue the others."

"Jump in the skiff, we'll all find them," Durjaya said, turning toward the boat.

Before he could jump in the boat, Wolf had the rifle in his hands and walked up behind the two young men, "That won't be necessary, as you can see, I can do it alone," he said sternly. "Now back away and I'll take the boat."

Durjaya and Johnny noticed the gun in his hands and thought it wise to listen to the man. They held their hands in plain sight and backed away from the boat, "Okay, take the boat. We'll wait here," Durjaya replied, surprised to think the stranger would shoot them.

"Good boys," Wolf grinned. "Stay away from the water and I'll be back soon."

Durjaya and Johnny watched helplessly as the stranger jumped in the boat and sped off around the bend.

"That guy gave me the creeps," Johnny said, throwing a stone in the water as he sat in the sand.

"He's up to no good. He's going to kill them when he finds them," Durjaya replied bluntly, taking his bowie knife out of the sheath. "We've got to follow the trail."

"What makes you think that?"

"I heard a phone conversation between Mayer Nick Myers and my father. He wanted my father to kill them after they killed AlliCroc so there'd be no connection between him and the reptile."

"That's insane! Why would he do that?"

"Politics."

33

The Everglades Sanctuary was the closest thing to safety but was at least five miles away. Chief Bhim led the way through the rain-soaked swamp. He knew the area like the back of his hand, but never walked through it. He dreaded the fact that they'd have to swim through some areas, knowing it was infested by alligators.

"Keep a lookout for gators," Bhim warned.

"Count on it," replied Virgil, trailing eight feet behind the chief.

"I wish gators were all we had to be concerned with," Bloodfoot retorted, looking like he could kill them with his bare hands.

"You still think it's alive?" Chuck sighed. "Damn well sure of it."

"Just keep walking and keep your eyes peeled," Virgil ordered, stopping the conversation and hoping like hell Bloodfoot was wrong.

They continued walking with little excitement, except when Don screamed like a little girl falling off her bike, when a large python tried to wrap itself around his leg. With one sweeping motion, Bloodfoot grabbed the snake behind the head and sliced its head off in one clean sweep of his trusty knife. Small alligators popped their heads up now and then but never tried to attack.

The sun still looked like a dim lightbulb, and the rain drizzled throughout the morning; the swamp still felt like a sauna. To the annoyance of Bloodfoot, Bob began wheezing and coughing, causing his broken ribs to be so painful that they had to stop and take a break every half-hour.

"How much farther Chief?" Virgil asked, sitting on a log and trying to light a wet cigarette.

"We're about half-way there," Bhim answered, clearly worn out. They were getting ready to start walking again when Bloodfoot suddenly crouched down low and held his hand up for everybody to follow suit.

Looking around, the crew couldn't see what the pirate apparently saw. Finally, Chief Bhim silently walked over to him with a puzzled look.

"What is it Bloodfoot?"

"Shhhhh," he replied, with a finger over his mouth.

"What the hell is it Bloodfoot?" Bob whispered with an agitated hiss before breaking into a gut-wrenching cough.

"Bhim's a goddamn Indian hunter and he doesn't see anything!"

Bloodfoot whipped around and grabbed Bob by the back of the neck with one hand and put another hand over his mouth and grumbled in a low, threatening growl, "It's not what I see, but what I smell. The reptile is up ahead. Make another sound and I'll snap your neck."

"Take it easy Bloodfoot," Virgil intervened, grabbing his arm. "Are you sure it's here?"

"It's here."

Virgil quickly squatted down and peered ahead. He had no reason to doubt the man who seemed to be enjoying the horrid situation. He looked over to Bhim and saw beads of sweat dripping from his forehead and a timid look on his terrified face. "Maybe we should let Bloodfoot lead," he sneered.

Bloodfoot stood motionless for what seemed eternity, sniffing the air like an animal, "The reptile is just past the embankment over there," he finally said, pointing a finger.

"Any suggestions?" Virgil whispered, checking the ammo in his shotgun.

Bloodfoot slowly withdrew his hunting knife and tested the sharpness with his thumb. "Okay, here's the plan and it's not open for discussion. The reptile knows we're here and that's a fact," he assured them.

"What makes you think it knows we're here?" Randy questioned. "Yeah, if it knows we are here, why doesn't it attack?" Chuck added. "Bloodfoot's right, it knows exactly where we are," Don spoke up. "The damn thing is smart as hell. It wants to surprise us when we walk over the embankment; believe it or not, it enjoys torturing its prey before the kill."

All eyes turned to Don with confusion, "What the hell does that mean?" Bob asked, his eyes twice their size.

"It's playing with us. It could kill us any time but first, it wants to smell our fear," replied Don, sitting back and waiting for the inevitable.

The goose bumps ran up the back of everybody's neck, Bloodfoot quickly spoke before the crew could decide to make a break and run the other direction, "Okay, listen up... It knows we're here. I want you guys to make a little noise so that it can focus its attention over here. Meanwhile, I'll sneak around to the other side and with any luck, take it by surprise," Bloodfoot said, with the first sound of fear in his voice.

"You think you're going to kill it with your knife?" Virgil asked with dismay.

"If it turns and directs its attention over here, I can come from behind and bury this knife right between its eyes," Bloodfoot replied with conviction.

"You're nuts," said Virgil.

"It's our only choice," Bloodfoot retorted.

Before anybody else could protest, they heard the sound of an outboard motor idle up from behind. Their smiles of relief quickly vanished when they saw the occupant aiming a sinister-looking rifle at them.

"Greetings gentlemen," Wolf said as he stepped off the skiff and walked over. "Drop those guns and raise your hands where I can see them."

"Who the hell are you?" Virgil asked.

"The name is Wolf. Consider me your worst nightmare," he replied in a casual tone.

"Myers!" Bhim blurted.

"Ah yes, you're very astute Chief. I didn't plan to kill you along with these fine gentlemen, but of course, I can't leave any witnesses."

"Where did you get my boat," Bhim demanded, noticing the Sanctuary skiff he arrived on.

"I believe your son Durjaya?...and his buddy lent it to me. I left them just around the bend a few miles back. Of course, I'll have to go back and kill them too," Wolf smiled wickedly.

"You won't get away with this!" Bhim erupted.

"Oh? I can and I will. You see, I wasn't supposed to kill you guys until after you killed the overgrown reptile. But, since I've watched you bumbling fools since you got in this godforsaken swamp, it has occurred to me that it will kill you guys first."

"What will Nick Myers say when he finds out you've killed us and AlliCroc lives?" Randy asked.

"See this rifle? It's a Barret M82A1, loaded with .50 caliber armor-piercing bullets. If your dumb-ass mayor gave you one of these, you would have blown that reptile's head off long before it killed all those pathetic victims," Wolf snickered. "But of course, these things are next to impossible to acquire. To answer your question, after I kill you guys, I will walk over that little hill and blow the reptile to kingdom come."

Wolf held his weapon on the men and slowly walked up the hill to take a look at the reptile, "The first person to twitch gets it," he warned as he turned to glimpse AlliCroc.

Bloodfoot had his knife hidden in the palm of his hand with the long blade hidden behind his wrist and inner forearm. At the same instant that Wolf turned his head to glimpse the beast, he quickly grasped the blade and prepared to throw it.

"Whew! That monster looks much bigger up..." *(Thud!)* Wolf's last words were cut short as Bloodfoot's bowie knife flew through the air and struck deep into his chest.

Wolf's eyes bulged with a surprised look on his face as his lungs refused to take a breath. He helplessly tried to take a step forward but collapsed and fell backward down the other side of the embankment.

With lightning speed, AlliCroc charged over like a freight train and grabbed the dead man in its colossal jaws and violently shook its head from side to side, tearing Wolf to pieces. Virgil and Randy ran for a clear shot and began blasting at the reptile with their shotguns while the other men scattered for safety. Again, the shotgun blasts seemed to do little more than irritate the creature as it continued to devour its prey.

"Damn shotguns won't do the job! We've got to get Wolf's gun with the armor-piercing bullets!" Virgil shouted.

"Who the hell's going to get it! AlliCroc's standing on the damn thing?" Randy retorted as he feverishly dug in his pocket for more shotgun shells.

Before Virgil could answer, Bill came out of nowhere and charged toward the back end of the feasting reptile and plowed into it like an NFL linebacker. With one hulking arm wrapped around the reptile's back leg and the other around the tail, Bill hung on for dear life, shouting obscenities at the top of his lungs as the reptile's armored plates sliced through the flesh of his arms. AlliCroc whipped his tail viciously from side to side to throw the attacker off, but Bill wouldn't budge. It turned and began snapping its enormous jaws at the intruder, missing him by inches before going into a death roll. At that point, Bill let go and grabbed Wolf's gun, throwing it over toward Virgil and ran for cover.

AlliCroc immediately gave chase. Nobody was prepared for the velocity and power of the agitated creature as it hissed and growled while closing the gap toward Bill.

The crew hit the ground and covered their ears as a sudden round of blasts tore through trees and blew holes in the ground behind AlliCroc before finally hitting its mark. What sounded like blasts from a canon came from Virgil as he stood at the top of the hill and fired the Barret M82A1. The last shot fired hit the unyielding monster in the hind leg and blew it off completely.

AlliCroc gave out a guttural roar as it flipped over in pain. Two more shots penetrated its belly as the beast gave a mighty roar and headed for the cover of water. Virgil's arm lost all feeling from the recoil of the massive weapon but brought the gun up in his sights once again to finish the job. He had a clear headshot just as the beast was about to go underwater and pulled the trigger. *(Click),* the gun was empty.

"Goddamnit!" he shouted in rage, throwing the weapon at the fleeing beast.

Bloodfoot quickly ran past Virgil, slowing only to grab his bowie knife out of a remaining piece of Wolf's torso before diving on top of AlliCroc as it dipped below the surface. The last thing the crew saw was Bloodfoot plunging the knife into the reptile's eyes before they disappeared under the brackish water.

Two full minutes went by, and the men gathered near the river's edge, somberly waiting for Bloodfoot to appear. The disturbed water started to smooth out and the ripples vanished as it looked like Bloodfoot had finally met his match.

"Where the hell is he? I saw him plunge the knife deep between that son of a bitch's eyes," Chuck said, reloading a shotgun and looking at the water with an intense look on his face.

"He's gone," Virgil replied with remorse, putting a hand on his shoulder and guiding him back a few feet.

The men began to walk back up the embankment and take stock when they heard water splashing toward them from the other side of the hill. They turned and aimed the two shotguns in the direction of the incoming disturbance when Durjaya and Johnny burst through the sawgrass.

"Don't shoot! It's me and Johnny!" Durjaya shouted with his hands up. Chief Bhim ran and grabbed his son by the shoulders before giving the two of them a rapturous bear hug, "Son! I thought I'd never see you again!"

Durjaya and Johnny looked around over Bhim's overbearing arms and asked, "Where's that guy with the rifle?"

"He's gone," Randy murmured as he slowly walked by.

The men began to walk away when Bloodfoot suddenly crashed through the surface. Blood poured from open wounds that seemed to consume his entire body.

"Bloodfoot!" they shouted in unison, dropping everything and running over to help him out of the water.

"Get him out of the water and set him down by that tree!" Virgil shouted, marveling at how the pirate was still alive with all the blood loss.

"I'm alright Captain. The reptile didn't get me. These are just flesh wounds from those sharper-than-hell scales on that reptile," Bloodfoot grinned.

"Did you kill it?" Don asked uneasily.

Bloodfoot reached into his waistband, and pulled out a six-inch tooth and tossed it at Don's feet, "It's dead. Your freak of nature will never kill again," he replied, exhausted.

"Let's get out of here," Virgil said, lighting another camel cigarette, "Think you can make it old man?" he gestured to Bloodfoot, trying to get a rise out of him.

"Lead the way Virge," the pirate replied with a sinister look, too tired for a snappy comeback.

34

A week had passed and the crew of the Horizon were sitting with Captain Bloodfoot in the Anchor bar, celebrating the demise of the gruesome reptile. It was late on a Thursday evening, but the place was packed with well-wishers and a few reporters trying to get into the conversation near the dingy booth at the far end of the bar. Carlos did a good job keeping a bouncer close by so that the booth remained undisturbed.

"Well Bloodfoot, I've got to hand it to you," Virgil said. "Without you, there's no doubt that monster would've slipped away. I salute you!" he bellowed and lifted his shot of apricot brandy high in the air. Everybody at the table followed suit and gulped down the potent liquid.

"Much thanks, Captain," Bloodfoot grinned. "But I can't take all the credit. If not for each and every one of you at this table, I think we'd all be dead. Here's to living on the edge!" he replied, lifting another round of brandy toward the ceiling.

Bill and Chuck were by now completely inebriated but held their own at the farewell party, for tomorrow morning at sun up, Captain Bloodfoot and his crew of pirates were to set sail for Jamaica.

"Too bad Officer Taylor couldn't be here," Chuck slurred.

"Yeah well, he's tending to some hanky panky business. Seems that the kite-boarding woman was released from the hospital today and asked that Randy help her home. He called about an hour ago and told me to send his regards because he wasn't going to make it here," Virgil grinned.

"Can't blame him; she's a beauty," Chuck smiled.

"I'll stop by and see him in the morning before I depart," replied Bloodfoot, a bit put off that Randy was absent.

"I'm sure he'd like that."

"One good thing, at least I won't have to see Don anymore. One more day with him and I think I would have killed him," Bloodfoot continued.

The day the crew finally walked their way to the Everglades Sanctuary, Don hitched a ride from the same helicopter that took Bhim to a hospital for a chest exam and grabbed a cab to his hotel, where he cleaned up and left town faster than a dog in heat.

"I don't think he'll ever show his face in this town again," added Virgil, refilling the empty glasses.

"Wish I could be here when the mayor gets back from his sudden vacation and see the look on his face when the cops arrest him," Bloodfoot said, pounding his empty glass on the table.

"We'll see how that unfolds. Seems a little suspicious how he ups and leaves when Randy called him at the Sanctuary," Chuck said, drinking his final round before falling flat out on the floor.

"Virgil, I'm a little concerned about your lightweight crew," Bloodfoot frowned as he moved his boot with his latest trophy tooth away from Chuck's head. "Your crew can't hold their liquor!" he roared with laughter.

"I'll drink to that!"

Epilogue

Mayor Nick Myers was sitting at his desk when he got the call from Officer Randy Taylor. He listened carefully while the officer explained how AlliCroc had been killed. He began to sweat heavily when Randy told him that the hitman that he'd hired was also dead and that he was going to personally come to his office and have him arrested. He panicked and hung up the phone when his secretary knocked on the door before entering the room.

He quickly stood up and turned toward the window. Wiping his brow, he turned to her and notified her that he was taking a vacation, effective immediately. When questioned, he stammered out of the room, shouting that he had to take his wife and kids on a vacation.

The following afternoon, the Myers family pulled into the campgrounds at Myakka State Park, located on the upper Gulf Coast. Nick's wife was at the wheel in their twenty-six-foot Winnebago. She registered under her maiden name and proceeded to site 008.

It took less than an hour to unload the canoe and hook up the electric and water lines. Nick held his promise to take a little canoe cruise before sunset. With his ten-year-old son

Brian and eight-year-old daughter Emily, Mr. and Mrs. Myers launched the seventeen-foot canoe at the small boat ramp, "There are a few gators here for the kids to see, right?" Nick asked a Park Ranger, with a slight wink of the eye as he struggled to hold the canoe steady at the launch.

"Oh, there should be plenty out there," the Ranger replied. "Just keep your eyes peeled as you cruise along through the sawgrass, and keep your hands and feet in the boat at all times," he smiled.

The kids put their life vests on and stepped into the canoe. Nick's wife, Elizabeth, was waiting in the front with the paddle in hand as Nick pushed off the dock and stumbled to the seat in the rear, nearly flipping the canoe over.

They slowly cruised through the river and admired the quiet calm of the wilderness with nothing around but sawgrass on the muddy banks and small alligators poking their heads up every now and then. They passed a loan kayaker as they rounded a bend and exchanged pleasantries, Nick nearly ramming the kayak when he found that he could barely steer the canoe.

A few minutes later, they rounded another bend and gasped at the largest reptile they'd ever seen. It sat on the bank of the river as if bathing in the sun.

"Oh my God! Look at that thing Nick!" Elizabeth gasped, her eyes unable to comprehend the massive reptile.

"Wow Dad! Take a picture!" Brian said, trying to sound like he wasn't scared to death.

The moment Nick locked eyes on the monstrous reptile, he knew exactly what it was. He was staring eye to eye with the other AlliCroc, the one that got away.

He panicked and tried to turn the canoe around but buried the bow head-on into the sawgrass. Engulfed in terror, Nick began to wheeze.

"Dad, are you alright?" Emily cried.

"Get on the sawgrass and run!" he screamed as he stood up and nearly trampled his family.

The sawgrass had grown two feet under the murky water and gave a false impression that there was dry land where they had stopped.

Nick lost his balance and flipped flat on his back, spilling his family into the alligator-infested water. He heard a tremendous splash and looked up to see the humungous reptile barreling over. His last thought was that, with a monster so big and vicious, he barely felt pain when the reptile chomped into his torso, biting him in half.